Paul and Carol Go to Guatemala

a novel

by Catherine Gigante-Brown

Cover and interior design by Vinnie Corbo
Author photo by Peter Brown

Published by Volossal Publishing
www.volossal.com

Table of Contents

4

To the people of Guatemala
and their generous spirits.
And to "Paul."

Jumpstart

Immediately, I'm paralyzed with fear. I can't stand, can't move, can't breathe. When I'm able to suck in a lungful of air, I scream, "Paul!" But he can't hear me in the squall so I scream it again, even louder, "Paul!"

He turns and makes his way to me. I hope he can't see the tears streaming down my face in the mist. But he does. "You're overreacting," Paul says as diplomatically as possible. But then a gust lifts his 200-pound frame and pushes him three feet away from me, toward Pacaya's edge.

When I detect fear on Paul's face I start to panic. "We're screwed, aren't we?" I sob. He doesn't answer. Even our guides struggle to remain standing.

Paul clings to me. "You've got to move," he shouts into the abyss. When I shield my face with the hood of my sweatshirt, I find that at least I can breathe. Breathing is good. Breathing is important. "Don't let go of me! Please don't let go of me!" I beg Paul. He doesn't.

With each step, I think, 'We might make it. We just might make it.' I keep repeating this to myself, a silent mantra, a prayer.

~

What the hell am I doing climbing an active volcano in Guatemala? Is this some sort of test? But who am I kidding? The only reason I'm here is because Paul is here.

But I'm getting a little bit ahead of the story…

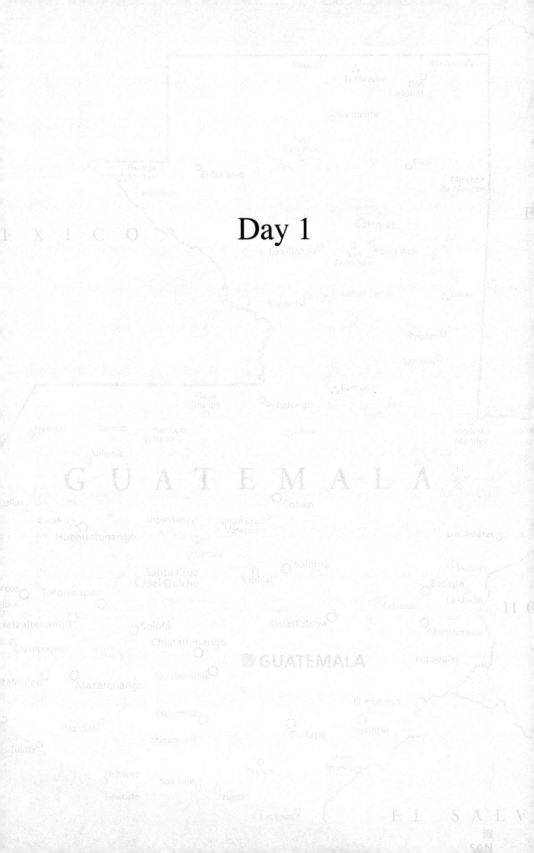

Day 1

I've never seen JFK Airport like this before. And I've been traveling for more than 25 years.

I've never packed for a trip like this before. All of my belongings are in one large, green backpack. I bought it at a store called Tents and Trails, which is nestled on Park Row in lower Manhattan. Tents and Trails is a cramped, ratty camping store a stone's throw from the Twin Towers and is out of place among the skyscrapers. Just like I will be out of place in Central America.

Plus, I've never gone on a trip like this before: to Guatemala, a mysterious land I know little about. Jungles. Monkeys. Mayan ruins. Still in the pangs of a waning civil war. "Don't you know that Americans get kidnapped in Guatemala?" my mother asked a few days ago, her voice sharp with fear.

"Didn't you see *Missing?*" my father followed up with before I could respond to my mom, taking a deep drag on his Chesterfield.

"*Missing* happened in Chile," I told them patiently. But it didn't make a difference. My folks believed what they wanted to believe.

"Of my top 100 countries to visit," my father said. "Guatemala would be 99th on that list. I would never go there."

But my boyfriend asked me to go to Guatemala with him, so here I am.

And on my own personal list of "nevers," I have never dated a man like Paul before. He is both rough and smooth around the edges. A drinker, a thinker, and ruggedly handsome in a way that still steals the breath from my body. Since we've been dating, Paul has gotten me to do things I wouldn't normally do, things far outside my comfort zone. Like hike from hut-to-hut in New Hampshire's White Mountains (the highest peaks east of the Rockies) and ride the Cyclone roller coaster in Coney Island in our native Brooklyn.

Now, Paul has convinced me to come with him to Guatemala, a place as wild and unpredictable as he is.

Of course, I said 'yes.'

Who wouldn't?

~

It is dark, misty and cold at six o'clock this wintery morning. The car service driver seems annoyed that Paul and I are going somewhere—anywhere!—and that he himself isn't. As the old Buick bolts into the rain-slick streets, the purple sedan is the only speck of color on the gray urban landscape.

When we arrive at JFK, the sun still hasn't risen and the sky is still a bottomless indigo. Our flight to Guatemala City is scheduled to leave at seven. Fat chance. The check-in line extends beyond the Lacsa Airlines terminal door and floods onto the airport's concrete sidewalk.

Paul scowls through half-closed eyes. Almost a year into our relationship, I am well aware that he isn't a morning person. But he is crankier than usual standing out in the frigid, pre-dawn November air with a 40-pound pack pulling on his shoulders. "Lacsa," he growls. "Who ever heard of Lacsa Airlines?"

"It's the national carrier of Costa Rica," I say, a bit too perkily. Paul grunts in response.

The line is composed mostly of women, children and babies. Paul has made it clear that he doesn't like kids very much. But at least the babies are quiet, swaddled tightly in blankets. Quieter than the adults are.

In addition to the bodies, there are boxes. I've never seen so many people traveling with so many boxes. Most are shrink-wrapped. There are Sony television sets, Schwinn bicycles, Fedders air conditioners and Black & Decker mini fridges. One carton is so warped and pitted that it's disintegrating. "Looks like it was stored on someone's fire escape," Paul notes.

"It probably was," I agree. Paul has a uniquely fresh, sarcastic way of looking at life that often makes me smile. How did I get by before him? I don't know. What will I do when it ends? Because all things invariably end, right?

But I just can't think of that now. Not when Paul and I are leaving for unchartered territory—both geographically and relationship-wise. Romances flounder on even the best of vacations. They buckle under the stress of lost reservations, missed trains and food poisoning. And most often, these are trips to gated, cushy, all-inclusive resorts in semi-civilized countries. Exactly what this trip is not.

Guatemala is raw and undiscovered and in the final throes of its 30-plus year revolution. Communication is sketchy there. Transportation is a challenge. Except for a couple of nights, Paul and I don't have reservations anywhere. You see, he wants us to be spontaneous. Me, not so much. In the morning, I like to know where I'll be laying my head that evening. Is that too much to ask? Apparently so.

But I force myself to be positive. I can't put the kibosh on this trip before we even leave the tarmac. I'm trying to be hopeful. Because without hope, what is there? Where will this three-week trip into the Great Unknown lead us? Damned if I know.

~

My friend Tony claims he would never visit a country whose name he couldn't spell.

My friend Joe (the guy who'd introduced me and Paul) keeps insisting we're going to Honduras, as though all Third World Central American lands are interchangeable.

"Why Guatemala?" everyone wonders.

"There are volcanoes in Guatemala," I answer.

"There are volcanoes in Hawaii," my friend Thomas responds.

I shake my head and say, "But there are also rainforests in Guatemala."

"There are rainforests in plenty of other places," Thomas shrugs.

But find one singular country that has volcanoes, rainforests AND Mesoamerican ruins AND Caribbean beaches. Not to mention the elusive and resplendent quetzal, Guatemala's glorious national bird. People don't know what to respond then.

Five hours from New York City by air, Guatemala is also incredibly inexpensive. Our roundtrip airfare costs less than 600 dollars each. Roughly five or six of their "dollars" (called "quetzals," not to be confused with the bird of the same name) equals one of ours. Paul estimates that 21 days in this pauper's paradise will probably cost us less than 2,000 dollars. That wouldn't buy us a week at a Club Med. If we even wanted to stay somewhere like that.

But the main reason I'm going to Guatemala is because Paul is going. Because I simply cannot comprehend spending three weeks without him.

Paul and I have known each other for a decade. And during that time, we not-so-secretly lusted after each other. Following the failure of my marriage and the breakup of Paul's doomed four-year relationship, we finally consummated our long-term lust. At first, it was a booty call to get all that messy longing out of the way so Paul and I could move on with our lives. But to our mutual surprise, it turned out to be much more than a booty call.

Paul and I clicked. We connected. In a way that neither of us could have fantasized. We are better together than we are apart. And 11 months later, we're going on a multiweek adventure together. Who would have thunk? Not us.

In my time with Paul, I find myself smiling and laughing more than I ever have before. I've never felt so comfortable in my own skin. I've never felt so content with myself. Whoever that happens to be at the moment.

But Guatemala? Really?

~

Standing in line at Lacsa's JFK terminal, Paul and I learn the true meaning of the Spanish phrase, *"Más o menos."* Which means "more or less." Which usually means "more or more." As in, more time...slower...longer.

Central Americans live by a different time clock than North Americans do. For example, our flight is supposed to leave at seven, *"más o menos."* It turns out to be closer to nine. I have the feeling this won't be the last time we'll hear those three words on this trip.

Paul and I are some of the few people in the Lacsa line who don't speak Spanish. We're outsiders in our own country, so to speak. As luck would have it, one of our Anglo compatriots is standing behind us. He wears a backwards Yankees cap and has the sort of Queens County whine we're trying to ditch.

Baseball Cap Guy gestures to a machine that crisscrosses security tape over luggage. "What's that for?" he moans.

"It stops people from going through your bags," Paul offers, uncharacteristically chatty at the ungodly hour.

"Nothing's safe down there," Baseball Cap Guy says dolefully.

'With that kind of attitude, why the hell are you even leaving your own living room?' I want to ask him.

But I don't say a word.

The airplane's first stop is Cancun. Whispering quietly, Paul and I bet that Baseball Cap Guy is headed for a fancy-pants, all-inclusive. We can't imagine him in Guatemala. And that's fine with us.

~

It's almost eight when we finally check our backpacks and board the plane. The flight attendant addresses Paul in English and me in Spanish. My black hair and olive complexion are probably responsible. Lighter skinned and sandy haired, Paul is actually half Cuban and speaks pigeon Spanish. My knowledge of the language is practically nonexistent. When the people behind us complain *en Español,* I understand only a sprinkling of words.

There are some benefits to being in a country where they don't speak your lingo. "The beauty of it is that we can goof on people to their faces and they'll never know," Paul philosophizes.

"But they can do the same to us," I remind him.

Making fun of people behind their backs is one of Paul's and my favorite pastimes. The pickings are so ripe here we can't resist. First, there's the lady with bad hair (*pelo malo,* Paul tells me) and Eskimo boots. And who could pass up the opportunity to comment on the senior citizen with coyotes, chili peppers and cacti decorating his shirt? Then there's the man decked out in a hideous plaid jacket with the cold, dead gaze of an ax murderer.

Yes, the opportunities for bilingual ridicule are ripe. The game occupies our warped minds until the plane prepares for an 8:30 departure. Over 90 minutes late. *Más o menos.*

The aircraft rattles and rumbles as it bolts down the runway, quickly gaining speed. I dig the fingernails I don't have into Paul's wrist. (I chopped them off with a clipper yesterday so I'd be more streamlined and easier to maintain. Paul, on the other hand, always

However, is it love? Lust? Both? Or something in between? Yes, to all of the above.

~

This morning is my first experience with a trickling, tepid, Central American shower. In Guatemala, it is the gold standard but it would be considered subpar in the US. The Colonial's "hot" water is heated by an exposed electrical wire. Not the safest practice, mixing water and electricity. But it seems to work. Most of the time. Sort of.

Before I actually get into the shower, Paul tells me about a man he met years earlier while traveling in Costa Rica. The guy was curious about the coil he saw above the showerhead so he touched it. And when he did, the poor fool was hurled across the bathroom from the jolt of electricity. "Why did you tell me this?" I ask Paul.

"I just want you to be careful, that's all," he says.

When I step into the lukewarm spray, I'm cautious not to stretch my hands too far above my head by accident, even while lathering my hair.

The showerhead unceremoniously juts out of the bathroom ceiling. The water runs down the concrete floor to a drain in the center. It smacks of the shower rooms in B-movies, the ones where they hose down a female inmate then menacingly approach her with a broom handle. Afterwards, when I mention this to Paul, he laughs. "You're right," he says as he peers into the bathroom.

The shower isn't as bad as I thought it would be. Although the stream isn't strong enough to wash all the sticky soap from my body, I notice as I dry myself with a rough, white towel. I'm filmy but at least I'm clean.

Yesterday, Lacsa promised they'd have more information about our luggage late this afternoon. Until then, instead of moping around, Paul and I decide to enjoy Guatemala City as much as possible. Our original plan had been to catch a bus to Tikal today and explore its Mayan ruins. We try not to stress out about our trip being pushed back a day. "Plans are made to be broken," I offer.

"Besides, we're on vacation," Paul points out. "It's all an adventure."

"Right," I agree. "We're supposed to relax and not get bent out of shape over minor setbacks like this." I sound so persuasive that I almost convince myself it's true. Except my sticky panties keep reminding me that it isn't.

us. He wears a backwards Yankees cap and has the sort of Queens County whine we're trying to ditch.

Baseball Cap Guy gestures to a machine that crisscrosses security tape over luggage. "What's that for?" he moans.

"It stops people from going through your bags," Paul offers, uncharacteristically chatty at the ungodly hour.

"Nothing's safe down there," Baseball Cap Guy says dolefully.

'With that kind of attitude, why the hell are you even leaving your own living room?' I want to ask him.

But I don't say a word.

The airplane's first stop is Cancun. Whispering quietly, Paul and I bet that Baseball Cap Guy is headed for a fancy-pants, all-inclusive. We can't imagine him in Guatemala. And that's fine with us.

~

It's almost eight when we finally check our backpacks and board the plane. The flight attendant addresses Paul in English and me in Spanish. My black hair and olive complexion are probably responsible. Lighter skinned and sandy haired, Paul is actually half Cuban and speaks pigeon Spanish. My knowledge of the language is practically nonexistent. When the people behind us complain *en Español,* I understand only a sprinkling of words.

There are some benefits to being in a country where they don't speak your lingo. "The beauty of it is that we can goof on people to their faces and they'll never know," Paul philosophizes.

"But they can do the same to us," I remind him.

Making fun of people behind their backs is one of Paul's and my favorite pastimes. The pickings are so ripe here we can't resist. First, there's the lady with bad hair (*pelo malo,* Paul tells me) and Eskimo boots. And who could pass up the opportunity to comment on the senior citizen with coyotes, chili peppers and cacti decorating his shirt? Then there's the man decked out in a hideous plaid jacket with the cold, dead gaze of an ax murderer.

Yes, the opportunities for bilingual ridicule are ripe. The game occupies our warped minds until the plane prepares for an 8:30 departure. Over 90 minutes late. *Más o menos.*

The aircraft rattles and rumbles as it bolts down the runway, quickly gaining speed. I dig the fingernails I don't have into Paul's wrist. (I chopped them off with a clipper yesterday so I'd be more streamlined and easier to maintain. Paul, on the other hand, always

17

bites his nails to the quick.) "I hate this part," I grimace through my teeth.

"I love this part," Paul smiles.

It's going to be an interesting trip.

~

Paul and I have a saying we came up with when we were in New Orleans this past May. As we stood, ankle deep in mud in the middle of a downpour during the outdoor Jazz and Heritage Festival, we'd look at each other and say, "Could be worse…could be raining."

On this trip, the catch phrase will pretty much be, "Could be worse…could be in Guatemala."

~

Hours behind schedule, we arrive at Guatemala City's La Aurora International Airport. But our luggage doesn't. Yes, Lacsa has lost our bags.

Up until now, Paul and I are proud of the fact that we shoved everything we could possibly need into one humongous backpack apiece. Only to discover that both of our backpacks are missing. Why couldn't they have lost someone else's TV or blender? (Tons of appliances are piled off to the side, waiting to be claimed by their owners.) Why did they have to lose all our earthly possessions?

La Aurora is the tiniest international airport either of us has ever been to. It only has two baggage carousels. One of which isn't working. How is it possible to lose anything in an airport so small?

There's no use in being angry or yelling at anyone. Paul and I don't have enough command of Spanish to get pissed off without sounding like Ricky Ricardo in a forgotten I Love Lucy episode.

After filling out a lost property report, we sit down to have a drink. A Gallo (the local beer, whose name means "rooster") for Paul and French wine in a tin can for me. As upsetting as being luggage-less in a foreign country is, we can't help shaking our heads and laughing. What else can we do?

We have nothing but the clothes on our backs, my shoulder bag and Paul's daypack. But at least we still have our passports, cash and travelers' checks slung in the money wallets around our necks. At least I still have that emergency condom in my purse so the day (and the night) won't be a total loss. And I have my journal, a purple-covered, eight-by-five, wire-rimmed notebook. Because I want to remember every detail about this trip, I promise myself that I'll write in my journal daily. We'll see.

~

Paul and I hail a cab and head toward the less-expensive hotels in Guatemala City's Zona 1. It's a journey of about five miles. Our chariot is an ancient, rusting Chevy. Chunks of the upholstery are eaten away and our feet almost push through holes in the floorboards which the driver tries to camouflage with filthy rubber mats. "This is where old American cars go to die," I tell Paul.

The streets of the capital are cluttered, both with vehicles — cars, trucks, food carts — and people. They are young, middle-aged, ancient and everything in between. A huge street festival is just winding up. We later read in the *Prensa Libre* that we stumbled upon the aftermath of a parade sponsored by Disney and Coca-Cola. It featured both life-sized figures from Walt's flicks and free soda. As if Third World children on the verge of poverty need either.

The people in the streets wear all manner of dress — from traditional Guatemalan *huipils* (blouses) and skirts to t-shirts embossed with slogans for American products they probably can't afford. Some women are squeezed into Spandex while others wear 1970s thrift store rejects that were ugly then and are even uglier now. Guatemala City, I decide, is a crazy-quilt of things that don't go together yet somehow work. Sort of.

What also strikes me is the sheer number of children. Maybe this is because the Disney cavalcade was geared toward kids. But everyone has at least one child. They are carried in arms and wrapped in bright pieces of loomed cloth. They are strapped to backs in colorful slings and shawls which I later learn are called *rebozos*. They are dragged by the hand or else run alongside their parents, trying desperately to keep up.

Above the swarming streets, an old brick aqueduct traces the entire length of the main road. And along the aqueduct calmly walks a soldier in his camouflage uniform, carrying an M-16 rifle. No one else seems to notice, as if this is a normal occurrence. I poke Paul and point to the armed militia man. He says, "Welcome to Guatemala."

The Chevy we're riding in comes to a dead stop. In his choppy English, our cab driver says that a merge up ahead is causing the traffic jam. Outside the car windows, vendors sell everything from candy to ice cream and roasted ears of corn on sticks, still in their husks.

"Qué es eso?" Paul asks the driver when we see people sipping Coke from paper straws inserted into plastic bags. *What's that?*

In deft Spanglish, the driver explains that the soda has been emptied from their bottles into Baggies. In Guatemala, trash is a problem and recycling is expensive. So instead of throwing them out, glass bottles are reused. This much is clear from the scratches and nicks in the well-worn crates of beer and soda bottles stacked beside the street vendors.

Drinking soda from a plastic bag will become a common sight on this trip. As will many other things I've never witnessed before.

~

Traffic starts to ease. Paul tells our cabbie that the airline has lost our luggage. The man seems extremely troubled by this. More upset than he should be. He furrows his brow and offers an earnest, *"Lo siento."* This means "I'm sorry." Later, we realize that by mistake, Paul used the word for "dresses" instead of the word for "clothes." Maybe this explains the strange expression on the driver's face—he was trying to picture Paul in a mumu. Not a pretty sight.

The cab drops us off outside the Hotel Centenario which is practically next door to the Palacio Nacional (National Palace). But even though we have a fax confirming our reservation, the Centenario has no accommodations for us.

Frustrated, we cross the street and head for the main square, Parque Centenario. We sit on a bench to figure out our next move. A man approaches us with a shoeshine kit. But when he spots our hiking boots, he grumbles and turns away without a word.

Wooden soap boxes are set up throughout the park. From some of them, Evangelists spout in Spanish. At others, people sing. Paul and I are surrounded by a festive, hectic atmosphere, two unilingual clowns in the midst of a Latin American three-ring circus.

We decide to brave the crowds and head toward a cluster of Zona 1's reasonable hotels. Swirling through a kaleidoscope of people, places and things, all around us vendors sell food, sneakers, t-shirts and toys. They peddle everything imaginable in the clogged, congested streets. We literally have to weave between the bodies to make any progress. There are stares because we stick out like proverbial sore thumbs in our western clothes, taller than most Guatemalans.

We pass hawkers selling cassette tapes of American songs they can't possibly know the meanings of. Creedence Clearwater Revival's

"Have You Ever Seen the Rain?" blares on a cheap boombox. It is bizarrely appropriate here.

On one street corner is a huge cardboard carton filled with puppies. Some nap peacefully while others try to escape. On another, there are two soldiers cradling their ever-present M-16s like mothers clasp their babies.

The Hotel Colonial is diagonally across the street from police headquarters, which looms like an incongruous castle. The Colonial's lobby is tiled, clean and full of dark, heavy furniture.

But when Paul and I get to our room upstairs, it's disappointing, musty and tattered. With faded blue roses on the wallpaper, Room 13 reeks strongly of disinfectant. Which is always better than smelling like cat pee. But since we're tired, dirty and possession-less, lucky Room 13 suits us perfectly.

~

Finding a half-decent restaurant late on a Sunday afternoon in Guatemala City is nothing short of a miracle. The Colonial's eatery isn't open. Altuna, a grand, expansive place, smells alluringly of garlic and spices. Its aromas make our mouths water. But a waiter tells us that they're about to close. We think. With our crappy command of Spanish, we can't be too sure. But maybe it's just our pathetic, "they-lost-our-luggage" look that gives us the appearance of American hobos which makes the waiter send us packing.

There are loads of fast-food spots lining the *avenida* but Paul and I agree that after airplane food, we want something delicious.

PS, we don't get it.

Soon, we're standing in front of a restaurant we passed up in the beginning of our search. It's a grungy "vegetarian" café that serves meat. Peeking inside, the peeling wallpaper is thick with grease. The cloth table coverings are badly stained. The torn menus are "older than me," as Paul says. It is exactly the type of establishment guidebooks warn you against entering. The kind of place in which your mother tells you to wipe down the silverware. The sort of place that screams, "Cholera!" in a nagging voice. But La China is only a half-block from our hotel. And besides, we're starving.

Inside La China, a man sleeps with his head on one of the tables. Is this our waiter? Should we wake him? A baby screams in a back room. Later, a little girl rolls around in a walker, teething on a plastic bag as her mother serves us our supper. La China is passable at best. At least we don't get sick.

For some unexplained reason, Guatemala City has an unnatural number of Chinese restaurants. Especially for a Latin American country. As its name implies La China's menu has an Asian flair. My steamed vegetables emote a "La Choy" meets "Franco American" brown gravy essence. Paul's chicken is edible, albeit a bit rubbery.

~

The diesel busses tearing through Guatemala City's streets sound like airplanes as they pass. These vehicles aren't sleek like the ones back home. Instead, the capital is filled with a legion of old school busses, Blue Birds probably too antiquated to use in the States anymore, but they suit GC just fine. Their diminutive seats are tailormade for Guatemala's small-statured populace.

Each bus is personalized by its driver. They have crazy names like "Love Machine" painted on the front in primary colors. Trinkets— beaded necklaces, rosaries and small dolls—hang from their rearview mirrors. The Blue Birds never come to a full stop; they just slow down. Paul and I take note of this as we dodge between them to cross the avenue. The air is choked with fumes as a continuous line of busses rumble along the broken roads.

The streets of Guatemala City are a lot like the streets of New York City, only narrower and crumblier. They aren't as dirty as they are back home but somehow, they're more desperate.

In one way, the people are more intense than New Yorkers, maybe because they're poorer. They don't have much to lose. This is poverty and squalor on whole new level. Yet, in another way, the citizens are friendlier, more patient, more eager to help, to understand. More so than New Yorkers.

~

Even with our limited language skills, Paul and I manage to find toothbrushes in an open-air pharmacy, and in our choice of designer colors. Plus, some contact lens solution for me. But oddly enough, they don't sell plastic contact lens holders. "We'll improvise," I tell Paul hopefully.

Our next stumbling block is trying to explain to the man at the Hotel Colonial's front desk that we need two small drinking glasses to store my contact lenses. Except Paul doesn't know the word for "contact lenses" in Spanish. Instead, he uses *ojos*, which means "eyes."

The desk clerk grudgingly hands us a pair of shot glasses from the bar, studying me intently. I swear he thinks Paul has just told him that I have a glass eye. The man examines my face, trying to decipher which eye is real and which is fake. When I wink at him, he turns away.

Back upstairs, the closer I inspect our room, the more I realize how threadbare it is. "Don't look too hard," Paul suggests. It is sage advice.

The Colonial's accommodations seemed adequate at first, when our bellies were empty and our bodies were travel-weary, before we got our second wind. But upon closer scrutiny, there's a cavern in the center of one bed's mattress. "It's all fucked out," Paul tells me. The room's other bed is solid but it's only a single.

Wood accents decorate the length of the wall, adding a sophisticated touch. In Guatemala, mahogany and teak are as plentiful as pine is back home. The rainforests are full of these trees. Or at least they were at one time. Soon, I suppose I'll get used to seeing these fine woods in the shabbiest of Guatemala's hotels. But at this point, in our journey, they appear luxurious.

~

Paul and I lay side by side on the chintz bedspread, reading. I, for some reason, decided to bring the hefty *The Adventures of Huckleberry Finn* as my literary companion on this trip. I'd always meant to read it, especially because of Hemingway's comment that all great books can be traced to *Huck*.

My travel partner has taken a thin but emotionally-weighty tome called *Ever After*. Paul keeps reading me excerpts. How I love when he does this! The gentle timbre of his voice in the night air of a peculiar, exotic land soothes me as Paul murmurs softly, so as not to wake our neighbors on the other side of the Colonial's paper-thin walls. I am like a beloved child being treated to a bedtime story—one that is cared for, catered to, delicately indulged. Or a cherished lover Paul needs to share these poignantly poetic words with. Which, I guess, I am.

But soon, both of us grow tired of reading. We seek the comfort of each other's arms as we usually do at bedtime. We are relatively new lovers, still discovering, still exploring.

There's a weighty double dresser in one corner of the room, across from the bed. It has a pockmarked mirror on the door. Paul and I watch our twined bodies by the glow of an amber utility light. This is a bonus, despite the huge divot in the center of the mattress.

That's when I remember that I transferred the emergency condom I usually carry in my shoulder bag to my lost backpack. To lighten my load, so to speak. Without hesitation, I take Paul into my mouth. He doesn't seem to mind this change of venue.

Afterwards, we try to sleep, but once again, Guatemala City proves to be like Manhattan: the city that never sleeps. Bells ring. A barrage of fireworks explode. A chorus of dogs bark. I feel Paul get up in the middle of the night and climb into the nearby single bed.

Abandoned, I call to him. "Either I keep falling off the edge or into the hole," he explains, then drifts off.

Near dawn, far off in the wilds of Guatemala City, a woman shrieks. It is piercing, urgent. Funny, how a scream sounds the same in Spanish as it does in English. It needs no translation.

Day 2

I would kill, or at least maim, for a fresh pair of underwear.
Paul and I have been wearing the same clothes since six yesterday
morning. At least the weather isn't too warm so we aren't sweaty
messes. I don't smell too foul. Yet. But what will we do if the airport
doesn't find our backpacks?

I'm not as upset as I should be. If I were in a similar situation
with my ex-husband, I'd be screeching at him and he'd be roaring back
at me. But being with Paul is different. He has a strangely calming
effect. I feel like nothing terrible will ever happen to me on his watch.

Yes, Paul is different than Alexander. Very different, I keep
reminding myself. But then again, with Paul, *I* am very different. I
hope he knows that most women would be freaking out if they had
to slip into their crusty, old socks for Day Two and had to go without
simple luxuries like hair conditioner and antiperspirant. But I think
Paul realizes this.

Sometimes Paul doesn't say anything but he notices everything.
And he tries hard to hide how taken he is with me. But he is. I'm sure
he is. It's there in the way he looks at me, although he tries to sluff it
off as my imagination. But it's not all in my head. "You read too much
into them," he smiles when I call attention to his weighty glances. But
there's no mistaking it.

However, is it love? Lust? Both? Or something in between? Yes, to all of the above.

~

This morning is my first experience with a trickling, tepid, Central American shower. In Guatemala, it is the gold standard but it would be considered subpar in the US. The Colonial's "hot" water is heated by an exposed electrical wire. Not the safest practice, mixing water and electricity. But it seems to work. Most of the time. Sort of.

Before I actually get into the shower, Paul tells me about a man he met years earlier while traveling in Costa Rica. The guy was curious about the coil he saw above the showerhead so he touched it. And when he did, the poor fool was hurled across the bathroom from the jolt of electricity. "Why did you tell me this?" I ask Paul.

"I just want you to be careful, that's all," he says.

When I step into the lukewarm spray, I'm cautious not to stretch my hands too far above my head by accident, even while lathering my hair.

The showerhead unceremoniously juts out of the bathroom ceiling. The water runs down the concrete floor to a drain in the center. It smacks of the shower rooms in B-movies, the ones where they hose down a female inmate then menacingly approach her with a broom handle. Afterwards, when I mention this to Paul, he laughs. "You're right," he says as he peers into the bathroom.

The shower isn't as bad as I thought it would be. Although the stream isn't strong enough to wash all the sticky soap from my body, I notice as I dry myself with a rough, white towel. I'm filmy but at least I'm clean.

Yesterday, Lacsa promised they'd have more information about our luggage late this afternoon. Until then, instead of moping around, Paul and I decide to enjoy Guatemala City as much as possible. Our original plan had been to catch a bus to Tikal today and explore its Mayan ruins. We try not to stress out about our trip being pushed back a day. "Plans are made to be broken," I offer.

"Besides, we're on vacation," Paul points out. "It's all an adventure."

"Right," I agree. "We're supposed to relax and not get bent out of shape over minor setbacks like this." I sound so persuasive that I almost convince myself it's true. Except my sticky panties keep reminding me that it isn't.

"I mean, it's not like everything we own is lost in limbo," Paul says with a forced grin.

~

The Hotel Colonial's cafeteria is quaint and adorable. Arranged on a glass case are postcards and packs of cigarettes, both for sale. The two ladies behind a counter dote on us. The older one wears a hairnet and is clearly in charge. The younger one is her helper and our waitress. Her waist-length hair is pulled back into a tight, shiny ponytail.

We watch the women prepare our breakfast with interest. It's like sitting in a friend's home as they make you a meal. Only this kitchen is lots bigger than a typical household setup. The walls are tiled white and the tiles sparkle. The women chatter amicably to each other, and to us, in Spanish as they cook.

Paul and I sit at a heavy plank table with matching chairs. The meal is good, simple—eggs over easy with refried black beans on the side. In the weeks to come we will grow accustomed to black beans with almost every meal. Not only will we get used to them, but we will come to expect them. And like most things in Guatemala, we will ultimately crave them.

~

After breakfast, we try to reach Paul's former roommate Glenn but have no luck. Although Glenn's telephone number is in Paul's missing backpack, Paul manages to contact the language school Glenn is affiliated with out of town. Fingers crossed that they give Glenn the message but with what we've seen of Guatemala's efficiency so far, it's doubtful they will.

Glenn is a Latin American History major working on his thesis in Quetzaltenango (nicknamed "Xela" from its old Mayan name "Xelaju.") Before Paul and I left Brooklyn, we promised Glenn we'd call him as soon as we arrived in Guatemala so we could coordinate our itinerary for the last week of our trip. Glenn has managed time off from his research so he can show us some of his favorite spots in the backwoods of Guatemala's Western Highlands.

Hopefully Glenn isn't sitting by the telephone, waiting for our call. Between our arrival delay, our lost luggage and the iffy pay phones, this is the first chance we've had to call him. But more than Paul and I do, Glenn knows how things work in Guatemala. Which is hardly ever.

29

~

Trekking in Guatemala City, amid the bus exhaust, the sea of buildings and snarled traffic, you sometimes forget that you're nestled in a beautiful valley surrounded by volcanic peaks. But whenever I peek down a side street, I am reminded of this because the stark blue shadows of Sierra Madre de Chiapas stare back at me. Knowing these mountains are close makes the city's fumes easier to deal with.

With every step there are more oddities: the profusion of old cars, for one, both American and European, even Volvos. Also, no matter where you go, there are armed soldiers. I still can't get past the fact that they all carry machine guns. For me, it isn't the fact that they have automatic rifles, but the thought that these weapons are so accessible, poised in their hands, ready to be used at a moment's notice. This will take some getting used to.

~

Today is earmarked for sightseeing. Paul and I head toward the Palacio Nacional but on the way, we come to a vast church. It's made of white stone and has two bell towers with a smaller clock tower burrowed in between them. "For a couple of lapsed Catholics, we have an unnatural interest in churches," Paul remarks.

He's right.

But still, I tell him, "It's just architecture. Not theology."

The sheer size of the Catedral Primada Metropolitana de Santiago takes my breath away. Inside its cavernous belly, people pray at individual altars dedicated to particular saints. The worshippers are fervent, immersed in their own world of supplication and devotion. We admire the cathedral's vaulted ceilings, the patterns of light streaming in the tall windows, the red banners strung throughout, then leave the others to their prayers.

Outside the cathedral's doors, peddlers sell homemade candles and curiously enough, birdseed. A little girl stands on the steps, engulfed by a flock of pigeons, giggling with delight as she feeds them.

Our next stop is the Mercado Central. Guatemala City's central market is partially underground, similar to a parking garage, and is supposedly earthquake-proof. Like any public stairwell in any large metropolis, the concrete steps smell strongly of urine. But it feels like home, like a dank corner in a New York City subway.

Not counting street vendors, of which there are many, this is our first taste of a typical Central American market. Booths filled with weavings and pottery are squashed close together. They press against others which sell varieties of corn, grain and dried beans. There are also baskets of spices, avocados and all sorts of vegetables, some so local and exotic, I have no clue what they are.

At about ten on a Monday morning, things are just getting started. This early, Paul and I are the only *gringos* present. Although the selection of handmade crafts is tempting, we opt to hold off until later in our travels to buy souvenirs. If we get them this early in our trip, we'll have to lug them around for almost three weeks. And we still have no luggage to put them in.

~

The Palacio Nacional is impressive. It was built by then-president General Jorge Ubico between 1939 and 1943, right before he was ousted from power in 1944. At the cost of 2,800,000 quetzals (with an exchange rate higher than today's 5.5 quetzals to every US dollar), it's sumptuous, especially by Guatemalan standards. Decorated with polished brass and wrought iron, the ceiling is supported by mahogany beams. There's marble throughout, as well as carved columns, elaborate lanterns, frescoes and a bunch of courtyards.

All visitors have to walk through a metal detector to enter the Palacio Nacional. The security guards stop a group of a dozen indigenous people. They are neatly dressed in traditional clothing: the women wear *huipils* and cotton skirts while the men are in button-down shirts and pressed pants that reach a few inches above their ankles. This group is searched more painstakingly than Paul and I are, even though we look like unkempt bums in our rumpled, day-old Westerners' clothes.

This is our first experience with prejudice toward Guatemala's native people. But not the last. It's so blatant that it makes us uncomfortable. Paul and I swap angry glances but not words. The Guatemalan Indians, with their proud bearing, their jet-black hair, their broad cheekbones and their smooth, caramel-colored skin, don't bat an eye. Perhaps it's because they're used to being treated like this. But we aren't used to seeing it. I hope we'll never be.

Paul and I turn and mount the palace's wide marble staircase. We wander from room to room unfettered, peeking into cordoned-off reception areas, admiring architect Rafael Pérez de León's Moorish design. The main ballroom boasts a chandelier with four gilded quetzals carved into it. (The feathered sort, not the monetary unit.)

Likenesses of Guatemala's national bird stare off into four different directions: north, south, east and west. There's also said to be a stuffed quetzal in the room but we can't find it and there are no guards to ask.

Briefly, Paul and I tag along with a tour group. We roll our eyes at the guide's watered-down version of the Spaniards' invasion of the New World. It sounds so neighborly and friendly, like a social visit. Plus, there's no mention of the two S's the Spanish were kind enough to bring as gifts: syphilis and smallpox.

~

Next on the agenda is a cab ride to the Museo Popol Vuh. This museum's name refers to the Mayan creation myth. Paul and I take a glass elevator up to the sixth floor of an office building. There sits a limited but noteworthy assortment of Mayan art and a smorgasbord of ancient artifacts. In 1977, Jorge and Ella Castillo donated their private collection to Universidad Francisco Marroquín, which still oversees it.

We walk among a slew of ceremonial masks, pottery and burial urns. I've never seen a burial urn before and have no idea what they are. "You mean, the Maya shoved their dead into these big jars?" I ask Paul, shocked.

He's even more stunned at my stupidity. "No," he says carefully and slowly, as if speaking to a simpleton. "The urns held their cremated remains. Then the urns and ashes were buried."

"Oh," I say, blushing. I'm sure this question has taken me down a notch in Paul's book. Quietly, I squint at the note cards, written in Spanish and spotty English, as if they hold the key to secrets I don't know.

Museo Popol Vuh displays a sacred book of the K'iche' people which was saved from destruction by Spanish priests. This is surprising since Catholics tried to quell every vestige of pagan ritual possible. As though this could make K'iche' beliefs cease to exist. In many ways, it only made them stronger.

Some Mayan customs are bizarre to modern-day "civilized" folks like us. One exhibition's placard claims that the losing team of a game fondly described as "Death Ball" would either be decapitated or tied together and rolled down the side of a pyramid as punishment.

Apparently, the Maya also liked hot cocoa—they invented it. But I don't think marshmallows were around yet. I'm too afraid to ask Paul, though, for fear he'll think I'm a jackass.

We watch part of a film which is narrated in English, oddly enough. It describes the Popol Vuh mystery. In the Popol Vuh, not only is the world created, but the Hero Twins are victorious against the Lords of Xibalba (the Underworld, literally "the place of fright"). Sounds like a comic-book movie.

The bulk of the cards accompanying the artifacts at Popol Vuh aren't translated into English—and if they are, the translations are hilarious—so we can't get the full effect of the exhibits. However, Paul and I eavesdrop again as a Spanish-speaking guide translates the placards for his tribe of well-coiffed, older ladies. "I bet they're the pampered wives of foreign businessmen," I offer to Paul.

He picks up without skipping a beat. "Sucking up the local color while their husbands slave away at the Canadian Embassy," he says.

"Charging souvenirs and expensive lunches on the company card," I embellish.

"Then their husbands get canned when some pencil-pusher figures it out," he tells me.

From the start of our relationship, Paul and I have slipped into this weird order of behavior. By now, we have become adept at crafting elaborate pasts, presents and futures for total strangers. It's an amusing diversion.

~

After Museo Popol Vuh, Paul and I change travelers checks at the bank on the ground floor. As expected, there are armed guards.

We get lunch at a place on Avenida La Reforma. The thoroughfare itself reminds me of New York City's Park Avenue because it's wide and spacious, intersected by a strip of green grass. Although our Spanish still sucks, Paul manages to communicate preferences like "without ice" (*sin hielo)* and "without meat" (*sin carne).* He is more daring experimenting in this language than I am, maybe because he grew up with a Spanish-speaking mother. Yet Paul won't acknowledge his growing prowess. He gets embarrassed whenever I compliment him. About anything. Often, he tries to change the subject or belittles his accomplishments. Like now.

Similar to the legumes at breakfast, the black beans served with our lunch are also refried but these have a faint chocolaty taste. They go well with the little corn cakes, guacamole and the omnipresent tortillas we are served.

33

Paul and I sit at a table which borders the street. Nearby, a light-haired American couple fasten an obviously Guatemalan baby into a stroller. Did these people venture south of the border to buy this child from parents who could no longer afford to care for it? There are rumors of such things happening frequently. Whether or not it's true, the complicated scenario Paul and I construct for the family dovetails nicely into reality. And it helps pass the time as we wait for our sweet *postre*.

~

Another walk, another outdoor market. This one is closer to the airport, which we are slowly making our way toward. Paul and I mentally gird our loins for the possibility of wearing the same clothes for a third day. "We might have to get all Guated out," Paul warns me.

"Guated out?" I ask.

"You know, dress like locals. Or else go to a *ropas Americanos* store."

"I am *not* wearing second-hand clothes," I insist. "American or not."

~

To our amazement, when we get to La Aurora's Lacsa counter, we discover that our backpacks have been located. It turns out that luggage was deliberately removed from yesterday's flight because the airplane was too heavy. (*'But why couldn't they bump a couple of TV sets instead of our stuff,'* I ask myself.) Our packs were then sent to La Aurora on this morning's flight.

Never was I so thrilled at the prospect of fresh underwear. Never was I so delighted to get a 30-pound pack onto my shoulders. I vow not to complain about how heavy my bag is but know I will. In the coming weeks, I'll be huffing and puffing from its bulk, wondering why I took all these pairs of socks with me.

Like everything else in Guatemala, getting our backpacks is unnecessarily complicated. An airport worker takes us downstairs, wielding a large ring of keys. We descend staircase after staircase like we are going into the bowels of hell. Or maybe Xibalba. "I didn't know airports even *had* a downstairs," I whisper to Paul.

"Maybe he's taking us somewhere to rob us and kill us," Paul suggests.

Maybe my parents were right.

Hundreds of bags are in the bowels of La Aurora, locked into cages. The attendant reads numbers from a scrap of paper then proceeds along the row. Finally, he locates the correct section. After several tries, he finds the corresponding key and unlocks the pen. Then he disappears inside. "We'll never see him again," Paul sighs.

But the attendant eventually reappears, dragging first Paul's backpack, then mine, grunting under the weight. Paul slips him a few quetzals tip for his troubles. Then the man leads us back through the labyrinth of suitcases and boxes, and upstairs.

Before we leave the airport, Paul and I arrange for a one-way flight to Flores the following morning. At least we can recoup for our lost day and fly there instead of taking the bus. Saving time justifies the extra expense.

Though she claims she speaks English, the woman at the Tikal Jets counter stumbles over *Inglés*. Our bad Spanish succeeds in confusing her even further. Maybe it's our Brooklynese accents but the poor woman is flustered. She stammers over Paul's simple last name—Black.

Paul tries to politely enlighten her, asking what color her hair is. She has no clue. *"También negro,"* he grins. *Also black.* But she still doesn't see the connection. Paul smiles again to get her to relax but this makes her even more nervous. Maybe she thinks he's flirting. Maybe she thinks we want a threesome. All Paul is trying to do is help. The woman is relieved when our credit cards are approved and we walk away, tickets in hand.

~

Some mysterious force keeps us from Restaurante Altuna. Since it's closed on Mondays, we decide on El Gran Pavo, which translates to "the great turkey." But alas, there's no turkey on the menu. Instead, it serves first-rate Mexican food. Two full-course dinners of steak, fish, plus two beers, a gigantic fruity drink, dessert and coffee cost only 20 US dollars. El Gran Pavo is pretty but almost empty, as most restaurants in Guatemala City seem to be. How do they stay afloat?

For some reason, this broken-down metropolis is inexplicably romantic. In a sentimental mood, Paul asks a strolling photographer to snap a Polaroid of us. It comes out awful. My eyes are customarily closed in pictures and this one is no exception. But we buy it anyway.

Into El Gran Pavo comes a brood of Europeans. From their conservative clothes, we gather that they're from some sort of religious sect. "Jehovah's Witnesses?" I wonder.

"Bruderhofers," Paul suggests with confidence. But I'm too tired to ask what a Bruderhofer is.

The group is pushy. They rearrange tables to their own liking without the staff's permission. Do they realize that they're being rude, that they're making the owner uneasy? The real question is, do they care?

In El Gran Pavo's adjoining room, a pair of roving guitarists play for a quartet of drunks. Sensing this could get ugly very quickly, Paul and I pay our bill and escape.

The streets are dimly lit. There's a sinister air, like one you get at Central Park after midnight. But it's barely nine and the *avenida* is empty. I still feel safe at Paul's side, as though no harm will ever come to me when I'm with him. I don't understand why but he always makes me feel this way. And I like it.

~

Back at the Colonial we finally get in touch with Glenn by phone. We solidify our plans to meet up with him and his girlfriend Rachel in Xela on December 3. This gives Paul and I a week and a half on our own to do whatever we choose. With Glenn and Rachel, we'll rent a Jeep to explore undeveloped, off-the-beaten path villages in the Western Highlands.

Honestly, I'm a little overwhelmed at the thought of the perfect freedom we'll have in the coming weeks. We're unchained. Unmoored. We can go anywhere we want in this crazy country. It's a little unnerving.

If Paul feels the same way, he doesn't show it. Before we left Brooklyn, he made a hand-drawn grid on lined paper and penciled in the sites he hoped to visit before we hooked up with Glenn and Rachel. I have a heavily-Highlighted copy of *The Real Guide* where I've read and reread about these places. Plus, like the well-trained, former Catholic school girl that I am, I scribbled copious notes in the margins.

But instead of being excited about the possibilities, I'm paralyzed with fear. There are too many choices! Too much can go wrong! But then I remind myself how lucky I am. Who has this kind of flexibility in their life? This type of elasticity to travel to wherever they please? For as long as they please? And to travel with a man like Paul at their side? Not many. Not any, in fact. Just me.

~

Up in our room, Paul and I decide against taking a side trip to Belize after the pyramids of Tikal. Since neither of us scuba dives, there isn't much sense in going. The main reason to visit Belize is to dive because their coast is an underwater playground, second only to Australia's Great Barrier Reef.

Plus, Belize City is downright dangerous. Stories circulate of tourists being held up at knifepoint in their hotels and of entire dive boats getting robbed. "Besides, it's probably better to check out one country at a slower pace than to rush through two," Paul suggests.

I agree. But only because Belize sounds more terrifying than Guatemala. Which is saying a lot.

There's nothing quite so soothing as curling up beside someone you love. Or someone you *think* you might love. The sensation of Paul's body wrapped around mine, carving into the crook of my spine, is indescribable. Comforting and stimulating simultaneously.

It's a matter of minutes before I turn, pressing him into my belly. In mid-kiss, Paul smiles, hopefully knowing how good being desired feels. But neither of us says it. Ever. At least, not yet.

Afterwards, we sleep.

Day 3

Tuesday, November 23, 1993
Guatemala City/Flores/Tikal

Because it's my grandmother's birthday, I convince myself that
nothing bad can happen to us today. It's my first thought before I open
my eyes this morning.

Wishful thinking.

~

Paul and I wake at five and catch a cab to La Aurora at 5:30.
We arrive to a closed hurricane fence's gate. Wrong airport? Not
exactly. The one with flights to small, regional cities like Flores is right
next door to La Aurora. It's a tinier, military-type base. The pervasive
armed soldier stands behind the locked front gate, his ever-ready rifle
almost an appendage.

The sun is just beginning to rise. The sky has a greenish tint
above the Sierra Madre de Chiapas Mountains. A group of us,
tourists mostly, wait expectantly outside the gate. Like us, many
are taking chartered flights up north to Flores in the Petén, a vastly
uninhabited region.

In sheer landmass alone, the Petén occupies about a third of
Guatemala. Yet it contains less than two percent of the population. The
main attraction in the Petén is Tikal's Mayan ruins, about an hour's
drive from Flores. Miniscule compared to the capital, Flores is the
Petén's largest city.

Finally, the sentry standing guard opens and closes the gate by hand. He lets in ragtag clusters of workers and other locals. The rest of us stand outside until six, when the airport officially opens. And when it does, the caravan sweeps toward a row of Cheap Charlie airline terminals. We go past huge hangars, their doors gaping in wide yawns, displaying helicopters, propellor planes and other aircraft. "Most of these are kind of...old," I note.

Paul nods. It's still too early for him to talk.

The airplanes look especially battered, browbeaten almost. Is Guatemala where old planes—as well as old cars—go to die too?

~

All last night I tossed and turned in bed, worried about taking a flight on such a pint-sized plane. I'm not the most confident flyer in the universe, nervous and jittery in the air. I function best on flat, sure, solid ground. Not climbing a mountain. Not swimming. Just walking on straight, strong bedrock. Whenever I'm airborne, my body instinctively tells me, 'Hey, you're not supposed to be up here!' And I don't relax until there's earth beneath my feet.

The Tikal Jets desk is as sterile and welcoming as the New York State Department of Motor Vehicles. A woman sits at a metal table, taking tickets from the people who crowd the lobby. When our turn comes, she can't find our name on the handwritten passenger list, even though Paul and I have tickets.

Their first flight to Flores is booked solid and there's no room to squeeze us in. The black-haired girl who'd made our reservations yesterday at La Aurora (the same one who'd been so uncomfortable with Paul's good-natured joking) cowers in the corner, hoping we won't notice her. But we do.

By now, Paul is about to explode. Through his teeth, he asks me to get him a cup of coffee from the urn that bubbles in Tikal Jets' sitting area. There's coffee, sugar, spoons but no cups. Typical. When I report back to him, java-less, Paul plops into a plastic chair, simmering. I keep my distance; I know better. He needs a cup of mediocre coffee in him before he can even think of being polite.

It's difficult, if not impossible, to have a satisfying argument with someone in a foreign tongue. Body language—i.e., an angry glare, a hard-set jaw—is not without its merits but they still aren't the same as irritated words. Paul manages to convey, "This is bullshit!" (*"Esto es una mierda!"*) *en Español* with a certain degree of conviction.

But bullshit or not, there's still no room on the flight.

~

Paul's ire prompts the woman at the metal table to ask a minibus driver to take us to a rival airline at another terminal so we can try our luck there. The thought of a second day stranded in diesel-infested Guatemala City is too horrible to bear this early in the morning. But it doesn't look like we'll be able to get to Flores today. So much for Nana's birthday being lucky.

The first airline we check at Terminal 2 says only one space is available on the next plane out. "You and your wife could take separate flights," the minibus driver suggests.

When Paul frowns, the driver leaves to check a different airline. I raise my eyebrows at Paul and mouth the word "wife." He half-scowls. "It's official," I tell him. "We're married now."

Paul eyes me, amused. "Pilots can marry people," he corrects. "But not the guy who drives a van in the airport."

I laugh but in reality, I am terrified. Not of the prospect of marrying Paul but of flying solo in a prop plane. What if separate flights are our only option to get to Flores? I can't imagine flying without Paul, especially on such a crappy, little airplane. And what if Paul can't get on the next flight out? Then I'd be stranded in Flores by myself. Besides, whose wrist would I dig my fingernails into at takeoff? And what if the plane crashes? Then I'd die alone.

The driver returns with excellent news. There are plenty of seats on an Aerovías flight. They even volunteer to hold the plane for us.

Paul dashes to the Tikal Jets office to process our refund. When he tells the woman what airline we're taking to Flores, she's surprised. *"Ellos son muy malos,"* she stammers. *They are very bad.*

Paul snickers in response. "You messed up my reservation," he tells the woman. "How bad could they possibly be?" The woman says nothing.

Because he's been so helpful, Paul tries to give the minibus driver a tip but he refuses to take it.

~

Although the Aerovías staff is professional and courteous, they are by no means the slick, streamlined flight team TV commercials are made of. Instead, Aerovías has a rough-around-the-edges quality.

It's a lot like Eddie's Airways from the Jerry Lewis movie *The Family Jewels*. Eddie's slogan was "the airline for the birds."

In the film, Eddie does everything—fuels the plane, flies it, is the flight attendant. The Aerovías staff works almost as hard as Eddie does. The two stewardesses wear uniforms that don't match—they're just shabby skirts and blouses. One flight attendant is rather large. Her abundant thighs brush the sides of the seats as she plods down the narrow center aisle.

The inside of the airplane is only steps above a Guatemalan taxicab. The material on the chairs is worn thin and the plastic paneling on the walls also shows signs of wear. "It reminds me of an old Brooklyn city bus," Paul offers.

"Shush," I tell him. Paul is right but I won't admit it. Not now. Maybe after we safely land in Flores. *If* we do.

~

The airplane holds approximately 50 but it is only half full and there are no assigned seats. "Where should we sit?" I ask, my voice trembling. I hope Paul doesn't detect this.

"Near the emergency exit," he responds, dryly.

My heart skips a beat and not with love. A German tourist sitting behind us laughs at Paul's remark. I don't.

Takeoff and the flight itself are relatively smooth. Not nearly as bad as I expect. The scenery is spectacular, especially when Guatemala City falls away and the countryside comes into view. From this height, the mountains look craggy and cut, as if by an X-Acto knife. Like a topographical map instead of an actual landscape. *Fincas* (farms) and a handful of houses dot the land. A river meanders through the hills. But soon, the cloud cover becomes thick and chunky, blotting out everything below.

Guatemala must be where old breakfast drinks go to die too because the flight attendants serve Tang. The astronauts' favorite drink is also Aerovías' sole beverage choice. I settle back and attempt to relax for the remainder of our hour-long flight.

But as soon as I close my eyes, Paul jostles me awake. "I found this in the pouch in front of me," he says, waving a wrinkled newspaper.

"Nice," I say to him and shut my eyes again.

Paul shoves the paper at me. "This might explain why our flight isn't full." I take the paper from him, still not getting what he means.

"And why that Tikal Jets chick said Aerovías is *muy malo*,"
he continues.

He points to an article near the top of the page. It says that two
days prior, an Aerovías flight crashed in the Petén. On the very same
route we're traveling. Veiled in clouds (like now!), the pilot slammed
into a mountainside. Thirteen died on that ill-fated flight, including an
American Peace Corps worker.

I start to sweat and grab hold of Paul's hand. I don't let go for
the rest of the flight. But Paul doesn't seem to mind. He keeps holding
on. Tight.

~

After circling in the sky above Flores for almost an hour,
we finally land. In one piece. Without crashing into a mountain. As
they do in most Latin American countries, the passengers burst into
spontaneous applause when the wheels touch down. I finally release
Paul's hand and wipe the perspiration on my pants.

The weather is totally different than it was 300 miles away in
Guatemala City—warm, tropical and pleasantly humid. Paul and I
walk across the tarmac with the herd of others toward the terminal.

Plopped in the jungle, the Flores airport has two short runways.
The terminal itself is like an immense shed. In it are counters for the
handful of carriers that serve the region. There isn't even a baggage
carousel. Our luggage is wheeled over by handcart and cast onto a long
table for passengers to grab in a free-for-all. "Hey!" I say when a man
takes Paul's generic blue pack.

"Brooklyn's in the house," Paul tells me. Embarrassed, the
man heaves Paul's bag back onto the table and locates his own almost-
identical one.

"You can take the girl out of Brooklyn…" I begin, sliding into
my forest green backpack.

~

Only three hotels are on the grounds of Tikal National Park
itself. Before we left Guatemala City, Paul called and checked for
vacancies. We managed to score a room at the Hotel Tikal Inn. At 37
dollars a night, it's cheap by New York standards but considered pricey
in Guatemala. But because of its proximity to the ruins, we decide it's
well worth the cost.

Paul and I hop a Tikal-bound minibus. Also aboard is a young
Britisher who's been up since three a.m. Understandably, Colin isn't

talkative and immediately dozes, shielded by his safari hat. The single-lane highway is full of bumps, bruises and craters. I don't know how Colin can rest but soon he's softly snoring into his hat.

Lining the road to Tikal are lots of small houses. In another country, I might be inclined to call them shacks but by local standards, they're well-appointed. Some are made of thatched material while others are built of concrete blocks. Still others, on the edge of Lake Petén Itzá, are half submerged.

On the surface, the people in the Petén don't seem to have much. They're not exactly poor but let's just say they're dancing on the poverty line. Theirs is a simple, basic existence. I guess if that's all they've ever known, it's all right. They don't know what they're missing. If they *are* missing anything. But to me, it seems kind of sad, hollow.

As the minivan zips by, we pass kids playing in the dirt with sticks. They seem happy. Their feet are bare, their clothes shabby. But they're content. I'm not sure if I should feel sorry for them or not. In some ways, their modest, uncluttered lives might even be better than ours.

The town of Flores is a symphony of animals. There, chickens, turkeys, pigs, horses, oxen and dogs roam freely. Sometimes they wander into or lie in the middle of the road. Everyone takes this in stride; they simply go around the creatures. Few vehicles travel along this fast-paced, one-lane highway. We see pickup trucks and occasionally, other tourist vans. The most common method of transportation is by foot. People walk beside the road, carrying bundles on their heads or on their backs.

Before we reach Tikal itself, all three of us passengers are asked to get out of the van at the park entrance and pay a fee. It's all very serious and official. There's probably an armed soldier lurking close by. We do as we are asked, dole out the Tikal National Park fee and get back into the minivan.

~

The redundantly-named Hotel Tikal Inn—is it a hotel or is it an inn or is it a hotel with an inn-like atmosphere?—is situated on prettily-landscaped grounds and modestly decorated in a Mayan motif. (Meaning there's an abundance of bare-chested warriors sporting armbands and feathered headdresses.) We arrive at 11:30 and are told that our room won't be ready until one. The desk clerk agrees to let us leave our backpacks with him.

Paul and I convince the kitchen staff to make us an early lunch before we set off into the jungle. Our British companion is too tired to eat. Colin snoozes on a bench, using his backpack as a pillow.

The dining room has an open kitchen where women in hairnets and white paper hats bustle. Since the hotel/inn has no telephone, the desk clerk/waiter/Jack-of-all-trades listens to a crackly short-wave radio. He says *"Cambio"* each time he finishes speaking. *"Cambio,"* I know, means "change."

Outside, there's a sudden downpour, an attribute the Petén is famous for. Violent, quickly-changing weather is no surprise here. Paul and I watch the skies sizzle with rain. I feel lucky to have shelter, even if it is under a thatched roof. Yes, I am pleased with life in general. For the moment.

There are often times like this for Paul and me. Times of quiet solitude. Times when he and I say nothing to each other. Times when nothing needs to be said. Nothing in words, that is.

Yet, this silence is not from boredom; it's from contentedness. From knowing it's not always necessary to clog the air with words. Paul and I share the same opinion about so many things, there's a *déjà vu-ness* of having known each other, of having been lovers, in another time. That's when we look at each other and smile. Knowing this.

Lunch is basic but good. Broiled chicken for Paul and eggs for me. I am vegetarian—for now—and wonder how long I can keep up being meatless in a country that prides itself on serving *pollo, pollo e más pollo. (Chicken, chicken and more chicken.)* I will probably fill my cholesterol quota until the year 2000 during my stay in Guatemala. But there are worse things.

The rain stops by the time Paul and I finish eating. With small daypacks containing water, raingear and little else, we venture past Tikal's *comedor* stalls whose vendors sell wares we do not need. The entrance to Tikal National Park is steps away.

~

The ruins of Tikal are impossible to adequately describe. Photographs don't even do them justice. To appreciate these immense Mayan pyramids, you have to stand in front of them and silently ponder them, investigate them, run your fingertips along their rough stones, press your face into the rock and breathe in their essence. Once you feel sufficiently dwarfed and insignificant in their shadows then maybe you can begin to comprehend them.

Then again, maybe you never will.

Tikal is an ancient city that dates back to the fourth century BC. It is the oldest place I've ever been. Tikal is full of nonchalant grace. Of spirits. Of awe. The sheer size and visual impact of the ruins' gigantic forms rising up from the jungle floor would humble anyone. It renders guttersnipes like us speechless. Paul grabs hold of my hand as we gaze out at the ruins then look at each other then look some more at the massive temples before us.

Nothing could have prepared me for the sight of my first pyramid. At the base, it resembles a mound of dirt and grass but at the top there's rock and a steep staircase leading up. So far up, it's almost vertical.

Paul and I just stand staring, not knowing what to say or do. But then we climb one of the ruins. Of course, we climb it. Like restless children, we can't wait to climb it.

Although there are guards randomly stationed throughout the park, there's no supervision to speak of. Paul and I are free to scale the ruins as we please. Unlike dusty museum relics, there are no barriers to keep visitors away, no bannisters to prevent them from falling off the sides of pyramids once they have mounted thousands of precipitous steps to reach the top.

Paths wind lazily through the park leading from one ruin to the next. Occasional signs spotlight an ancient ceiba tree or the route to a particular temple. But besides those few guidelines, Paul and I are free to wander.

There you are, minding your own business, walking along a trail when, BOOM!, out of the greenery comes a huge ruin that seems to grow out of the ground like a tree. The steps to the top are tall, spaced 12 to 18 inches apart. "Mayan steps," Paul starts calling them.

Because this is my first time in a jungle, I'm surprised it's so noisy. I didn't realize that a rainforest simmers with life. It's a breathing organism made up of other breathing organisms. All around us are bugs, lizards and birds, and they all make their own sounds.

Standing at the top of a ruin and absorbing the panoramic view is both empowering and humbling at the same time. And Temple I isn't even close to being Tikal's biggest. Paul and I go from one to the other, practically running.

Deeper in the jungle, there's a stillness. A peace. A balance. A sense that all is good, and all is as it should be. A sense that no evil could ever happen, anywhere, to anyone. If such wonderment as tall, stone pyramids could be created by the ancients, then anything is possible. Right?

When a new ruin materializes, it is like a brand-new miracle, fresh and different than the one before it. What made people want to build such impossible structures? What were they thinking?

~

There are so many ruins in Tikal that some aren't even fully excavated. Paul and I scramble up at least a half dozen of these stunning structures. After a while, we lose count. One of the most extraordinary is Temple IV. At the bottom, it could be a hill because moss and dirt and grass cling to the base.

We clamber along a series of steps and ladders leading to the top of Temple IV. At almost 250 feet tall, the journey up its side is precarious, even dangerous. But I know that going down will be even worse. I try not to think of this until I have to.

On our almost-vertical ascent, Paul and I pass a German family, bravely making the descent with their three children. The father has a screaming toddler clinging to his chest. This guy is a combo platter of gutsy and foolish as he holds the boy with one arm and braces himself with the other. He doesn't have a belt or a rope to secure the child to his body. If the man slips, his son could easily go tumbling from his arms. The little boy's cries are chilling. They bounce off the pyramid walls like a boomerang. The child will probably be traumatized for the rest of his life. I know I will.

But standing on Temple IV's uppermost platform and looking out over Tikal makes the harrowing elevation worthwhile.

At the top of pyramids like this, there are usually miniature rooms with wood framing the doorways. Most of these carved lintels were removed by a Swiss scientist in the 1800s to "preserve" them and are now on display in Basel, Switzerland. After the lintels were taken, all that remains in Tikal are plain timber arches with tourists' names etched into them. Stupid, selfish people who need to make a mark by defacing an ancient structure with something as meaningless as their own name. Some of these date back to the early 1900s.

I don't know how long Paul and I linger at Temple IV, just looking out over the park. He hooks his arm around my shoulder.

"Amazing, isn't it?" he says. There are no words for what this is so I just sigh. "I only take you to the best places," Paul adds. That he does.

We take photo after photo of the jungle and the ruins below, knowing they will be tame in comparison to the real thing. In pictures, you can't taste the wind or feel the infinity. Images of Tikal are inadequate, just like words are.

~

But more striking than Temple IV is the center of Tikal. The Grand Plaza is surrounded by four massive structures. A jigsaw of buildings, it is almost too much to take in at once. Paul and I make our way through the Plaza slowly, trying to digest the sheer mass of it little by little.

The Temple of Masks is still being unearthed, roped off and scaffolded. But its mirror image, the Temple of the Jaguar, is directly across from it, standing a dizzying 144 feet above the ground. Fully restored, it was used in a Nike TV commercial a few years earlier.

When Paul and I approach the Jaguar Temple, instead of a wiry runner puffing up its steps, a solitary nun picks her way down the high stairs, her white habit blowing in the breeze. She wears sensible, spotless tennis shoes, probably not Nikes. The sister bows a silent greeting to us and continues her descent.

"Race you to the top!" Paul shouts and takes off. I start up behind him but quickly lose ground. On the platform above, Paul waits for me, panting, but smiling.

When I get to the platform, a sense of vertigo greets me. Here I am, standing in the open, unprotected, above the trees, towering hundreds of feet above the jungle floor. The incline of the steps is so pronounced that the stairs aren't visible from the top of the Jaguar Temple. I have the sensation that I'm floating helplessly in space.

There's also a weird aura surrounding me. A spirituality. I am flooded by the overwhelming presence of the people who once lived here—and died here.

When the ruins were originally discovered, evidence of human sacrifice was found—i.e., the remains of severed skulls and full skeletons—plus treasures like jade and pearls. It is believed that Mayan priests sweated their brains out in nearby saunas to cleanse their souls before performing religious rituals.

Blood-letting was also a common practice at Tikal. Princes were said to pierce their penises, then emerge before their devoted subjects in a swooning state at the top of a pyramid. I mean, who wouldn't swoon when you've just punctured your Johnson with a stick?

Tikal's oldest structure dates back to 150 BC and its newest, to 700 AD. The reason the Maya disappeared from the face of the earth is unclear to historians. Whether the ancient civilization was destroyed by war, an epidemic or whether there wasn't enough food to sustain them or a natural disaster like an earthquake or a volcano wiped them out is still unknown. There's no explanation as to why they're no longer here. They just seem to have vanished.

~

Paul and I laze around on the manicured lawn in the center of the Grand Plaza, trying to process all we've seen. "My head's going to explode," Paul says.

"I know what you mean," I tell him. "Pierced penises. Lintels. Beheadings. The temples themselves. It's a lot to take in."

Beneath the grass that cushions our heads, there's said to be four layers of paving. And what lurks under all of that paving? It's pretty unbelievable, unreal. Being in Guatemala. Lying on the grass in an ageless city. All of it.

There are so many unexcavated ruins in Tikal. Still buried, they just look like piles of dirt but the signs posted in front of them tell you otherwise. Paul and I scramble up a covered pyramid, pulling ourselves along rocks and vines in an unpopulated section of the park. The climb isn't easy but it's gratifying.

A handful of others explore the grounds with us including oscillated turkeys—a cross between peacocks and pheasants. They let out bloodcurdling screeches whenever the mood strikes them. As Paul and I walk through the jungle, a sudden, mournful howl makes me jump. "What the hell is that?" I gasp.

"I don't know," Paul admits. "But it sounds scary."

Then there's a great woosh in the brush. Like a large animal running in thick vegetation. "Is that a jaguar?" I panic. "There are jaguars in the jungle, right?" I want the answer to be "no." But it isn't.

"Yeah but…" Paul admits. Leaves waft down from the treetops. Then Paul looks up and starts laughing. Grayish-black howler monkeys swing from branch to branch above our heads. They stop, gawp at us, open their mouths and shriek. Then they continue playing like schoolkids at the park, yawling in delight.

~

At dusk, Tikal crackles with even more life. The turkeys give
their weird, whip-o-will cackles. Other birds join in the chorus. I've
never seen parrots that aren't in a cage. Flying free, they zoom like
red and green dashes of paint in the muggy jungle air. We listen to a
hyperactive woodpecker and finally pick him out in a nearby tree.

"Let's stay for the sunset," Paul says suddenly.

"That's crazy," I tell him. "It will be dark afterwards. How will
we get out of here?"

"I have a flashlight," he reminds me. Reluctantly, I agree.

We choose the Temple of the Lost World (*Mundo Perdido*)
to be our vantage point. Hopefully it won't be too crowded up there.
More isolated than the others, the Lost World stands at 221 feet high.
We begin our ascent at about four in the afternoon. Halfway up, we
settle in a grassy spot to rest and sip some water. The oscillated
turkeys don't mind.

Paul and I continue up to the platform. It's beautifully serene. I
try not to worry about how we'll get down the side of the pyramid and
out of the park in the pitch blackness and focus on the moment. And
the moment is lovely.

The two-hour wait for the setting sun passes quickly. Slowly,
others make the pilgrimage and join us at the peak. There are about
a dozen of us in all. When the colors finally come, a gentle pinkness
floods the sky. It's not the dramatic purples and oranges we'd expected.
But still, we'll take it. Stretched across the sweeping, unobstructed
horizon, it is quietly magnificent.

The pinks bleed into reds. Our companions remark on the sky's
splendor in an array of languages. Two wealthy Americans watch with
their Belizean guide. There are even a few children, pensive and awe
filled like the rest of us.

From the Lost World, the forest canopy looks like bunches of
broccoli. There is nothing above us. We are at the top of the world.
You can almost see yourself as a god or at least a demigod when you
eyeball the earth from on high.

But then comes the descent. Paul holds my hand as we creep
down slowly, step by step. I want to kiss the jungle floor when we
finally reach it. Our group of spectators goes off into several
directions. Paul and I navigate the shadowy paths, aided by the light
of a three-quarter moon shining through the trees.

When we hit the Grand Plaza, the lunar glow reflects an eerie pink off the pyramids, as if tinged in pale blood. We rush through, sensing the presence of the long dead. I'm afraid we may never find our way out of Tikal National Park. When I tell Paul this, with great confidence he says, "Of course we will." After a few steps, he clarifies, "And if we don't, we have enough water and protective gear to survive the night."

"Is that supposed to make me feel better?" I ask.

"Yes," he tells me optimistically.

"Well, it doesn't."

I repeat to myself that Paul always manages to get us out of jams, whether we are lost in the city, in the country or on the grounds of ancient ruins. Unlike me, he has an impressive sense of direction, which will come in handy because he's managed to misplace the map of the park.

But soon enough, we pass the giant ceiba tree near Tikal's entrance. The lights of the *comedors* wink at us, silently mocking us, 'And you were worried you wouldn't find your way out? Here we are…here we are.'

~

Hungry, Paul and I choose the least-grungy eatery for dinner. A rat scurries by while we order. But the presence of rodents and other creatures can't be helped. We're in the jungle, after all. Although the *comedors* have roofs, there are no doors. The windows are flung open wide to let in the breeze. Anything can—and does—come in from the wild.

On the way back to the Hotel Tikal Inn, Paul and I pause to stand in an abandoned airfield, contemplating the inky sky studded with stars. Then we continue walking.

The magic of the pyramids follows us to our room as Paul and I slide into the cool sheets. The thatched walls don't touch the thatched ceiling. We make love quietly, the lines of each other's bodies as familiar as our own. But we are oddly altered in these altered surroundings, with unfamiliar food in our bellies and another language staining our tongues.

Far off are the phantoms of the ruins. And I feel the Mayan pyramids contemplating us too.

Day 4

Paul and I wake up with the sun to the sound of the jungle. It is alive with the voices of birds, too many kinds to count. Their calls melt one into the other. The plan is to have a quick breakfast then return to Flores to continue our journey. Santa Elena, a small town that joins Flores by bridge, has a bus station with coaches that go all over Guatemala.

Breakfast is the *típico* eggs, black beans, fried bananas and tortillas. It's tasty and filling. We have the misfortune of occupying a table next to a loud, overbearing Southern man. Picture Foghorn Leghorn, but with a hangover.

Over fried *plátanos,* Paul and I wonder how this bombastic Rebel happened upon sharing a room with two genteel gay gentlemen. But stranger things have happened.

As Paul and I try to enjoy our *desayuno*, Southern Man goes into exquisite detail about his bowel movements. He claims he can't have breakfast because whatever he eats turns to liquid shit. Then he proceeds to complain about how expensive the less-than-40-dollar a night hotel is. "His cowboy boots probably cost more than what a Guatemalan makes in a year," I whisper loudly to Paul.

"Most locals don't even have shoes," he points out.

"But do they even want shoes?" I ask.

Southern Man grouses about the hotel's beds, the showers, and just about everything it's possible to complain about. All this while grabbing one tablemate's spare piece of toast and dipping it into the other fellow's leftover coffee. "Y'all don't mind, do ya?" Southern Man drawls. I imagine the toast immediately transforming into molten fecal matter and push away my plate.

"Ugly Americans," I mouth to Paul. "They're everywhere."

~

Blue Bird busses, taxis and vans bound back and forth between Tikal and Flores throughout the day. Paul and I are anxious to get back on the road so we can hop a bus to Guatemala's Caribbean coast early the following morning. We opt for a cab rather than wait for an unpredictable minivan or public bus.

In the Hotel Tikal Inn's parking lot, we have our pick of chariots, each driver doing his best to outdo the other with bargain-basement prices. In the lull before the afternoon flights from the capital arrive, they are anxious to pick up a fare or two. Our best offer is 20 dollars for the hourlong drive—it cost us half that to go from Flores to Tikal in the van with Colin, the drowsy Britisher. But we go for it. Every other driver's price is higher.

José must have been a Pakistani New York City cabbie in a former life. He whizzes down the road at 70 miles an hour, beeping at cows and anything else that might slow him down. On the outskirts of Flores, José almost runs over an *abuela* on a bicycle. The old grandma flashes her middle finger.

As dangerous a driver as José is, he is equally as accommodating. He gladly takes us to a bank with a decent exchange rate. Then José ushers us over the causeway to Santa Elena to purchase our bus tickets for the next morning.

Heading back to Flores, I am courageous enough to ask José in Spanish which place is better—the Hotel Yum Kax or the Hotel Petén. Paul looks on, impressed, as José unscrambles my Spanish. *"El primero,"* he says. *The first.*

José is pleased with his 20 dollars as he drops us off at the Yum Kax. We're glad our errands are done so we can enjoy the charms of Flores.

The desk clerk gives us a room on the second floor of the Yum Kax because the first floor is flooded. So, the Hotel Yum Kax is not just *on* Lake Petén Itzá, it is also *in* the lake. How many hotels can say that?

One guidebook describes Flores as being dull and dusty. It claims that if you stay too long, dust will settle on your shoulders. But to the contrary, Paul and I find Flores nice so far. We are anxious to explore it.

~

Situated on San Andres Island, Flores' winding, narrow cobblestone streets lead to a stark, white, double-domed church in its center. Nearby, there's a nice restaurant with an enclosed patio on the lake.

Well before noon in a quaint, sleepy town, I can tell it's going to be one of *those* days—full of drinking, soul searching and amorous talk. One of *those* days when the things Paul tries so desperately to hide—i.e., the depth of his feelings for me—come gushing to the surface when tempered with alcohol.

I admit that I'm sometimes guilty of taking advantage of Paul's inebriated state and use (abuse?) these times to ask pointed questions. About life. About us. About us in each other's lives.

Paul orders a *Gallo*. I start with a Coke, then graduate to adding tequila and lime when there's no rum to be had. After two tequila-spiked Cokes, I pose, "In general, do you think people are happy?" and "Why do most relationships go sour after a couple of years?"

The first, Paul answers easily, starting with, "No..." The second, he initially says, "I don't want to talk about it." After which, he proceeds to talk about it. How some people are afraid to be content. How some people are convinced there's something wrong with someone stupid enough to love them.

"Some people, or you?" I press.

And so, the tone is set for a boozy, Hemingwayesque afternoon in a sunken town as lovers pleasantly argue while they try to decide what to have for lunch. Picture "The End of Something" without the mills and the fishing. But the strong, bright Flores sun makes everything blue and hopeful. Even our often-shaky relationship.

Boatmen occasionally approach our table, offering rides around the lake. At first, we refuse because it sounds too touristy. Until a particularly earnest young man comes by. Roberto apologizes for interrupting us and says he'd be willing to wait until we finish our lunch to take us on a tour. Finish it...we haven't even ordered it yet!

The waitress finally stops flirting with a deliveryman when she spots Roberto hovering. Maybe she realizes that she should be hovering too—to take our order. I decide on the fish *a la plancha* (grilled), caught in Lake Petén Itzá, while Paul gets venison *a la plancha*. Our meals are actually grilled on boards.

We've become used to waiting a long time for meals to be served, especially in modest eateries like this. Dishes are made fresh to order, one at a time. But Paul and I are in no rush, especially on this lazy Wednesday. And neither is Roberto. We ask him to join us at the table but he refuses, sitting along the shore near his boat, contentedly biding his time.

~

About ten feet long and three feet wide, Roberto's wooden boat has a striped awning on top. It reminds me of a larger version of those kiddie amusement park boats. The ones that circle round and round in concrete pools without going anywhere. Roberto's craft is coated with thick layers of blue and red paint which is chipped in spots. But it seems lake-worthy.

After lunch, Roberto helps us onboard. The motor isn't as fragrant or as noisy as I expect. We can easily talk above its purr. Lake Petén Itzá is beautiful—placid, vast, calm and deep azure.

"You are my teachers in English and I am your teacher in Spanish," Roberto tells us soon after we leave the shore. Awkwardly, we communicate with each other, carefully translating for each other, exchanging the words for flowers, for colors. We are like eager children, gently learning.

Our first stop is the Peténcito Zoo. (I'm pretty sure it translates to "little Petén.") It's a tiny place with chain-link fences that barely look strong enough to contain the animals. No warning signs are posted on the cages. No wrought-iron fences wrap around the cages themselves to keep visitors at a safe distance. I'm surprised when Roberto reaches forward to touch the hand of a spider monkey. *"Suave,"* he says.

Roberto motions for Paul and me to stroke the monkey's paw too. *"Sí, suave,"* Paul agrees.

"Soft," I tell Roberto in English after I touch it.

The second half of the Peténcito Zoo is located on the opposite side of the lake. It features tired crocodiles, parrots and other creatures indigenous to the area. The flowers planted between the exhibits are profuse, purple and swollen with life. *"Qué es?"* I ask my teacher. *What is it?*

"Bougainvillea," Roberto says.

"The flower's name is the same in English as it is in Spanish," Paul tells him. *El mismo en Inglés.*

For our *lago* voyage, we've taken along several beverages but our intrepid captain won't accept a beer. He agrees to one of the Cokes, however. We ride in the wake of a gay couple whose boatman is lethargic compared to ours. Their guide naps in his craft while his passengers visit the zoo. In contrast, Roberto takes great pride in the attractions he shows us.

~

The next site we visit is across the lake from Flores. Roberto promises it will be *muy especial.* The boat launch at the bottom of a dry, barren hill is underwhelming. "What's so special about this place?" Paul wonders. Roberto doesn't answer. All he does is smile as he leads us along the slope.

We pass clothes hung to dry on lines strung between trees. Wooden *tiendas* (stores) are propped beside the dock, their proprietors half asleep. Roberto passes their stands and continues uphill.

Steps are carved into the earth itself. Paul and I huff and puff while our spry, young guide jogs along the incline effortlessly. For emphasis, he pats Paul's stomach, "Lots of beers," Roberto says good-naturedly.

"*Mucha cervezas,*" Paul agrees. We all laugh because it's true.

At the crest of the hill is a treehouse-like structure. It doesn't appear stable. Several slats are missing on its stairs. We climb them carefully, watching our feet. We don't want to break a bone in this remote location. Or anywhere in Guatemala.

At the top of the treehouse, Paul and I are greeted with a gorgeous view of Flores stretched out in the mist. I gasp in delight. Paul breaks out into a wide grin. Roberto beams, pleased with our reactions.

From here, Flores looks distinctively European, resembling Florence or Venice. At a distance, its twin-domed church and brightly-colored buildings are stately and graceful instead of old and tired. Paul pulls me toward him in a kiss then hands Roberto his camera to snap a photo of us. Next, we take one of him.

On the way back downhill, we pass the gay couple. Again, without their guide. "Is it far?" one asks.

"Just a hundred feet or so," Paul says, gesturing over his shoulder.

"Imagine," cracks the other fellow, "A guide who literally *guides*. Where'd you find him?"

"The luck of the draw," I shrug. Then we go off in opposite directions.

~

Before we reach the boat, I ask Roberto if we can stop at a construction site we noticed during our hike. The hotel-to-be isn't anywhere near completion although tiles have already been laid on the floor. The swimming pool has been dug out. Greek arches support a communal balcony overlooking the lake.

Paul sighs, "In five years, we won't recognize this country."

"I hope you're wrong," I tell him.

"I'm not," he says. "People ruin everything."

An older man approaches us and exchanges a few words with Roberto. He explains that the man is the construction job's foreman. "Foreman of *nada*," Paul says under his breath.

Undeterred, the foreman proudly takes us on a grand tour of the site, opening doors, showing us where closets will be, revealing tiled but otherwise empty bathrooms, uncovering the future honeymoon suite. Since three of the proposed hotel's walls face the sea, it will be spectacular if and when it's done.

As the man talks, we nod profusely, pretending we understand. "Are you getting all this?" Paul asks me.

"*Más o menos*," I say. *More or less*.

Back at the dock, the gay folks' guide is snoring in his boat. We try not to wake him as we climb into Roberto's. But the sound of the motor makes him jump. '*Good,*' I think. '*Lazy bastard.*'

Motoring back to Flores, Roberto tells us that he is 20, but to me, he looks much older. I think most people in Guatemala give the impression that they're older than they actually are. Even the children have a certain old-soul-ness about them. Maybe it's the result of living a hard life. Maybe it's worry. I don't know. But Roberto also seems pretty happy, if not a little tired.

As we approach a cluster of homes, Roberto points out his family's cement box of a house on a hill in a town called San Benito. "There are many of us," he explains. "And I'm the only one who works."

Roberto drops us off at the dock outside of the Hotel Yum Kax. We thank him and pay him more than he'd originally asked. Grateful, he watches until we traverse the haphazard series of boards which lead us to dry land. Then Roberto starts the outboard and speeds away, waving.

~

Fishermen bring in their boats as the sun begins to sink beyond the horizon. They paddle along in *cayucos* (dugout canoes), some which look about to capsize with their next stroke. Paul and I visit the verandah of the hotel next to ours since the Yum Kax's terrace is underwater.

The sunset is astonishing. It's probably the most brilliant one I will ever see. As subdued as it was in Tikal yesterday, this one is showy, boastful and glorious. All bright, bruised pink and orange. It is otherworldly reflecting off the waters of Lake Petén Itzá.

Smoke rises from the surrounding homes as their inhabitants prepare supper. I will grow familiar with the fragrance of wood-burning stoves that fills the air at dinnertime throughout the whole of Guatemala. I will miss it when we get home. The aroma will become one of those things that unequivocally say "Guatemala" to me. One of those things that will make me feel warm and fuzzy whenever I come upon it somewhere else. The smell of a campfire will evoke this place, this moment, to me. And I will long for it.

~

At Bar Maya, when a German tourist snaps a picture of his wife at the table next to us, Paul asks if the man would like him to take one of them together. They do, and, in turn, take one for us.

"You're constantly doing nice things like that," I tell Paul when they go.

He shrugs it off, as he does most compliments. "Doesn't everyone?"

"No," I say to him. "They don't."

One of *those* days morphs into one of *those* nights. One of those nights when alcohol makes us feel less vulnerable in the feelings we feel for each other. One of those nights when Paul willingly volunteers the words, "I love you" as often as he raises a *Gallo* to his lips. One of those nights when I half-believe him. One of those nights brimming with spontaneous, easy talk. And not-so-easy talk.

Paul brings up the subject of marriage. Again. For a man who claims to never want to get married, he talks about marriage a lot. This confuses me. Until I realize that Paul does this out of insecurity. Insecurity that someone he wants to marry may not want to marry him.

I know insecurity well. It's my old, stubborn pal. You know, the one you've had since childhood, the one you've kind of outgrown but still want to keep. Because…because even if everyone deserts you, you'll never be alone. You'll still always have that one, crappy friend. Yes, self-doubt plagues me too.

Because I'm so insecure, I frequently find myself saying I don't want something that I need desperately—in the chance that I don't get it. This way, it will seem like I never really wanted it anyhow. A twist on the fox and the grapes—those grapes I can't taste are probably sour anyway.

~

Tonight, this is how Paul broaches the subject of marriage. He says, "Hypothetically speaking, if I asked you to marry me, what would you say?"

I am baffled. "Are you asking me to marry you?"

"No."

"Then what are you asking?"

"If I did, would you?"

I am extremely careful with my response. The last person Paul asked to marry him laughed in reply. Both times he asked. ("Why would I want to marry you?" Carrie had responded, rhetorically.) In Carrie's defense, Paul was 19 at the time; she was even younger. But this scarred Paul forever. Not only did Carrie turn him down, but she left to attend college in Texas and promptly got herself a new boyfriend. Then she got married. Had kids. Had a life. All without Paul.

I sometimes wonder if I remind him of Carrie. Not because our names are so similar (Carol…Carrie) but because it sounds like Carrie had an eccentric nature too. Paul repeatedly tells me that he and I are the same person, that I am a female version of him. I'm not sure I agree but the idea that *he* thinks so speaks volumes. That's why our relationship is so perfect and so messed up at the same time. We "get" each other but we also know each other's shortcomings. And fears. And tricks. Because of this, we can't lie to each other—or pull one over on each other.

So, on the terrace of Bar Maya in Flores, Guatemala, Paul sort of asks me to marry him. I take a deep breath and tell him, "I'm not sure I want to get remarried..." (PS, I was married for almost ten years and had only been divorced three months before Paul and I started dating.)

I take hold of Paul's hand and continue, "It scares me, how you can love someone to pieces in the beginning. Then it falls apart. And suddenly, you're at each other's throats, arguing about a lamp." I pause. I hope Paul understands what I mean. "But if ever were to do it again, I'd definitely marry you."

Paul smiles and kisses me. I'm glad he takes my answer in the spirit in which it was intended. My fear of marriage mirrors his own.

I mean, right now, things are ideal and easy and right between Paul and me. But how long before they turn? How long before he snarls the words "my wife" like so many men do? How long before I snap at him like a shrew for leaving a dirty glass in the sink?

"It's usually four years before my relationships turn to shit," Paul admits.

And yet...and yet the thought of marriage at its most sterling and perfect...the idea of being cherished, protected, yet still keeping your own identity and independence, working together toward common goals... that idea is pretty damned nice.

It isn't that I'm afraid of marriage; I'm afraid of a bad marriage.

I know that Paul sometimes studies me in my sleep like I sometimes watch him. I know he loves me in a deep, complex, complete way, as I do him. There is something so sure and certain and joyful about simply being with him. I've never experienced anything like it before. Even with my ex.

"Can't we just hang out like this forever?" Paul wonders.

I toy with a spot of moisture that stains my paper placemat. "I don't like the word 'forever,'" I tell him. "There's no such thing as forever."

"Sure, there is," he insists.

"Sooner or later, someone leaves. Sooner or later, things change. Sooner or later, someone dies. 'Forever' is a fallacy."

Paul says nothing. He stares out onto the darkened surface of Lake Petén Itzá. Neither of us can see it but we can feel its presence.

"Can't we focus on the right now?" I ask.

He nods.

Because the "right now" is wonderful. I want it to stay like this for as long as "forever" can be. Paul keeps me calm. He keeps me grounded. He makes me feel safe, even in the jungle, even in a revolution-torn Third-World country. Paul makes me feel protected. He makes me feel. Period.

~

I used to be so frightened of my ex-husband. Scared to be with him when he was teeming with rage. Even the love part, even in the beginning, there was a desperation to it. I was a teenager when Alex and I started dating and he was eight years older. I was 18 and insecure and terrified that no other man would ever love me. So, I stuck with him.

Alex was a struggling artist. He thought that if he "made it," well, that would mean he had value. If he sold enough paintings, it would somehow validate him. But what was "enough"? Nothing was ever "enough" for Alex. And if he didn't "make it," that meant he was a failure. As hard as I tried to convince Alex otherwise, it didn't work. He decided that his self-worth had to do with his success—or failure— as a working artist.

Besides that, Alex was deeply depressed. Sometimes suicidal. I tried to get him to a therapist but he refused. He was pissed off, angry at the world. And he was damaged by his rage. As naïve as I was, I thought that if I loved Alex, if I showed him how much I loved him, that I could save him. But that's not how love works. It's not a cure all. And besides, you can't save someone; they have to save themselves. They have to want to survive.

So, instead of me rescuing Alex, he began destroying me. He started to drag me down with him.

Alex was an anchor of despair. His sadness, his extreme feelings of worthlessness, began to chip away at our relationship, at me. My desire to live a happy life caused my husband to grow to hate me. Alex thought my wanting to be content was a personal affront to him. A slap in his face. Bit by bit, his crippling depression was obliterating me.

But Paul is not Alex, I have to keep reminding myself. This relationship is not *that* relationship. I tell myself this over and over again. I keep expecting Paul to hurt me or desert me but he hasn't. Not yet, anyway. But isn't that what I deserve? Someone walking out on me?

That's what Alex kept spitting into my face whenever he'd wake me up in the middle of the night in a rage. He'd say that I would make any man insane. That I would drive any man crazy. That I was a horrible human being.

Unfortunately, I started to believe him.

There are things from my past Paul needs to know but can't bear to hear. He needs to see my scars, my hurt, in the light of day but he refuses. "The past is the past," Paul says.

"Unless it becomes the present," I tell him.

~

What does this have to do with Guatemala? Nothing. Except this is the ghost that surfaces on this trip. The Ghost of Alex Past. But despite the specter of my ex rattling his chains like Jacob Marley, I think/hope Paul and I are going to grow closer as we travel through this puzzling and brilliant country together. Either that or we'll break up.

But no matter what ultimately happens to Paul's and my relationship, it's definitely experiencing a metamorphosis. A sea change. By the time we head home, I predict we will weather a series of seismic shifts. And this transmutation will either save us or kill us.

After all, we'll be at each other's side for three weeks solid. We'll cling to each other out of familiarity, out of desperation. And sometimes out of isolation. We're the only ones we have in a land full of beautiful, brown strangers. Will Paul and I get sick of each other? Will we want to run? Will we want to strangle each other? All of the above. Neither? I'm afraid of the answer.

~

Slightly drunk and tired of starry-eyed talk, Paul and I pursue dinner. We catwalk along a series of boards which lead to a restaurant that's in danger of being submerged in Lake Petén Itzá's overflow. It's lovely but modern and sterile, with floor to ceiling windows that open onto the swollen waters. Practically half the town seems to be flocking here. But to us, it has no personality, no distinctive character.

Because we're hungry, Paul and I sit at a table, but just for a moment. Then he says, "I can eat in someplace like this at home." I know exactly what he means. It could be anywhere, Peoria, even. So, we leave.

Down the street, a boy stands outside another restaurant. He calls out to passersby, hawking the food and the reasonable prices. He tries his best to entice potential eaters but most ignore him. Maybe this child is the owner's son. Or a street urchin, trying to earn a few quetzals for his efforts. Like our boatman Roberto, the boy does his job with such an agreeable nature, Paul and I decide to give the *comedor* a try.

Inside, we are greeted by mahogany paneling and a palm tree growing out of the center of the floor. There's a long, polished bar and paintings on the walls that were probably done by locals. El Florito also has a bookcase filled with paperbacks in a potpourri of languages. *Birds of Tikal* stands out. This eatery has a sense of place and definitely doesn't look like Peoria.

Our meal at El Florito is uncomplicated and solid. Paul and I talk with Pedro, the owner, after we finish. He speaks a handful of languages, including excellent English. Rightly so, Pedro is proud of his establishment and of the fine food it serves. He beams when he recalls the time Brooke Shields ate at El Florito. She was very down to earth, he adds.

Pedro then pulls out an autograph book of sorts. He says that he only lets his favorite customers contribute to it and scribble a line or two about the virtues of El Florito as well as their impressions of Guatemala. When he invites us to write in his book, we gladly comply.

Paul and I are on the road to blissful inebriation. Sufficiently lubricated himself, Pedro asks Paul to tell him successful English pick-up lines. Mind you, minutes before, Pedro told us that he was married and had five kids. But this doesn't stop his desire to learn American pickup slang. We teach Pedro words like "make love" and explain what "sloppy seconds" are. The man is so enthralled that he takes notes.

In return, Pedro gives us a quick synopsis of what women around the world are like in bed. Germans are cold and lifeless, he offers, while Anglos are too noisy. Pedro also says that Guatemalan women are very traditional—they don't practice oral or anal sex. It is "unaccustomed," as he phrases it.

The teenager tending bar also waits tables. We learn that his name is Hamilton, which is an oddity here. (Perhaps as odd as oral or anal sex.) Hamilton is adorable and head-over-heels in love with a girl named Lisa. To prove this, he has had her name crudely tattooed to his forearm. When I show Hamilton the cluster of roses and the heart etched near my shoulder, his eyes widen. It's "unaccustomed" for women to have tattoos in Guatemala, too.

Hamilton says he lived in Belize for five years and that he worked in Texas and Mexico for several months each. We're surprised that someone so young has moved around so much but Hamilton shrugs it off. "I go where the money is," he says.

Like Pedro, Hamilton is anxious to practice his English on us. He has a sweet, wounded cast to his gaze. I know this Lisa chick is going to break his heart. Then his handsome face will become cold and hardened. He will grow a tough outer shell that most men have and most women spend their lives trying to penetrate. But for now, Hamilton is sensitive and oh-so-cute in the gentle throes of first love. "Poor bastard," Paul says.

Then there's the Colonel, as everyone calls him. The Colonel is the nickname of the earnest boy who works the street and originally got us to come into El Florito. He's about ten years old and striking with blue-black hair that stands on end and distinctly *Indio* features. Namely, cheekbones so sharp they could cut glass. The Colonel's coffee-colored skin is flawless. He has an easy grin and flashing ebony eyes.

"He's a Mayan prince," Paul whispers to me. I nod in agreement. I bet the Colonel will grow up to be quite the lady killer with his good looks and outgoing manner. He's thrilled when Paul buys him a Coke.

This is something that constantly strikes me on our trip— Paul's unbelievably compassionate heart. Whether it's as seemingly insignificant as buying a street kid a soda or giving a pack of Marlboros to a homeless man who asks for a single cigarette, Paul has such a charitable nature.

But again, whenever I compliment him about his bigheartedness, Paul gets uncomfortable and quickly changes the subject. About the homeless man and the Marlboros, he quipped, "Oh, it wasn't such a cool thing to do. He'll just die of cancer quicker, that's all."

~

It is well before 11 when Paul and I head back to our room at the Hotel Yum Kax. We've got to wake up early and catch the bus to El Relleno at the mouth of the Rio Dulce at eight the next morning.

After we're done packing, Paul takes me from behind with two pillows under my hips and his hand cupped beneath me. I climax almost immediately, squirming on my belly, his hot whispers in my ear.

Then we sleep, curled into each other's bodies as Lake Petén Itzá's waters lap the swollen shores outside our window.

Day 5

Thursday, November 25, 1993
Flores/Santa Elena/El Relleno/Livingston

Today is Thanksgiving Day back in the States.

Paul and I are awake by six and checked out of the Yum Kax by 6:30. In town, people are already out and about, on bicycles or on foot, riding and walking to work. It is overcast as we head across the dirt and rock causeway that joins Flores to the neighboring town of Santa Elena. But it's so foggy we can barely make out the buildings ahead of us.

A handful of men are busy repairing the causeway itself, reinforcing it with sandbags, shifting shovelfuls of dirt so the bridge's foundation won't wash out with the next flood. The rains have stopped for a week now and the lake is slowly subsiding.

Though Paul and I are clearly foreigners, we are still greeted with early-morning *holas* and the occasional *buenos días*. We walk the mile or so to the bus depot, saying these words with practically every step. It's a custom I will grow to love—saying hello to strangers. In New York smiles and hellos do not come easy. Because in that city, nothing is given away for free, not even kind words. But in Guatemala, even among the very poor, pleasantries and politeness is shared with everyone like it's a birthright.

I'm glad we decided to stay the night in Flores instead of Santa Elena. The latter is more no-nonsense, not as picturesque. Santa Elena

73

reminds me of a dusty western town in an anonymous John Wayne movie, while Flores is prettier, slower, laid-back.

~

The bus depot is easy to find even without a cab driver to take us there. It's located on Santa Elena's busiest street. As with most towns in Guatemala, chickens and other barnyard creatures roam around, as if it's their unspoken birthright too. And I guess it is—until they end up as someone's supper.

We are the only outsiders at Santa Elena's bus station. Our style of dress and backpacks give testament to this. The depot is a fraction of the size of New York City's Port Authority but oddly enough, it has the same stiff plastic seats. It's basically a storefront with concrete walls painted white and turquoise.

The busses arrive on the curb-less street outside, letting off trickles of passengers who look tired and windblown. Which they probably are after riding the overnight coach from Guatemala City, a trip of about eight hours.

While I sit watching our backpacks, Paul stumbles off in search of breakfast. I try to read *Huckleberry Finn* as the other passengers look me up and down. One woman whips out her breast and nurses her toddler. She studies me while I study her.

I've noticed that the men tend to be friendlier than the women here. Paul claims this is cultural, that in Guatemala most women are raised to be subservient and guarded. It is the Latin American way for women to have downcast gazes, to be silent. When they work outside the home, in restaurants or shops, they are as quiet as possible, tend to speak only when asked a question, and hesitantly at that. They rarely initiate a conversation.

I agree somewhat with Paul's observation about Guatemalan women but not entirely. There's much more to it than that. When I feel the women's eyes upon me in the Santa Elena bus station, I also sense their envy and resentment. Because I can do things they can't—like travel. I have things they don't—like freedom. Although lower middle class by US standards, I would be considered rich here. I tour their country with a backpack while they work until sundown with a baby on their body. No wonder they're resentful. I would be too.

~

Paul returns from his *desayuno* pursuit empty-handed. He reports back to me about a food stand a block away that is too tiny to be called a *tienda*. It serves only *pan dulce* (sweet bread) and coffee. "The words 'to go' aren't in their vocabulary," he says. "You have to eat there."

He sends me off to find the food stand with his blessing and vague directions. The place is ultra-simple with barrels that serve as seats. They dole out instant coffee in a dozen mismatched cups which receive a quick wash in a pot of water after each use. This is exactly the type of place the NYC Board of Health warns against eating in. But I have little choice.

When we began our trip, Paul and I decided to pool our money. If there's anything left when we get home, we'll split it down the middle. For us, this method works perfectly. It avoids uncomfortable discussions like, "You had one more drink than I did" or "Your dinner cost 10 quetzals more than mine."

Clutching the colorful bills Paul has given me, I am like a child on her first errand. As per Paul's instructions, I ask for a *café* and a *pan dulce*. In a glass showcase, there are a few pastries to choose from. I point to the one I want. It's round and crusted with sugar. I sit and eat and drink Nescafé on a barrel like the rest of the customers then head back to the bus station, licking sugar granules from my lips.

We are still at the juncture in our relationship when the mere sight of Paul makes me smile. I often find myself seeking him out in a crowd, not because I'm afraid he'll disappear, but because I like his face. And when I find it, his mouth is usually painted with a slight grin at the sight of me. I hope we will feel this way about each other for a very long time. But things change; they always do.

As I approach Paul at the bus depot, I watch him reading *Ever After*. When I get closer, he looks up, sees me and smiles.

Yes, love is grand. Most of the time.

~

I take a seat on the outdoor bench and relieve Paul of his backpack babysitting duties so he can check out the local market that's coming to life nearby. It's only 7:30 and busses, like most things in Guatemala, are usually late. There's plenty of time before the eight o'clock special to El Relleno arrives.

This is why I'm so surprised when the bus pulls up in front of the terminal at 20 minutes to eight.

The driver checks the tickets I hold, mutters something in Spanish then proceeds to take our large backpacks. Effortlessly, he hands them up to a man who stands on top of the bus. The *ayudante*, or assistant, puts our packs on the roof with the other suitcases and baskets that are already there.

With Paul nowhere in sight, I quietly begin to panic. *"Un momento,"* I stammer to the driver. He responds in rapid-fire Spanish then climbs back onto the bus. And drives away. With our backpacks on top.

My brain hunts for words in a language I don't know. I feel sick to my stomach. Our bags are gone again! Paul is going to kill me! At a loss for what else to do, I chase after the bus, screaming, "Wait! Wait!" But the bus doesn't stop. It keeps right on going.

Near tears, I turn to the locals for help. They observe my hysterical antics with a glimmer of delight, like I am the Mexican comedian Cantinflas. "Where is it going?" I ask no one in particular.

A man talks to me in Spanish. *"No comprende,"* I wail. A woman joins the man in trying to calm me but I don't understand her either. "I don't speak Spanish," I sob like Mrs. Ricardo in *I Love Lucy*.

"Está regresando," the man says.

"I still don't understand," I cry.

The man takes pity on me and tries a pantomime. He stretches out his hand and draws a circle on his palm. *"Está regresando,"* he repeats.

Finally, I get it. "It's coming back?"

"Sí. Está regresando," he nods enthusiastically.

So, apparently, the bus isn't leaving. It's only going to pick up other passengers and will return soon. And sure enough, a few blocks down, there's the bus, kicking up a cloud of dirt as it heads back to the station.

When Paul comes toward me from the market, I run into his arms and bury my head into his shoulder. "What happened?" he asks.

"I just made a complete ass of myself," I confess. "I can't wait to leave this place." He laughs when I tell him the story.

Minutes later, I get my wish to leave Santa Elena. When the runaway bus returns, our backpacks are still lashed to the top. The fog, which was thick as pudding when we crossed the causeway from Flores, has burned off.

~

Because Paul and I board soon after its first stop, we find seats. But before long, it's standing room only. This bus is streamlined compared to the Blue Bird specials we saw in Guatemala City. And it's leaps and bounds above "chicken busses." By the way, they're called "chicken busses" because people literally come onboard carrying chickens.

As fancy as this bus is, it's still a far cry from the luxury coaches back home with bathrooms, air conditioning and multiple television screens. The bus to El Relleno has torn, uncomfortable vinyl upholstered seats and almost nonexistent shock absorbers. But it's still better than a "chicken bus."

The road between Flores and Tikal was a dream, well-paved for the upscale tourist traffic between the airport and the national park. But the road heading out from Santa Elena is a totally different story. It isn't as nicely maintained because it's used by locals and poorer tourists who can't afford to fly. Paul and I don't fit into either category. We take the bus by choice. Although we can afford plane tickets, we want to actually *see* the country—and not from 30,000 feet. On busses like this, we get to feel the country, too. We experience every rut in the road, every pothole.

Washed out by the recent rains, the dirt "highway" is eroded down to bare rock in spots like raw, exposed bone. The road is pitted and grooved with huge holes that are haphazardly filled with gravel. Some believe this to be the worst main thoroughfare in the whole of Guatemala. Later, I will discover a large welt on my thigh from being banged around on the bus.

It's too bouncy for me to write or read without getting nauseous. The loud diesel engine makes it hard to talk. The occasional overturned carcass of a bus rotting on its back in a ditch reminds us how treacherous the road actually is. As if we need reminding. In a few hours, my hair, skin and even my sunglasses are coated with a thin layer of grime from the open window. But it's the only source of fresh air.

A number of children ride the bus with us. Is November their "summer vacation"? Or are they not attending school?

A little boy boards with his mother. He stares at me like I come from another planet. In his eyes, I guess I do. I stare back at him just as intently. When the boy takes the seat behind me, his tiny fingers slide into the space between my chair and Paul's. When I grab them, the boy giggles. We repeat this silent game until he dozes off.

The bus stops often to pick up passengers who wait alongside the road and at scheduled stops. Whenever we come to a village, children sell us food through the open windows. Everything from oranges with delicately-carved skins to home-cooked snacks and soda in plastic bags.

At one stop, Paul gets off the bus to stretch his legs. He comes back with a bag of Coke and two *tamales*. A dollop of cornmeal surrounds tomato sauce, vegetables and a smidgeon of chicken. This mixture is steamed in a corn husk which you unfold like a secret and eat. I've never had a *tamale* before; it's delicious.

~

About four hours into our seven-hour trip, the bus driver announces that we'll stop for about *viente minutos*. Twenty minutes so he can rest and have a meal. "I've got to use the bathroom," I tell Paul.

"Ask the *ayudante* where it is," he says.

"I don't know how. You do it."

"Listen," Paul begins. "We're going to be here for weeks. I'm not going to ask where the bathroom is every time you've got to pee. But I'll teach you how to ask for it yourself."

This sounds reasonable.

And Paul does teach me. Slowly and patiently. Soon I am confident in saying, *"Dónde está el baño?"* The *ayudante* listens carefully to my Brooklyn-accented Spanish then motions to a cluster of cement boxes which serve as an outdoor market. Beyond them are two outhouse-type structures, one for men, one for women.

The restroom consists of a toilet bowl propped over a hole in the ground. No flusher, no water, no sink, no paper. Luckily, I carry Kleenex with me at all times. (I even brought a roll of TP from home which is already misshapen in my backpack.) Guatemalan toilet tissue, when available, is disturbingly rough.

At another stop, the bus is detained by several men in military uniforms. They board, study the passengers then leave. This will happen a total of four times throughout the trip.

Except once, the soldiers bark in Spanish and the male passengers begin filing off the bus one by one. When Paul hesitates, they yell at him to join the others. I grab his arm. "It's all right," Paul tells me, prying loose of my grip. He goes down the steps, carrying his passport in hand like the others do.

The remaining soldiers halfheartedly rifle through the bags on the overhead racks. Even the militia men in Guatemala are slight, most of them shorter than me. They look as harmless as children. Except for their M-16s. And they seem very young and tired, tired of this civil war which has already gone on for more than 30 years. Longer than many of them have been alive.

Minutes later, the militia send the men back onto the bus. Paul tucks his passport into the pouch around his neck. "See? Nothing to worry about," he says. He stashes the pouch under his t-shirt. I breathe a sigh of relief and settle onto his shoulder.

~

I'm impressed by the *ayudante*'s skills set almost more than I am with the bus driver's. The *ayudante* has a myriad of jobs while the driver has just one—don't crash the bus. Not only does the *ayudante* handle baggage and stow it on top of the vehicle but he also collects fares and tickets, plus somehow keeps track of who got on and where, who paid and who didn't.

In astonishment, we watch our *ayudante* skuttle onto the bus's roof. While it's moving. Carrying a suitcase. "What is he? Half monkey?" Paul asks me.

A stunt like this would be dangerous on the New Jersey Turnpike but on Guatemala's terrible, chewed-up roads, it's a suicide mission. I wonder how many *ayudantes* die tumbling from bus tops as the vehicles bounce and swerve, the helpers diligently stowing and retrieving parcels from above, undaunted.

The road is so bumpy I think I lose my spleen around Dolores. But I can't be sure.

~

The trip from Santa Elena to El Relleno is about 125 miles yet it takes more than seven hours. That's how bad the highway is. But time passes quickly, even without television. A live-action *telenovela* transpires on the bus, the cast of characters changing constantly. There are tears, giggles and quiet arguments, mostly in Spanish. Paul and I are among the few non-Guatemalans on board.

An unconventional fashion show also keeps us occupied throughout the ride. We see traditional *huipils* from different parts of the country (each region has its own unique pattern), western-style clothes, even *ropas Americanos*. This means "American clothes" and it refers to used clothing from the US sold in second-hand stores here.

The bulk of the clothes donated to charities in the States end up in Guatemala. In Guate, American thrift shop wares are a status symbol.

Besides *ropas Americanos* there's Spandex. Lots of Spandex. ("Spandex is a privilege, not a right," Paul quips.) And there are ruffles. Far too many ruffles. There's cotton and Polyester. There's every sort of clothing imaginable in combinations you wouldn't think possible.

Men, women and children are equally disbursed among our fellow travelers, some carrying handmade crafts to sell at their final destination. Some are visiting their families in neighboring villages. You can always tell because they carry just-cooked food in pots and baskets. And it smells amazing.

At Poptún, three loud kids say goodbye to their *abuelita,* who waves back especially energetically for such a little, old lady. This trio is so animated during the bus trip, it's clearly hard for them to sit still. "Grandma is probably glad to get rid of them," Paul yawns, then falls back asleep.

~

The countryside around us is lush. The terrain is hilly and sparsely populated, except for the occasional village along the route. All around us, people go on with their lives, working the fields and carrying everything conceivable on their heads. Most are barefoot. This is odd to me at first but when I realize that my own hiking boots are caked with mud, being barefoot makes sense. Cleanup is easier on bare feet.

The houses on the route are glorified shacks. In some front yards, children bathe in plastic tubs. As the bus roars by, they stand up naked and wave at us. We wave back.

Guatemala is an impoverished country which survives mainly on farming. People tend to grow enough to feed their families then sell the rest. They live in the same uncomplicated way they did 50 years earlier. Are these people lucky or poverty-stricken? Are they to be envied or pitied? I still can't decide. I guess good fortune is in the eye of the beholder. Most of these people seem content. Or else too busy to stop and think about whether or not they're content.

Past Poptún, a bunch of tourists board, fresh from Finca Ixobel. *The Real Guide* describes it as a working farm run by two Americans, Mike and Carol Ann DeVine. But a traveler back in Tikal told us that Finca Ixobel is now run by only one American—Carol

Ann was widowed when Mike was murdered in 1990. It's rumored
that the Guatemalan government suspected Mike of being a spy so
they disposed of him. But who actually killed Mike has never officially
been proven.

This doesn't stop the *finca* from being a popular spot for
tourists. With a clear pond, treehouses to explore and guest houses
to rent, it's nestled in the cool mountains and offers plenty of home-
grown foods to eat. Finca Ixobel does sound idyllic. But then there's
the matter of Mike's murder.

"Look up," Paul tells me when the bus starts moving again. I do.

Besides the *ayudante,* passengers are also riding on top of the
crowded bus, jockeying for position among the baggage. Their bodies
cast shadows on the road. It must be an unnerving but invigorating
way to travel. But one I won't try. However, I'm sure Paul is itching to.
"Don't you dare," I tell him.

"Riding inside is scary enough," he answers, surprising me.

~

Paul and I are slowly making our way toward Puerto Barrios,
which we hope to reach in two days' time. One route is to switch
busses in Morales, take another bus for three or four hours to
Livingston then hop a ferry across Amatique Bay to Puerto Barrios,
one of a handful of Guatemalan towns on the Caribbean coast.

But in *The Real Guide* Paul has found a quicker, more palatable
route to Puerto Barrios. It suggests hiring a boat in El Relleno
and traveling downriver on the Rio Dulce to Livingston, our final
destination for today. It sounds like a pleasant enough water voyage.

El Relleno is slightly more than a mass of tired market stands.
It's so cluttered and confused that it brings to mind photographs I've
seen of Calcutta. Finding a boat to hire is no problem. The minute we
step off the bus, Paul and I are bombarded by ferrymen trying to one-
up each other with better prices.

We share a boat with four other tourists from the bus: two
Germans and two Swiss traveling together. The boatman is asking 50
quetzals a head, which comes to less than 10 dollars a person. Paul and
I think this is a fair price. But one of the German ladies complains. "A
guy on the *finca* told us to spend no more than 40 quetzals," she huffs.

Paul shrugs. "That's a difference of two dollars."

"Yah," she says.

"The trip is two hours long," Paul adds.

"And your point is?" she presses. Paul gives up. I bite my tongue at a complaint coming from a woman who has the luxury of traveling for three months. (She bragged about this earlier on the bus.) Meanwhile, the boatman is working hard to earn each and every quetzal.

Our captain says something in Spanglish. "He promises to take us on a tour too," I tell the woman.

She snorts. "They always say that." Reluctantly, the woman finally agrees on 50 quetzals.

The boatman's helper, Choocha, hoists our backpacks into the center of the vessel. Its wooden slats serve as our seats. The boat fits 12 but even with eight and all of our backpacks, there's still plenty of space. Before we set off, we refuel, then speed away.

Between the octet of us, we speak a quartet of languages. There's chatter in each tongue as we putt past tall trees and greenery. The now-familiar scent of cooking hearths waft above the odor of fuel. Daylight is fading, making everything glow soft and muted. "This place is like no other place," Paul says. His topaz eyes are bright with the delight of being somewhere magical.

Guatemala is so many different lands melted into one. The emerald chaos of the Petén. The diesel-tinged claustrophobia of the capital. The promise of the sights we haven't yet seen: the Caribbean, the volcanoes, the vastness of Lake Atitlán, the lush Western Highlands. Paul is right about Guatemala being like no other place. And I've got a hunch it won't be the last time he says this.

~

The trip along the Rio Dulce is striking, much more agreeable than a long bus ride. The "sweet river" gives the impression of the open sea but this is only an illusion. It's actually a wide waterway that leads to a lake which leads a bay which leads to the Caribbean.

As I stare out into the open blueness, a nameless freedom fills my every pore. This odd joy strikes me at unexpected moments throughout the trip. It is the remarkable sensation of smiling on the inside. Judging by Paul's beatific face, he feels it too.

The further we ride into the Rio Dulce, the rougher and choppier the water becomes. The wind is strong. It sears our faces. The boat leaps from wave to wave like a frog from stone to stone. Our captain hands us a plastic tarp to protect us so we'll stay dry. But we let the tarp fall back down, choosing instead to be baptized by the mist. It feels good after the hot, dry bus ride.

Paul grins into the breeze, his baseball cap turned backwards on his head. Now I know for sure that he feels it too—that contentment, that euphoria of simply being alive in astounding surroundings, on a rickety boat heading into the great abyss. The wonderment of this flash in time.

The Rio Dulce is dotted with speedboats, sailboats and yachts, playthings of the rich from Guatemala City, those who live their lives behind high walls. Since it's Thursday, most of the watercraft are dormant, docked in marinas, awaiting their weekend warrior captains. My favorite is a sleek catamaran named "Wet Dream."

Moored among these elegant vessels are the boats of poor fishermen. From these raw dugouts, they throw hand lines, hoping to catch fish to sell or eat. The juxtaposition of the wealthy and the lowly is so clear in this country of opposites. Somehow, it's more stark in El Relleno than it is in Guatemala City.

~

The Rio Dulce opens into a lake called El Golfete. On the lake's northern shore is Biotopo de Chocón Machacas, the government-sponsored manatee reserve. These huge sea cows are notoriously shy and seldom seen, especially by boats with noisy motors like ours. We also don't spot jaguars or tapir which supposedly are plentiful in the forests that line these shores.

A mass of birds fly overhead and perch in the trees nearby. We catch sight of both black and white herons, large yet graceful. Parakeets whiz through the breeze in flocks, with the skill of airplane squadrons doing maneuvers. At one point, our boatman turns off the motor. We drift toward an overgrown island and are engulfed by frenzied chirping. He smiles at our sense of wonder then fires up the motor and moves on.

After El Golfete, the Rio Dulce reappears. We are overcome by a sulfurous odor not unlike Elizabeth, New Jersey. Our captain-turned-guide manages to communicate that this area is plentiful with thermal pools. He invites us to put on our bathing suits and go for a soak. Not far off is a second boatload enjoying the soothing waters. Although it's inviting, I'm hesitant.

Paul rifles through his backpack for his trunks. "We're going to change in an open boat? In front of strangers?" I ask.

He shrugs. "If you want to go into the hot springs, sure."

"What about our stuff? Our passports," I worry.

"They're safe with these guys," Paul tells me.

But I'm still not convinced. "What's to stop them from leaving us here?"

Paul sighs. "Nothing." He pulls down his jeans. "Have a little trust in your fellow man."

I find my bathing suit in the top flap of my backpack and strip as quickly as possible.

One by one, we ease over the boat's edge and into the warm water. The German women, I note, have more body hair than their male companions. But the thought slips from my mind as soon as I submerge myself in the relaxing waters. The boatman and his assistant sit at the bow, waiting for us to get our fill.

The natural hot springs are shallow enough to stand in. Depending on where you sit, the temperature varies. In some sections, it's unbearably scorching, like a pipe is pumping in boiling water. Paul and I find a spot between blistering and lukewarm. We sit on submerged tree branches and algae-slick rocks. Although the cove is odorous, it's also heavenly. Steam rises from the surface, making us lazy and languid, coaxing the travel dust from our skin, from our hair, from our souls.

Paul pulls me close in the acrid water. "There is no place like this place," he whispers.

After we heave ourselves back into the motorboat and strip out of our wet bathing suits, we continue inching down the Rio Dulce. The terrain transforms from lowland to a haunting gorge, bordered by high cliffs, verdant with vines and vegetation. I am dwarfed and insignificant by the sheer scale of the backdrop. None of us speak. It's too awe-inspiring.

~

We go about 20 miles downriver before we there's any sign of Livingston. Close to town, small boats are anchored to the shore. For fishing or ferrying tourists, I'm not sure.

The sky is gray and the sun is beginning to set. Livingston itself is somewhat leaden in the distance. I spot a big, square concrete pier. "This is probably where the ferry to Puerto Barrios docks," Paul tells me.

But instead of going to the big dock, we pull up alongside a plank. It isn't easy scrambling off the wobbly boat, especially clutching my heavy backpack. I'm afraid I'll drop it into the water and that it will sink like a rock.

When a pair of thin, cocoa-colored hands grab for my pack, I gladly pass it over. The hands belong to a boy of about 15 or 16. He speaks to us first in Spanish then in a jigsaw puzzle of English. Tired from a full day of travel, we permit this boy to be our escort through Livingston for a few quetzals.

The town seems easy enough to navigate. Its main street, Calle Principal, runs into the dock. Along that street there are many hotels to choose from. We tell the boy the name of an inn we read about in our guidebook. He nods and slows his pace so we can follow him.

Livingston is not your typical "white sandy beaches" Caribbean spot. It's a town where people live and work, not a village created for the tourist trade. It's a town where women scrub their clothes by hand in the communal laundry's cement tubs. Livingston is not the sort of quaint locale depicted on glossy brochures or in TV commercials. It is gritty roads and warped wood-frame houses that look fragile enough to collapse in a strong breeze. But I like Livingston because it's real and because it's not Club Med.

The boy leads us off the main road to a pink, two-storied building on a cliff above the Caribbean. Casa Rosada has definitely seen better decades. In French, the boy flirts with a young Canadian woman reading a paperback on the hotel's buckled front porch. The owner is MIA. "We want a nicer place," Paul tells the boy in Spanish. "Without a shared bath if possible," he adds.

"*Es posible,*" the boy assures him. He says that the Hotel Tucan Dugu is 80 American dollars a night.

"Not *that* nice," Paul laughs. "Something in between. *En el medio.*"

Again, the boy nods. He knows the perfect guesthouse. We backtrack down the dirt road to a rubble-strewn stone lane. The boy passes two women and tries to charm them in Italian. I'm impressed with this mini, Third-World Romeo. The holes in his sneakers and his worn pants don't deter his *machismo*.

We leave behind the grand Hotel Tucan Dugu, a sprawling, opulent palace. It's so luxurious that it's indistinctive—it could be in

Hong Kong, Aruba or Mumbai. We're seeking a more authentic inn, something that reflects the flavor of the country, so we move on.

But where is this boy taking us? "He's going slit our throats in an abandoned shack," I whisper to Paul, who sighs at my apprehension.

An alley leads to a wide, two-laned residential street. There are a row of trees and shrubbery in the center. This end of Calle Principal is more affluent than the other yet it's still lowkey. The homes are better maintained, though chickens still wander the street, clucking and fussing.

The three of us stop at a neat, white house. A sign bolted to the wall announces Hospedaje Doña Alida in fancy script. We walk inside to find a washtub set up next to the reception desk. And there stands Doña Alida. She talks briefly with the boy then greets us. Doña shows us a nice room with a bay view but single beds. It costs about 10 dollars a night.

I muster the courage to ask if Doña Alida has a room with a *cama matrimonial.* She and a housekeeper within earshot giggle like schoolgirls when I request a double bed. Luckily, Doña Alida has another room but it's twice as expensive — 20 dollars a night. She's happy to show it to us.

In the growing twilight, the lady of the house leads us down a spiral staircase overhung with bougainvillea. At the bottom of the steps is a cottage perched over the Bay of Amatique. The room measures about ten-foot square and is stuffed with a king-sized bed positioned beneath a wide window with an expansive view of the water. There are open shelves for our luggage and even a small refrigerator. The room also has a bathroom with a cold-water shower. It's a tiny paradise at the end of a long travel day. We take the key from Doña Alida, give the boy a tip and settle in.

~

Livingston is plentiful with eateries and none of them are near capacity. Hungry and tired, Paul and I have dinner at Comedor Coni back on the main street. We are the sole patrons of a waitress who never smiles. The restaurant is large and newly-painted in turquoise. It is thoughtfully decorated with hand-woven tablecloths.

I'm getting used to eating fish with their heads on, their eyes gaping at me. The unfortunate whitefish on my plate is tasty and meaty, cooked with curry. It's served with fresh vegetables and rice.

Paul's fish is done with Oriental flair and is just as tasty. "This is our Thanksgiving dinner," I remind him.

"It's not bad," he says. "Only different."

We both miss our families. This is the first Thanksgiving away from home for the two of us. We reminisce about how more than 20 generally crowd our respective holiday supper tables. Then our mood turns quiet. "Let's try to find a phone after dinner," Paul suggests.

~

There's a long line at the Guatel office. Since almost no one has home telephones, the best way to make infrequent (and expensive) phone call is at one of Guatemala's many telephone storefronts. And because quetzals exchange hands, an armed guard is stationed inside.

Paul and I have a tough time communicating with the Guatel operator in his Plexiglas cage. Finally, we understand that we must complete an information sheet before our call can be made. The sheet asks who you're contacting, how you'll pay for it and where you're staying. Why they need to know all of this, I haven't got a clue. Sign language, pigeon English and jumbled Spanish fill in the blanks and we manage to fill out our forms.

The operator reaches Paul's family immediately. He is called into a see-through cubicle and manages to speak briefly with everyone who has gathered at his grandmother's house for Thanksgiving. With Paul sealed into the transparent room, I can't hear what he says but there's a joyful spark in his eyes. It makes me happy to see him happy. So happy, I well up with tears.

Although the operator tries over and over, no one answers the phone at my parents' apartment. They're probably on the road, driving from my grandmother's house to theirs. I don't bother having the operator call my grandma's number. I hang up, feeling like an orphan. As Paul and I walk back to our cottage in the dark, I want to cry.

I hear a gobbling noise on the road in front of us. At first, I think I'm imagining it. Then the sound comes again. "Did you hear that?" I wonder. Before Paul can respond, a thin, Central American tom turkey bobs into the street. He stares at us defiantly. It's almost as if he realizes it's Thanksgiving in the United States and that we celebrate by eating his brothers.

"There's our Thanksgiving dinner," Paul laughs. The turkey flees upon hearing this, cackling angrily with every step.

~

Paul and I make love in our room with the lights off, facing the sea. We try to do it soundlessly so our sighs won't sift to the beach below. I'm on my knees and he is behind me. The windows are open so the breeze can saturate our bare skin. Primal and sensual, there are moments I can't decipher where Paul ends and I begin, where the sky and the pinpricks of stars end and our bodies begin.

When we finish, it's only 8:30 but we're exhausted from all the miles we've traveled, both by land and by sea. The hard bed, which is actually a pair of twin beds pushed together, draws us in. We avoid the line of demarcation in the middle. But at least the bed's center isn't cavernous like the Colonial's. "We'll be wide awake in the middle of the night," I yawn before I nod off.

"Shush," Paul whispers. "Or you'll make it happen."

Just as I predict, he and I are wide-eyed at one a.m. Sensing each other's wakefulness, we talk in the blackness for almost an hour. Then we fall out again.

I sleep until dawn.

Day 6

Friday, November 26, 1993
Livingston

I wake to the crowing of roosters and the sound of the sea. Paul snores right through both. From our bed, I watch the sun rise then put on one of his semi-clean t-shirts. I like smelling the scent of his skin on mine.

Because I don't want to disturb Paul, I sneak out onto the verandah to write in my journal. The Bay of Amatique is at my feet. Last night's three-quarter moon crawls further up into the sky. I don't want to forget this. Any of it.

I've become the national snack of Guatemala, my sweet, Anglo skin luring mosquitoes from far and wide. My body is dotted with at least three dozen bites, mostly below my knees, mainly souvenirs from Tikal.

My multitude of mosquito bites make me glad I decided to take anti-malaria meds. I have to pop a total of six Larium once a week for six weeks in order for them to work properly. I vow to swallow them religiously, gulping down the Larium at the same time, on the same day, every week before, during and after the trip.

The post-dawn clouds are oddly illuminated. It must have rained overnight. I give up trying to distinguish the line between the sky and the bay that opens onto the Caribbean. The water laps gently at the beach. An occasional boat stutters by. I observe all of this from a wobbly chair that is painted white. When I shift my weight, a slat pops out. "Probably from termites," I hear Paul's voice say.

"Good morning." I turn to greet him.

He kisses the top of my head. "I want to write a postcard to Mark," Paul yawns, heading down to the porch below, which has a table. I've gotten used to writing on whatever surface is available—my knees, the arm of an unsteady chair, the back of a book.

I take a break to wring out our bathing suits, both of which are still damp from yesterday's soak in the Rio Dulce's thermal pools. Minutes after I hang them over the railing, Paul reappears. "They're dripping on my head," he laughs.

But I think he comes upstairs just because he wants sex. Not that I'm complaining. I don't know what it is, but we've been making love more than usual. Maybe it's Guatemala's sluggish heat, the thick, tropical air, the lushness of life here. Maybe it's the exoticness of being in an enigmatic, untamed land. But why question it? I just go with it.

~

Afterwards, we shower, dress and go back to Calle Principal on a quest for breakfast. At 7:30, the Guatel office is already open. "Why don't you try your folks again?" Paul suggests. "Your mom's an early riser."

I don't need convincing.

The same operator is on duty from as last night. He had the foresight to keep the information sheet I'd filled out, somehow knowing I'd be back.

It's weird but good talking to my parents. Weird because they're 5,000 miles away and in a much different place than I am. I'm not sure they'd appreciate how wonderful it is down here, they of the benign, predictable vacations to Disneyland and Cooperstown. I'm so emotional talking to them but I can't find the right words to express how beautiful Guatemala is. And at least I don't feel like an orphan anymore.

Even at this hour, Livingston is wide awake and at work. Paul and I walk up the hill and delve deeper into town. We have breakfast in a side-street eatery with no name. A step from being shabby, it has battered tables and chairs but tries its best to look jaunty. There are scrubbed, shiny plastic tablecloths and the walls are decorated with fans made from drinking straws and their wrappers. This adds a peculiarly festive touch.

Paul shakes his head. "No matter where you go in the world, you'll find pictures of two things."

"Which are?" I push.

"'The Last Supper'," he begins, "and 'Dogs Playing Poker.'" Sure enough, there's a black velvet tapestry showing a half-dozen pups seated around a card table. The collie has the best hand.

This *comedor* is the type frequented by locals. Though not a large place, most of the tables are filled. Including one with a party of 12. The people are neatly dressed and could easily work in an office, if there are any offices in Livingston.

At a distant table sit a few police officers. One of them, I keep seeing throughout town. He's thin with a youthful face and barely looks old enough to drive, let alone carry a gun.

At the counter, a grubby man with no left arm stares at me while he scratches his stump. Is it my imagination or does my tattoo, on the very arm he is missing, grab his attention? My magenta rose is where the man's left forearm used to be.

Breakfast at the *comedor* is *típico: huevos* but not with tortillas. Instead, there is toast. Maybe this is because of Livingston's Caribbean, as opposed to *sabor Latina Americana*. But there's the ever-present, savory puddle of black beans that I've grown to expect— and jones for.

I'm still surprised at how weak the coffee is in Guatemala. For a country whose Western Highlands are brimming with *fincas* noted for their aromatic beans, there's a profusion of watered-down Nescafé. "Real coffee is probably too expensive for dives like this to serve," Paul suggests. "And I bet the Guatemalans make more money exporting it then selling it here."

~

After we eat, Paul and I set off on a short trek to a waterfall called Las Siete Altares (the Seven Altars). *The Real Guide* claims it's a three-mile walk along the beach, totally doable. We decide to first venture through Livingston, then search for a shortcut to the shore.

But when we do, the road in town quickly changes from badly paved to heavy dust. No hotels are out here, only plain concrete, crate-like buildings. Some are painted tired pastel colors in an attempt at cheerfulness. But it doesn't quite work. Others have flower gardens out front. Still others are unadorned and crumbling. There are a couple of *tiendas* for the locals, their fruits and vegetables displayed in rows of woven baskets on the ground.

The people in Livingston are friendly but they look as careworn as the streets. We hear polite *holas* and a chorus of *buenos días* as we pass. There are plenty of nods and smiles for us, white *diablos* who have meandered off the straight-and-narrow and are invading their private lives.

Unlike any other part of Guatemala, there are a large number of Blacks in Livingston. Caribbean Blacks. As with most immigrant groups, fantastical stories and folklore about them abounds. Accusations of voodoo and cannibalism run rampant. Many of the women in Livingston speak a language called Garifuna which is supposedly incomprehensible to men. I keep telling Paul that I understand Garifuna perfectly. He only half believes me.

Garifuna is an Arawakan language used by less than 200,000 people in Belize, Honduras and Nicaragua as well as Guatemala. Livingston is a hodge-podge of Indian, African and Spanish cultures, so Garifuna is a good fit.

On our walk, Paul and I pass no men. It is women and children exclusively. And almost every woman balances a basket on her head with great skill. It's a useful talent which keeps both hands free plus doubles as a sunbonnet. Some ladies prefer to rest the baskets directly on the tops of their skulls while others cushion the baskets with a rolled-up length of cloth. Young girls master this skill too, occasionally grazing a hand up to steady their cargo.

Many have babies fastened to their backs with shawls. It's a far cry from those multi-compartmented baby backpacks Gerry sells in Babies"R"Us but the tied scarves work remarkably well. Peasant women have been carrying children this way out of necessity for ages—so they can work in the fields and go about their chores hands-free. No fancy, expensive kid carriers, just strong cloth they weave themselves.

Young children are curious about Paul and me and flash toothy grins at the two oddly-dressed travelers when they see us. One with hair that is almost blonde (Paul) and the other with a flower etched into her arm (me). Some kids are feisty enough to say hello while others giggle shyly and hide their faces in their mothers' *cortes* (skirts). They play with sticks or roll tires down the road, their faces happily streaked with mud.

~

Paul and I are faced with a dead end far up in the hills where Livingston abruptly stops. We can't find an outlet to the bay that doesn't cut across private property or plunge down a jagged hill. We're high above the water now and inland, approaching a hot, empty soccer field instead of a beachside road. We decide to backtrack through town to the shore. Wasted time? Not really. We're exploring. It's all an adventure. Plus, there's no such thing as a wrong turn when you're on holiday. All turns are correct when you have no direction.

Again, we pass the same two women talking in the road. They still speak in the hushed tones of Garifuna but pause to greet us a second time.

Further down, a pair of men work on rethatching a hut's roof. "Everyone seems to be building something," Paul says. The concrete frames of hotels are everywhere. Rebar is exposed like raw nerve endings. It extends to second stories which may or may not exist in the near future. Around us, wheelbarrows are filled then emptied then filled again. The tap-tap-tapping of hammers spice the air like woodpeckers.

"Will we recognize this town in five years?" I wonder, echoing Paul's words in Flores.

He doesn't answer.

~

Back on Calle Principal, Paul and I head toward the shore. It is in the opposite direction of the small pier where we'd arrived in Livingston yesterday. We pass a handful of *tiendas* and residences, mostly flimsy, wooden one-or-two-roomed structures. We get glimpses of the people inside, catch sight of the flicker of television screens, hear the sounds of pots clanging. Then we finally reach the beach.

The sand is black here but not the black of Hawaii's volcanic powder. The sand in Livingston is black from filth and overuse. Small fishing boats rest on their sides, painted with the names of old wives and past lovers. The shoreline is strewn with waterlogged leaves and trash. Paul and I follow the guidebook's directions and walk north, toward Belize.

Along the route, we are confronted with more construction. These homes will be sumptuous if they're ever finished. Huge, they have commanding views of *la bahia*.

Paul and I talk of many things as we walk along the beach toward Las Siete Altares. He brings up what he'd like to do when he retires from his City job. "We'll come back to Guatemala," he says whimsically. "And we'll open a bar/restaurant somewhere."

'We,' I think. 'Will we still be together when you retire?' But I let the "we" pass. "A bar/restaurant sounds like hard work," I tell him.

"Play along," Paul says.

I do. "Okay. What will we call it?"

Paul ruminates for a few steps. "Blackie's," he decides.

"Too racist," I say.

"But my last name's Black," he tells me.

"But still."

Digging our toes in the sand as we go, Paul and I daydream about Blackie's—what it will look like, what sort of food we'll serve. "It will be a warm, welcoming place," he says. And with Paul at the helm, I know it will be.

I picture Blackie's having a definite tropical flavor: lots of natural fibers, accented with special pieces we've collected in our travels—weavings, masks, ceramic vases and bowls. Blackie's would be the type of pub where people feel at home. "We'll serve peasant food," I tell Paul. "The kind of stuff we grew up on."

Paul and I cook dishes like this for each other all the time, delicious bits of our childhoods. Hearty recipes from Cuba and Italy that our mothers and grandmothers made for us. Escarole and beans, *picadillo* (a type of hash with chopped meat, onions, garlic and green pimento olives), thick lentil soup, rice and beans and *plátanos*. This is the type of comfort food that would be on Blackie's menu.

But no matter what we serve, no matter what Blackie' looks like, Paul and I decide that we would be very, very happy there. Our skin would be tanned to a toasty shade and we would have no worries, no fears. '*And there would be no exes haunting me,*' I add in my own head.

In walking distance from Blackie's, Paul and I would build a big house by the sea with a porch that wraps around it like a belt. There would be hammocks, a window seat, a fireplace for those rare, chilly evenings and a huge kitchen with an industrial stove. Our bed would have a view of the water and there'd be a balcony where we'd watch the dawn, sipping strong coffee in the morning. And a garden. There would definitely be a garden. With lots of dazzling flowers. "And we'd have a gazebo," I say.

"I always thought gazebos were useless," Paul tells me, kicking up a pile of wet sand. "You know, wasted space."

"Stop being an architect," I begin, then add, "Not ours. We'd find some use for our gazebo. A music pavilion, maybe."

Paul and I keep walking, keep dreaming. When we finish, he sighs, "That's a lot to ask for."

"But we deserve it, every bit of it," I say. "We work hard... when we work."

"And we play just as hard."

Here we are, two Brooklyn kids who grew up in cramped city apartments now living out of rucksacks. We're in a strange and wonderous land with nothing but a couple of packs, the money that hangs in pouches around our necks and a deep, serious love for each other which we're reluctant to admit.

~

The face of the sand gradually shifts. It is cleaner, wider, white instead of dark. Palm trees crane their necks toward the sun. Fallen coconuts are the only litter now. Plus, there's driftwood and even some seashells.

We pass a tiny woman in traditional Guatemalan dress. She has sharp, proud cheekbones and russet-colored skin. The lady purposely turns from us and calls to her young son, pulling him to her side. The boy stares at us but is silent. "Shy or hostile?" Paul wonders after they pass.

"Shy," I tell him emphatically.

More grand homes are under construction along the shore. Grander than we imagine Blackie's will be. The workmen acknowledge us as we pass. Nearby is a bungalow colony of huts. We can't figure out how you gain access to them except from the beach. Or could there be a road leading down from the hills?

But there are more important matters at hand when Paul and I hit another dead end. The beach is suddenly cut in half by a river of about 30 feet wide that drains into the bay. Although *The Real Guide* suggests wading, the water seems too deep and murky to negotiate safely. Swimming across would mean our cameras and our quetzals would get wet.

Standing on the shore contemplating our options, Paul and I spot a boy taunting his little brother on the riverbank closest to us. A miniature canoe lays on its side near them. "I think this kid makes a living paddling stranded tourists across the river," Paul says.

The ten-year-old proves to be a seasoned businessman. Paul bargains with Miguel, sparring amicably in Spanish. They finally agree on the price of three quetzals (about 50 cents) for each of us. But the kid warns that he'll charge us additional quetzals on the return trip.

Miguel ferries us across the river separately in his rough-hewn boat. I squat in the bottom because there's no seat. It's a wobbly ride, until Miguel catches his stride, establishing a steady rhythm as he shifts his paddle from one side to the other.

I stand on the opposite shore, waiting, as Paul steps into the boat. Miguel groans dramatically under Paul's weight. Before they reach me, the boy pulls a bunch of yellow fruit from a drooping tree branch and tosses Paul two. They resemble waxy grapes but taste bitter. All three of us spit them out, making faces. We say goodbye to Miguel and continue our pilgrimage.

In order to return to the beach, Paul and follow a path that leads through a thick forest. Soon, the gentle surf comes into view and we can once again walk along the shoreline. This is the first time we notice warning signs posted in Spanish. They look foreboding. "Basically, they say 'Private Property. No Trespassing,'" Paul explains.

"But how else can you get to the waterfall without walking along the beach?" I ask.

"Ah, that's the million quetzal question," he counters. (Actually, the preferred method is renting a boatman, we later learn.)

Since we've already walked about a mile and a half, Paul and I decide to keep going and play dumb (which won't be too hard) in case we're stopped by the authorities.

We approach a cluster of palm huts where a somber-faced man is patching his overturned boat. He wears a pair of filthy BVDs and nothing else. The man scowls at us as he works. He doesn't respond to our *holas*.

Two mangy dogs stroll toward us on the beach. There's nothing odd about strays since Livingston might be populated by more stray dogs than humans. These particular mongrels are skinny and flea-bitten. From afar, they give the impression that they're dopily friendly. Paul and I keep walking.

When I turn, the dogs are closer, gaining on us. Suddenly, one lunges and begins barking. The other bares his teeth, snarling, poised to bite. The man, far off now, doesn't call them away.

Not one to back down from a challenge, Paul wheels around and barks right back at the dogs. Startled, they stop in their tracks momentarily then continue advancing. Paul grabs a piece of driftwood and flails it wildly, yelling to scare the dogs. He and the strays stand there growling at each other before the dogs finally back off, flashing us dirty looks.

"That bastard sent them after us," Paul mutters. He takes the stick with us, just in case they come back.

"You were like a caveman," I tell him in awe. "Thanks."

~

It isn't far to Las Siete Altares from here. The trail winds into the jungle then opens to an inlet. And there lie the falls, which are more of a dribble as opposed to a gush. "That's it?" Paul wonders.

"I mean, they're pretty but..."

"This is what I risked my life for?" he says, incredulous. We both crack up, laughing.

Seven separate steps of rock rise from the base. Under each step are unappealing pools of water. It seems more like an off-kilter, tiered wedding cake than seven altars. At least to me.

Instead of scrambling up the slick rocks, Paul and I climb down through *la jungle*. It's a difficult descent, grabbing onto vines and dead trees that give way the minute you put your weight on them. Clumsily, I slip several times. Paul worries that I'm hurt but I'm only frustrated. "In 30 minutes, we moved all of ten feet," I sigh.

Two German tourists chomp on watermelon, following our struggle like it's the "Movie of the Week." But Paul and I forge on. Without flipping the Krauts the finger.

Las Siete Altares feels as frigid as it looks. Although I duck behind a tree to change into my bathing suit, I'm not brave enough to go any further than dipping my toes into one pool. Paul, on the other hand, dives right in. But this is *típico* of how he and I operate: he's impulsive while I proceed with caution. Except in this relationship, where I've thrown all caution to the wind.

Paul floats on his back, surveying his surroundings. "This place is lousy with Germans," he says, smiling. (Luckily, no Germans are within earshot.) It's an observation we will make often during this trip.

In our defense, the Huns *do* seem to be everywhere. They're also the most frugal of all the travelers we encounter. They bunk in the rattiest guesthouses, eating fruit for lunch rather than give the local *comedors* business. And they have at least triple the vacation days Americans do, so Germans travel for long periods of time on a strict budget.

There are now about ten people lolling around in the lower pools. Guide boats arrive with doughy tourists too uninspired to hike. They just observe Las Siete Altares from the bay. Around the falls, we are treated to a buffet of languages and accents belonging to: an affluent family from Guatemala City, two young British fellows, a solo Asian woman, their local guides and, of course, Germans. One cute Britisher swan dives into the lowest, deepest pool. Paul and I relax on the rocks, girding our loins for the long walk back and the inevitable mongrel attack.

To our surprise, the mutts don't chase us this time. They doze in the hot afternoon sun beside their owner's hut. Their master still fiddles with his boat in his tighty-whities. We get yet another nasty look from him and from his most fierce charge, Cujo, who menacingly opens his left eye as we pass.

Further down the beach, Paul and I swim in the clear, tepid water as comfortable as a bathtub. "This is paradise," he says.

I have to agree.

A cluster of women wade out into the Bay of Amatique, baskets of laundry balanced on their heads. Although they hold up their skirts, the water only comes up to their knees and they're further out than we are. "That little bastard!" Paul says.

"What?" I wonder.

"*Mira*," he tells me. "Those women are walking out to the shallows to cross. I bet there's a sandbar. You don't need a boat to get across the river." He shakes his head, smiling.

"And we paid that little creep to row us," I say.

"All of 50 cents each," Paul points out. "Good for him. He got over on us."

As Paul and I splash through the water on our return trip, the boy sits in his *cayuco*, watching us. He raises his fist and yells something unintelligible. We laugh at what is probably a half-hearted curse. The boy laughs too.

Since we've run out of drinking water, Paul and I stop at a beachside *tienda* to buy some. A drunken, tattered man approaches, trying to bum a cigarette from the stand's owner. Quietly Paul asks

me for the pack of Marlboros I always carry for bartering purposes.
I hand it to him and Paul hands it to the man. Surprised, he thanks us
profusely then leaves to smoke in solitude.

~

Back in Livingston, Paul and I eat lunch on the Happy
Fish's patio. Hungry dogs nudge us with their snouts. Finally,
Paul throws them the shells from our peeled shrimp which they
chomp enthusiastically.

Not far from the dogs, children watch our table. A pair of waifs
literally lick their chops nearby. We try to ignore them while we eat,
which is difficult. I can feel their eyes on my skin. Before he pays our
bill, Paul asks the owner to give the children some warm tortillas and
add it to our check.

At the ice cream parlor next door, an obviously well-off
Spanish-speaking family with a young son arrives. A Guatemalan
street kid tags along, talking and giggling with their child. When the
rich lady gives the tagalong boy a cone overflowing with bubble gum
pink ice cream, his face lights up.

As the boy savors his ice cream, two of his friends appear. Out
on the street, more children gather. In less than a minute, there are 11
children clustered around the rich couple, their son and his new friend
at the sweets shop. The kids jump up and down, begging for ice cream.
"Helado! Helado!" they cry. The woman doesn't know what to do.
Finally, she and her family walk away, trailed by the hungry street kids.

~

Following a lazy afternoon of naps and sex, Paul and I decide
on dinner at the African Hotel. For some reason, their restaurant is
built to resemble a Moroccan castle complete with moats and towers.
The décor is Turkish, heavily tiled, sporting Hebraic letters and a Star
of David chandelier. Yet, reggae music plays in the background. In the
midst of the Caribbean, this mishmash of Ottoman Empire meets Israel
meets Jamaica is oddly incongruous yet satisfying. Kind of like us.

As in many Livingston eateries, we are asked to write down
our order for the waiter. Some restaurants give paper checks while
others indicate your tab on the page of a marble composition notebook.
Because the African Hotel is somewhat upscale, it has lined pads. But
upscale or not, a persistent pooch still parks himself under our table.

The waiter tries to hide his smirk when I order my peasant
meal of salsa over rice and beans with fried banana and fried eggs.

Perhaps the waiter is condescending because it's the cheapest item on the menu. But it's also one of the few vegetarian offerings. The food is tasty, with an island flair. The black beans are slightly different, served with crispy, caramelized onions. Paul has chicken with a curry vibe and no ridicule on the side.

Walking back through town, we pass a reggae bar full of dancing bodies. Five percussionists flail on bongo drums and turtle shells. The rhythm is infectious. The musicians' energy practically levitates the cinder block building which houses the bar. Paul and I peek into the open door, aching to enter but aren't daring enough to break the silent barrier which tells us not to. The guidebook warns about going into pubs like this—robberies are common. It also says solo women should be wary walking on Livingston's beaches after dark. So, we don't, even together.

Instead, we try the bar at the opulent but sterile Hotel Tucan Dugu. It's empty except for us, six toucans in cages and several turtles in a moat. After one drink, we leave and end the evening with sugary *licuados* (smoothies) at an open-air stand on the main drag.

A walk to the pier brings us to a family who guards their belongings, furniture and all, which have already been loaded onto the morning ferry. The first one leaves for Puerto Barrios at 5:30 a.m.

~

In the courtyard of our hotel, we meet Doña Alida's husband and their two sons. They study the moon through a telescope and politely invite us to join them. The glowing lunar surface is breathtaking. *"Que linda!"* we exclaim. Doña's husband and children beam as we look into their telescope. They know they're giving us a special gift.

The five of us communicate as best we can, stumbling over each other's native tongues, attempting to describe the beauty of the moment and the face of the Earth's satellite.

Paul wonders how to say "moon" in Spanish. *"Luna,"* I tell him before Doña's men can answer. They're all impressed, especially Paul. I too wonder how I came up with the word so quickly. Maybe Guatemala is rubbing off on me.

Afraid to overstay our welcome with Doña's family on the patio, Paul and I head back to our bungalow, soothed by the bay breezes into sleep.

Day 7

Saturday, November 27, 1993
Livingston/Puerto Barrios

Yes, Guatemala is truly a country under constant repair, and the Hospedaje Doña Alida is no exception. Today, we are awakened by the sound of hammers and saws rather than the gentle music of the surf as we had been the day before. The workers are building additional bungalows behind ours. Paul is right. In five years' time, we will hardly recognize this place.

Breakfast this morning is quick and at the same stand we'd had our *licuados* the night before. The same staff scuttles about to serve us. "Don't they ever sleep?" I ask Paul.

He takes a gulp of his *café con leche*. "They probably close at midnight then open up by seven."

"What sort of life is that?"

"I bet they're just glad to have jobs," he says.

The same cowering, misshapen man with the limping gait, large head and mangled tongue serves us. He's conscious of the way he looks, of the way he speaks. There is a Quasimodo-ish gentility about him, an eagerness to please. When the man leaves, I whisper to Paul, "I've seen lots of deformed people in Livingston. Especially with problems in their legs and bones." Paul nods. "Why is that?" I continue.

"Poor diet," he ponders. "Bad medical care. No prenatal care. Abject poverty. Take your pick."

Paul and I sit at a wobbly table on the street. Dogs beg at our sneakered feet before our *desayuno* arrives. One bitch with grossly-distended nipples is so bold as to prod my bare leg with her snout. She must be very hungry.

Breakfast at this simple food stand is delicious and different. A giant pancake (they call it a tortilla) dripping with yogurt and fresh tropical fruits like papaya, bananas and mango topped with honey. It pleads for a first-rate cup of coffee. But there is none to be had, just sad sugar water doused with warm milk.

Ten feet off, people set up booths for a celebration. If it's going to happen tonight, we might decide to stay on in Livingston an extra day. Paul asks our waiter, who says the festival is weeks away, in honor of the Lady of Guadeloupe. "Two weeks? To build a few booths?" I say to Paul when the waiter leaves with our empty plates.

"*Chica,* things move very slowly in Guatemala," he reminds me.

~

After we check out of Doña Alida's, Paul and I take one last stroll around Livingston. On Calle Principal, we pass a group of large, white women. "Park Slope lesbians?" Paul ventures. I shake my head and sigh—like Ugly Americans and Germans, they're everywhere too. The women flaunt stubby braids in their short hair. Local ladies earn extra quetzals making *braicitas* (Spanglish for "little braids") for tourists who think they're chic by corrupting African hairstyles in a Latin American country.

Paul and I pass more famished children, more dogs, more people limping and on crutches. "I guess we've seen all we can see in Livingston," he nods. We head toward the pier, wearing our huge backpacks.

A poster warning against the evils of cholera catches my eye. The words are paired with explicit cartoons depicting intense thirst, stomach cramps and rice-water stool with a fishy odor.

Despite the cholera poster, Paul defiantly orders *ceviche* at the Happy Fish. It is my first time having the dish. "Raw fish," I say. "Here goes nothing."

"It's not raw," Paul explains, taking a spoonful from the parfait cup it's served in. "The lime juice cooks it." I'm doubtful until he swears, "My grandmother makes it all the time. It's incredible."

Paul's teaspoon is poised outside my lips. I open my mouth and chew. He's right; it *is* delicious. Firm, fresh seafood marinated in lime and seasoned with scallions, salt and pepper. There are also bits of tomato, celery and avocado We order another, which goes down just as easy.

~

I am writing these words in my fuchsia notebook on the ferry as it chugs from Livingston to Puerto Barrios. An armed immigration official does his best to read my journal over my shoulder. Or pretends to read it, since I'm confident he can't read English. Maybe he's trying to unnerve me. But it doesn't work.

The ferry ride across Amatique Bay at the mouth of the Caribbean takes 90 minutes. This boat is smaller than the Circle Line back in New York, which doesn't even carry vehicles like this one does. Manhattan's Circle Line just rings around Manhattan, as the name implies. And this boat is much older than the Circle Line is.

Suddenly hungry again, Paul and I buy coconut bread from a coffee-skinned woman onboard. It is rich and decadent, a cross between fudge and peanut brittle and sweet as sugar cubes. As we eat, I notice that the woman who sold it to us has open sores on her legs. When I nudge Paul to show him, he shrugs. "Just enjoy the ride."

I try.

~

The Real Guide says that Puerto Barrios was established in the 1880s and used to be one of Guatemala's major ports, if not the largest. The United Fruit Company, which still horribly exploits its workers, was once based in Puerto Barrios. It controlled the town and the railroads as well.

Today, the neighboring port of Santo Tomas is larger, more modern, more streamlined and because of this, gets more business than Puerto Barrios does. However, in some aspects, Puerto Barrios is still booming. It still bears souvenirs from its seafaring era—strip bars, whore houses and salty, old boozers. All the things Paul and I love.

Not counting Guatemala City, Puerto Barrios is the biggest metropolis we've visited so far on this trip. Following a languid Caribbean town like Livingston, we find nothing quaint or cozy about Puerto Barrios. But there are fewer stray dogs, so that's a plus.

Beyond the dock, Puerto Barrios' Saturday afternoon market is sooty and congested. From the ferry, Paul and I jump directly into a cab—a Toyota wagon rusting (of course), with one side window's glass missing. Since the banks are closed, the driver takes us to Carmen, a lady who runs a dry goods store and also changes money. It's risky but we have no choice.

The bank's exchange rate is 5.7 quetzals but Carmen begins with her own private rate of 5.3. Paul charms her up to 5.5, claiming he got six on the streets of the capital. A blatant lie, but Carmen buys it.

Our driver is a fast talker and speaks English well. Every other word out of Carlos' mouth is "fuck." He blames his potty mouth on living in a south Texas border town and serving three years in prison for drunk driving there. The police also found an ounce of marijuana in Carlos' car which he swears wasn't his. (It never is.)

Carlos is quite the character, cursing his lungs out, finessing his way around Puerto Barrios' potholes while spouting racist remarks. One gem is, "Who wants to live in Livingston next to a nigger?" I want to tell him that some people wouldn't take too kindly to Carlos' dark brown skin but bite my tongue.

He takes us to the bus station so we can buy tickets for the express to Guatemala City tomorrow. We're heading back to the capital because busses to virtually every part of the country leave from GC. So, it's a choice spot to begin our gradual journey to the Western Highlands and Glenn in Xela.

After the bus depot, it's on to the Hotel del Norte, located well outside the clatter of Puerto Barrios. The del Norte is about seven blocks from the bus terminal and will be an easy downhill walk to the station tomorrow morning.

On the way to the del Norte, Carlos gestures to the crude homes we whiz past. "Under each of these roofs, at least six people live in two or three rooms," Carlos claims. His parting words to us are a joke of sorts:

"What are the two things a nigger is afraid of?"

His answer: "A knife and water."

I need a long shower to purify me after Carlos' racist cab ride.

~

The Hotel del Norte is a big wood-frame building, which, like most of Guatemala, has seen better days. But it still manages to maintain a certain refinement and charm. It's situated on a substantial plot of land and overlooks the bay. Scrupulously neat, the del Norte smells of fresh paint. The bulk of it is painted bright white but the shutters and moldings are loden. Like a wandering eye, the del Norte's worn staircases warp toward the left. Enclosed porches drape themselves around the hotel's two stories.

Inside, the Hotel del Norte is filled with a fine sampling of old, dusty wood. The bar, the dining room's huge credenza and the check-in desk's mahogany, though ancient, are polished to a high sheen. Although there are no rooms with private baths left, we still go for it. Since we need to catch the 7:30 bus the next morning, we figure that few of the other guest will be up by then, so the shared bath will be all ours. "We just need a place to rest our heads," I say.

But when the desk clerk tells us the room has twin beds, I roll my eyes. "I hate twin beds," I whisper to Paul.

"I'll visit you," he promises.

Our room is utilitarian but spotless. Like a high-class bordello, it has a washbasin, presumably for washing body parts. Our room also sports a small table upon which is a card that discourages bringing "disreputable people" back to one's lodgings. In English *and* Spanish. "Do they mean prostitutes or people like us?" Paul wonders.

"Probably the first one," I venture.

As Paul and I order drinks on the Hotel del Norte's screened-in porch, I detect another distinct Hemingway vibe. It could be from the scruffy beard Paul is growing. I ask for a rum and Coke *sin hielo* (without ice). It arrives in a heavy tumbler with plenty of lime and a huge t-shaped ice cube. When the waiter leaves, I fish the ice from my drink and fling it out the door. "What part of *sin hielo* didn't he understand?" I ask Paul.

"Maybe it's your accent," he suggests. I stick out my tongue at him in response.

We sit and drink and grin and watch the thick, gray water.

~

Today marks the one-year anniversary of our first date. (If you can call a "booty call" a date.) Paul and I talk about how good this past year has been. Toasting me with his *Gallo*, he says, "Thank you." This is perhaps the best toast I've ever heard.

This pleasing afternoon is filled with quiet revelations. "Whenever I travel with someone, I usually need to be by myself for at least one night," Paul confesses. "You know, go out alone just to have some space. Even when I'm traveling with a guy. But I don't feel that way with you."

I nod. "I don't feel that way with you either," I agree. "You don't get on my nerves. Yet."

With my ex-husband, vacations were never a vacation from Alex's piss-poor attitude. From his constant complaining about the shitty hand life had dealt him. Instead of making the most of the cards he had, for example, Alex would endlessly bemoan his failed career as an artist but he was totally unwilling to try and find happiness in something else. For a couple of days, the trip might be fine but then the timebomb of Alex's discontent would be hovering on the periphery, threatening to explode.

It was always the same story with my ex, no matter where we were...the Bahamas, Bermuda, California. I'd end up crumbling in tears, just like I did at home—but in a prettier place. There was no talking to Alex, no reasoning with him. It was impossible to break through his pungent sadness. It got so bad that I felt like I was smothering. I felt like he was picking me apart, bit by bit. From the inside out.

The truth is, I never should have married Alex. Oh, I loved him at the time. In the beginning. I loved him too much, in fact. That's the only reason I think people should marry: for love. At least that's what I was taught growing up. I didn't care that Alex was a struggling artist, that we might never have a house, a new car or other luxuries. I didn't care that I might have to work my whole life to support him and his dreams. It was Alex's abject pessimism that dismantled us. His self-hate. It poisoned him and me and everything around us. I would have stuck by him through anything. Anything but this.

How can you respect someone who doesn't respect themselves? How can you convince them that a life of struggle, of trying, is better than giving up? Than suicide? You can't. I finally learned this after 15 years of being Alex's partner and almost 10 years of being his wife. I had to get out. I had to leave him before he totally destroyed me, destroyed my spirit. And I barely got out alive.

The damage had been done in Alex's childhood, long before I came into the picture. He was the fruit of two people who didn't love each other and the victim of his mother's own discontent. Alex was what happens when sadness and anger are relentlessly drilled into a young skull. In the beginning, I was stupid enough to think my love, my devotion, could change that, could transform him. Well, it couldn't and it didn't.

But what Alex's sadness *did* change was me. My love dissolved into duty and pity. If I left this man, he would have nothing. How could I abandon him? Somewhere along the line, I lost sight of what his self-loathing was doing to me. I lost "me" in the mix.

A marriage is two people trying, not one. The cold reality struck when I realized that I was seeking happiness outside my marriage. That's where I got my laughter, my joy. From friends and family, not from Alex. I was being emotionally unfaithful to my husband with others. What's the difference between this and being physically unfaithful to someone? Not much.

Therapy didn't help. When Alex ultimately agreed to go to a marriage counselor, he told us, "This isn't a problem with your marriage…it's a problem with him. *He* needs therapy; that's what's wrong with your marriage." Although Alex eventually tried seeing a therapist on his own, it didn't help.

When I told Alex I couldn't take it any longer, he said, "Good. Go. Walk out on me like everyone else has. The art galleries, my manager…" Then Alex refused to sign divorce papers for six months. After me begging and pleading for half a year, it suddenly dawned on him. "You're really miserable with me, aren't you?" Alex finally said one August day.

"Yes!" I sobbed. That's when Alex finally signed our divorce papers. Immediately after, he hurled his wedding band across the room at me. But by that point, I didn't care. I was numb. There wasn't a thing he could do or say that could hurt me anymore. I had to escape. I had to save what was left of me.

Then came Paul, three months later.

The friend of a friend, Paul and I had known each other for a dozen years. We'd flirted at parties, gave each other books to read. *Interview with the Vampire, Blue Highways*… Our first "date" was supposed to be a one-time fling to consummate our long-term lust. To get each other out of our respective systems. But it was good. Too good. One "date" with Paul became another. And another.

So, against our better judgement, here we are. Still together. In Guatemala.

~

Why do I keep skipping back to Alex? I'm in a poor man's paradise with a great guy and I keep obsessing about my ex-husband and my failed first marriage. Maybe I do it because I'm afraid I suck at relationships. Maybe because I'm afraid Paul will grow to hate me, too. Just like Alex did.

I force myself back into the here and now. Back onto the porch of the Hotel del Norte in Puerto Barrios, the second-best port in Guatemala. I am here with Paul. The sun is starting to set. It is beautiful and I am happy. Finally.

Paul downs his *cerveza* and smiles at me. I smile back. "Will you still look at me like that when you're 60?" he asks.

"I sure hope so," I tell him.

~

Maybe it's the drinks, the tainted ice cube, memories of Alex or the *ceviche* from lunch. Maybe it's drinking two *ron y Cocas* on an empty stomach. But by suppertime, I'm definitely queasy. And mad at myself because I want our first-date anniversary supper to be special. It is special, but not in the way that I'd imagined—I spend most of it in the bathroom.

As I dash back and forth between the restroom and the table, Paul sits alone in the grand dining room among the mahogany and the starched, linen tablecloths. The credenza, which is about 20 feet long and at least 10 feet high, is magnificent. I try to focus on the beauty of the room rather than the fireworks in my belly. But it doesn't work.

Although it kills me, I barely touch the *langosta ajillo*. Paul's *caracol* (sea snail), served flattened out, is so rubbery he can't eat it so he happily tears into my garlicky lobster.

Back in our room, I'm nauseous, seasick, hot and tired. Paul sits on the edge of my bed, rubbing my belly, cooing to me in Spanish. *"Ai, mi vida...mi novia..."* It means, "Oh, my life...my girlfriend..."

"You're so sweet," I groan. "I really appreciate this, I do. But I just want to puke in private."

"I understand completely," Paul says. "I'll be downstairs if you need me."

Kneeling over the toilet bowl, I picture Paul sitting at the del Norte's long, handsome bar, having a *cerveza* alone. Though the urge to hug the porcelain has subsided, I lay on my bed in the dark for a little while longer.

Our room is right by the communal bathroom. At dinnertime, it's very busy as toilets flush and doors slam. Thirty minutes later, I still haven't nodded off and am feeling better. Especially after I brush my teeth. I head downstairs.

There's no sign of Paul at the bar, which is now overrun by Germans, their guttural words flooding the air. It isn't the same placid place it had been two hours earlier.

I stand on the porch. The sun has already gone down. The water gently laps the rocks. The park adjoining the del Norte's grounds is a favorite spot for young couples to coo and kiss. Its gazebo sees its fair share of traffic. Children play on the swings. Others kick a soccer ball. Even Paul-less, I am very content at that moment.

~

A huge cargo ship sits at a faraway dock, a different pier than the one our ferry arrived at this afternoon. This dock has to be at least a city block long. Large wooden cartons are being unloaded by a pulley system. Bananas, someone says.

Still no sign of Paul, though. Now I feel mild distress at being left alone in a strange country. But an odd type of excitement accompanies it too.

Soon enough, I spot my lover's familiar, loping gait and his crooked, uncomplicated smile. Paul was about to check on me when he saw me musing on the verandah, he tells me.

Together, we head toward the dock. It's about ten boards wide, and like a broken-toothed leer, has a bunch of slats missing. Crossing them successfully requires a light, tapdancing motion. Paul does a fleet-footed, tipsy shuffle across the boards, gingerly stepping over the loose ones.

We sit with our feet dangling above the water as the ship unloads its cargo onto the other dock. Our conversation ping-pongs back and forth between the Chiquita ship and our relationship. "Who makes most of the money on bananas?" I ask.

"Not the farm workers," he admits.

"That's a hell of a lot of bananas," I tell him, watching crate after crate lowered to the dock.

We observe in silent awe. After a long pause, Paul says, "The neighborhood kids used to tease me that my mother came to New York on a banana boat from Havana."

"Did she?" I wonder.

He shakes his head. "An airplane. To JFK. But it was called Idlewild back in 1949. She came to Brooklyn to live with her father and his new wife."

"That must have been tough," I say.

"It was. She was only 11 at the time. Didn't speak any English."

Inside the boxes, the green skins of unripe bananas peek through the slats. "This is kind of cool, isn't it?" I offer. "Weirdly relaxing."

"Mmmm," Paul says.

In between our words, we kiss like schoolkids, like the locals in the gazebo. I'll never see Paul — or bananas — the same way again.

He leaves to get a beer and comes back with a club soda for my still-delicate stomach. Even though I didn't ask for one. How did he know I'd changed my mind after he'd gone and now wanted a drink? Sometimes Paul and I are like *The Corsican Brothers*. In the Dumas novel (and in the movies), they were conjoined twins, and although separated at birth, they could still read each other's emotions. I guess what Paul and I both want — and fear — is the same. But we refuse to own up to it.

~

When they're done unloading the cargo ship, next they stack containers onto it. Watching the banana boat load and unload is apparently *the* thing to do in Puerto Barrios on a Saturday night. Families gather to see the spectacle. A crew of teenage girls giggle and playfully berate each other. Sweethearts, groups of kids, clusters of young men...and then there's us. We don't fit into any of the pigeonholes but they still welcome us.

The container compartments of trucks are snapped up by a gargantuan magnet contraption and are then arranged one on top of the other on the ship. It is like the hand of a giant, unseen boy is playing with his Matchbox cars on the open sea rather than on his bedroom floor. We are all hypnotized as we watch with wonder.

~

After a while, Paul and I walk into town. We want an agreeable bar to sit in and enjoy cocktails. But we can't find any that fit the description. There are lots of whorehouses that serve alcohol and feature upstairs rooms at the end of long, red-lit hallways. But that's not what we're looking for. We immediately leave these establishments as soon as we realize what they are.

Pigally is promising, but it's empty except for four hookers (oldish, plump and not too attractive). They perk up when they see Paul then visibly deflate when they notice me behind him. There's a female bartender and her female helper who clears tables.

The barkeep speaks to Paul in Spanish. About me. She wonders if I am Hispanic because I'm black-haired and dark-eyed. Then she asks if I'm his wife. First, he answers, *"Sí,"* then "No." Next, the bartender inquires if I am a special one. *"Muy especial,"* Paul nods. I turn away, embarrassed.

We leave Pigally when a rummy perches on a barstool beside Paul and tries to become his best buddy. Many locals speak English in Puerto Barrios, at least a little bit. Maybe it's the transient nature of the seaport town.

When Paul pays our tab, he gives the drunkard a couple of quetzals. The barmaid is pissed off that the lush has driven us out. But other drinkers will soon take our place. I'm sure of it.

There's a club further down the street that charges five quetzals (about a dollar) admission per person. Once inside, Paul and I feel like we're trapped in a 1970s-time warp. A Bee Gee's knockoff group sings "You Should Be Dancing" from the *Saturday Night Fever* soundtrack then leave the stage after that tune.

The DJ is way too loud. "If it's too loud, then you're too old," Paul shouts over it. He and I dance to bad, American disco music. We're the only *gringos*. Luckily, a halfway-decent seven-piece band comes onstage and plays a few Latin numbers. Although the dance floor is crowded, no one applauds between songs. Is this a Guatemalan tradition or rudeness? When Paul tries to order a shot of tequila, he's informed that liquor is sold by the bottle, not the glass. "Let's go someplace else," he says.

"We've got to get up at six tomorrow," I remind him.

It doesn't take much convincing to steer Paul home. He falls asleep almost immediately in his single bed. I hear his flow of breath change and know he's no longer awake. But I, on the other hand, lie there for some time, shadows painting the walls, as I listen to the mournful cry of foghorns.

Day 8

Sunday, November 28, 1993
Puerto Barrios/Guatemala City/Antigua

"There are too many *gringos* in Guatemala," says an old
drunk to his friends in Spanish at a 24-hour diner in Puerto Barrios
at seven a.m.

Paul and I ignore him. Maybe the man is upset that we don't
appreciate his singing/screaming along with the lovelorn songs he
plays on the jukebox. The sounds that come out of his mouth as he
alternates between sucking on his beer and spitting out sappy lyrics are
horrendous. But he obviously doesn't think so. Neither do his buddies.

My travel partner and I are booked on one of the Litegua line's
"luxury" busses that will take us back to Guatemala City where we'll
hop another to Antigua, our final destination for today. It's a stunning
colonial town about an hour's ride from the capital. But it will take
about six hours to get from Puerto Barrios to GC.

~

At the Puerto Barrios bus station, a woman with a beat-up red
Igloo cooler sells sandwiches and cold drinks. "No soda in a plastic
bag?" I say to Paul as he passes me one of each.

"Disappointed?"

"Sort of," I admit. I'll definitely miss not getting food and drink
from open bus windows. But maybe we can buy snacks from street
hawkers on the road.

During the trip, I write in my journal for almost two hours before I take a break. Paul alternates between reading *Ever After* and dozing.

Litegua boasts the fastest, finest Pullman buses in the country. I'm not sure if this is true but our vehicle is several steps up from the other busses we've been on. There still isn't air conditioning but at least no luggage or people decorate the roof. Wonder of wonders, there's even a bathroom and assigned seats. Time passes quickly and unremarkably.

Between Puerto Barrios and Guatemala City, the roads are paved and smooth. Guard rails bracket particularly hazardous curves. The ride is almost bounce-free, unlike the stretch from Santa Elena to El Relleno. Paul keeps trying to read what I'm writing in my notebook and I keep covering it. "I promise you, it's nothing exciting," I tell him. "It's just a journal." He gives up and continues reading *Ever After.*

The little girl sitting across from us looks freakishly like me when I was her age. She has a straight black pageboy haircut with sharp bangs, big, dark, somber eyes and beige skin. When I mention this to Paul, he studies the child intently. He tries not to stare in a creepy way as he looks for the "me" in her.

The countryside is a muddle of different terrains: dry, arid hills mixed with flat plains and stands of cactus. The sharp mountains in the distance may have been volcanoes at one time. Although it's pretty, my lids soon grow heavy. I take a nap, my head bobbing on Paul's shoulder, dreaming of green.

~

There's no mistaking the outskirts of Guatemala City. Squalid is the most charitable description I can muster. Cement-block houses are stacked one on top of the other, balancing on hillsides. We pass a Shell Oil sign riddled with bullets. Welcome to the Wild, Wild West.

Paul and I arrive at 12:30 in Guatemala City and walk briskly toward the Antigua busses. The travel gods smile upon us because we manage to catch the one o'clock shuttle. And even that isn't soon enough for us to leave the capital.

Waiting in line to board the Antigua bus, we see a man selling sodas. He wears a t-shirt that reads, "Ask me about my Heiney." Which is short for Heineken beer as well as the nickname for a "butt." Paul and I burst out laughing. The man scowls at us until Paul explains what Heiney means in English. *"Es el culo,"* Paul says, pointing to his rear end. *It's the ass.* The man is horrified and starts taking off his shirt.

The decrepit Blue Bird bus smells vaguely of gasoline and has broken, gashed seats. In front of us sits a young couple with a newborn who cries almost continuously, his voice a plaintive bleat. Many, like this family, are traveling to Antigua just for the afternoon with daypacks and shopping bags, taking a Sunday jaunt to the country as people in large, crowded cities often do.

Before the bus leaves, a man boards, waving a fistful of drug prescription forms. He says he doesn't have enough money to fill them and begs for quetzals. The man leaves when he collects a few. Another beggar replaces him, asking for contributions to aid El Salvador. He sings his tale of woe in Spanish, his eyes rolled back in his head. The man's expression is feral and unhinged, like the one Hitler wore in his rabid newsreel speeches. When no one puts money into the panhandler's battered box, he retreats, grumbling.

Slowly, the Blue Bird creeps through Guatemala City. The center of town isn't as crestfallen as Central, just industrial. I watch a man carry a new, full-sized mattress (still wrapped in plastic) on his back. The bus curves through the suburbs, past a shop that sells sinks and toilets in a kaleidoscope of hues. There's also a public bathhouse. "What is this, the 1930s?" I ask Paul.

"Remember," he says, "a lot of people don't have running water."

As the Blue Bird climbs the hills, the road grows curvier and steeper. We pass clusters of white crosses which indicate roadside death sites, then a large marker. I catch the year 1992 and little else. "This must be where the Mexican dance troupe died," Paul says.

I recall reading that the dance company's driver was speeding to get the Ballet Folklorico to their gig on time. The brakes failed and the bus went careening into a canyon, killing 25 out of the 41 on board. When Paul retells this tidbit, I shudder. "Glenn saw the Ballet Folklorico once," he continues. "He said they weren't very good."

I elbow Paul. Hard. "Are you trying to make me feel better?"

"Yeah," he admits. "In a way."

"Well, try again."

Throughout the trip, the *ayudante* keeps shouting, "Antigua! Antigua! Antigua!" He yells it out the open door whenever we pass people lingering on the road. "Why does he keep doing that?" I finally ask Paul.

"Doing what?"

"Yelling where we're going. I mean, it's written on the front of the bus."

"Lots of people here can't read," Paul reminds me.

~

One quick turn off the paved road and the streets suddenly become cobblestoned. This, and the bus's descent into a green valley, signals that we're approaching Antigua.

Situated in a fertile basin, the town is ringed by volcanoes, two of which are still active. Established in the 1540s, Antigua was actually Guatemala's third capital. But 20 years later, it was ravaged by its first major earthquake. Ignoring this fact, a number of religious orders established themselves here and built elaborate churches and convents.

A second big earthquake struck in 1717, then two more a few months apart in 1773. This prompted the capital to be moved to its present location of Guatemala City, about 25 miles southwest of Antigua. Although it's nowhere near as beautiful as Antigua, at least GC is geographically stable.

The skeletons of wrecked churches and other colonial buildings pepper the streets, accented by lush bougainvillea. Ruins are adjacent to people's homes. The hollow skulls of broken nunneries exist serenely beside thriving businesses, the heaps of rocks virtually ignored. Life goes on around them. Antigua is striking and amazing but in an entirely different way than Tikal is. It's on a smaller, more manageable scale.

The bus lets us off at a terminal which also serves as Antigua's main market. The *ayudante* hands our bags down from the roof. On the return trip to Guatemala City, his cry changes. Instead of "Antigua! Antigua! Antigua" it is now, "Guate! Guate! Guate!" because the bus is headed back to Guatemala City.

~

Paul and I arrive in Antigua six and a half hours after we boarded the Litegua bus in Puerto Barrios. My pack feels unbelievably heavy. Maybe this is because I've barely worn it in the past several days. At 2:30 in the afternoon, I'm cranky, tired, hungry and headachy.

Since street kids spout the virtues of a *hospedaje* nearby called Casa de Santa Lucía, we figure there's probably something wrong with it. Paul and I hit the town, looking for reasonable lodgings. There's no shortage of hotels but they're either flea bags with sexed-out mattresses or luxury behemoths out of our price range.

Paul leaves me and our packs near a ruin while he explores the possibilities without the burden of his heavy bag—or me. He can tell by my face that I'm exhausted. At times, I lag a half block behind. I welcome the chance to sit on the curb and wait until he gets back. When he reports his findings to me, we hit the *avenida* again.

Posada Don Rodrigo is modest from the street but when we step inside, it's anything but. Before we can refuse, the desk clerk has the bellman show us a room. Paul and I follow him through the manicured courtyard where a marimba band plays and pampered folks listen. These are exactly the sort of people we don't associate with back home and definitely don't want to hang out with when we're away.

In his elaborate, ribboned and braided uniform, the bellman leads us to a tremendous suite which sports two large, four-posted beds, tiled floors, a fireplace, an opulent bathroom and a mini balcony overlooking the room itself. "This is 80 dollars a night, not 80 quetzals a night, right?" Paul asks the bellman. (Eighty quetzals would be about 16 dollars.) His face registers polite shock. "*Sí,*" the bellman nods, trying to bury his surprise. We're seriously in the wrong hotel.

Back at the reception desk, the clerk drops the price to 50 dollars in the time it takes us to sling our packs onto our shoulders. We admit that it's still out of our budget. In Brooklyn, 50 dollars buys you five hours in a no-tell motel. But in Guatemala, 50 dollars is exorbitant.

As Paul and I leave, we notice that the bellman has returned to his post at the front door. He still wears a slight smirk from our reaction to the room's price. In the best Spanish he can muster, Paul tells him, "That room was nicer than my apartment back home." The man nods. Now he understands.

The prospect of stumbling around Antigua's gentle hills weighed down by our packs is not an attractive one. So hastily, we decide on a *hospedaje* nearby for 37 dollars a night. Down the street from the ruined El Carmen church, it's 13 dollars cheaper than the opulent Don Rodrigo but more our style. Plus, *desayuno* is included.

The El Carmen Hotel features a lovely restaurant in its enclosed courtyard. Each room has its own bathroom (with scorching water) and televisions (with cable and remote). Amenities like these seem out in place in such an antiquated town. They're as out of place as the automobiles that choke the colonial streets are.

With the exception of the capital, there are few passenger cars in Guatemala. Sure, there are plenty of delivery trucks—*Gallo* and Coca-Cola reach even distant towns, including Livingston and Tikal— but passenger cars are scarce. However, in Antigua, there are lots of private cars and even traffic jams, on a Sunday afternoon.

It's also bizarre seeing people using cordless telephones on the street since most people in Guatemala have no house phones. "Rich businessmen from the capital," Paul guesses.

"The kind of people who stay at the Don Rodrigo," I agree.

Another oddity in Antigua: high-quality, soft, toilet paper that isn't the texture of fine-grained sandpaper. We're thrilled that the El Carmen boasts the former. As disgusting as it sounds, we've gotten used to throwing soiled bathroom tissue into the trash can, not the toilet. The reason is that Guatemala's delicate plumbing can't handle it. Even the almost-ritzy El Carmen's pipes are no exception. There's a sign requesting the proper disposal method, in several languages.

Our room is hung with weavings, decorated with handmade rugs, local crafts and other handsome accoutrements. "This is far too nice for the likes of us," Paul says.

"Speak for yourself," I tell him.

After we settle in and wash up, Paul clicks on the TV and channel-surfs like a man possessed. "No television for a week and the minute we've got one in our room..." I begin, grabbing the remote from him. I turn off the TV.

Antigua awaits.

~

Unlike any other city we've visited so far, Antigua has a unique, old-world Spanish charm. Toppled remnants of churches and monasteries speckle every other street corner. They aren't guarded. They aren't cordoned off. People are free to climb them. So, Paul and I do, going from one to the next like chimps.

In the middle of town is Parque Central, a neatly-kept square in full bloom. And in the middle of Parque Central is a charming but unusual fountain. Four stone maidens stand in its center, water spritzing from the nipples of their proud, swollen breasts. We nickname this the Tittie Fountain. No doubt a fertility symbol, it's still jarring in this ultra-Catholic, ultra-conservative country.

"She's my favorite," Paul says, nodding toward the statue with the strongest, most defiant streams of water.

"I can see why," I admit.

We have a late lunch in a German restaurant facing Parque Central. It's called Weiner something or other. With a Teutonic menu, a Southwestern/Santa Fe décor, REM piping through the speakers and traditionally-dressed Guatemalan women waiting tables, the Weiner doesn't know exactly what it is. But the prices are decent and the menu is a refreshing change from *típico* fare.

I order spinach dumplings sprinkled with chopped peanuts, surrounded by steamed vegetables drizzled in a mustard sauce and ringed with succulent fresh tomato slices. Paul orders a Black Forest version of *ropa vieja* (which translates to "old clothes"). The shredded spiced beef over rice is delicious. Dessert is crepes smothered in jam and a cup of coffee, real, live, bona-fide brewed coffee.

Because of the large number of American students who settle in Antigua to study at its many Spanish-language schools, there are amenities here that you find nowhere else in the country. Like video bars, for example, and the aforementioned ballsy coffee.

Most restaurants sport bulletin boards which alert students to Anglicized activities and the Weiner is no different. A poster advertises the movie *Slacker*, an indie film Paul and I have been dying to see.

To walk off our big lunch, we stroll through town, delighted with the wonders each new block brings. Ruins, ruins and more ruins. Paul and I stumble upon the venue that's supposed to air *Slacker*. It's a small hotel on the edge of town near the remains of the San Francisco church. But the workers inform us that their VCR is broken so there will be no showing of *Slacker* tonight. Such is life in Guatemala.

~

Antigua is dotted with a blend of restaurants and ruins, upscale shops and street vendors. It's a striking contradiction of opposites. A row of women sell similar dishes from carts—fresh guacamole, fragrant chicken wrapped in floury tortillas. It smells great but we're still stuffed from lunch.

On one block, we find a shop that has spectacular mahogany furniture. Inside, we lust after a gorgeous rolltop desk priced at 1,500 dollars. The tables, dressers and beds are too massive for my tiny Brooklyn apartment. Besides, the shipping cost would be prohibitive.

But still, I can dream. "Maybe we could put stuff like this in Blackie's," I tell Paul.

"Maybe not," he says, glancing at the price tag on an end table.

Outside, the sun has long set. The line of food vendors is gone, replaced with legions of itinerants, ready to bed down in Parque Central. They lay on its brick walkways, covered by rags, not even blankets. There are women, children and families here, and it's heartbreaking to see. Especially in a city as prosperous as Antigua with fine hotels like the Don Rodrigo. And our own El Carmen.

As the moon rises higher in the sky, it lights the cone of Volcán Fuego, which smokes in the distance. Paul and I search for a sociable sort of bar, one where people sit on stools and actually talk to strangers. Most pubs have private tables where people only talk to people they know. After a week of traveling, it would be good to compare notes with other travelers. But we come up empty.

In our quest for the perfect watering hole, Paul and I circle the same streets. We're growing weary of our aimless wandering. In the dark, all the ruins look the same. The stone canyons take on an eerie glow at night. It's not as menacing as Tikal but similar. "Do you feel it?" I ask Paul. "The spirits?"

He shakes his head. "I don't," he tells me."

"Really? I think this must be what it's like in Athens or Rome. You get a sense of the people who walked the streets before you did."

"There's a Jamaican saying, 'The ghost knows who to scare.'" Paul says.

"It's not scary," I try to explain. "But there's just a…a presence."

He shakes his head again. "Still no."

We both forget the name of the street El Carmen on. "It has a ruin on the corner," I joke.

Paul kisses me. "They all have ruins on the corner."

Somehow, we manage to find the hotel.

At the start of this trip, Paul stopped shaving. With his new mustache and mutton chops, he takes on another persona. I consider him in the twilight of our room, scrutinizing the strong lines of his face, newly cushioned by blonde tufts of sideburns. It's almost as though I'm with a different man. There's a dusky, mysterious quality to him. The intensity of his eyes is accented now. He is a deeper, darker Paul.

Is it because of all the rum and Cokes? Because of the mystical land itself? But our tumbles have become more passionate here. Afterwards, though, there is always peaceful sleep in each other's arms. There's always that.

Day 9

Monday, November 29, 1993
Antigua

I am awakened by a swift kick in the middle of the night. It jolts me out of my dreams. I have an LSD flashback and immediately think of my ex-husband near the end of our relationship. Of the times Alex would wake me up at three in the morning, screaming into my face about wanting to kill me then kill himself. Then, the next second, Alex would be sobbing, begging for me to forgive him and wondering why I wanted to leave him.

But Paul is not Alex, I tell myself. Again.

In bed, in Antigua with Paul, I almost cry with relief that I am with Paul in Antigua. Paul has never hurt me. (*'Not yet,'* Bad Carol's voice rings in my head. *'Not yet.'*) This is the man who helps me into my backpack every morning. This is the man who watches my face fade into slumber. This is the man who comes to my apartment when I feel sad, even when I tell him not to. This is the man I'm probably going to marry. Maybe. We'll see.

Paul apologizes for drop-kicking me in his sleep. He holds me close as he tells me about the dream which prompted his nocturnal attack. In it, two street thugs were terrorizing us. When they lunged at us, Paul let loose with a drowsy roundhouse which caused him to knee me in the base of the spine.

As Paul adjusts his arm, he knocks down a wall hanging. We lay there in the stark blackness, giggling under a six-foot long weaving in a picture frame. After we crawl out from under it, we make love.

My own dreams on this trip have been turbulent ones—twisted scenarios of money problems and people problems. In these disturbing night visions, I keep telling myself that I'm on holiday, that I should be enjoying myself, that I shouldn't be worrying. Will the checks I'm promised for projects be waiting for me when I get home? Will I get more assignments after almost a monthlong hiatus? Such are the woes of a freelance editor. It's so bizarre to dream of Brooklyn then wake up in Guatemala. Disorienting, even.

As an independent contractor, I hold on fiercely to my freedom, to my ability to take time off whenever the mood strikes me. This is one of freelancing's perks, besides having no health insurance and no paid vacation. My trip to Guatemala is the longest one I've taken. Ever. And I deserve it. I think.

At its best, freelancing works like a well-oiled machine. At its worst, it means starvation. I silently vow to find a steady part-time job when I get back. But I will do this kicking and screaming emotionally. Part of me hopes I don't have to actually *do* it. I know I'll fight it every step of the way. I don't want to be pushed to choose between freedom, happiness and money. Happiness shouldn't be a struggle, should it? Happiness should be a given.

~

"*Soda in a Plastic Bag,*" Paul says emphatically as we dress for the day. "That's what you should call it. Your journal about Guatemala. It sums up the country in a nutshell."

"I don't know," I tell him. "I kind of like *Huck Finn in Guatemala.*" I wave the thick paperback at Paul for emphasis. "It seems to fit." After all, Paul and I are Huckleberry Finns of a feather, traveling together.

Here are some more inconsistencies I've noticed about Guatemala:

- Pepper is rarely on restaurant tables but there's no shortage of clumpy salt cellars;
- Guatemalan sugar is raw, brown and coarsely granulated, and doesn't fully dissolve in their tepid instant coffee;
- There is absolutely no water pressure. Not in the lukewarm/cold showers, not in the sinks. Likewise, for

toilets. I'll just say that the water pressure doesn't exactly
do its job with American-sized poops.;
- Here, they strain the pulp from orange juice. But back in
  the US, thick OJ marked "Homestyle" and "Grove Stand"
  are selling points.

When I share all of the above observations with Paul, he
laughs. "That's a good start," he tells me.

~

Well-rested, Paul and I are raring to delve into Antigua.
Following our complimentary breakfast of posh pancakes, fruit and
coffee in the El Carmen's courtyard, we pack and move to more
reasonable accommodations at Posada Asjemenou.

This *posada* has a large, nondescript door facing the street and
doesn't look like much from the outside. But walking through its arch
is like passing into another world. There's a fountain in the middle
of a terra cotta courtyard, trees, plants and lots of bougainvillea. The
Asjemenou has about 15 units but none with private baths. However,
in this instance, quaintness outweighs convenience.

Our room is very nice yet simple. The tiled floors keep us cool
from the dusty heat outdoors. Big, old wooden furniture compliments
the homespun art on the walls. There's even a communal TV salon
with comfortable couches and coffee tables covered with magazines in
a dozen languages. It's inviting and homey.

The Asjemenou is located beneath the Santa Catalina arch
which was originally constructed so the cloisters from the convent
could walk to the school without being exposed to the harsh realities
of the outside world. The arch is all that remains of the Santa Catalina
convent, which was destroyed in an earthquake in the 1700s. The
posada is built where the convent once stood.

On the half-hour, the clock embedded in the Santa Catalina
arch rings somewhat mournfully. With every toll, I swear I feel
the nuns' disgruntled spirits, mourning their wasted virginity, their
shrunken, unused wombs. But then again, maybe it's my imagination.

Paul and I spend the day exploring ruins, climbing collapsed
steps and venturing beneath crumbled porticoes. Even in their
devastated states, the wrecked buildings of Antigua are oddly
exquisite. They are landscaped to perfection with reverence and
respect. Florid bougainvillea, lush roses, daisies and other flowers

decorate the shells of buildings like life-sized floral masterpieces, a tribute to what Antigua once was.

There are so many fallen churches and convents within Antigua city limits one melts into the other. Especially in my poor memory. Was it La Merced or the church of Santa Rosa with two fountains in its courtyard? "I can't remember," Paul admits when I ask him. They are both equally as enchanting; their former worshippers equally as dead. So, what does it matter which one it was?

~

After lunch, Paul and I head for the outskirts of town. Our destination is a hill that is said to have a spectacular view of Antigua. *The Real Guide* warns that tourists have been robbed on the long, lonely slog to the top. "Are you sure about this?" I ask Paul at the base.

"Yes," he says confidently. I repeat to myself that Paul would never put me in harm's way and that he is not one for false bravado. When he says something worries him, I listen. When he says not to worry, I don't. For some reason, this hike—and the promise of *banditos* doesn't—so we forge ahead.

In the waning late afternoon sun, we pass cement houses, strolling farm animals and wary inhabitants who scrutinize us then offer halfhearted greetings. I prepare myself for the distinct possibility of a thug jumping out of the bushes. But there's no such distraction, just my usual struggle hiking uphill.

At the apex stands a graffiti-covered monument and two armed policemen guarding it. Although they try their best to look stern in their short-sleeved blue uniform shirts, they resemble boys playing dress-up. Paul good-naturedly coaxes one of them into taking a photo of us with Antigua sprawled in the background. When Paul turns the camera on them, they grin like schoolkids. The view, with the mountains and volcanoes in the background, is dramatic.

Going back down the hill, I notice burned piles of garbage on either side of the path—reminders that Guatemala is a stranger to recycling: most people set their trash on fire to dispose of it. Plastic, tin cans, newspapers, it doesn't matter. They just burn it. Or try to. The remains litter nature trails with no regard to land preservation or conservation.

People here are more concerned about living in the present rather than the impact on the planet. Considering the reckless abandon with which they chop down their forests for firewood (with no eye toward replanting), the future of environmentalism here is stark.

~

In town again, Paul and I finally manage to find a pub where people sit at the bar and talk to each other. The Mistral is a popular expat hangout with CNN blaring in the background. Besides conversing with English-speaking travelers, the main attraction is Monday night football, which will happen later on.

After some nonchalant, world-class eavesdropping, Paul and I discover that Peace Corps workers have a fondness for the Mistral too. We listen with interest as one speaks with an older gentleman. PC Man says that until recently, he and his compatriots earned about 1,000 quetzals a month (approximately 200 US dollars), which was just raised to 1,200 quetzals.

PC Man reveals this to his aging composer companion who is escaping it all in Guate. I listen intently as I simultaneously appear to be engrossed in CNN. I then share my recent discoveries with Paul on the adjacent barstool without being overheard. It's an acquired skill.

PC Man says he works with Guatemalan women and children in a neighboring village, the crux of his efforts being pediatrics. Peace Corps workers like him live at the people's level, i.e., no frills. I imagine this is to gain the locals' trust and to experience life through their eyes.

True to this minimalist credo, PC Guy pays 140 quetzals a month to rent a cold-water cement box home. He didn't shower during his entire time in the village. Instead, he took sponge baths. His one luxury was his membership at a local gym in Antigua with showers and a pool. He signed up for a two-year stint with the Corps but recently extended it by six months to finish a writing project.

These two men speak of the repercussions of "coming out" and how a conventional, Catholic country like Guatemala doesn't take too kindly to homosexuals. The older one admits that he sold everything he owned in the States to emigrate to Guatemala for the financial freedom, for the sense of adventure. I find their stories more interesting than anything on CNN.

Eventually, the seemingly mismatched couple leaves the Mistral together. Ever the romantic, I ask Paul, "Did they come all this way to find each other? Is it destiny?"

"Or just one hot night in Antigua?" he counters.

At any rate, how these lovebirds of a feather managed to flock together in Central America is quite amazing. Ain't love grand? Or at least lust is.

Taking Peace Corps Guy's space on the barstool beside me is a gnarled, weathered, scrawny fellow with a West Coast drawl. He sighs, "*Qué lástima,*" when he discovers that the bartender has run out of Marlboros. *What a pity.*

"He looks like an old Marlboro man himself," Paul whispers to me.

Without him asking, I pass Paul the pack of cigarettes I always carry with me. He passes them to Marlboro Man, whose name turns out to be Dave. His face lights up like a Christmas tree upon seeing the cigarettes. Subsequently, Dave becomes our new best buddy.

He tells us that he's retired and originally from Southern California. Dave's in Antigua to study Spanish for a couple of months and lives with a local family. He's been in Antigua six weeks already. I wonder what the conventional Guatemalan clan renting him a room makes of Drunken Dave.

"What brought you to Guatemala?" Paul wonders after taking a swig from his *Gallo*.

Dave shrugs. "The Maya, I guess." He goes on to say that he's always been fascinated with Mayan folklore and over the years, has traveled to various Central American countries to visit their ancient ruins. "Plus, Guatemala is dirt cheap," Dave adds.

He seems like your average American alcoholic—until Dave starts spouting his far-fetched theories. It starts with, "The Maya were giant extraterrestrials—that's why their temples have such tall steps." Paul and I plaster polite expressions on our faces as we listen. "They could levitate too," Dave continues, his eyes widening. I nudge Paul in the ribs. "Oh, and there were also 18-inch-tall Mayans," Dave tags on for good measure.

Upon hearing this, Paul cracks up. "It's true," Dave swears, hand to heart. "Anthropologists found fully-developed, adult, 18-inch-tall human skeletons in underground tunnels that ran between their temples."

"And exactly who were these 18-inch Mayans," Paul wonders.

"Messengers for the giant extraterrestrial Maya," Dave says without missing a beat.

By this time, Dave's obvious insanity has become worrisome. Now it's Paul who nudges me in the ribs. He turns from Dave and whispers, "Let's ditch this guy; he's a nutter."

Instead of listening to him any longer, Paul turns his attention toward Denny, on his left, while I try to dump Dave, the raving lunatic. Luckily, a bleached-blonde exchange student catches Dave's red-rimmed gaze. But not before Dave lifts his gums to show me his recent dental work. It's a sight that will haunt me for months.

Paul's newfound friend Denny is girlishly attractive with bright blue eyes, coppery hair and lips too full and sensuous for a man. Originally from Ohio, Denny is also a Peace Corps worker. He's scheduled to go home to Dayton in a couple of days.

Since his college major was forestry, Denny helped the people in a nearby village plant a Christmas tree farm. Most of the locals earn only 300 quetzals a month. In Guatemala City, these trees can bring in from 100 to 500 quetzals apiece. A Christmas tree farm is a solid investment for the future. The sale of just a handful of trees can bring in the equivalent of a half-year's income.

Denny's one regret is that he won't be here to see the fruits of his labor harvested. Listening to him speak so passionately, I tell Denny, "I can picture you coming back to Guatemala in ten years with your wife and kids, just to see how the farm turned out." This makes him smile. It's a fine smile.

Then there's Dan, with his long, slicked-back hair, a gaunt Michael Bolton clone with the spark of Jesus in his stare. (What is it with all of these "D" names tonight?) Dan has just spent a year in Nicaragua for a religious institution, teaching English to 600 or so kids. His students were of the Miskito people, one of Central America's many indigenous ethnic groups.

Paul and I buy Dan a *Gallo*. He stares blankly at the cobblestoned streets of Antigua beyond the Mistral's door. "Guatemala is rich compared to Nicaragua," he says wistfully. "At least the homeless here have shoes." Dan rubs his eyes. I can't be sure if he's crying. When he looks at me looking at him, I lower my gaze and contemplate the lime in my *ron y Coca*.

When Dan first came to Nicaragua, he said he'd been a 230-pound linebacker. Now he's down to a trim 168. "Were you sick?" I ask.

Dan shakes his head. "There's no junk food in Nicaragua. No double-thick pork chops either."

"Lots of rice and beans," Paul tells him.

"Did you like the work?" I wonder.

Dan's face lights up. "The people were incredible. So giving, so kind." His eyes dim with something like clouds. "But...but their poverty got to me. I felt like I couldn't really help them."

"You taught them English," Paul reminds him.

"Yeah but...then what?" We don't know how to respond. Dan raises his *Gallo* and clinks it with Paul's in a silent toast to the Miskito people.

"What was your favorite thing about it?" I ask.

Dan thinks for a second. "Showing them how to play American football," he says. "They loved it. They were actually terrific at it. But it was tough to get a game going."

"Why?" Paul asks.

"Somebody's mother always needed him to chop wood. Or somebody else had to sit at home with a sick brother. Another kid was always too hungry and weak to run. It's like they weren't even allowed to be kids," Dan laments. He struggles to make sense of it all. "I tried to give them some shred of hope in their piece of shit lives."

"It sounds like you did," I tell him.

"Maybe," he admits. "But toward the end, I found myself wondering, 'What's the point?'"

Dan tells us that he let his hair grow wild and sprouted a thick beard (which he's since shaved off) to look unattractive to his female students. But it didn't work. The girls still flirted with him unabashedly. Many were still in their teens with children of their own already. They couldn't comprehend the concept of celibacy which Dan, as a hardcore Christian, lived by.

"'Why don't you have a girlfriend?' they kept asking me," Dan recalls. "I tried to stress the importance of education, not fornication. 'Get educated in Managua then come back to help your people,' I'd say. But they just couldn't grasp it."

Paul and I let Dan talk away. He's thrilled to finally be able to speak English to people who understand every word. It's been more than a year since he's done that. Dan stares outside and cracks a smile. "Electric lights *and* paved streets," he says. "I can't believe it."

After traveling to Mexico for a Christian youth conference, Dan goes home to Minnesota in time for Christmas. "What will you do there?" Paul asks.

"Sit in the mall and watch the girls go by," Dan says vaguely. "That would be nice."

~

When we invite Dan to come with us to an Italian bistro down the street, he agrees. The restaurant is long, narrow and crowded. Dan inhales a hunk of *focaccia*. "I haven't had bread like this in over a year," he apologizes. Then he demolishes a plate of chicken parm. "Ditto," Dan says. It's like watching Henry the Eighth go to town at a banquet. I bet Dan will be back to his linebacker weight in no time.

Both Dan and Paul help me finish my pizza. The dough is authentic but the cheese is non-mozzarella, probably *queso blanco*. Paul has an unusual *spaghetti carbonara* with chopped *chorizo* (a cured, fermented sausage) instead of bacon. Dan has a little bit of everything.

To my dread, Dan mentions that he shares Paul's desire to scale Pacaya, one of the active volcanoes that rings Antigua. Dan even pulls out a rumpled flyer. The thought of scaling a rumbling volcano terrifies me but I don't want Paul to do it alone. What if he dies up there all by himself? What if he meets his dream Amazon goddess hiker? I am going up Pacaya with Paul, scared or not.

When Paul and I pick up the tab for drinks and dinner, Dan is extremely grateful. (It's less than 20 dollars for the three of us.) We promise to meet at the Mistral at one the next afternoon and head over to the tour office to book the sunset Pacaya trek. We shake hands on it then Dan makes his way to his hostel.

~

It's a clear, crystalline night. Paul and I walk back to our *posada* holding hands. The moon is high and full and bright in the sky. We sit for a moment in the hotel's tiled courtyard. Around us, the thick, hardy bougainvillea blossoms are almost black in the darkness. Here, poinsettias are large, woody and treelike, not spindly plants in foil-coated holiday pots like they are back home. The courtyard is studded with many-pointed poinsettias too.

Paul and I study the changing face of the sky. The wispy clouds shuffle so quickly through the cobalt that they seem to run. The stars are plentiful, uncountable. In my alcohol-induced haze, I'm not sure it's the same sky we see in Brooklyn. A second couple sits in the courtyard under the covered walkway, not even under the stars. They don't notice the magic.

"There is no place like this place," Paul says, staring at the sky.

I don't feel the need to respond. This is one of life's perfect moments when you are flooded with a warm joy, a contentment in simply being. These are the times that somehow give you a sense of validity and purpose. Like when you watch the setting sun reflect pink on the face of a Mayan ruin. Or when you drift off beside someone you love. Or feel a child clutching your arm in complete, utter trust. Or ponder the bursting moon in an Antiguan sky.

I know that Paul fell in love with me in one of these moments, only I am not sure which moment it was. It might have been months earlier, in my Brooklyn bedroom, when naked and on my knees, I recited my favorite poem for him. William Butler Yeats' "When You are Old." It goes like this:

> When you are old and grey and full of sleep,
> And nodding by the fire, take down this book,
> And slowly read, and dream of the soft look
> Your eyes had once, and of their shadows deep;
>
> How many loved your moments of glad grace,
> And loved your beauty with love false or true,
> But one man loved the pilgrim soul in you,
> And loved the sorrows of your changing face;
>
> And bending down beside the glowing bars,
> Murmur, a little sadly, how Love fled
> And paced upon the mountains overhead
> And hid his face amid a crowd of stars.

Yes, Paul might have fallen in love with me right about then. He could have become enamored with my pilgrim soul, whatever that is. I could tell by the way he looked at me. He constantly says that I read too much into his looks but a look is a look. Especially one like that.

Paul and I have had a handful of such moments during our week in Guatemala. Ripe with weighty stares, piquant scents, memorable images, unforgettable stories. They form a collage of colors and faces, some as vivid as the woven *huipils* the women wear. Others are as shadowed as the shroud of mist which now covers the smoldering peak of Fuego, the volcano that lives nearby.

In the Asjemenou's courtyard, Paul and I sit and watch the sky in the midnight chill of Antigua. The stars are chunks of crushed crystal in a cerulean silk scarf. "If I ever get married again," I confess to Paul. "I'd like an engagement ring to remind me of this place: a sea of tiny diamonds around a sapphire."

As if on cue, the clock in the Santa Catalina arch chimes. "We should catch some z's," Paul says.

We retreat to our room and make love as though it is an urgent and necessary thing, like breathing.

I seem to wake with each chime of the arch's clock, every 30 minutes or so, troubled by the virgin spirits of the nuns. Do they wander through our room? Are they stalking us, even now? Unlike me, Paul sleeps like a happy child, snoring contentedly, unaware.

Day 10

Tuesday, November 30, 1993
Antigua

Paul and I walk through Antigua, trying to decide where to eat breakfast. Suddenly, a man comes running down the street near Parque Central, clutching a tote bag. About 10 feet behind, a police officer chases him. Then another man pursues the cop and the thief.

Out of nowhere, the policeman stops, draws his revolver and fires a warning shot into the sky. I gasp and grab Paul's arm. "How could he shoot his gun in the middle of a crowded street?" I cry.

"This is Guatemala," Paul says. "Anything goes."

The robber squints over his shoulder, smirks at the cop and rounds the corner. The policeman tears after him, pissed off now. There are more gunshots, then silence. "What do we do?" I ask Paul, trembling.

"What we were going to do," he tells me. "Get some breakfast. I'm hungry."

A few minutes later, the would-be robber reappears. This time he's led down the street by the two men: the one he robbed and the cop. The thief's hands are tied behind his back with a crude rope. (Handcuffs are a luxury in Guatemala too, I guess.) He struggles against his restraints. Annoyed, the cop kicks the thug in the ass. Twice. The officer is probably more angry that he had to chase the thief several blocks than he is about the guy robbing someone.

"Maybe they'll hang him in Parque Central," Paul says optimistically.

But they don't. They just lead the *bandito* into an official-looking building near the square.

~

Paul and I have breakfast at Doña Irena's. It's two levels with an open courtyard and a bulletin board announcing local services and events. Doña's even has a bakery—and an armed guard out front. Both American and European tourists frequent the place so it's important to keep them safe.

We order our meals from a printed card the hair-netted waitress hands us and are served quickly. It's a feast of fresh fruit, granola, yogurt, the muffin of the day and steaming cups of a particularly brazen coffee. Then we're off to explore other ruins Paul has heard about.

On the outside, the convent known as Las Capuchinas is pretty commonplace. There's nothing special about its flowering courtyard and now-dry fountain. But inside, it's extraordinary. Las Capuchinas has 18 private chambers for the now-defunct sisters, each with its own individual plumbing system. "I thought nuns' poop was carried away on angels' wings," Paul says.

"That's what they told us in Catholic school," I agree.

These tiny cells are on the top floor of a two-story circular tower. On the lower floor are 17 smaller recesses, each with odd metal rings set into the stone walls. "A storage area? A laundry room?" Paul wonders.

"A torture chamber for naughty nuns?" I speculate.

"The Catholics love SM," he points out. "The Catherine Wheel, self-flagellation…"

Paul and I slither through spaces in walls that no longer exist. We walk on broken rooftops that spill into the courtyard. Some areas, like the living quarters and the mortuary, are reconstructed to show what they would have looked like when they were in use. Models of nuns, knees bent in prayer in their cryptlike chambers or laid out on a subterranean slab, are especially creepy.

As we peer into a cramped cell, there's the haunting sound of a female voice raised in song. It is soft, low and almost imaginary. "Do you hear that?" I ask Paul for reassurance. Luckily, he does.

Is it piped-in music to add to the convent's solemn mood? That might fly in Disneyland but not in an 18th century Guatemalan nunnery.

Intrigued, Paul and I follow the strains of "Ave Maria." It leads us downstairs and along corridors until we come upon a round lower chamber. A group of German tourists stand with their backs pressed to the curved wall, intently listening as their guide sings the hymn. It is pure and beautiful, so beautiful I have to chew on my lip to keep from crying. "I'll never forget this as long as I live," I whisper to Paul.

The tour guide takes a deep breath when she finishes singing. She blushes when we burst into spontaneous applause. Her charges break out into German songs, followed by rondos. "Row, Row, Row Your Boat" is not nearly as magical as the guide's heartrending "Ave Maria." The magic is broken as magic often is.

~

Next, we head to the ruins of San Jeronimo. The minute we see them, Paul announces, "These are my favorite."

"Maybe because they look like your wreck of an apartment back in Park Slope," I say. Paul gives me the side-eye as we explore further.

While San Jeronimo's façade is still intact, the interior is a jumble of huge blocks which have toppled inward. It's a yard full of toys a messy child forgot to put away. Paul and I play like hyperactive kids ourselves.

Down a dirt path behind San Jeronimo's ruins is the carcass of the church La Recolección. We overhear a tour guide telling his charges that during the devastating earthquake of 1773, hundreds of people rushed into the huge church for shelter. Being devout Catholics, they had faith that God would protect them. Instead, the walls of La Recolección tumbled on top of them. No one bothered to remove the bodies. "So, essentially, what you're standing on is a graveyard," the guide explains. Then he encourages the sightseers, "Take your time. Look around. But hurry up."

"This is why we don't take tours," Paul reminds me.

"Except when we have to," I tell him. He immediately gets the reference.

"But there's no other way to climb up Pacaya," Paul explains. I could happily live my life without scaling an active volcano but obviously, Paul can't. And where he goes, I go.

~

147

Before meeting Dan at the Mistral, Paul and I zip back to our hotel and quickly switch rooms since one with a private bath has become available. Although it isn't as attractive as the old space, it's worth it to have our own toilet for a few extra dollars.

Into a small backpack, I shove my sweatshirt, Paul's GORE-TEX jacket, my camera and a bottle of water, all for the Pacaya hike later that afternoon. Then we're off again.

Dan is late. He shows up as we're finishing lunch and joyfully digs into Paul's leftover fries. (Dan says he hasn't had French fries in over a year.) Dan worries that his worn cowboy boots won't cut the Pacaya ramble. But they were all he had besides sandals; he'd given his hiking boots to the local priest before he left the Nicaraguan village. "Your cowboy boots will be fine," Paul assures Dan. "I don't think it's a rough hike."

And indeed, the posters all over town make the Pacaya excursion sound like a relaxed jaunt in the park. Blurry snapshots show kids and *abuelas* doing it. Xeroxed Pacaya flyers are as profuse as coffee shops in Antigua. They suggest bringing water, a snack and wearing tennis shoes. "Piece of cake," Paul says. The three of us feel well-prepared. All except for the snacks part.

Paul volunteers to go back to our *posada* and buy sandwiches from its small but functional kitchen. Dan and I head to the tour office to reserve spots on our volcano trip. He and I manage this without a hitch then wait for Paul there.

But it's getting close to the two o'clock departure time and still no sign of Paul. The minibus driver says he'll pick up other passengers at various hotels around Antigua then swing back for me, Paul and Dan.

Minutes later, I spot a man a full head taller than anyone else. Paul. I could recognize him—and his walk—anywhere.

"Sorry," Paul tells us. "I forgot to tell the waitress I wanted the sandwiches *para llevar.*" Dan screws up his face, trying to decipher Paul's garbled Spanish. "To go," Paul explains.

"No wonder she messed it up," Dan tells him. "Your accent...it could use a little work."

Paul ignores Dan and continues his story while we wait for the minibus's return. "The hostess had the sandwiches done up nice on a plate then I had to ask her wrap them in wax paper. I mean, do I look like I can eat three sandwiches by myself?" As I open my mouth to respond, Paul says, "Don't answer that."

When the minibus comes back, only one true "seat" is left. The driver ceremoniously hands me a piece of foam to cushion the hump between his and the empty passenger's seat. Much bigger than me, I insist that Paul take the last real seat, the passenger's seat, aka the death seat. Dan, who's barely 22, is content to sit on the floor. My hair brushes the ceiling as I settle onto the foam padding.

At first, Paul wasn't going to board the bus at all. He didn't want to be uncomfortable on the long ride to Pacaya, which is about 30 miles south of Guatemala City, which is an hour away from Antigua. But Dan's gentle prodding, combined with Paul's unexplainable need to climb a spewing volcano, changes his mind.

The closer the minivan bumps toward Pacaya, the more scared I become. My Aunt Shirley would shake her head and say, 'You're not from the hikers.' And I'm not. How am I going to hike up a volcano?

Besides, I'd lied to my mother about it during our brief phone call the night before. "It's not an active volcano, is it?" she'd gasped.

"Of course not," I told her. "Do you think I'm crazy?"

P.S. I *am* crazy.

~

Instead of backtracking to Guatemala City and driving on a civilized, paved road, our navigator takes a route which makes the dodgy path from Santa Elena to El Relleno seem like a superhighway.

The backroad to Pacaya is almost 20 miles of boulders and weathered dirt, decimated by the rainy season. There are holes so large a child could curl up in one untouched as the minibus passes over it. At times, the van's nose points directly into cavernous ravines.

I wrap my arm around the back of Paul's seat to brace myself. The driver's teenage assistant sits on a makeshift chair, his back to Paul, and keeps banging his head on my forearm. Paul's knees keep crashing into the dashboard. "How are you doing?" he asks me, his jaw clenched.

"Next question," I say.

Maybe it's my unfair perspective because my seat is perched higher than anyone else's, but the road looks unbelievably dangerous. Especially for a van packed with 13 people. (I try to ignore the unlucky number.) We're a veritable League of Nations—Dutch, Belgian, British, Guatemalan and American.

I panic quietly on the inside. What if the brakes fail? What if we meet the same fate as those Mexican ballerinas? I grit my teeth and try to enjoy the surroundings as we pass anonymous communities, horses carrying bundles of kindling, women washing clothes in rushing streams and children who stare at the minivan in wonder.

The driver parks outside a *tienda* which borders a bleak, unfriendly village called San Francisco. Chickens and pigs mill about. A stray dog attaches himself to our group. "I bet he has fleas," someone suggests.

The *tienda's* owner eyes all of us. "Is he trying to calculate how much our stuff is worth in case we don't come back?" Paul wonders.

"Stop," I tell him.

"You're not scared, are you?" he asks.

"Shush," I say.

Up until now, our companions' moods have been jovial and light. But when the driver takes a hardhat out of the van, there's dead silence. Paul, Dan and I stare at each other in shock. "What happened to the flyers that say all you need is a sweater, a snack and sneakers?" I croak.

Paul reminds me. "In Guatemala, anything goes." Then the teenage guide stuffs a winter parka into his backpack. "Holy shit," Paul says. "That's something my grandmother would wear."

"Do we need a winter coat?" I panic. "All I've got is a sweatshirt."

"Relax," Dan tells me, helpfully. "We'll be fine."

There's only one other woman on the Pacaya hike besides me. She's a Britisher from Leeds with calves of steel. Back in town, Pip had been promised there'd be four armed guards accompanying us on the ascent. Paul tries not to sneer then turns and whispers to me, "And she believed them." In our short time here, we've learned that Guatemalans will say almost anything to make a sale. *Más o menos*.

The only arms our guides have are attached to their bodies.

Then Pip goes on to explain that in 1991, 20 tourists were robbed and three of the women were raped in an expedition much like ours. Although treks in the two years following have gone on without incident, we're still wary. I silently wonder which would be worse: being robbed or making it to the top of Pacaya.

Probably the latter.

~

Geologists estimate that Pacaya first erupted 23,000 years ago. After being dormant for more than 70 years, it suddenly piped back up in 1961 and has been exploding ever since.

Led by our teenage guide, our climb starts out at too fast a pace. For me, at least. Immediately, I am wracked with stomach cramps. My heart thrums painfully in my chest. I feel like I'm going to pass out which would be extremely embarrassing. "I need to stop," I tell Paul.

"But we've only been hiking five minutes," he says, a smile growing on his lips.

"Don't you dare laugh at me," I warn him. "I'll rip your heart out with every last bit of my strength."

Abruptly, Paul stops laughing.

I'm shocked at myself. I've never spoken to Paul like this before. Being ridiculed brings back the ghosts of my past: my ex-husband and his mocking brand of torment, and my father, when I couldn't tell my right from my left as a little kid. But since Paul doesn't want to hear about my demons, he also doesn't know my triggers. He doesn't know he might strike a nerve until he already has.

After considering the tortured lines of my face, Paul asks the guides if we can take a break. The others in our group seem relieved. A gray-haired Belgian suggests we relax the pace. I wonder if he is saying this out of consideration to me or because he's winded too? Great, at age 34, I'm hiking like an old man.

At first, I'm mortified at the thought of holding up the others. But then I ask myself, *'Why do you care what a bunch of strangers think?'* But I do. I always did. As far back as I can remember. I would much rather inconvenience myself than another person. One of the pitfalls of having an Italian-American/Catholic woman's martyr upbringing, I guess.

~

We begin climbing again, this time, at a more leisurely speed. The path is littered with cowpies and snack wrappings. I still can't understand how people can be so callous as to destroy nature trails with garbage. Do they want future generations to be playing in mounds of trash?

Near a barbed wire fence, a young girl leads a pair of huge bovines downhill. The child ponders us scornfully; she is working and we are playing where she works. As they pass the line of humans, one cow goes to the left and the other goes to the right. We're almost squashed between them. Did the girl train them to do this? Or are the cows pissed at us too?

A slide show of terrains shift by as we pick our way up Pacaya. There's dense forest, thick brush, scant woods. Everything from rocks to dust to twigs crunch underfoot. The guide wearing the hardhat lags behind and studies the shadows for possible intruders. Not including him, I am the last in the pack. Seasoned hikers, Paul and Dan are always near the front.

As we approach the apex of the volcano, the landscape changes from dry greenery to a black, lightweight lava gravel. Defiant clumps of flowers stretch their pink faces out of the rubble and toward the diffused sunlight. Seeing this gives me faith and hope. If flowers can survive this high up then maybe I can too.

Our guides stop so we can admire the sweeping view. But the closer we are to the cone, the more enveloped we become in a layer of mist. Fingers are crossed that the fog will clear by the time we make it to the top. Every few steps, it seems to get colder. Paul and I duck into our jackets. The younger guide swaddles himself in his *abuela's* parka.

Then I hear the sound of the surf. But we aren't anywhere near the ocean, I remind myself. "What the hell is that?" I ask Paul.

His eyes grow bigger. "Pacaya."

Another blast. A much bigger one. This time, the ground trembles. We all jump simultaneously. You half-expect a rain of rock or a gush of lava, that's how near this eruption sounds. But it turns out we're at least an hour from the cone.

Suddenly, the incline becomes steep, almost a 45-degree angle. "How are you doing?" Paul asks.

"I want to go back," I tell him.

"For real?"

"No," I sigh. "Going back will probably be worse."

~

Now we are clambering straight up. The lava rocks crumble beneath our feet. It's almost impossible to get a foothold. All of us huff and puff and slip backwards with each step. Suddenly, I'm not the last person in our party anymore. One British guy tries to pass me then pants in defeat. "I can't even overtake you," he gasps. The worst in the lot? That's pretty bad.

We wade through a smoking ashtray of soot and finally hit rocky, stable ground. It resembles what I imagine the dark side of the moon is like. Big boulders are precariously situated on the edge of a ridge. The erupting cone seems to be higher up and immediately to our right. I hear booming but still can't see a thing.

Occasionally, a cloud clears and I spot a ribbon of lava. Fluorescent orange in color, it oozes down the side of Pacaya's cone. But the spectacular fireworks the tour office proudly displays on sandwich boards in Antigua are nowhere to be found.

We sit in the misty, frigid wind, waiting for the sun to set. Why? Because after twilight, Pacaya's eruptions are even more dramatic, the guides promise. "Can you believe it?" I ask Paul. "We're sitting on the side of an active volcano waiting for sundown."

"Who would think we'd be spending the last day of November in 1993 on Pacaya," he says, unwrapping his sandwich. I can't tell if he's being ironic or not.

Paul hands me and Dan our *tortas*. "If someone had told me that, I would have thought they were crazy," Dan agrees.

"But here we are," Paul echoes. He kisses me. It tastes of spicy mustard and sweet ham.

Much like I did at Tikal, I worry about how we'll actually get down the slope. But for now, I try to concentrate on the stark beauty of Pacaya. The trickles of glowing lava. The eruptions that rattle me to the core. It's something you'll always remember if you're foolish enough to scale an active volcano in the semi-darkness. If you're lucky enough to survive it.

Before us, some brave, stupid souls ventured into Pacaya's caldera directly beneath the cone and wrote their names in chunks of hardened lava. Some in our group scramble higher to be closer to the cone. People they know who'd done the trip weeks earlier said they stood at the rim and peered directly into the shaft itself. But our guides warn that Pacaya's recent surge of activity makes this impossible to do now. *"Es muy peligroso."* *It's very dangerous.*

Pip says that recently, an experienced tour guide with 18 years under his belt lost his life when a wayward rock from a badly-timed explosion pelted him in the head, killing him instantly. This is why our own guide wears a hardhat. But shouldn't we be wearing them too?

~

153

We sit on our own separate rocks in the cold, like frogs on frozen lily pads. Paul and I huddle together, shivering, hugging each other for warmth. "It's miserable up here, isn't it?" he says in consolation. I nod.

On top of Pacaya, it's wet, gusty and nasty. Plus, we're eternally blanketed in clouds. And our snacks are getting soggy. Even worse, at our shrouded elevation of 8,200 feet, we can't even see the sunset. Hell, we can barely see ten feet ahead.

A bad omen: the scrappy stray dog who started trailing us has given up. "Even Devil Dog had the sense to leave," Paul notes.

"Maybe he put a canine curse on us," I tell him.

Our feckless leaders are distracted, flirting hard with Pip, the British girl. They aren't anxious to leave. But the rest of us are. Spontaneously, Paul begins chanting *"Pacaya es mierda."* The others join in enthusiastically. *"Pacaya es mierda."* Yes, Pacaya is indeed shit. At least this afternoon.

The guides don't like our chant much but at least they get the message and we start moving again. We head further up, toward Pacaya's crest. Inching toward a slender ledge, we hunch our bodies against the elements. The wind is so powerful that I'm almost blown off the side of the volcano.

Immediately, I'm paralyzed with fear. I can't stand, can't move, can't breathe. When I'm able to suck in a lungful of air, I scream, "Paul!" But he can't hear me in the squall so I scream it again, even louder, "Paul!"

He turns and makes his way to me. I hope he can't see the tears streaming down my face in the mist. But he does. "You're overreacting," Paul says as diplomatically as possible. But then a gust lifts his 200-pound frame and pushes him three feet away from me, toward the ridge's edge.

When I detect fear on Paul's face I start to panic. "We're screwed, aren't we?" I sob. He doesn't answer. Even our guides struggle to remain standing.

Paul clings to me. "You've got to move," he shouts into the abyss. When I shield my face with the hood of my sweatshirt, I find that at least I can breathe. Breathing is good. Breathing is important.

"Don't let go of me! Please don't let go of me!" I beg Paul. He doesn't.

The wind almost takes us countless times but we fight it. Crouching together, we practically crawl to the stone wall where the others are clustered, waiting for us. Their faces are painted with the terror I feel inside. They've been charting every inch of our struggle. "Glad you made it," Pip calls into the gale.

"I am too," I admit to her.

Our tour guides speak little English. But Dan, who is fluent in Spanish, volunteers to act as our translator. His face drops when the older guide explains something to him. Then Dan repeats it to us, stone-faced. "He says that in our descent, we will be sliding down the side of Pacaya," Dan tells us as calmly as possible.

"Sliding?" I shriek. At first, I don't think I hear Dan correctly in the howling air.

But he repeats himself for our benefit. "Yes, sliding," Dan nods.

"That's insane," I say. Around me are a chorus of protests. The others apparently agree how crazy this is.

Paul squeezes my hand to reassure me. "You can do this," he whispers.

"Do I have a choice?" I ask him.

"Sure, you can die on Pacaya or…"

"…die on the way down," I finish. "Remind me why we're here," I start. "Forget it, don't answer that." With great effort, we stand.

Dan's voice rings out amid the eruptions and the raging winds. He confirms, "They say to stay close together and to walk in single file." I cross my fingers and say a silent prayer as we begin our descent.

~

Our group slowly proceeds down Pacaya's slope, our feet shuffling through thick, volcanic ash. It's similar to skiing—without skis. With every slide, our boots sink a foot into the lava gravel. There's no chance of being tossed over the side by the breeze now. Buried in the gravel, yes, but not being blown away.

My hiking boots fill with pebbles and my thick, wool socks offer little protection. I can feel the skin peeling neatly off my heels. Blisters sprout instantaneously. My contact lenses scream, dried out by the relentless blowing. Snot pours from my nose. It doesn't help to blow it because the faucet starts flowing immediately after I wipe. But by that point, I don't care. I just want to get back to Antigua. Alive.

Armed with a flashlight, I can only see a few feet ahead. Which is fine because it means I can't gauge how dangerous this is. As long as we stay on the route, we'll be all right. At least that's what I keep telling myself.

Paul leads us off trail to take a shortcut and catch up with the others. Suddenly, the ground evaporates under our feet. We stumble. "Where the fuck are you taking us?" I snap. This is the second time I've talked to Paul like this. In the same night. But in my defense, I am terrified.

"I'll never hurt you," Paul says. "Don't worry."

"Not on purpose," I tell the wind. But I worry. I still worry. Except, with each step, I think to myself that we might make it. We just might make it. I keep repeating this to myself, a silent mantra, a prayer, in my head.

And my pleas are answered. The earth beneath my hiking boots changes from ash to dirt to solid rock. I sense that we're close to the base of the volcano. The air stops screaming. Paul gestures to a pinprick of brightness ahead of us. "See that?" he asks.

"Yes," I sigh. The lights of the *tiendas* blaze in the distance.

I can't believe we survived. I want to kiss the ground. I want to sob with relief. But instead, I walk. I walk until we reach the row of shops. "You owe me a Coke," I say to Paul.

He smiles. "You're a cheap date." He comes back with sodas and two bags of chips. A pair of children watch us eat. Paul holds the second bag of TorTrix out to them. They take it and scuttle into the shadows like rats. Some of our compatriots empty the rocks out of their boots. Others stare at the outline of the belching volcano, probably as shocked as I am that we made it down.

~

On the ride back to Antigua, our companions joke about how terrible the Pacaya hike was. How cold, how wind-beaten. The Belgian man agrees that the flyers the tour office hands out left us ill prepared and ignorant about what to expect. "But if they told the truth, maybe people wouldn't go," Pip says.

The older guide's face tenses as he drives. He speaks more English than he's led us to believe because he clearly understands our complaints. "You should have known," the driver finally says in carefully-chosen words. "When you climb a mountain, you are going up. Of course, it gets colder, no matter how warm it is down below."

He pauses, gathering more courage. This could mean his *propina,* his tip, but he is livid. "When you go swimming, you bring your bathing suit, don't you?" He says nothing else for the duration of the bumpy ride.

"Has he ever seen the flyer?" I ask Paul.

Paul shakes his head. "Let it go. We made it, didn't we?"

~

Back in Antigua, a bunch of us stop at the bar across the road from the Posada Asjemenou to celebrate our survival. Over pitchers of beer, we bitch and moan. "We should go through town ripping down those posters the tour office puts up," someone suggests.

"We didn't see a damn thing up there," the Belgian man says.

"We'll demand our money back," his friend chimes in.

"Yeah, all seven dollars of it," Paul whispers, tepid *Gallo* breath in my ear.

"I'd say we got our money's worth," I counter.

Then Dan brings us back to our senses. "Who are you kidding? Tomorrow, you'll be telling everyone how great Pacaya was. And in a couple of days, you'll want to do it again." We all laugh. Because it's true.

The Brits ask us if New York City is as dangerous as everyone says. "You just climbed an active volcano," Paul tells them. "What can be more dangerous than that?"

"Point well taken," Pip concedes.

Paul has gotten a second wind but I'm beat from our pleasure trip and from my raw fear. Besides, my feet are howling in my hiking boots. I beg out early. "I'll be home soon," Paul promises.

It's an easy walk across the cobblestone street to the Asjemenou. The large wooden door is locked. I ring the bell to rouse the night clerk. I can't bear wearing my boots any longer so I unlace them and dump a pile of small rocks onto the ground. The nightwatchman opens the door and looks at me knowingly. "Pacaya?" he asks.

"*Sí,* Pacaya," I tell him.

Once inside, I rinse the ash from my hair and creep naked between the crisp, white sheets. Exhausted, I struggle to find sleep but can't. I have the unnerving sensation that I am still sliding down the volcano. Paul comes in at about one, curls around my body and promptly falls asleep.

Day 11

Wednesday, December 1, 1993
Antigua/Panajachel

Antigua is so delightful we could easily stay here for the rest of the trip. But we've promised to meet Glenn in Quetzaltenango in less than a week. It will take several days to reach because we want to check out a few other towns along the way, so we have to leave Antigua today.

Paul and I wake at six to catch the semi-express bus to Panajachel. The five-dollar fare, which we paid at the tour office in advance, leads us to believe that it's a special, streamlined van. But this turns out not to be the case. Paul's face drops when he sees our transportation to Pana. "It's just a souped-up Blue Bird," he grumbles.

"Well, it's only two bucks to ride up there," I tell him, gesturing to the bus's roof, where plucky tourists, natives and luggage travel.

"I'll take my chances down here," he says.

The Blue Bird bounces through comely country, catching the same bumps as the roof travelers do. When a man boards with a machete, he leaves it on the floor at the front of the bus. No one bats an eye. Except me. When the man leaves, he picks up his machete again like it's as *típico* as a Macy's shopping bag.

The terrain is hilly and there are more crops than cattle in these parts. As I point this out to Paul, he reasons, "I bet the soil is better." The dirt is as dark as the coffee it grows.

Alongside the road, besides the usual baskets and bundles pedestrians carry on their heads, I see a man balancing a kitchen table and four chairs on his back. It's fascinating to watch him gradually peck his way uphill.

The bus grows crowded soon into the two-hour-plus trip. Lots of women and babies are onboard. The usual three passengers squish into seats meant for two. As a rule, the Guatemalans are smaller than Westerners are—both in height and girth—so this tends to work out fine.

With no seats left on the Blue Bird, a boy edges into the tiny space beside me. At first, he is wary but his mother nods that it's all right and nudges him toward the chair. But he still gives me the hard eyes. *"Está bien,"* his mom encourages. *It's okay.*

About six or seven years old, the child looks far too wise for his years as he cautiously sits next to me. Eventually, he falls asleep on my shoulder.

"Su novio," Paul jokes from the other side of me. *Her boyfriend.* The child's mother hears and smiles.

"He's not my boyfriend," I insist. "He's too old."

~

Today, I'm slightly melancholy. Still hung over from climbing Pacaya, maybe. I'm worried about anything and everything that could possibly go wrong on this trip: that we'll run out of money (we're currently below budget); that we'll be murdered in the Western Highlands; that Paul will grow bored of me; that I'll grow bored of him. You name it, I worry about it.

I'm displaced and travel-weary. It was good to spend more than one day in one spot, especially a city as beautiful as Antigua. But still, Paul and I are moving around so much and living out of our backpacks that I feel rootless. I'm strangely untethered, adrift.

At night, I dream of home: of my parents, my sister, my niece and nephew. I dream that I'm back in my ground-floor Sheepshead Bay apartment and that Paul is still in Guatemala. I dream that he finds a gorgeous, indigenous woman and decides to stay, having lost patience with my nonsense.

What nonsense? Wait, aren't I pretty uncomplicated? No, everyone is complicated. Everyone has their own bullshit others have to deal with. And there comes a time when people get tired of it. When will Paul get tired of mine?

Here I am, in a magical land, on holiday, worrying.
Will I ever be happy?
Probably not.

~

Paul and I wrestle with the idea of stopping in Chimaltenango
because two short order cooks at Pete's Waterfront Alehouse back in
Brooklyn come from there. Before we left, they gave us the name,
address and phone number of their uncle. But we have no photos, gifts
or money to deliver so we figure it isn't worth the side trip. Besides,
Chimaltenango is like a junior Guatemala City.

By the way, "tenango" at the end of a city's name literally
means "the place of." That's why it comes up so frequently in
Guatemalan geographical names. Chichicastenango—the place of the
nettles. Quetzaltenango—the place of the quetzals. Chimaltenango—
the place of trees. And so on.

The two-and-a-half-hour bus ride seems endless. Especially
after a woman with a bundle on her back squeezes into the seat beside
me recently vacated by my young boyfriend. A kid sitting there is one
thing but a full-hipped woman is quite another. I start to seethe until I
see the tiny, tawny fist of her baby popping out of the red *rebozo* that
straps around her chest and back. The woman smiles bashfully at me. I
grin back. All is forgiven.

~

The Blue Bird leaves us in the center of Panajachel, which is a
bit grimy around the edges. There's no sign of Lake Atitán, supposedly
one of the most picturesque bodies of water in the world.

Since it's only ten in the morning, Paul and I decide to have
breakfast first and seek lodgings later. Steps from the bus stop is a big,
greasy *comedor*. "Just our style," Paul says, settling in. We have the
usual: fried eggs, black beans, fried bananas and tortillas on the side.
The jukebox plays bad country music loudly. It keeps speeding up,
slowing down, then grinds to a crushing halt, only to crank back
up again.

After considerable searching, we find a decent hotel within our
price range. In Panajachel, they're either $1.50 a night with a cold-
water shared bath or palatial resorts featuring color TV and manicured
grounds for 60 dollars a pop. There's no middle of the road.

Pana is a haven for the great unwashed: scruffy Europeans
and Americans. In contrast, the Guatemalans are cleanly-scrubbed

and neatly dressed, no matter how poor. These filthy travelers would be hippies if it were the 1960s but they're 30 years too late. Their uncombed hair, mucky feet and grubby ragamuffin clothes stand out among the locals. And not in a good way.

The draw of Panajachel, of course, is the beauty, but also the cheap eateries where these low-budget tourists sit sipping coffee for hours. Like I said, accommodations are also reasonable. Then there's the potent and economical marijuana the town is famous for.

By sheer, dumb luck, we stumble upon the inn Pieter, the Belgian fellow from the Pacaya hike, recommended. The Hotel Martita has newly-refurbished $20-rooms with hot water private baths. Plus, it's a half block from the lake. We also discuss the possibility of having our laundry done with the woman who runs the Martita as she nurses her son. *"Es posible,"* she says. For anything's possible in Pana.

Paul and I head toward Lake Atitlán along Calle Principal, which is lined with food carts and cheap *posadas*. Relatively early in the day, people are still setting up their wares alongside the road. Not really stands, not really stalls, these tentlike structures at least offer them shelter from the sun.

Florid blankets and *huipils* blooming with flowers are suspended from poles or are folded on tabletops. The *huipils* are different here in Panajachel—their signature shades are in the muted colors of autumn, as well as the usual rainbow of hues.

"We can shop later," Paul tells me as we continue to Lake Atitlán. Hungry children follow us, begging for quetzals. They sell half-broken crafts and plead with us to let them shine our shoes. We keep walking.

Our first glimpse of Lake Atitlán leaves us speechless. Sapphire waters touch the navy-blue mountains surrounding it. A steady breeze ripples the surface. The Guatemalans call this *Xocomil,* "the wind that carries away sin." When I tell this to Paul, he wonders aloud, "Will it take away mine?"

"Depends on what you've done," I say. He doesn't volunteer information and I don't ask. Maybe I don't want to know.

~

There's no shortage of eateries in Panajachel: upscale restaurants, open-air cafés, food stalls. Paul and I sit at a bistro with tables outside. We order a drink and a *ceviche* each. Panajachel shines in the early afternoon light. We gaze at the lake contentedly as we eat our marinated fish.

Our waiter cops an attitude when we try to break 100-quetzals for a 40-quetzal charge. He stomps over to the café next door to break the bill.

While he's gone, a shoeshine boy approaches our table. He asks to shine my black Reeboks for five quetzals. (About a dollar.) The child is reed thin. His clothes, worn and dirty. "My sneakers will only get dusty again," I say to Paul.

"The point is, he gets to eat," Paul tells me.

The shoeshine boy's eyes are pleading, earnest. *"Por favor, señorita,"* he begs. *Please, miss. "Por favor.* I do a good job."

"Sì," Paul says to him. The boy's face beams as he takes a small brush out of one pocket and a tin of shoe polish from the other.

I've never had my shoes shined before. I'm embarrassed as the child kneels at my feet. "Just relax," Paul nods.

The boy slathers the black polish onto one sneaker with his bare hand then buffs it with the brush. He scrubs with gusto, applying a great deal of elbow grease. Then he says something to Paul that makes him laugh. All I can understand is *"Muy, muy mejor."*

So, I ask, "What did he say?"

"For 10 quetzals, he can do a much better job," Paul smiles. "That's roughly two bucks."

"Everybody's a hustler," I sigh.

Paul shrugs. "Maybe his father beats him if he doesn't bring home enough money. Maybe he doesn't even have a father." Then he adds, "When I was a kid, I used to shine shoes on Ninth Street." That explains a lot.

"Tell him we'll give him the 10 quetzals," I say.

The boy asks a friend for additional tools, various brushes plus a dollop of clear polish. Gently, the child tugs on my feet, raising them one by one onto his beat-up wooden box, then placing them back onto the café's concrete floor. His bony hands are soothing as they massage the leather. When he's finished, my Reeboks gleam.

Paul hands the boy 50 quetzals. His eyes almost pop out of his head. *"No cambio,"* Paul tells him. *No change.*

"Muchas gracias," the boy gasps then scurries off before *el Yanqui* can change his mind. He quietly argues with his friend about splitting the money.

"Do you realize what you just did?" I ask Paul. He shrugs. "You gave him about 10 dollars for a shoeshine."

"To us, it isn't much," Paul says. "But to that kid, it's a fortune."

~

Until now, we haven't bought souvenirs—for us or for others. Even though we've seen some wonderful crafts along the route, we don't want to lug them around while we travel on busses and carry our belongings on our backs. Since we'll be meeting Glenn and Rachel soon in Quetzaltenango and will traveling by car from there, we figure Panajachel might be a good spot to start buying mementos of our trip. And since Christmas will only be a couple of weeks after we get back, who wouldn't want a unique holiday gift from Guatemala? (No one in our family, that's who.)

Heading down Calle Principal, we're bombarded by sweetly seductive sales pitches accented by charming come-ons. The sellers start with outrageous prices ("One hundred quetzals!") then drop them to *"Casi libre!"* (*Almost free!*) We go from stall to stall, comparing wares.

Panajachel is famous for its clothing, for its trademark geometric patterns in a wide spectrum of colors. Paul and I buy all sorts of cool things: baby jumpers, shorts, shirts, purses, placemats, vests, headbands and barrettes covered with bold fabric. A pair of adorable sisters, about 10 and 12 years old, say, *"Una quetzal"* (about 20 cents) when we ask to take their picture. Meanwhile, we just bought about 35-dollars-worth of stuff from them.

"Everyone's a businessman," Paul jokes. "Even little girls."

But how can we refuse? Giggling, the sisters squeeze into a wheelbarrow and pose. Their wide grins of crooked teeth are brightened even more by their multihued *huipils*.

Paul and I drop off our purchases at the Hotel Martita. The temptation to make love before we set out on our adventures is too great to resist, so we don't.

~

Back on the street, we continue to explore. So many restaurants. So many coffee houses. There's even a shop that specializes in making scaled-down models—of anything. Plus, there's a bookstore and a couple of motorcycle-rental storefronts. The going rate is 25 dollars for 24 hours. "That's dirt cheap," Paul says. "Might be the perfect way to see Lake Atitlán."

"Sounds great," I tell him, though I've only been on a motorcycle once before. Clinging to Paul's back along the Belt Parkway.

We grab an early supper at a café on busy Calle Principal. The dinner special is too tempting to pass up: soup, rice, veggies and grilled shrimp for six dollars. Sitting outdoors, we watch busses chug past. Street vendors pack their wares and head home. It's the start of a pleasant night to end a pleasant day.

More wandering after dinner, this time to upscale crafts stores. We attempt to follow the directions on a flyer announcing a new pub. Finally, we find it, not far from an old, sprawling, whitewashed church.

After a quick peek inside the church, we venture into the bar. "I've been in dives before," Paul says. "But this has to be the worst." Brand new, Bill's is already falling apart. The paint is fresh, but a nauseating shade of green. There's also no electricity, only sad candlelight. The owner is a tall, skinny, wizened fellow named Bill who hails from Philadelphia. He professes to have the best cheesesteaks in town—probably the *only* cheesesteaks in town.

Paul and I sit on old barrels. "Is it safe to drink here?" I ask him. "You've got to admit, it *is* sort of gross."

"The alcohol will kill the germs," he says. "One drink and we're gone."

Hora Feliz (Happy Hour) brings us two-for-one cocktails and the usual tawdry cast of characters. Like Gus, a wiry-haired fellow from the States who lives across Lake Atitlán in San Pedro La Laguna. Gus says he comes to Pana once a month just for Bill's famed cheesesteaks.

When Paul asks Gus what he does in San Pedro, he responds, "Live." End of a not-so-polite conversation. "He's probably on the lam, running from someone or something," Paul says to me as the guy hobbles off to *el baño*.

"Probably from himself," I suggest.

A gnarled rummy at Bill's tells us he's in the import/export business. "That usually means they're selling drugs," Paul whispers over my shoulder.

The rummy belches. "Textiles," he says after a long pause. (Did he invent that on the fly?) He also says he came to Pana to have his teeth fixed. Which is a popular attraction in Panajachel, besides smoking pot.

Paul and I head back to the Hotel Martita early. We dutifully take our quinine pills to stave off malaria. We've been doing this every Wednesday for the past few weeks. Paul settles down to read *Ever After*, which he says is equally as captivating as it is disturbing. I abandon *Huckleberry Finn* yet another evening in favor of keeping up my journal.

Day 12

As we dress this morning, Paul and I revisit the possibility
of renting a motorcycle. Since no busses make the trip around Lake
Atitlán, we agree that the best way to tour it is to circle it on a dirt bike.
Okay, I agree less enthusiastically.

Post-breakfast, we go to Bigsa Moto-Rent on Calle Principal.
It's an easy and pain-free transaction. The flyer says "We don't keep
your passport." It's true, but they keep your credit card as collateral
instead. This is in case you damage the bike or skip town. Leaving
your physical credit card seems fair enough, if not a little unorthodox.
But we've already learned that anything goes in Guate, Guate, Guate.

Paul inspects every moto in the shop and chooses the one with
the best tires. It happens to be a white Yamaha 250. An experienced
motorcyclist, Paul has owned quite a few. (He currently has a Honda
Nighthawk 700 S.) But he's never ridden a dirt bike before.

"Piece of cake," he says. "Same as a motorcycle but it's just
got a smaller engine." I look at him like he's speaking Greek. "A 250
engine has less balls than my 700 back home," he clarifies.

"But does a 250 have enough balls to get us around the lake?"
I ask.

"Sure," he tells me.

The man in the rental shop claims that the 100-kilometer ride will take us ten hours at best. "Ten hours to go 60 miles? Why?" Paul asks him.

The man shakes his head woefully but doesn't answer. When Paul asks again, all the man says is, *"El camino es muy malo."*

"Just how bad is it?" I wonder. But the man still won't respond.

Outside the shop, I give Paul a weighty glance before climbing on the bike behind him. "What?" he says.

"Ten hours?" I tell him.

"That's for amateurs," he insists, a bit too confidently. "I've ridden my motorcycle cross-country. Twice."

"But this isn't your motorcycle. And this isn't your country."

Paul plops a too-big helmet onto my head before snapping on his own helmet. I recheck my small pack which includes water, my camera, the guidebook, the phrasebook and light jackets. Clutching a map of Lake Atitlán the man in the bike shop gave us, Paul and I set out toward the lake.

I press my cheek to Paul's back and hang on tight. His skin is warm beneath my fingertips as I nestle against him. I love the sensation of the breeze in my face. We weave around the locals who flock the streets to set up their stands. My heart is light. I know this is going to be a great day.

~

Paul easily finds the road out of Panajachel. It snakes lazily out of town. There are almost no cars on the outskirts. We pass an occasional pickup or delivery truck. After all, *Gallo* and Coca-Cola must quench the thirst of the masses. Even in the Third World. Especially in Panajachel.

As we approach an old man leaning on a wall, he rubs his forehead, studying us curiously. Then he lifts his hat and gives us a stiff bow. To return the greeting, Paul taps his horn in a short beep. The dirt bike seems to amuse everyone we pass.

The views along this initial stretch of road are spectacular. The robin's egg blue of the sky is dusted with cotton-ball clouds. It's a real Cecil B. DeMille panorama. Lake Atitlán's waters are a bottomless azure, almost as dark as the night sky. The lake is lighter around the shore's jagged edges and inkier toward the middle. Perched in a volcanic caldera at a 5,000-foot altitude, it's said that Lake Atitlán's depth is immeasurable, even with modern equipment.

The surrounding hills and coast are rocky, craggy and rough. It's easy to see that they were formed by volcanic activity. The soil is deep brown and covered with lush emerald foliage. All along the road's edge are sprays of delicate yellow flowers. Buttercups? Daisies? We haven't a clue.

The road isn't paved exactly but fairly smooth. It's covered with a mixture of fine gravel and larger pebbles. Heftier rocks are lined up along its sides like an improvised guardrail. It feels good holding Paul around the waist. The clean smell of his skin, the heat of his body...it all feels secure, dependable. Even in a strange place where strangers can vanish. Especially here.

It's hard for us to talk over dirt bike's engine. I try shouting above it. "This is what heaven looks like," I yell. Paul dips his head in acknowledgement.

Every so often, we pass a road sign indicating an inland village but we don't veer toward it. However, we do pause to take photos. And to read what *The Real Guide* has to say about these towns. We could have easily stopped 10 more times but we've seen lots of churches, lots of markets. We move on.

~

Ahead is a village called Santiago Atitlán. We hope to make it there by lunchtime. Throughout the Guatemalan civil war, Santiago Atitlán suffered unspeakable violence. In 1990, 14 people, ranging in ages from 10 to 53, were massacred and another 21 were wounded when the Guatemalan Army opened fire upon an unarmed crowd of several thousand Tzutujil Mayas. December 2 is the three-year anniversary of this atrocity. Which is today.

And back in 1981, a Roman Catholic priest was assassinated by a right-wing death squad in Santiago Atitlán. At various times since then, the Army has dragged scores of men out of their homes in the predawn hours and murdered them, convinced that the people of the village were guerilla sympathizers.

The president of Guatemala signed a letter promising that this kind of brutality would never happen again. The letter is proudly displayed in Santiago Atitlán's town square. We want to find this letter, to pay our respect to all the villagers who were killed and their families.

From the main road, a crude path swerves downhill to the town itself. We are greeted by arbors decorated with evergreen branches.

Christmas is several weeks off, so that might be the reason. Or are the boughs to commemorate the dead on this somber anniversary? The arbors silently welcome us, casting off their sweet scent as we pass beneath them.

First impression: Santiago Atitlán is an old town, laced with tradition and antiquity. There are only a couple of cars on the street. The chief mode of transportation is by foot. A market buzzes in the street ahead. There are stares as we ride toward it. Paul suggests we park the noisy dirt bike in an alley and walk the rest of the way. "So we won't be as conspicuous," he explains.

"Good luck with that," I tell him.

Of average height in the US, Paul and I are giants in Guatemala. We are almost a foot taller than most of the indigenous people. "Well, we can try to blend in," I say. "But do we sort of stand out."

~

Santiago Atitlán is a village mostly of women and children. They still haven't recovered from the wounds of the massacre three years ago. The inhabitants aren't overly friendly. It's as though their misery is palatable. Perhaps they're wary of foreigners. But whatever the reason, this is the first town in the entire country where Paul and I have felt unwelcome. The people's sad, blank eyes silently say, 'You don't belong. Please leave.'

"Let's get out of here," I whisper to Paul.

"It's fine. We're fine," he tells me. "Besides, we've got to find the president's letter in the square."

Paul takes my hand as we walk through the market. I hold my head high but I'm scared. The locals study our faces and after we pass, I can feel them staring a hole into my back. Women suckle their babies, still gawping. Children, usually smiling and quizzical, turn away from us.

In the mazelike market itself, Paul and I step beneath sheets of plastic meant to shield shoppers from the sun. The plastic is strung from pole to pole and droops in the middle. Paul's hair brushes the top of the improvised ceiling. At five-foot-ten, he is the tallest human being for miles.

In their stalls, women peddle dried beans, cloth, fresh produce, anything imaginable. Another section smells rancid, like blood. This is the fresh meat market. Huge sides of beef hang from the rafters, unrefrigerated. Flies buzz and dogs hang about, hoping for scraps.

Paul and I leave the market without making a purchase. We're still searching for the presidential letter. We manage to find what looks to be the center of town but there's no sign of the proclamation in the concrete square. It would be too complicated, too sensitive to ask someone about it. One misplaced word might insult the entire village. It's a difficult day, a difficult subject. We dip in and out of a church, wondering what to do next.

What I want to do is leave. But Paul wants to see Maximón.

~

The main attraction of Santiago Atitlán is the shrine of Maximón, aka San Simeon. He's the patron saint of smoking and drinking. As if smoking and drinking needs a patron saint.

In Guatemala, the mix of Catholicism and paganism is a potent one. The Maximón folklore is particularly colorful. He's said to have been inspired by a Franciscan friar with a tendency to chase local women when he was soused. As punishment for his transgressions, the friar's legs were lopped off below the knees. This explains Maximón's stumpy lower appendages whenever he's depicted in art.

Traditionally, Maxi is shown in Western attire, wearing a felt hat. He's a wacky combination of things the indigenous people both hate (*gringos*) and love (tobacco and alcohol). Only two or three shrines devoted Maximón are left in all of Guatemala.

As if reading our minds, a street urchin approaches us tentatively and wonders, "Maximón?"

"*Sí,*" Paul tells her. The girl gestures that we should follow her. She's scarecrow thin and dressed in rags. The child takes us through a blur of gritty streets, up and down hills lined with houses that seem ready to disintegrate. The girl's legs are spindly but strong. Her face and clothes are dirty. Her hair is matted and stringy. As she plows ahead, she hugs her soiled knitted shawl to her bony shoulders. She's so pitiful, I'm afraid I'll start to cry.

"When do you think is the last time she's eaten?" I ask Paul. He doesn't answer. "How do you say 'Are you hungry?' in Spanish," I press. Again, *nada.*

After a few steps, Paul says, "We can't ask her that. It would be insulting."

"She's a kid. Who cares? Besides, she's probably starving."

Paul motions for the girl to stop at a *tienda*. There, he buys a pint of Venado, a local rum with a buck's head on the label. It's a tradition to give Maximón a gift when you visit him. Paul buys something else I can't make out.

The girl patiently waits for us alongside the store. Children approach her, jeering. Perhaps they tease her because she's so filthy, so unfortunate, and they are not. As Paul and I emerge from the *tienda*, the children scatter like leaves. All except for our little waif.

"Vamanos," Paul tells the girl. *Come on.* Then he puts out his hand and slips a small package into her twiglike fingers. It's a cellophane sleeve of Chikys. The girl considers the vanilla sandwich cookies and hides the packet under her battered shawl. Shyly, her gaze meets Paul's. She nods a silent thanks, then picks up the pace, almost running.

I bite my lip to hold back the tears. "Thank you," I tell Paul, my eyes brimming.

"What?" he asks.

"You know what," I say.

The girl takes us over rocks, up a curving path then down. Children call to us as we pass. "Dollars! Dollars!" they yell, sensing we're Americans. We ignore them and follow our impish guide. Other kids say things we can't understand but their tone is taunting. "Why do they keep torturing her?" I ask Paul.

"The strong always prey on the weak," he says. We blow past them, trying to keep up with the girl.

In about 15 minutes, we reach a shack at the crest of a hill. Its front door is covered by a heavy, red velvet curtain. The girl gestures to the door, indicating that we should go inside. This is the Mayan idol Maximón's haven and children dare not enter.

As Paul holds aside the curtain, we slip into the shrine. We are engulfed by darkness in the middle of the day. All of the windows are covered. Candles are the only source of light. When my eyes adjust, I'm face-to-face with a life-sized replica of Maximón, who might actually be leering at us. "Is it my imagination or..." I start.

"Yeah, he's goofing on us," Paul says.

Coins and quetzals lay at the wayward saint's truncated legs. To his left is a table and around it, sit the keepers of Maximón's shrine. These men are the *cofradìa*, a special religious society, a brotherhood of sorts. Paul hands one of the attendants the Venado and explains, *"Por Maximón."*

But it's most likely for them, not Maxi. The man thanks Paul. It's barely 11 in the morning and the attendants are all falling-down drunk. We leave a fistful of quetzals at Maximón's stubby feet.

"How will we find our way back?" I ask Paul.

"She'll be there. The girl."

"How do you know?" I wonder.

"Because we haven't paid her yet," he says.

Sure enough, the street child is still outside. She brushes Chikys crumbs from her face then asks. *"Ve ahora?"* Go now?

"Sí, vamanos," Paul tells her. *Yes, let's go.*

The child ushers us back through the labyrinth of streets to the center of Santiago Atitlán. When we get to the cement town square, Paul asks her, *"Cuanta?"* Sheepishly, she asks for five quetzals (approximately a dollar) but Paul gives her a 20-quetzal bill. The girl glances to either side, making sure no one is watching. Then she bunches up the money and shoves it down her tattered blouse. She thanks us and disappears.

"To the lake," Paul says.

~

The further we move from the market, the fewer people resemble us. Our surroundings become less hospitable. The houses are smaller, more ramshackle, the people lingering outside scruffier. This is a village where bitterness grows like roadside flowers. The soil of Santiago Atitlán is fertile for acrimony.

Gangs of boys line the street. They scrutinize us with cold, hard eyes. I sense Paul's growing discomfort as we head toward the lake. But we say nothing to each other about the village's ominous vibe. We hunker down and keep going.

As we pass, a young boy says, *"Tu puta."*

Paul bristles. "Did that kid just call you a whore?" His body stiffens. "That little fucker..."

I squeeze Paul's hand. "Just let it go. Please." He sighs deeply. I squeeze his hand again, this time harder. "They're only children. They don't know what they're saying." Only they do.

Paul complies with my request. We keep walking.

~

At the dock, there's no boat in sight. The ferry comes to Santiago Atitlán a few times daily. From here, it hits several villages along the lake. Since no one has cars, the ferry is an efficient travel method. We head back through town, looking for lunch.

Close to the street where we left the dirt bike, there's a *comedor*. Although simply-furnished, it's like entering a magical land. The scent of evergreens greets us at the door because its floor is carpeted with loose pine needles. The scent is so heady it's almost dizzying. The worn, wooden furniture is painted in kindergarten colors and the chairs don't match. But this only adds to its charm.

A Guatemalan camera crew carries their equipment through the restaurant. They must be staying in the *posada* upstairs. Are they doing a story about the anniversary of the 1990 massacre? A pair of Germans come from the same direction. They sit and eat while the camera crew loads their van.

Paul orders chicken and I go for tostadas topped with a perfect guacamole. The woman who fills the *comedor* with such wonderful smells—pine needles mingled with the scent of crispy, roasted fowl—observes from the kitchen doorway as her son toddles between the diners' tables. The boy says "Okay!" over and over. It's probably the single word he knows in English. Maybe he thinks it means "Hello."

In the *comedor's* restroom, I'm surprised that its toilet is no more than a cement basin fastened to the floor. But at least there's running water. Meaning, it flushes. Via a rope suspended from the ceiling. Paul and I are soon out of the *comedor* and bowlegged on the motorbike again.

~

According to the map, we are roughly halfway around Lake Atitlán. But Santiago Atitlán has the last gas station until Sololá, which is less than four miles outside of Panajachel, our final destination. "We'll probably make it back to Pana on one tank," Paul estimates.

"Probably or definitely?" I ask.

"Let's stop for gas," Paul tells me. "Just to be sure."

The gas station is a mile down the road but is out of regular gas. Luckily, the delivery truck is there with a fresh supply. Another man patiently waits for refueling. He leans against his pickup truck, knowing this could take a while. But it's a cool spot to stop, situated between Lake Atitlán and the blue, blue mountains. A boy leads a herd of cattle through a gate, swatting their bottoms with a stick. It could be a Winslow Homer painting come to life if not for the brown child in it.

The man delivering the fuel and the gas station owner kneel beside a hole in the ground. They painstakingly measure the gas level with a long pole. Then they climb on top of the delivery truck and insert the same long pole into the truck's receptacle, measuring the gas level.

Between this measuring process and the actual refueling, Paul and I wait almost an hour. Before we leave, the man with the pickup truck tells us that the road is bad for cars but impassible for motorcycles. After he leaves, Paul says, "He's just trying to scare us."

"Well, he did," I tell him. "Should we turn around?"

"I don't give up," Paul replies. "On anything."

~

The road meanders through the hills. At times, Lake Atitlán isn't visible but hidden in the brambles. Other times, it lurks far below us. We pass an occasional person but no vehicles of any type. "Why aren't there cars or trucks?" I ask Paul when we stop to take a photo. He shrugs.

But soon, the road answers my question.

Almost immediately, its surface grows pitted, strewn with large rocks, or small boulders, depending on your perspective. Paul swerves on the bike, trying his best to avoid huge potholes. But this is an impossible task because the road itself has become one long series of potholes.

I cling to Paul's belly as the dirt bike leaps from one small ditch to the other. A few times, the bike stalls but he manages to get it started again. So far.

We pass a group of children. Paul stops and asks a boy if this is the road to San Pedro, the next village. *"Sí,"* the boy responds, a worried expression on his face. *"Pero el camino es muy malo,"* he adds.

"Didn't the guy at the bike shop say the same thing?" I ask Paul.

"Probably," Paul nods, flashing the smile that melts me. Then he turns to the boy, *"Pero es posible?"* But is it possible?

The child's brow furrows even more. *"Sí, es posible, pero..."*

"Meaning, it's possible but you're crazy," I suggest to Paul.

"That's one translation," he says. "But I never back down from a challenge."

The children gape at us in disbelief. *"Gracias,"* Paul tells the boy. Then we are gone in a shower of gravel and dust.

At parts, the road seems like it's been chewed up then spit back out. And those are the better parts. The "highway" is so chopped and hacked that it would be difficult to walk, let alone ride. The pedestrians we pass are amazed we're attempting to navigate the lake on a vehicle. I'm in awe of Paul's control of the dirt bike. We don't go down once but there are lots of close calls.

However, we do stall. A lot. Too many times to count. The back tire often skids out from under us but Paul's strong, sturdy legs always grip the ground to hold us upright. After hours of struggle, I sense that Paul is getting tired and his patience is growing thin. We creep only a hundred feet before the tires shoot out a spray of rocks which send the tires whirling. Then the motor dies and it takes a bunch of tries to restart it.

When we stall at the bottom of a hill, Paul asks, "Would you mind walking to the top?" I dismount the bike while he starts to roll it to the apex. Whenever Paul tries to ride up the slope solo, the rear wheel spins out. My body on the back acted like an anchor. Yet the weight of the two of us going uphill on a nonexistent road was too much for the bike to handle. It's a cruel Catch-22.

Shades of green envelope us on either side. Bushes and trees sweep inward, as though trying to swallow the road itself. At times, this sorry excuse for a highway is the sole sign of civilization. Other times, we seem horribly lost. But there's only one route around Lake Atitlán: to follow the garbled road.

At one point, the bike lurches and my fingernails accidently graze Paul's chest. "Quit clawing me!" he snaps.

I'm taken aback. Paul's sudden nastiness shoves me toward tears. I chomp on my lip and remind myself how hard this is for him, physically and mentally.

The bumps propel me forward on the motorcycle seat. I keep sliding as far to the rear as I can but the jolts constantly fling me forward and into Paul. "Move back!" he yells. I do. Repeatedly.

As uncomfortable as the ride is for me, Paul must feel an unbelievable sense of responsibility. He's promised me that nothing bad would ever happen to me in Guatemala. Now he may actually have to live up to his pledge.

Every time we stall, Paul curses, sometimes in a shout and sometimes under his breath. His arms and legs are probably screaming—from supporting us and the bike. Thankfully, we can see San Pedro in the distance. On the map, it's the biggest village before Sololá and Panajachel. Yet in reality, San Pedro is small and unremarkable. But that's all right with us.

~

Tired and dusty, we're incredibly grateful to make it to San Pedro. We stop for a cool drink and a short rest. My Coke is sickly sweet but refreshing as hell. "I think we should spend the night," Paul sighs, sweaty and exhausted.

"But we don't have clothes. Or a toothbrush."

"You'll survive without clean undies," Paul tells me. "At least I hope so."

"I did in Guatemala City," I point out. "I'm sure I can here."

After that, I bite my tongue. We have no soap, no shampoo. We're running low on quetzals too. Because of its size, I doubt San Pedro has a bank to change money. Plus, we've already paid for our comfortable, new room with a bathroom back in Pana. But I can see how tired Paul is. I feel guilty for being such a passive, useless passenger. "Sure," I tell him. "We'll stay here. It will be fun." Famous last words.

~

Paul and I wind slowly through San Pedro on the dirt bike. We head down the hill toward the shores of Lake Atitlán. Although a number of people walk the streets late this Thursday afternoon, San Pedro isn't a Mecca for nightlife. This is where Gus, the wiry-haired man we met in Panajachel lives. No wonder he treasures his once-monthly cheesesteak at Bill's dive.

Today, the big happening in San Pedro is the girls' basketball game. It's going on in a cracked court near a nondescript church. We briefly pause to take it in. Townspeople also stop to watch the game, and occasionally turn to watch us watching it.

Continuing downhill, the *comedors* we pass are less than tempting. The village itself lacks the panache of Pana. But San Pedro is real. No gimmicks, no fake façades. Paul and I approach a cluster of *posadas* on a strip not far from the lake and the ferry landing. We ask about vacancies at the Hotel San Pedro. It's the largest on the street but its accommodations are spartan by any standard.

A man in the hotel office offers to show us another room he occasionally rents. "Jail might be better," I whisper to Paul as the guy unfastens the padlock to a cement cell to reveal a rusty bed frame inside. We politely turn down the man's offer. He suggests the hotel next door, the Hospedaje del Sol, and is kind enough to take us. But there's nothing sunny about the Hospedaje del Sol, which means "Lodging of the Sun."

On our behalf, the man speaks to the owner. A few rooms are available. We accept one with a stone floor, one bed and chipped furniture. There are bars on the windows and a barred slot on the metal door. "You got your wish for a jail cell," Paul smirks.

"It's like one of those solitary confinement holes in an old Humphrey Bogart movie," I tell him.

"But there's a private bath," Paul points out.

"With a cold-water shower," I frown.

I lose a coin toss and have to go downstairs to ask the proprietress for a bar of soap. I keep repeating the word over and over in my head. *Jabón, jabón, jabón.* I remind myself that in Spanish, the "j" sounds like an "h." Like in José.

I find the *hospadaje's* owner in the courtyard with her family, snapping string beans into a bowl. I excuse myself and ask her for *jabón.* There's a delay of several seconds before she can decipher my accent. Then she gestures for me to follow her to the office. I stand outside and wait near a large cage of monkeys. They screech and yell. *'Do they understand Spanish too?'* I wonder.

The woman unlocks a desk drawer and extracts a tiny cake of soap as though it's a holy thing, like a Communion wafer. I thank her and leave. Behind me, the monkeys scream in both English and Spanish.

~

Paul and I are tired but it's too early to turn in for the night and too late for a nap. Instead, we venture back into town but on foot this time. We leave the dirt bike in the hotel's courtyard. It's incomprehensible to ride it any more today.

The girls' basketball game is still in progress. There are no *tiendas,* no establishments that might sell toothbrushes or toothpaste. We walk back to the shores of Lake Atitlán. The sun will be setting soon and the sky is crossed with pink scars. "I'm sorry for snapping at you back there," Paul apologizes.

I squeeze his hand. I won't say it's all right because it isn't. "But you have no idea how fucked we were," Paul continues.

"I trust you," I tell him. "I know you'll always take care of me, no matter what. Besides, you know what you're doing on a motorcycle."

Paul rolls his eyes at my blind faith then kisses me. We haven't brushed our teeth since eight this morning. I crunch on grit whenever I talk. I hope Paul doesn't get a mouthful of grime in our kiss. But if he does, he doesn't say.

We follow a narrow foot path along the lake. Up ahead is a row of simple eating establishments. Or it could be a mirage. "Dinner with a view," Paul says.

"Sounds nice," I admit.

A boy comes up to us, leading a horse on a rope. He wonders if we would like to ride the next morning. Paul tells him that we're catching the ferry at eight. The boy nods and leaves. "We are?" I ask Paul. "Taking the ferry, I mean."

"I can't deal with that road anymore," he sighs.

"El camino es muy malo," I tell him. He laughs and grabs my hand.

"Have I told you that I love you?" Paul asks.

"Not recently," I say.

We come to an open-air *comedor* covered with a tarp canopy. Surrounded by a three-foot rock wall, we can admire the lake while we have supper. My first rum and Coke goes down easy. Once again, I sense this is going to be one of *those* nights—full of soul-searching, sweet words, private disclosures and alcohol. Lots of alcohol. And I'm right.

My hair is pulled back into a short ponytail. Wisps curl around my face. I don't wear makeup. Just a relieved smile to be off the motorcycle and with Paul on the shaky ground of love. He looks at me strangely, grinning. "What?" I ask. "What?" Paul doesn't respond, only keeps smiling.

The sun sets coral and gold above the black, bleak waters of Lake Atitlán, so vast they seem part of an ocean. Paul takes a photo of me as I sit on the step of the *comedor,* cradling a drink.

In a while, we order dinner. The radio plays the equivalent of Spanish elevator music in a land of few elevators. Wildflowers sit in plastic containers on each plastic tablecloth. Grungy Europeans with stringy blonde dreadlocks sit at a nearby table. "There ought to be a law," Paul says. My face questions him and he gestures toward the Europeans. "Dreadlocks on white people. If our kid ever came home with dreadlocks..." he begins.

'*Our kid?*' I let it go.

I marvel at the slew of meals being prepared in such a rustic kitchen. The stone hearth is fueled by firewood. The waiter carefully writes the day's menu on a chalkboard. It is unexplainably pleasant, all of it: the smell of the wood stove, the flowers, the drink, Paul. Even our dreadlocked neighbors. A flood of contentedness fills me. But maybe it's the alcohol.

As our food arrives, a group of English-speaking people enter. Paul and I try to guess what country in the UK they're from, then give up. It doesn't matter. They ask permission to share our table, which is long enough to host the Last Supper. Paul glances at me. "It will be good to speak English to people other than each other," I agree.

Turns out our tablemates are a mix of Australians, New Zealanders and from various parts of Great Britain. Sandy, with his perfect teeth, blue eyes and a daft sense of humor, is paired with Lyndal, a stuffy schoolteacher. Paul takes delight in annoying her, which is easy, because everything seems to bother her.

With Sandy and Lyndal are Brits Mal and Jessica, a cute, athletic blonde who works in market research. Mal is employed by a London trucking company. They introduce us to Wally, a peculiar, red-haired Aussie who is supposedly pecking out a novel. He complains about the power generators constantly failing and blanking out his computer screen while he writes. Or tries to. Wally soon leaves to join other friends at a rival food shack next door.

The conversation threatens to become raucous, our voices raising in laughter and polite argument. They all sip liter bottles of *Gallo* while I down *Cuba Libres*. "How long are you on holiday?" Sandy asks.

"Three weeks," Paul says proudly. "You?"

"Er, five months," Sandy admits sheepishly.

"Five months," I gasp.

"That's not right," Paul tells them. "Damn Kiwis."

We talk of our travels: ferries, "luxury" busses, Blue Birds. "Lyndal won't ride anything unless a live chicken's onboard," Sandy jokes.

"It's true," she says.

They've done at least 100 hours on local busses and anticipate more bumps and bruises. It's all friendly and jovial until the gang starts bashing Americans for their gratuity-giving policies. "You blokes ruin it for everyone!" says Mal. "Now they expect us all to give tips."

"The people here are so poor how could you *not* tip?" Paul scolds. "But tipping adds up when you're on holiday almost half the year!" he blurts.

Next, the conversation stumbles upon men and their nasty habits. "Oh, they're perfect gentlemen the first month," begins Jessica. "Then, after they've got you hooked, they start farting and belching up a storm."

The men retaliate by going on about how women hold in their gas and how unhealthy this is. We all howl as the Guatemalan staff watches, not quite understanding. The waiter plies them with *Gallo* and me with rum. Sandy orders the vegetarian platter I asked the *comedor* to create for me and enjoys it immensely. "The next time we come here, it will be on the menu," he says. "They'll call it *Comida Carol*."

I go off in search of the restroom but discover there is none so I squat, hidden in the tall brush across the road. When I return, I sense that the group has been talking about me. "Were they pumping you for dirt on me?" I say into Paul's neck. He doesn't respond, just wears a silly, "you-caught-me" grin. The others won't make eye contact with me.

When Lyndal uses the bushes, Sandy takes the opportunity to complain about her hiking mania and her desire to drag him up nearby Volcán San Pedro. Paul's face lights up at the chance to climb a second volcano. *"No más, por favor,"* I beg. *No more, please.*

After we tell Sandy the *Reader's Digest* version of our trek up Volcán Pacaya, he says, "No flipping way!"

~

Soon, it's time for us all to stumble back to our mutual hotels, especially if Paul and I want to catch the early ferry in the morning. We stop to kiss in the lunar light. The moon is a crescent sliver but glows defiantly, illuminating the earth below. Stars spill through the murky sky. "I love you," Paul tells me as we scale the stairs to our room. I'm not sure if I should believe him.

185

"I love you too," I breathe. He probably won't remember it tomorrow.

Paul opens up the little metal compartment on our door and presses his lips between the bars. "Attica!" he cries, just like in *Dog Day Afternoon*. Then, "Warden, I want a reprieve." Followed by lines from every B-prison movie he can remember.

"It doesn't look *that* much like a jail cell, does it?" I ask. But it does.

"Silencio!" one of our neighbors pleads. *"Basta!"* Silence... Enough.

We lay down on the bed, kissing, cuddling and talking. No condoms, so no sex. Without warning, Paul blurts out, "I don't want to marry you." But I think he really *does* want to marry me. Only it scares him.

"Uh, I didn't ask you to marry me, did I?" I confirm.

"No, but..."

"Then why are you always bringing it up?"

Paul is adamant about not wanting to be tied down, about not wanting to give up his freedom, about not wanting children. Blah, blah, blah. I think he's fighting his own demons. In fact, I know he is. Who isn't?

Perhaps it's from the dusty, difficult dirt bike ride but suddenly, I burst out crying. "Why do you have to be so mean?" I sob.

"I don't know," he says, hanging his head.

"We're barely going out a year," I tell him between tears. "I don't pressure you into anything, do I?"

Paul shakes his head. "I pressure myself," he answers.

"Well, stop it!"

I'm sure the *cervezas* are doing the talking and worse, that Paul won't recall this conversation the next day. But I will. In fact, I won't be able to forget it.

I sob harder, maudlin from all the rum. Paul holds me and begs me to stop crying. "I never want to hurt you," he says.

"That's exactly what people say when they hurt you," I sigh.

Did I want marriage? Marriage doesn't guarantee a thing — fidelity, happiness, security. Marriage assures none of that. I lived that lesson already with Alex and won't live it again. I want things to stay like they are with Paul, to stay good. Why does that scare him so much?

Soon, Paul is snoring softly beside me, still clinging to my waist. But I am wakeful, angry and confused. Why does he insist on messing with my head?

We talk intermittently through the night. Whenever he rolls over or shifts his weight, he starts yapping. I am a knot of tension, uncomfortable on the small, lumpy mattress. Absentmindedly, I masturbate and shudder quietly beside Paul but the physical release doesn't help. I finally nod out after a few hours.

Before dawn breaks, a symphony of howling dogs leads to a symphony of roosters. Sleeping in fits and starts, I worry about missing the ferry because our alarm clock is back in Panajachel. I worry about getting the motorcycle safely onto the ferry. I just plain worry.

Soon morning comes and the sun rises as it always does. Some things never change. Until they do.

Day 13

Friday, December 3, 1993
San Pedro/Panajachel/Quetzaltenango

Before I even open my eyes, Paul asks, "Are we still friends?"

I half-smile and tell him, "Yes." I'm shocked he remembers the night before. But that would be a heap of drama to forget.

~

The prospect of taking a cold shower this morning doesn't thrill me. As I run a brush through my dirty hair, I pick up where I left off in the Worrying Department:
- that we'll miss the ferry;
- that we'll catch the ferry and it will sink;
- that the motorcycle won't fit on said ferry;
- that the motorcycle will fall off of said ferry, and
- we'll have to ride back to Panajachel on that terrible road.

You know, the usual.

~

Paul and I are quiet and awkward with each other after my sobfest the previous evening. Our awful breakfast of glue-paper pancakes doesn't help. They stick in our throats even more than our words do.

Paul hates making me cry. By the slump of his shoulders, I can see that he's sorry. I'm not mad at him, though. Just slightly wounded.

The feeling will pass. It always does. But I will always remember the words that were said. And I guess he will too.

Jessica and Mal arrive at breakfast soon after we do. Paul and I say hello to them but that's all. The alcohol withdrawal renders the four of us sheepish.

Unbeknownst to us, Mal had been sober for six months before he gracelessly swan dove off the wagon last night. In the morning light, Mal's face bears the delicate scars of a cruel hangover.

~

The day promises to be bright and clear. The eight o'clock ferry blows its horn on the pier, jarring us out of our silent thoughts. We go to meet it.

Paul carefully walks the dirt bike along the narrow, rickety dock. He and the workers struggle with its weight as they lift the motorcycle in unison and haul it onto the boat. I cross my fingers as they heave it over the foot of air between the pier and the boat's edge. Miraculously, *el moto* does not disappear into the azure of Lake Atitlán.

The dirt bike is secured in the aft while we take seats midship. The other passengers stare at us as if we're transporting a purple aardvark. We ignore them. The ferry itself is cobbled together with wooden planks and doesn't seem particularly seaworthy. "Will this thing make it across the lake?" I ask Paul.

He lowers his sunglasses and gives me a hazel stare. "I'd like to think so."

A cluster of men toy with the ferryboat's engine. It sputters, coughs then stops completely. Then the men fasten masking tape and a shoelace to select moving parts. I half-expect one of them to attach a wad of chewing gum to the belt. After almost an hour of tinkering, the finicky engine purrs contentedly. The passengers applaud. "Only in Guatemala can you fix an engine with a shoelace," Paul notes.

The ferry makes several stops along the shores of Lake Atitlán. Eventually, I stop counting. No signs tell the names of villages when we land at each small pier. There are no announcements from the crew. Every village seems almost identical as the next. I try to follow our journey with my fingertip tracing the guidebook's map but give up.

At each stop, Guatemalans bearing baskets filled with crafts are anxious to board. Most wear traditional dress, the women in *huipils* and flared skirts, the men in shabby calf-high pants and cotton shirts.

Others are decked out in their finest *ropas Americanos*. The ferry workers alternately collect the fares and help people onto the boat. Other passengers ride on the roof for the view.

It doesn't take long for Paul to slip through one of the windows and hoist himself on top of the boat with the others. Soon, he knocks on the glass for me to join him. I'm hesitant at first but it's an easy scramble, even on a moving ferry.

Below, the engine is noisy and pumps the claustrophobic cabin full of dizzying gasoline fumes. The benches, with space for a couple dozen passengers, fill quickly. The floor is crowded with baskets and backpacks. So, the roof is a nice change. It's breezy up top and brilliantly sunny.

Paul studies me from behind his shades but I pretend not to notice. Sometimes his gaze makes me feel even more naked than when I'm actually naked. Like now.

~

At San Pablo La Laguna, an American named Bob hoists himself onto the ferry's roof with us. He speaks fluent Spanish, albeit with a Californian drawl. He says goodbye to Orso, his black, bearlike dog, who wags his tail excitedly on the pier. Bob looks like he's standing at attention even when he's propped up on his elbows. "Ex-military," Paul ventures.

"Currently a spy," I tell him. "Ponytail, funny hat. That's his disguise."

Paul rolls his raingear into a pillow and lays down on the deck. I try to write in my wire-ringed notebook but it's too bouncy, the scenery too distracting. Bob stares me down, aching to grill me. "I'm a writer too," Bob finally tells me. "A screenwriter." He's ready to burst, dying to reveal what his script is about but I don't ask. Is every American tourist in Guatemala a writer?

"I'm just an editor," I tell him. "This is my journal."

"Inside every editor is a writer waiting to get out," Bob says sagely.

"Not this editor," I insist.

Bob clearly doesn't find me the least bit interesting so he switches the conversation back to him. "Now, if I can only get in touch with Chuck Norris's people," he laments. "I'd be rich and famous. Instead of only rich."

I chuckle politely and continue writing. "Hollywood wants to turn my novel into a screenplay," Bob says.

Paul smirks behind his sunglasses. "That's great," I tell Bob.

"Did you ever think of publishing your journal?" Bob asks. "People love travelogues."

"It's private," I respond. "Just for me. Just so I remember."

"Remember what?" Bob wonders.

"Everything," I say.

Paul sits up and removes his shades when Bob says he used to be a mercenary before retiring to Guatemala. "Bingo," Paul says quietly to me so Bob can't hear. They talk about wars, real or imaginary, while I consider the homes on stilts, the beautiful, chiseled faces of the indigenous people and the rolling, leafy hills bathed by the wind that washes away sin. Midmorning, the soul-cleansing breeze of legend is calm. I feel dwarfed by the volcanic crags surrounding Lake Atitlán, like I'm in a fishbowl, sailing on a play boat.

Bob soon leaves, eager to ply his stories on unsuspecting travelers below deck. Paul and I lay back and study the lapis sky. His hand brushes my face and I ask myself, *'Where would I be if I didn't have these nail biter's fingertips to touch my face?'* Lost. That's where.

The ferry stops at a village called Santa Cruz La Laguna. From the dock, we see a majestic, unmistakable place named Hotel Arco de Noe, or the Noah's Arc Hotel. Only it more closely resembles a Swiss chalet rather than a biblical boat. The guidebook says the place is run by an Austrian couple. It's exactly the type of ethnic pastiche you'd expect in Guatemala.

Impressive houses are built into the hillside, practically carved into the rock. The road to these homes is so steep it's hard to imagine a car, let alone the road itself, making it. "Maybe there's a secret path," Paul says dreamily.

"Can you imagine waking up to this view every morning?" I ask him.

"No, I can't," he says. "I have a view of a brick wall back home."

~

The next stop is Panajachel. Paul and I climb back into the ferry's window to disembark. We are astounded that the motorcycle is still standing. After all the passengers leave, it's the dirt bike's turn to come ashore. It takes more effort getting the motorcycle off the boat than it did getting it on. The procedure is so slow and laborious, I turn away again.

This is when Paul realizes that the motorcycle's key is missing. "Are you sure you didn't put it in your pocket?" I ask.

"No," he says, patting himself down. "I left it in the ignition."

Did one of the passengers mess with it? Bob? Or one of the workers?

On sandy, solid ground, Paul shakes his head. "I'm not pushing this piece of shit through town," he balks. I stay with the bike while Paul trudges to Bigsa Moto-Rent on foot. What if someone tries to take the disabled bike? What if? What if?

Suddenly, I'm hit with a blast of cold water. Is someone trying to create a diversion to steal the motorcycle? No such luck.

A shoreline water pipe has burst, courtesy of the people who were using it as a bench. The weight of their bodies breaks the joint where two parts of piping were haphazardly welded together.

Water spews 10 feet into the air, soaking the crowd until the pressure subsides. People part like the Red Sea, dashing out in all directions. The bike is getting soaked too. I try to move it but it's too heavy. I take refuge on drier land, guarding the motorcycle from afar.

When Paul finally returns, swinging a spare key on a scrap of string, his face literally drops. I run up to him, trying to explain what happened. "You could have at least saved the helmets," he snaps.

Our headgear is waterlogged. They jiggle back and forth in a muddy puddle. "Sorry, I didn't even think of it," I apologize.

I help Paul pull the motorcycle out of the watery deluge. After we dry it off, it won't start, even with the new key. Paul bounces up and down on the gas pedal, trying to coax it to turn over. Maybe the obstinate bike senses Paul's rage because it finally does start. I jump behind Paul, hanging onto our dripping helmets with one hand and his waist with the other. "Someday we'll look back at this and laugh," I offer.

"Not any day soon," he says.

Although the man at Bigsa is shocked at our drenched clothes, he's more concerned about his soaked helmets. In fragmented Spanish, we explain what happened down at the pier but he doesn't believe us. He probably thinks the helmets fell into Lake Atitlán.

But regardless of what he thinks, the man charges us 10 dollars for the lost key—renting the bike for a day is only 25 dollars. But at least he tears up Paul's credit card imprint and hands back his card. We pay without argument. "Yeah, 10 bucks for a key sucks," Paul admits as we walk to the bank. "But where else can you rent a motorcycle 24 hours for 35 dollars?"

"Only here," I say.

More than a week into our trip, the sight of an armed guard at the bank doesn't even make me blink. We change some cash and travelers' checks before our trip to Quetzaltenango later today and head to the Hotel Martita.

A warm shower, the brushing of teeth and a final walk through Panajachel sets us right following our stressful ferry ride. After lunch, Paul and I seal up our backpacks, including our freshly-laundered clothes from our proprietress. We tell her why we didn't "come home" last night—because we were waylaid in San Pedro—but I'm not sure she understands.

~

The 2:30 bus to Quetzaltenango (shortened to "Xela") leaves from the center of town. It's already half full when we arrive before two. Paul and I are lucky to snag seats. By the time we pull away from the curb, there's the usual three people stuffed into spaces meant for two. More bodies pack the aisles.

During the two-and-a-half-hour bus ride and numerous stops, we pass grand mountains and seas of supreme greenness. Guatemala's countryside is so striking that it's beginning to border on redundancy. If only they could harness this beauty and somehow sell it. Rich in natural splendor but poor quetzal-wise, most Guatemalans live well below the poverty level.

The bus drives past waves of grain, coffee plantations, workers, walkers, a gorgeous array of intricate *huipils,* children playing beside the road and women scrubbing clothes in streams. I'm bounced into a semi-sleep on Paul's shoulder until we arrive in Xela.

~

First impression of Quetzaltenango: it's ugly, gray and citified. The Minerva Terminal, an open-air bus station, is congested and confusing. When the *ayudante* hands our backpacks down from the top of the bus, Paul grabs mine and helps me into it. There's something very sensual about wiggling into the straps, almost like dressing in public.

Our next hurdle is to grab a taxi. To reach the main street, we walk through the crowded market, careful not to knock over people with our cumbersome packs. No cabs are to be had on the street so we head back to the Minerva Terminal.

A minor argument ensues with a Texan and his entourage who are also waiting for a taxi. The man insists he was there first. Except the driver wants to take Paul and me because we'll be traveling further and it will mean more money. "Hey dude, I don't want to fight," Paul tells the guy. "I'm on vacation. You take the cab." The driver is pissed off but takes the lesser fare.

Tex and his friends drive off with our most sincere blessing. "Assholes," I say to Paul.

The next cabbie wants to charge us 25 quetzals; the first driver had quoted us only 15. We wave him off. The third cabbie has no side windows but a more economical price.

Before we even leave the Minerva Terminal, our driver sideswipes another car. After curses, fists dramatically waved and minor damage to both vehicles, our cabbie shrugs and is on his way. There's no exchange of personal information, no contacting the police, no nothing. "Do you think they have car insurance in Guatemala?" I ask Paul.

"Fat chance," he says.

~

We pass Quetzaltenango's Monumento a la Marimba (Marimba Monument), strategically placed in a traffic circle. Xela, Guatemala's second-largest city, swells with cars. It has a touch more charm than the capital. Xela natives pride themselves on their formality and their politeness. Later, Glenn tells us that Xela poisons their stray dogs once a year. But politely, very politely.

Soon enough, the cab driver finds Glenn's street. His place is on a bleak, industrial-looking block. When we ring the bell, Glenn's girlfriend Rachel answers the door with a big hug for Paul. She and I have never met before so Rachel's greeting for me is not as affectionate but it's still warm.

Four years ago, when Paul and Glenn were roommates, the three of them practically lived together. That virtually makes them... well, I don't know what it makes them. But they're familiar with each other's quirks, habits...and ghosts.

197

Rachel is cute and slim with short, chestnut hair and dark eyes that sparkle with intelligence. Though not tall, she gives the impression of being lanky. Her long, slender hands seem too large for her body. They move through the air with the nimbleness of a dancer's as she talks. Rachel wears what Paul calls "ragamuffin clothes:" tatty, comfortable and not necessarily matching garments. But on Rachel, it works. She's sexy in a haphazard way.

Glenn rents a room in a large house from a woman who takes in students. Xela is a popular spot for Spanish-language schools. These institutes are supposedly less commercialized and more authentic than the ones in Antigua. And like Antigua, it's common for families to host student boarders.

Included with Glenn's room is the use of a slightly-crumbling courtyard and a communal kitchen. Glenn cooked professionally back in Brooklyn so he uses the kitchen a lot. "Chef" is one of his many "used-to-be's." His actual living space is a large but very messy room with a fireplace, bed, desk and piles and piles of papers rising up from the floor.

Fresh from his Harvard University graduation, Glenn is in Quetzaltenango on a grant, documenting indigenous peoples, their languages, customs and histories. He'll be in Xela for a total of two years and only arrived this past summer. Part of his research consists of poring over official documents stored in government archives. Polling records and commerce records, for example. These papers chronicle who came in and out of Xela and what they were carrying. They go as far back as the 1800s, when the city began keeping track. There are leather-bound ledgers, thick folders and loose papers filled with looping, antique handwriting strewn throughout the room.

To our disbelief, Xela's government office has permitted Glenn to borrow the actual, irreplaceable paperwork from their archives. They sit heaped on his bedroom floor. "He can't even find socks that match," Paul whispers to me. "I wouldn't trust him with original records."

Rachel, a film editor, has taken a few months off to spend time with Glenn in Guatemala. She's traveled around on her own while Glenn does his research. Her latest trip was last week, to Huehuetenango, to study Spanish. She also spent time in Chiapas, Mexico.

Vigorously scratching her calf, Rachel informs us that earlier this afternoon, she was diagnosed with scabies. "What the hell is scabies?" Paul asks. "It sounds like something dogs get." Given their long history together, Paul can pull off talking to Rachel like this. Even Glenn can't.

"It is," Rachel smiles, "but humans can get it too. It's a skin mite. Highly contagious." Luckily, Glenn didn't come down with scabies because Rachel has been gone for weeks and they haven't had physical contact. Yet.

"How did you get it?" Paul wonders.

"Could be from someone she sat next to on a chicken bus," Glenn offers. "No one knows." Immediately, my own skin starts to itch when I recall all the Blue Birds Paul and I have been on.

Since Glenn has no space to put us up, Rachel names a handful of respectable, reasonable accommodations nearby. Before Paul and I set off to investigate, we agree to meet back at Glenn's at six. This will give us time to find lodgings and settle in. It will also give Glenn time to finish a report he's in the middle of writing.

Paul and I don't get past the lobby of the first hotel. If you could call it a lobby. It's a shambles. Even worse than Glenn's room.

Further down the block, the second place seems more hospitable and less like a fallout shelter. We breeze past a Canadian struggling to phone home in the lobby. The receptionist lets us choose from a number of rooms. We decide on one with a New Orleans bordello motif. It has a red rug, a red bedspread and red velvet curtains. It is a tacky work of art and right up our alley.

~

Ditching our backpacks, Paul and I take a quick survey of Quetzeltenango. We spend time exploring the streets around our hotel and check out the plaza in the center of town. Upon closer inspection, Xela is pretty, expansive and old-fashioned, especially for a city its size.

It's getting close to six and Glenn has promised to cook us supper. Paul and I are on a mission to find a cake to bring as dessert but come up emptyhanded. As it turns out, Glenn left the archives late, after the vegetable stands closed, and he couldn't buy the greens he needed for dinner. He suggests we go to a nearby restaurant. Our stroll doubles as a walking tour of Xela.

More about Glenn: he's about six-foot-tall and gangly. He slouches in a bashful sort of way and has a nervous laugh to go with it. Glenn's thin blonde hair stands up like a baby chick's. He's extremely smart—graduated from City College with a 4.0 GPA and won a scholarship to Harvard. He's down-to-earth and gentle. A bit goofy and awkward but entirely lovable. Think, a light-haired version of *The Nutty Professor.* It's easy to see what Rachel sees in him; it's the exact opposite of what I see in Paul.

Xela is more inviting at night. Its shadows hide some of the grime and dirt. The streets melt one into the other like a maze. Without Glenn to guide us, we'd surely get lost. Xela's sidewalks are cracked and narrow. Maneuvering them requires minor gymnastics, a combination of leaping up, jumping down and walking single file.

Glenn tells us some of Xela's history. He talks about the people he's come to know and the family he used to live with when he was studying Spanish at the Proyecto Lingüìstico Quetzalteco. Now Glenn's too busy to sit in a classroom; he learns Spanish on the fly. Quetzaltenango is his teacher, as is the whole of Guatemala.

When he can escape his studies, research books and stacks of 300-year-old paperwork, Glenn travels with likeminded souls through the Western Highlands and other remote regions, sometimes riding the tops of busses. In Tikal, he and a couple of friends bribed the guards so they could camp out on top of a ruin. Another time, he hiked for days in the mud to visit exiled Guatemalan nationals who were living in hiding, in fear of the guerillas.

The four of us cut through Xela's plaza. It's bordered by an old cathedral that's decorated with rows of pollution-ravaged saints who look down on us with solemn distain. A Christmas tree is strung with lights on one end of the plaza's park, giving it a magical glow. At the other end of the plaza, Glenn points out the empty ground floor of a historic building. "This would make a great spot for a restaurant," he says.

When we pass a post office, I push a bunch of postcards down the mail chute. "I've never known anyone who's done that," Glenn admits.

"Let's hope for the best," I tell him.

~

At first glance, the bistro Glenn takes us to gives the impression that it's upscale but the prices turn out to be very reasonable. As we eat, we compare notes on our various travels. We're psyched about our new adventure that will start tomorrow. "We'll go to some cool villages in the Western Highlands," Glenn promises. "There's some people I'd really like you to meet."

After a meal of simply-prepared fresh fish, we call it an early night. Glenn and Rachel walk us back to our hotel. The plan is for them to come by the next morning at about eight. From there, we'll head to the car rental shop together. "Sounds like a plan," Paul says.

I'm exhausted from our travels by ferry, motorcycle and bus. But not too tired to straddle Paul in the heavy, red-velvet darkness of our room.

Yes, life is very good sometimes.

Day 14

Saturday, December 4, 1993
Quetzaltenango/Aguacatán

Paul and I are up and out before eight. We wait for Glenn and Rachel across the street from our hotel, under a tree that sprouts delicate white flowers. The bus depot must be nearby because noisy vehicles plow through at a constant pace, belching diesel fumes. Wild violets crawl up the hurricane fence that wraps itself around the warehouse behind us. I want to pluck a sprig and tuck it behind my ear but rifle-bearing police officers keep passing on foot patrol. Maybe they think we're up to mischief. Maybe they're right.

"Glenn is always late," Paul notes. But it doesn't matter. We're on Guate time and the clock is meaningless here. Especially in the Western Highlands.

Since Quetzaltenango is in the mountains, the morning air is pleasantly chilly, refreshing after the arid breeze of Panajachel. The sun shines steadily. Sunshine makes a world of difference to everything, everywhere, doesn't it?

When Glenn and Rachel show up at about 8:20, she rolls her eyes, "Of course, he waited until this morning to pack," she begins. "Then he couldn't find clean socks."

"Some things never change," Paul sighs.

Rachel admits, "It's one of his best qualities."

Glenn has made the arrangements for the rental of an SUV.
It will cost about 200 dollars for the week, which we'll split four
ways. But before picking it up, Glenn leads us to the second-best
hotel in Xela.

"Their American-style breakfast is cheap," he says. "And good."

As we approach the hotel, we notice a Maya Tours bus parked
haphazardly on a hill. Inside the restaurant is a group of oddly-dressed
German tourists. A blonde wears a *sari*. Another wears a *dirndl*
dress. "She looks like the St. Pauli Girl on the beer bottle labels,"
Rachel remarks.

"Not as pretty, though," I add.

"Or as busty," Paul notes.

We drink real coffee and eat pancakes, ringed by slices of fresh
papaya and mango. The restaurant's interior is lovely. The tablecloths,
utensils and chairs actually match, a rarity for Guatemala. Except for
the Mayan artifacts on the walls, it could be anywhere. But the service
is achingly slow so we know we're still in Guate.

In the car rental office's parking lot, we meet a little, red Suzuki
Samurai, our chariot for the following week. A two-door model, it's
very basic and has a manual transmission. Out of the four of us, only
Glenn can drive a stick shift, so he's our chauffeur by default.

Glenn and Rachel drop us off at our place while they return
to Glenn's so he can finish packing and locate fresh socks. Since
Paul and I are already packed, we savor our last moments in the
whorishly-decorated hotel suite. But even after a romp, we still have
to wait for Glenn and Rachel downstairs.

~

Paul lashes our backpacks to the Suzuki's roof rack while
Glenn and Rachel stash their bags behind the back seats. Since she will
act as navigator, Rachel takes the passenger seat. At first, the back row
is comfortable but after only a few miles, my butt can feel the outline
of every spring. The raw metal floorboards have holes drilled into
them—so you can hose mud out of the inside, I guess—but I can see
the road underneath us, which is disconcerting.

Truth be told, it's a tad cramped in the Suzuki. I'm pretty much
fine, but Paul, who's about five inches taller than me, is contorted.
"Are you okay back here?" I ask.

"I'm fine," Paul says. At first.

Glenn has a bunch of interesting stops planned for us today. I expect the roads to be poor and washed out, and I'm right. Travel is slow, full of pregnant pauses, but this works for us; we're in no rush. We take breaks often to suck up the vistas and snap photos.

A thoughtful chauffeur, Glenn always tells us where he's thinking of stopping in advance. He asks if we're all right with visiting this church or that ruin before going there. He's a gracious and well-informed tour guide.

Our first visit is to a textile and glass-blowing cooperative in a nearby town. Cantel Fabrica is a half-hour's drive from Quetzaltenango. The name "Cantel Fabrica" translates to "Cantel Factory." The village is a by-product of the *fabrica* itself and has sprung up around the cooperative.

The glass operations are amazing, a perfect example of how recycling can be profitable. The factory's wares are wonderfully unique: bulky, chunky, raw, filled with blemishes like bumps and bubbles, but oddly attractive. Not one goblet, candy dish, ashtray or vase is the same—or perfect—but it's their very imperfections that make them so lovely. Kind of like people.

The glass they use to create these pieces is all recycled. The green comes from 7Up bottles, the blue from Nivea jars and the amber from beer bottles. The clear glass, which makes up the main body of the finished product, is fashioned from melted-down Coke and Pepsi bottles. The recycled glass is then fired, shaped and blown in a factory behind the *fabrica's* showroom.

In Spanish, Glenn asks the woman behind the counter if we can tour the factory itself. *"Es posible?"* he wonders. The woman nods. She shows us to a huge, cavernous, warehouse-like structure filled with ovens. It's infernally hot, like I imagine hell might be.

The men who stoke these ovens stand in their dingy underpants, grinning uncomfortably at Rachel and me. This is how they work, in their briefs, because it's so unbearably sweltering in the factory. No protective clothing, no fireproof garments so they won't get burned. It's just them in their bare skin and their baggy, grayish Fruit of the Looms. "I'd call them tighty-whities, except they're not white," Rachel whispers to me.

I give Rachel a small smile. "Let's go outside," I suggest. "We don't want to embarrass them." We pass the time surveying the mounds of broken bottles sorted into piles by color. When Paul and

Glenn join us, we go back into Cantel Fabrica's showroom. We want to buy everything there but can't decide on anything. "Imagine having a hundred dollars to spend here," I tell Paul. "You could buy glassware for your whole house."

"Yeah, but shipping would probably cost more than the stuff actually does," he figures.

There are pitchers, tall and short cups, shot glasses, casings for light fixtures. There's any glass item you can imagine. Paul buys a candy dish for his Aunt Lorena. For about three dollars, I get my parents a blue ashtray. And for my grandmother, I choose a statue of the Virgin Mary crafted from pale blue and clear glass. Rachel ambitiously buys a wine set for a Christmas gift. I wonder if it will make it back to Brooklyn in one piece.

And Glenn, our clumsy but lovable tour guide, walks into an arrangement of pitchers on the floor, shattering a few. *"Lo siento,"* he apologizes, reddening to his earlobes.

The clerk shrugs, *"No es nada,"* and sweeps the broken glass onto a pile for reincarnation. *It's nothing*.

~

Three miles past Salcajá is a village called San Andrés Xecul. It looks *típico* except for the church. In a country of churches, this is truly one-of-a-kind. The colors are so bright and vivid, it could have come out of a Marvel comic book. In the middle of this dry, dusty town, it's the largest structure for miles. The church's walls are painted in explosive tempera colors. Picture a house of worship designed by Crayola.

"This is unbelievable," Paul says, climbing out of the Suzuki's cramped back seat. It's the most curious church I've ever seen. We take a closer look.

Instead of having tired, whitewashed skin like most of Guatemala's churches, the exterior of La Iglesia de San Andrés Xecul is a brazen yellow. Its trim is cherry red. The figures of saints and angels are rosy and electric blue, their faces and the angels' wings are bleached pale. Decorative flourishes of green leaves and red geometric patterns stud the sides. The church has two bell towers and a big, swirling crucifix that stretches for the sky.

At first, the church seems outlandish but when I think about it, the color scheme is perfect. It's constructed with the simplicity of a child coloring a picture for someone they revere (i.e., God) with a stack of gaudy Magic Markers. The riotous palette is an unadulterated declaration of love from people who don't have much to offer except their devotion.

Inside, the dimly-lit church's walls are paneled with mahogany as many churches here are. It's such a contrast from the technicolor exterior. From the high ceilings and cement arches, it's cool inside.

When I first step in from the blinding sunshine, it's so dark I can barely make out the glass-encased figures of saints lining the walls. Like oversized dolls, the statues are dressed in clothing. It's somewhat unnerving that the bodies are also life-sized and have human hair. They exist in an uncanny limbo between religious icon, human being and plaything.

Something jolts me out of my thoughts. A woman's voice is raised in song, melancholy yet beautiful, as she sings a hymn in Spanish. Clear and strong and gorgeous, the hymn is so exquisite that tears choke my throat. But it's also so private, between her and God, that I feel like I'm eavesdropping. (It's so different than when the tour guide sang in the convent.) I know the others feel the same because we start to leave without saying anything to each other. Paul comes up beside me, hooks his hand around my waist. His eyes are full and wet. "There is no place like this place," he says once again.

~

Directly across the road from La Iglesia de San Andrés Xecul is an arbor of evergreens like the one which led to Santiago Atitlán. Beyond the arbor is nothingness, just taupe dust that radiates heat in the early-afternoon sun. The town abruptly ends here.

Too early for lunch, we buy sodas from a cart and look briefly at the display of weavings a woman has set out on a blanket. Soon we're back on the road, the Suzuki lurching and bumping along. The curls on top of Paul's head graze the inside of the roof. There's no padding, only strips of bare metal. On particularly rough stretches come the painful sound of skull striking steel. Paul's skull. "Fuck," he grumbles.

"Sorry," Glenn tells him.

"Maybe you should drive a little slower," Rachel suggests. The condition of the road is a matter for concern; it's actually just the skeleton of a throughfare with the bones of rocks peeking through. To call it a road would be too generous. "Please, slow down," Rachel begs when Glenn doesn't. He responds with an uneasy titter. We are clearly at Glenn's mercy. Maybe he even delights in the fact. But maybe not. Maybe I'm imagining it.

We turn from San Andrés Xecul's dirt road onto the main road. It's in slightly better shape. Heading north, in a couple of hours, we manage to cover about 40 miles.

Outside of Huehuetenango, we stop for gas and split the tab. Paul hands Glenn our share from our pooled resources while Glenn and Rachel quibble over quetzals. Because she can stay in Guatemala only until her money runs out—then she'll have to go back home and back to work—Rachel is carefully counting each quetzal she spends. And since Glenn is living on a student's limited budget, he is equally as vigilant.

There's a restaurant right next to the gas station in Huehue. It resembles a Guatemalan truck stop but we go inside anyway. Decorated with local crafts, woven blankets, framed *huipils* and pottery complete the hominess picture.

As we wait for our meal, a marimba band sets up their equipment and plays for the Saturday lunchtime crowd. I order a savory seafood soup, although Paul warns, "We're nowhere near the sea." I take my chances and go so far as to spoon some into Paul's mouth for a sampling. He eats his words while I take quiet delight watching his tongue, his mouth, as I feed him.

After lunch, we wander through the streets of Huehuetenango, seeking the road to Zaculeu. Still struggling with the clunky stick shift, Glenn manages to stall the Suzuki while we're chugging up a hill. We begin rolling backwards before he can pop it into gear again, almost running over an old man with a bundle on his back.

Quietly, politely, the ancient gentleman curses us. *"Lo siento,"* Glenn calls out the window. *I'm sorry.* The old man gives us a halfhearted shake of his fist to continue scolding us silently. Glenn responds with his edgy giggle then rolls up the window.

Rachel almost has a litter of puppies at Glenn's close call, then swiftly regains her composure. "This is where I studied Spanish," she says in a shaky voice, nodding to a small stone structure we pass. "This is the hotel where I stayed," she tells us as we pass another.

"This is where you got scabies," Glenn jokes. Rachel is the only one who doesn't think it's funny.

~

The ruins at Zaculeu are less than three miles west of Huehuetenango but because the road is so bad, it takes us a jolting hour to travel two miles. The landscape is pretty, though, and the conversation lively, so the time passes swiftly, quicker than the miles do.

Zaculeu was once the capital of the Postclassical Mam kingdom—the Mam are a preconquest indigenous people still found in Guatemala's Western Highlands as well as southwestern Mexico. The Zaculeu ruins are meant to be striking remnants of that early civilization. "But don't expect Tikal," Glenn warns us.

In 1525, the Spaniards arrived in the area, led by Pedro de Alvarado's not-so-famous younger brother Gonzalo. The siege went on for several months, during which the Mam were reduced to starvation. When the Spanish entered Zaculeu, they found 1,800 dead Indians and the survivors chowing down on the corpses. Because of the bad juju, Zaculeu was abandoned and Huehuetenango was established nearby. Oddly enough, the name of the new city, Huehuetenango, translates to "the place of the ancients."

The choice Gonzalo gave the surviving Mam was to either peacefully convert to Christianity or be murdered. (And the Spaniards thought the Indians were savages!) Understandably, the Mam chose the lesser of two evils.

The Real Guide describes the archeological site of Zaculeu as resembling an aging film set, and that's pretty accurate. In 1947, the ruins were "restored" by the United Fruit Company as a gift to the Guatemalan people. For some unknown reason, they coated all of the buildings with a layer of white plaster, which is now chipping. Occasionally, the original surfaces of the ruins break out like wildflowers fighting through cracks in city sidewalks.

In the 1940s, excavators discovered numerous artifacts including ornamental metalwork, jade and unconventional burial techniques. The corpses at Zaculeu were either crammed into huge urns (yes, really), cremated or interred in vaults. The museum on site is informative and the storyboards are translated into English for our benefit.

Zaculeu's grounds are manicured and nicely kept but the short squat ruins themselves do have a Hollywood soundstage vibe. They look like leftovers from *The Ten Commandments*. I half-expect to find Charlton Heston swaggering around in robes and a beard.

It's a gorgeous afternoon. The never-ending valley and heavy cloud cover are pressed to a melodramatic sky. The perfect setting for exploring, Paul and I climb the tallest ruin and look out from the top. "What do you suppose the view was like in the 1500s?" I ask.

"Probably about the same it is now, except there are more houses today," he says. "And that damn bus that keeps following us." Sure enough, the Maya Tours bus is in the parking lot, not far from our humble Samurai, the passengers scattered like flies.

Back in the SUV, Glenn backtracks to Huehuetenango in search of the eastbound road that will take us to Aguacatán, our destination for today. Huehue itself is crowded with Saturday shoppers who walk down the two-laned highway with absolutely no regard for motorized traffic. Finally, via trial-and-error and conflicting directions from locals, we're soon zipping down a pitted dirt road again.

Rachel flips through our copy of *The Real Guide* with interest, rattling off all the places she's been. She spots the bright orange marks from my Highlighter pen and snickers. I thought making notes would be helpful; Rachel says it's anal. Paul and Glenn think my Highlights are hilarious too. "Is there anything you *didn't* Highlight?" Paul wonders.

Earlier in the trip, however, Paul complimented my note-taking prowess. Is he suddenly turning on me? A classic example of three-against-one? I take this criticism as cheerfully as possible but silently I'm hurt. I try to shrug it off. Otherwise, it will be a very long week.

~

On the map, Aguacatán is 12 miles from Huehuetenango but on the chewed-up road, it seems much further. It takes us three hours to travel a mere inch and a half on the map. But it's an all right, if not bouncy, ride. Surrounding us are mountains. Past the side of the road, the hills drop into sheer cliffs. There's nothing between us and the birds but air, sweet, fresh air.

The highway is so snug that when an oncoming delivery truck or pickup needs to pass, one vehicle usually has to stop. On the roads of Guatemala there's a cautious politeness; the opposite could mean death. One, if not both, of the vehicles could be belly-up in a ravine due to someone else's stubbornness. The evidence is all around us.

A glutton for punishment, Rachel asks Glenn, "Tell us about the Mexican ballerinas again."

"Please don't," I beg. "Not now."

I am in the back of a tin box hurling down a dirt road with no guardrail in a Third World Country. Please. Don't.

Paul grabs hold of my hand on the plaid upholstery in an attempt to soothe my worries. Until Glenn hits a rock and Paul's head hits the ceiling. "Son of a…" He rubs his crown.

"Lo siento," Glenn giggles.

I expect Rachel's fingerprints to be permanently etched into the Suzuki's dashboard. She keeps clutching it for dear life whenever we head into a sharp turn it's impossible to see around or when Glenn comes too close to the edge and pebbles rain down into the abyss. Things always look worse from the front seat. Unless you're in the backseat of a two-door Suzuki.

"Why did they name this car the 'Samurai,'" Rachel asks out of nowhere. "Didn't the samurai crash their airplanes into ships?"

"That's the kamikaze," Glenn reminds her patiently.

"The samurai were warriors," Paul says. "Military nobility."

"This one's a little fighter," Glenn says, patting the dash. "Don't you think?"

Although I try to hold back, I can't. I blurt out, "I read in *Consumer Reports* that the Samurai has a tendency to flip if you take a turn too fast."

"Like Glenn's doing now?" Rachel says.

I don't answer. And Glenn doesn't slow down.

Our pleasant, if not harrowing, ride is punctuated by Rachel's frequent gasps, startled exclamations and Glenn's chuckles. Someone else might rap Rachel in the jaw but not Glenn. True love, I guess. But given the condition of the roads and Glenn's inclination to speed, Rachel's reaction is perfectly valid.

The countryside is lovely, though. Glenn keeps pointing this out, perhaps to distract Rachel. But she's undistractable. Like a cat toying with a wounded mouse, once Rachel sinks her claws into something, it's hard to wrestle it away from her. Case in point, she'd much rather goof on Paul than appreciate the panoramic views. This seems to have a more calming effect on Rachel's raw nerves than the tranquil scenery. But it wears mine to a frazzle. I mean, who wants to hear about their boyfriend's ex? And why would Rachel bring her up? Just to hurt me? And Paul?

Out of the blue, Rachel asks, "How's Leah?"

Paul sucks in some air then responds. "How should I know?"

"Aren't you still in touch?" Rachel pushes.

"Why should I be? That was a million years ago," Paul says calmly to Rachel. "You think more about Leah than I do."

Rachel rummages through her shoulder bag, perhaps looking for a ball gag for herself. "So, whatever happened to Leah?" Rachel asks, undeterred. "Married? Kids?"

"I don't know and I don't care," Paul tells her.

'But I do!' I want to shout. I sit on my hands and study the clouds instead.

Paul's ex-girlfriend Leah always seems to call whenever I'm at his apartment. Like a big, dopey puppy, she doesn't know when to stop. Leah's "dumb as a stump," Paul claims, but was such a sweet person he didn't have the heart to break up with her until being with Leah became unbearable. Over a year after their split, Leah still continues to leave messages on Paul's answering machine in a tone that's too cozy and familiar for my liking. "I'm going to go do the Walmart thang," she twangs. Do people really talk like that?

"Are you sure Leah knows it's over?" I ask Paul after hearing one of these voice mails. But he doesn't respond. Maybe to infuriate me even more.

I'd met Leah a couple of times in the four years she and Paul had been dating. At parties, at suppers at a mutual friend's house. And I remember feeling...disappointed. Leah wasn't the type of woman I pictured Paul being with. Nice-looking enough but too average, too old-fashioned. I wanted better for him. Someone like...well, someone like me, for example.

~

Aguacatán. Aguacatán. The road to Aguacatán is as rutted and worn as Paul's road to me.

On the final stretch to that faraway village in the Western Highlands, Rachel clutches the dashboard the entire trip while Paul's head bangs on the Suzuki's roof every few miles. Glenn's nervous giggle provides additional musical accompaniment. My hand cups Paul's knee. For physical or emotional support, I'm not sure which.

I keep telling myself that we are 5,000 miles from Leah's relationship-threatening phone calls. We are far from her homey country-western dancing at Denim and Diamonds and her nauseating quilting bees. We are far from Leah inviting herself along to visit

Paul's sister and her new baby. (Doesn't Leah realize she and Paul broke up?) We are far from the lunch where Paul told Leah that he and I were dating—where Leah had to pop a Valium upon hearing the distressing news. '*And why were they having lunch in the first place?*' Bad Carol asks Good Carol.

But I repeat to myself that I am at Paul's side in a battered Samurai which hugs the road in an unreal Third World wonderland. I am here, not Leah.

I clutch Paul's hand and rub his skin softly. He smiles, despite the bumps on his head. I am here and Leah is there. I always want to be here...wherever *here* happens to be. And never there, which is without Paul.

~

Highway 7W to Aguacatán weaves through the hills like thread. With enough prompting (pleading!), Glenn manages to drive slowly enough to satisfy all three of us. We are surrounded by unusual sights that will soon become commonplace: people walking alongside the road carrying humongous bundles, multicolored *huipils*, children who wave and beam broadly, men working on the road with crude tools, women working the fields with machetes.

Although it's late autumn in New York, it is Guatemala's summer. Schools are closed, on holiday, I think. Corn was recently harvested and other crops are almost ready to go. When we drive past fields outside Aguacatán, we are greeted with the fragrant scent of garlic and scallions, crops Glenn says the area is well-known for producing. "Something about the soil here," he tells us. The fields are ripe and lush and many are flooded, like rice paddies.

It's 4:30 and the sun is due to set by six. We want to be off this twisty, snakelike road well before then. "Should we stay at Aguacatán?" Glenn confirms. "Or should we go a little further to Sacapulas?"

"Is Sacapulas bigger?" Paul wonders. "Nicer?"

Glenn shakes his head. "They're both similar. Sort of rustic. Besides, it's just for one night." If Glenn, he of the mismatched socks and towers of papers, thinks Aguacatán is rustic, how bad is it?

P.S. it's bad.

Late on a Saturday afternoon, people are already preparing for Sunday morning's market. Stalls and wares line the main street, covered with blue tarp. Aguacatán itself is so small it only has a handful of streets. Glenn suggests we look for a hotel on the largest one.

Each village in the Western Highlands has its own trademark style of dress. By the colors of a woman's *huipil* and skirt, you can tell where she's from. In Aguacatán, the "uniform" is a navy-blue cotton skirt and a *huipil* that hangs loose rather than being tucked in. The *huipils* here are of white or pastel colors and are decorated with bands of ribbons as opposed to *huipils* sewn with multicolored threads. Older women wear *cintas*. A *cinta* is a traditional handwoven headdress wrapped around the hair, after which the tails of the *cinta* are arranged on top of the head.

Glenn guides the Suzuki slowly through Aguacatán's unpaved, people-congested streets. The second-best hotel in town, the Hospedaje La Paz, has a bicycle shop in its lobby. We forge on to the Hospedaje Aguateco, which our guidebook says offers the top accommodations in town. When we reach it, Rachel gasps in wonder, "This is the best in Aguacatán?"

Glenn laughs nervously. "Yep," he tells her.

I read aloud from *The Real Guide*. "The Hospadaje Aguateco is a simple, little place with small rooms off a courtyard."

"They make it sound appealing," Rachel says. "Except it's not."

But there are hardly any rooms left in all of Aguacatán because of tomorrow's market. To describe the Aguateco as a hovel would be too kind. It is a worn, wooden fortress built around a scrappy square of dirt where chickens peck for bugs and fight over dry slivers of grass. "Can we sleep in the Suzuki?" I whisper to Paul. "This is horrendous."

"It would be too cramped," he says. "This will be fine, I promise. Think of it like camping out."

Now, Paul and I are avid campers but the Aguateco is rungs below even the lowliest campsite. At least the dirt is clean dirt when you camp. This "dirt" is filth. At least we have a tent and our own sleeping bags when we camp out. Here, we'll be relying on their linens and their mattresses. I can't even imagine what kind of shape they'll be in. "I don't know," I sigh.

"There isn't much choice," Paul tells me.

A semi-drunken man in a t-shirt leads the four of us up an external set of creaky stairs. The porch that encircles the entire second floor is uneven, unsafe and too narrow to hold chairs. The doors to the Aguateco's rooms are wide open when unoccupied. I notice padlocks hanging from hasps outside of each room. Guests are given the keys to these padlocks when they rent accommodations.

With trepidation, I peek into our potential room. A summer camp bunk is luxurious in comparison. Scraps of cloth pretending to be bedsheets cover slim cots. The floorboards are unpainted, like in a barn. Cheap, plastic tablecloths are stapled to the walls and ceilings in lieu of wallpaper and paint. "Home, sweet home," Paul says.

Perhaps because of the shocked expression on my face, the man says he has other rooms available in the hotel. Stupidly, I ask to see them. Of course, they aren't much better. Paul suppresses a laugh. "At least there isn't a bicycle shop in the lobby," he points out.

Glenn tells the man that we'll take two rooms. Paul makes sure each one has a window. "This is a firetrap," the architect in him tells us. "It could go up in flames in a second." He gestures to the transom. "At least we can climb out of it."

Ours opens onto a bucolic setting. The village, fields and hills stretch out below. Walk six blocks and you're in farmland. It would have been charming if our view was the rooftops of Paris, except this is Aguacatán. And there is nothing charming about Aguacatán.

Rather than hang around in our depressing room, we decide to take a predinner walk through town. Since Rachel needs to buy a scabies-free bath towel, we head to the market. We buy mandarin oranges and eat them along the way, spitting the pits into the dirt like everyone else does.

But seed-spitting aside, the four of us still don't fit in. There are stares, especially from children. Maybe it's our western dress. Maybe it's because we are the tallest people in the maze of the market. Glenn's fine blonde hair, which stands up like chicken feathers, is rare in a country where bone-straight, blue-black tresses are the norm.

Glenn manages to procure a few packets of Chikys. He cracks the package and hands us each one. They're a ton sweeter than American cookies but still delightful. "This is my afternoon snack when I work in Xela's archives," he confesses. "My addiction." The fact that Chikys have made their way to the shelves of a dry goods store without electricity in a tucked-away village like Aguacatán is impressive.

I briefly picture the spindly girl in Santiago Atitlán, clutching her sleeve of Chikys and hope she liked them.

~

In one of Aguacatán's shops, women line up with baskets of corn, patiently waiting as a contraption whirrs and cranks. "It's a grinding machine," Glenn explains. "It crushes corn into meal and flour for tortillas and other stuff."

For such an inconsequential village, there are a number of Evangelical storefront churches. They're more crowded than Aguacatán's one unexceptional Catholic church.

Paul, Glenn, Rachel and I continue walking until we get to the outskirts of town. "Maybe we can hike up one of those hills," Paul says, looking toward the small mountains that encircle the agricultural village.

"I'm not sure that's a good idea," Glenn tells him. "This place can get sketchy after dark." Oh, great.

At the less-populated edge of town, the four of us are even more out of place. I feel that we're intruding, interfering with people's lives. Dogs bark forebodingly as we pass houses. Rachel visibly stiffens. "I was bitten by a stray when I was ten," she explains. We use this as an excuse to turn back.

A stroll in the opposite direction takes us through fenced-in fields of garlic. It smells pleasantly pungent. Some plots of land are heavily irrigated, flooded with water. We cross a footbridge which spans the Rio San Juan, only a trickle this time of year.

A visibly-wasted man approaches us, mumbling something undiscernible. It sounds friendly. In Spanish, at least. He follows us, wanting a handout. "Ignore him," Glenn suggests. "He'll go away." As we continue walking, *el borracho* gets bored and leaves, just as Glenn predicts.

When we reach the center of Aguacatán, it's almost a reasonable time for supper. A number of *comedors* line the street but Glenn is looking for somewhere specific. "They've got a fawn in the backyard," he recalls. But all the *comedors* look the same from the outside: unremarkable adobe structures, in a row, painted different shades. "Here it is," Glenn finally says as we pass one eatery for the third time.

Inside, the Café Shaddai has about eight tables, all of them empty. The room is dimly lit by the fading daylight. Cotton cloths cover the surface of each vintage aluminum and Formica table, leftovers from America's 1960s suburbia. The floors are bare cement but swept and neat.

At the other end of the dining room is a doorway which leads to a backyard. A woman in her late 20s eventually comes out to greet us. Marisol remembers Glenn from his previous visit and is glad he's come by again. He introduces the three of us in Spanish and asks if she'll take us on a tour of the grounds. Marisol is more than happy to comply.

Like most of Aguacatán, chickens and rabbits wander in the dirt yard. Exactly as Glenn remembers it, the Café Shaddai has a young deer on the patio. She's tied to a pole, timid but trusting and affectionate as we approach to pet her. The deer is a lithe, beautiful creature, her fur coarser than you might think.

Two other women and their children come out of a room off the patio. It turns out to be the Shaddai's kitchen. They watch us, chuckling softly at our delight. "You don't see this in Brooklyn," Paul remarks, patting the deer's head. Guatemala is constantly proving itself to be the source of tiny, unexpected joys.

Marisol tells Glenn something in Spanish. He repeats it to us in English. "She says the deer came from very far away."

"Is it a pet or for food?" I whisper to Glenn.

He pauses, thinks of how to say this in his second tongue and asks. Marisol's face registers shock. Glenn blushes then tells us what she told him. "The deer is part of the family," he says. "Like one of her children."

"*Lo siento,*" I apologize to Marisol, horrified at what I made Glenn ask. The kitchen women giggle and disappear into the heated concrete box.

Glenn asks Marisol if she could make us dinner. "Not venison," he jokes. The woman nods, smiles and we are redeemed.

Marisol serves a feast of chicken, rice, beans and tortillas. And for me, there is an egg instead of chicken. We are the only customers the entire evening, though people come and go, visiting the women in the kitchen.

Sometimes the female cooks appear from its depths to unabashedly flirt with Glenn. Like the people in the market, they're particularly fascinated with his cornsilk-colored hair. One would-be suitor asks Glenn to marry her. Rachel frowns. "Just what did you do the last time you were here?" she says through clenched teeth. Glenn's response is his nervous titter.

Over supper, there's jovial talk between Glenn, Rachel and
Paul about people I don't know and things I haven't experienced.
The three of them are part of a secret club I don't belong to. I attempt
to join in but can't find the opening. It's odd seeing another woman
make Paul laugh. Does he truly find Rachel amusing or is he just being
polite? Then I remind myself that Paul is never polite just for the sake
of being polite.

Does Paul think Rachel is attractive? She of the straight, perfect
hair, she of the straight perfect teeth. What about when he and Glenn
were roommates? Did the sound of Glenn and Rachel having sex
permeate the apartment? Did Paul hear her whimpering like a puppy
or screaming like a banshee? I'm afraid of the answer but still, the
question plagues me. Eating my runny egg, I try to fit in but feel like a
hopelessly square peg.

~

At the market, Glenn has taken the liberty of buying a deck of
cards. It would help time pass during quiet hours in villages with no
nightlife, he reasons. "Places like Aguacatán?" I ask.

"Yes," he admits. There are no bars, no clubs in Aguacatán.
Saturdays, people turn in early to wake at dawn for the sprawling
Sunday market, so there isn't much happening on Saturday night.

Back in their room, Rachel suggests we play Hearts, a game
I've never heard of. That's something else I don't have in common
with the three of them—I hate playing cards. I'm bad at most games,
probably because I don't get the significance of games. What do games
have to do with real life? What do they matter? How can a straight
flush possibly impact my existence? Maybe that's why I am so horrible
at game-playing; I don't see the point.

But Glenn, Paul and Rachel really want to play Hearts. By their
quick description, I gather that it's an evasion-type of "trick-taking"
card game. They claim it needs four participants to be any good. So, I
agree to be their fourth.

Hearts' rules are straightforward enough but no matter what I
do, no matter how I will myself to concentrate, no matter what strategy
I use, I still lose. But I don't just lose, I am slaughtered. I shrug it off,
but they're tremendously competitive, taking delight in their victories
and taunting the loser. Who's usually me.

I hate being given a handicap or having special concessions
made for me as Rachel shaves points off my score to even out the

playing field. (The one with the lowest number of "hearts" wins.) I hate allowances being made for me in any aspect of my life. In the grand scheme of things, being defeated at Hearts doesn't matter. But I don't want to be seen as "dumb as a stump" in Paul's eyes. In an odd way, I want him to be proud of me.

Hearts unearths the difficult card games of my childhood. A math whiz, my dad is skilled at card-playing. Unlike him, I had a tough time counting to 21 under duress when we played Blackjack as a family. "How the hell can you be waiting for a ten?" my dad would berate me, exasperated. "Didn't you realize all the tens were out already?" Apparently not. It was challenging enough keeping track of my own hand, let alone the cards others cast out.

So, Glenn, Rachel, Paul and I play Hearts. I hate it but we keep on playing. For hours. Although I try to take it good-naturedly, the tears well up when they poke fun at me. I keep drawing "the Black Bitch" (aka the Queen of Spades) time after time. Is the game fixed? Are they cheating?

At least there are some breaks in my constant losing streak when Paul goes off to find beers and Rachel and I hunt for a suitable snack. All we find are third-rate chocolates. Paul manages to procure some *Gallos* before we resume Hearts. I find it boring. I find it senseless. The minutes seem endless but I don't say a thing. I just keep losing. We play until about nine, then Paul and I return to our luxurious hotel suite.

~

As we get ready for bed, Paul and I don't comment on our wreck of a room. It's not necessary but implied because it's so damned ramshackle. We keep looking at each other and laughing. Then I have the pleasure of using the Aguateco's communal bathroom for the first time.

Urine-stained corners of New York City subway stations smell better. I hold my breath as I pee into a hole in the ground. There's no toilet paper. There's no sink except the one outside the room. This means brushing your teeth in the courtyard with the chickens but at least chicken shit doesn't smell as bad as stale human piss.

Our beds are patched together from leftover pieces of wood. They're cots, really, with filthy lengths of material imitating sheets. I can't bear to undress. I sleep in long johns, socks and my hooded wind shell. When I unbutton the hem, it goes down as far as my ankles. But even that's not long enough. I wish I could crawl into a plastic trash bag to protect myself from what might be lurking in the mattress.

Cringing, I stretch out on the scratchy blanket. "This is something you'd throw over a horse," I grimace. There's no light in the room, except for Paul's flashlight, no electricity, even. But maybe that's a blessing in disguise—the less I see, the better.

When Paul snaps off the flashlight, the room goes black. There isn't even a moon to shine through the lone window. This will mark the first day in Guatemala that Paul and I don't make love. I can't fathom it in this squalor.

As I drift off, I keep envisioning fleas, lice and a fine assortment of maggots burrowing into my tender crevices. "This is the kind of place where you get scabies," I tell Paul.

"You need skin-to-skin contact to get scabies," he yawns.

"Thanks for that," I say.

I picture Paul and me picking bugs out of each other's hair like monkeys. I listen for the sounds of mice scampering along the floorboards or gently gnawing at the walls but hear only silence. I'm afraid to close my eyes so I stare into the dark. "I can't sleep, can you?" I ask Paul.

"No," he says. "Not with you talking."

"Can I come into your bed?" I ask.

"It's barely big enough for one person," he tells me. "Just go to sleep."

"But my skin is crawling. Do you think the Aguateco has fleas?"

"No," he says. "Rachel's scabies probably killed them all."

The clock in Aguacatán's church tower chimes on the hour. I listen to Paul's breathing grow heavy then hear him sputter into startled wakefulness every so often. Once, he wonders, "Are you awake?"

"Why? Do you want some company?" I ask expectantly.

Paul sighs, "I'm not going to get much rest anyway. Come on." I can barely decipher him holding the threadbare blanket aside for me. Before he can change his mind, I dash across the floor, hoping not to step on vermin in my socks. Paul's body curls around mine, big spoon cradling little spoon. I feel safe and warm.

We sleep like angels in a sullied heaven.

Day 15

Past midnight, there's a banging on the huge, bolted door that
turns the Aguateco into an impenetrable fortress. Finally, after 30
minutes or so, the nightwatchman wakes up to let the person in. I hear
loud grumbling in Spanish then quiet until the roosters begin their
mournful crowing. "Why do the roosters sound so sad in Aguacatán?"
I ask Paul, who is breathing delicately into my ear.

"Wouldn't you?" he yawns. "This place is a shithole." We roll
over in a synchronized swimming maneuver in the single bed and try
to go back to sleep. He does; I don't.

At about six, come sounds of movement and life. Of people
dressing. Of a baby crying. Of the shower water running in a glorified
trickle. Of bodies shuffling through the dirt courtyard. Aguacatán is
waking up. Hospedaje Aguateco is the lodging of choice for vendors
from neighboring villages to spent the night before Sunday market
where they will sell their wares.

Paul and I doze intermittently, then are officially up at 7:30. He
tells me about his terrible dream where I am brutally attacked before
his eyes and he can do nothing to stop it. It was as though his arms and
legs were caught in a thick molasses. "One night without sex and this
is what you dream about?" I say, trying to make light of it.

He shakes his head. "It was horrible."

"Which was worse?" I pose. "The dream? Or waking up in this place?"

"No contest," he says.

For people from villages even more remote than Aguacatán, having running water and a cold shower is a treat. But neither Paul or I are nervy enough to face the dribbling, frigid showerhead. Baby wipes do wonders in a pinch. We can both hold out until the next town. Instantly refreshed, we dress, smelling as clean as an infant's freshly-swabbed bottom.

When we meet in the open-air hallway en route to brushing our teeth, Glenn tells us he thinks the room was just fine. "I slept like a log," he yawns.

Paul and I crack up. "See? I told you," Paul says. "Glenn is easy to please. Not like you, princess. You expect bedsheets...and a flush toilet."

Rachel gives us her daily scabies update, telling us more detail than is necessary. Further into the trip, I find that if we forget to ask Rachel, "So, how's your scabies?" each morning, she's sullen the whole day. Glenn sighs because he's heard about every itch, scratch and new lesion during the night. Paul and I feign interest.

~

Aguacatán's market has grown exponentially overnight. We explore it deeper this time. Again, we are the sole foreigners. We buy a sweet pound cake as a prebreakfast snack and some mini bananas. As Paul passes, a young girl says, *"Gringo?"* and points.

Her mother is horrified but Paul laughs and tells the girl, *"Sì, gringo."*

Outside the Café Shaddai, a woman with a baby on her back loads sticks into her arms. The kindling is fuel for the stove that will prepare our breakfast. The child is chubby and would have made a perfect sepia-skinned cherub if not for the florid rash decorating her cheeks.

Inside the café, my companions eat eggs with beans and tortillas. Since I had the same dish for supper the night before, I order something dubiously called "chow mein." It turns out to be soft noodles with chicken and vegetables in a light broth. I pick out the chicken and give it to Paul. It's strange breakfast fare but filling and tasty.

As we leave Aguacatán, traffic on the outskirts of the village comes to a standstill. There are rarely tie-ups in the far-flung Western Highlands—except for stops caused by military searches.

"What's going on?" Paul asks. Glenn shrugs as he inches the Suzuki forward. Then we see a pair of bulls fighting in the middle of the road. Everyone is afraid to drive past because the strapping beasts butt horns ferociously and rear up on their hind legs.

Foot travelers and drivers keep a safe distance as we observe *machismo* in the raw. The boy leading the bulls and cows into another field stands waiting, wise enough not to interfere. One bull considers our gleaming red Suzuki as though it's a matador's cape. "Is he going to charge?" Rachel pipes. Glenn giggles. But the bull thinks better of it.

The creature's horns and head are enormous. "He would have torn up the truck like a piece of cardboard," Paul says as the cows, the bull and his rival are led to greener pastures.

~

The road to Nebaj is narrow, bumpy and steep. The land on either side of us reminds me of the Grand Canyon with plunging gorges that extend as far as the eye can see and a lazy river carving through the base. Pines, scrub, vast stretches of grass and cactus are plentiful. The view is so glorious that we ask Glenn to stop a number of times so we can take pictures.

Paul chooses a plot of land where we could build Blackie's, raise a thousand brats and wake to Paradise every morning. "Here or in Livingston? I'm confused," I ask him.

"Both," Paul responds.

Glenn calls us back to the Samurai. "It's a long drive," he says.

On the bank of the Rio Blanco is Sacapulas, a village at the crossroads to many destinations. A cluster of market stands sell produce from the surrounding plains. There's also a section for livestock. Here, pigs and burros are tied with rope to a nest of trees. Interested buyers slap the animals' flanks and check their teeth. A soccer game is in full swing in a mucky field a hundred feet away.

We buy sodas in plastic bags and take in the game. Across the Rio Blanco, a cluster of women and children bathe, naked, in view of anyone who cares to look. Gauguin meets Renoir. Most people, except for us, opt to watch the soccer.

The Suzuki forges ahead to Nebaj. The village is off the main highway, about 13 miles down a bad road. Outside town is a civilian patrol hut. The radio is blasting and the lone guard's machine gun is tipped toward the road. Glenn whizzes past the hut, undaunted.

Despite the weaponry, Nebaj is pastoral, cupped in a valley situated high in the hazy mountains. It's bathed in what the locals call a *chipi-chipi*—a fuzzy, constant mist, too light to be a drizzle. We drive slowly along Nebaj's main street, which is unpaved and dusty.

Although *The Real Guide* names three places to stay in Nebaj, we can only find one: The Hotel Ixil. It's a large, newly-whitewashed building whose rooms surround a big, tiled courtyard. Unlike the Aguateco, the Ixil's patio is chicken-free. Instead of fowl, it has a flower garden plus two moldy fountains.

The accommodations are also tiled, huge, cavernous, with four single beds. We wisely decide not to share a room; each couple gets their own. At the proprietor's request, Glenn backs the truck into our own private parking space in the courtyard.

A street boy named César pounces on Glenn the minute he climbs out of the Suzuki. César has the heavy features of one on the cusp of Down Syndrome. He's affectionate, smiling and full of hugs. César remembers Glenn from his last visit to Nebaj. And who wouldn't remember a blonde-haired, light-skinned Brooklynite who speaks fluent Spanish?

~

We walk through Nebaj's streets, past the barber shop, whose curtained-off side room houses not a porn theater, but a mini cinema that constantly plays karate and action/adventure flicks. Their "bang! boom!" soundtrack spills onto the hard, clay streets, thick as syrup.

Moving past town square, Nebaj's few stores display faded wares in their streaked windows. Beyond the cement saltbox houses, past the open-air market, Nebaj becomes immediately rural. Glenn leads us along a road that branches off to the right, toward structures which are situated further apart than they are in the center of town. These homes have front and back yards. Some even have scraggly gardens.

Glenn points to a plain cinderblock building. "That's where I stayed with friends the last time I was in Nebaj." The house is owned by Juana Marcos, who we're on our way to visit.

"Then why didn't we stay there?" I ask.

"No electricity," Glenn says.

"Like the Aguateco?" Paul wonders.

Glenn shrugs, "Cleaner. A lot nicer. But I don't think Rachel would like it." She squints at Glenn as she scratches a newfound itch.

Several hundred feet down the road is the home where Juana and her family live. Glenn opens the roughly-hewn wood gate and goes inside. Pigs and chickens roam Juana's front yard. Her house is a typical cement box but with a porch along the entire length. It's very simple, unadorned and utilitarian. Juana is considered prosperous for the area. After all, she owns two homes, one of which she rents out to travelers.

Juana's son Jacinto comes out of the house, immediately recognizes Glenn and embraces him warmly. Then a squat, round woman bounds out the door. "Len!" she says, faltering over the "g" in Glenn's name. Meet Juana Marcos.

Her Spanish is oddly accented and comes slowly. Juana murmurs something to Glenn as she wraps her arms around his towering frame. She hugs him like he is her fair-haired Prodigal son come home to Nebaj.

Juana has a pleasing, moon-shaped, jolly face, and a ready smile that suits her. Her grin comes easily but can leave just as sudden as an unexpected breeze. In the next beat, she will be solemn and stone-faced again. Juana's Indian blood gives her prominent Mayan cheekbones and leather-toned skin. She wears a wide red *corte* (skirt), the bright *huipil* of the region, with its signature geometric pattern and a woven sash around her waist (called a *faja*). Juana's colorful matching *cinta* wraps around her head, partially masking her dark-as-ink hair.

An earnest, caring woman, Juana seems eternally happy. She carries herself with the dignity of an indigenous queen. Deeply spiritual, her kindness shines from the inside out. She's one of those rare people you immediately take a liking to—and have no idea why. While we are in Nebaj, Juana will treat us like family, feeding us and fussing over us as if we're her own children.

Although she's just met Rachel, Paul and me, Juana hugs each of us, even though she doesn't yet know our names. The sheer fact that we're friends of "Len's" is more than enough reason to embrace us. There's both love and strength in her arms as she wishes us each a ceremonious *"Feliz Navidad"* though Christmas is still several weeks off.

Juana's affection is uncomplicated and real. She shares the stark honesty of little César, even though she doesn't share his simple mind. Juana invites us to stay for a cup of *cabe* ("coffee" in her dialect). It is more a command than a question, her phrasing so insistent it would be rude to refuse.

While Juana prepares the coffee, we wait on her porch. Glenn explains to us that her native tongue is Ixil (one of 22 or so indigenous languages spoken in Guatemala) and that she is K'iche', of rich Mayan heritage. This explains her unusual accent, her slow and thoughtful *Español* with an Ixil twist. Glenn translates Juana's Spanish for us and our English into Spanish for her.

~

It is probably the longest cup of coffee in the history of cups of coffee. Before Juana actually makes it, she runs off, literally, then comes back breathless. "Excuse me," she apologizes, "but I had to chase the pig. He got loose." It seems that Rachel forgot to close the gate behind her.

Then Juana ducks back into her kitchen to boil water. Hopefully the chickens won't run off this time.

When it comes, Juana's coffee is the typical sweet mixture so prominent in Guatemala, especially in destitute regions. It's instant Nescafé tempered with milk and plenty of sugar, of which there is no shortage. With the *cabe,* Juana serves whole wheat buns. They're still warm from the oven.

Juana seems genuinely pleased to see us, pleased to have such exotic company. She insists on carrying her frayed kitchen chairs out to the porch one by one so we can sit and enjoy her coffee. She won't accept help from her guests.

Glenn asks Juana if it might be possible for us to have a *chuj* later in the day. A *chuj,* I soon learn, is a Mayan-Mam steam bath which is supposed to be purifying for the soul and good for the constitution. Glenn tells us there's a special stone structure in Juana's backyard for this very purpose. It sits a foot off the ground so a fire can be lit underneath.

Juana thinks a moment then says that Jacinto can have the *chuj* ready in the early evening. It takes hours for the wood to burn then die down to the smoldering embers that heat the *chuj* to the correct temperature. We should return around six, she says.

Then Glenn wonders if Juana could cook us the meal which traditionally follows the *chuj,* a dish called *bosh bol.* Glenn describes it as corn meal wrapped in a squash leaf, boiled, then dipped into a spicy salsa. "*Bosh bol* sounds a lot like Guatemalan stuffed grape leaves," Rachel says.

"Similar but not really," Glenn tells her. But he swears it's delicious. *Bosh bol* is also said to be cleansing for the digestive system.

The dish has a secret ingredient which Juana will tell no one. If she's able to find the proper herbs, she says she can make *bosh bol.* Again, Juana runs off. She soon returns with a fistful of greens. Juana tells Glenn that though it's past harvest time, she's managed to find the squash leaves required for the dish. She will be glad to prepare *bosh bol* for us.

Juana's teenage daughter Magdalena watches from the doorway as Juana proudly shows off the weavings the girl has made. "This is a horse, not a reindeer," Juana says emphatically as she fingers a scarf. She tells us how the local hotels won't let her sell her family's wares to their guests. This is all acted out quite dramatically, with imaginary slammed doors, stomping and such.

Magdalena listens, mooning at Glenn. She's a lovely girl, about 16, with *café con leche* skin and a cautious but radiant face. Magdalena wears Nebaj's customary dress but no *cinta.* She moves gracefully as she comes onto the porch to help her mother.

When we finish our coffee, Juana produces yet another object from the depths of her cement home. This time, it's a dog-eared, leatherette autograph binder. It's the sort of book high school seniors inscribe silly sayings into so their classmates won't forget them. Juana presents her book to me as sacredly as one might handle a Bible.

I open the binder and read other travelers' reflections about their time with the Marcos Family. They're written in numerous languages—Hebrew, Danish, German, English—and the words are glowing, genuine, sentiments that are heartfelt and carefully crafted. We promise Juana we'll add our reflections after tonight's *chuj* and supper.

Perhaps the most amazing thing about Juana's cottage tourist industry is that she isn't mentioned in any guidebook and she doesn't run ads for her services. Word of mouth is her sole means of advertisement. Yet, she manages to support herself, her four children and their children with what she earns. She always has a steady flow of guests.

We leave Juana with the promise of returning in a few hours.

~

Although Juana's coffee and rolls have satiated us somewhat, we're still hungry. It's two in the afternoon and we need a proper lunch so we head to the market. A girl points us out and says, *"Ve! Ve! Ve!"*

Glenn explains, "That means 'Look! Look! Look!'"

"I figured," Paul laughs. He smiles at the girl, who hides behind her mother's skirts as we crisscross through the congested marketplace.

For a village the size of Nebaj, they are surprisingly short on eateries. We pass a large *comedor* which gains Rachel's approval. There is one choice: chicken. I promise my poultry to my tablemates.

Outside the *comedor's* open front door, children and stray dogs jockey for position. One mongrel is so thin it's entirely possible he could collapse with his next struggled breath. Seeing this makes Xela's yearly dog poisonings seem humane. What can be done about the hungry children, though?

I fork strips of chicken from my plate onto a paper napkin. "You can't feed the whole village," Paul tells me with a full mouth. I put another piece of chicken onto the napkin. "I'm serious," he adds.

"He's right," Glenn says. "It will cause a fight."

"Between the dogs or the kids?" I ask.

"Probably both," he nods.

Reluctantly, I transfer the chicken onto Paul's plate and choke down my rice, beans and avocado slices, trying not to acknowledge the stares.

The sounds of John Rambo's machine-gun patter spills onto the street from the barbershop cinema as we return to our rooms for an hour's nap in the clean dampness. But first, a shower to rinse the imagined filth from the Aguateco off my skin.

The sheets are so cool that they feel wet until Paul's and my bodies heat them. Before sleep, I find Paul's flesh, fitting him into my fist, then into me. Damp kisses, searching tongues, hard and soft spilling one into the other then the sensation of falling, unraveling and landing with a thump.

~

Although Rachel and I hang socks and underwear on the clothesline strung between the pillars outside our rooms, we know they'll never dry in Nebaj's damp climate. Not in the fuzzy *chipi-chipi* that coats the mountain air. Not quite rain, not quite not.

Just before six, the four of us begin walking back to Juana's. It's already growing dark. Her porch's sensor lights snap on as we approach. Jacinto appears and invites us inside.

Juana's house is so upscale that it has a stone floor instead of swept dirt. The kitchen takes up most of the space in this two-roomed structure. A stove built from cement blocks and fueled by wood stands in one corner. A large cauldron sits on one of its burners. Its contents boil, a comforting aroma filling the air. Juana stands there, stirring. Christmas lights are suspended from the opposite wall. They wink at us, another testament to the fact that the Marcos Family has the luxury of electricity.

Juana leads us to her backyard, to a stone hut that measures about six feet by six feet square and is just as tall. She hands Glenn two candles, lights one, then the other, and leaves us alone.

Glenn balances the candles on the ground then begins undressing. He already knows the drill. "This is how it works," he explains, pulling his t-shirt over his head. "You take off your clothes, grab your stuff and get into the *chuj*."

"How?" I wonder.

He points to a small opening at the front of the *chuj*, no larger than a doggie door. "You crawl in," Glenn tells us. "On your hands and knees. One at a time."

"Together?" I ask.

Glenn nods.

"Naked?"

He nods again.

Paul is already down to his boxers. Rachel wears only her long peasant blouse. "Okay?" Glenn asks me.

"Okay," I tell him, slipping down my jeans. We try our best not to look at each other but look anyway.

Glenn manages the pair of candles while Rachel carries the soap and shampoo for the two of them. The last to go in, I tuck my toiletry bag into my armpit and creep along the wooden plank propped above the dirt, crawling on all fours.

Inside the *chuj*, it is unbearably hot, almost too hot to function. Every inhalation is a struggle. It's like someone is holding a wet cloth over my nose and mouth. My first instinct is to panic, to scream. I suppress the desire to cry out and force myself to take slow, measured respirations. But the panic returns.

"I have to get out," I whisper to Paul, my voice wavering. "I can't breathe. I'm smothering."

"You'll be fine," he insists, squeezing my hand. "Relax. You'll be fine. I promise."

I'm a scuba diver without the proper gear. I'm a landlocked fish sucking in drippy air instead of water.

Eventually, I become accustomed to the flickering candlelight. The *chuj's* ceiling is about five-foot-high so there isn't enough room to stand up straight. Paul and I sit on a ledge at one side of the *chuj*. Glenn and Rachel sit on the other. A series of water jugs in different sizes surround us. "Some are cool," Glenn explains. "Some warm and some are scalding."

"What do we do with them?" Paul asks.

"You mix the water in these bowls..." Glenn gestures to the tower of ceramic dishes Juana has left for us. "...until it's the temperature you want. Then you dump it over your head."

"Why?" Rachel asks.

Glenn doesn't answer. He just takes one of the vessels, mixes water from two jugs and pours it over his scalp. The water spilling from his body hits the heated rocks, causing them to sizzle. "That's why," he tells Rachel. "The cold water on the hot stones makes it even steamier. It's good for your lungs and also opens your pores. Gets rid of the toxins."

Paul and I take turns washing each other. There's something so sensual and primal about this, something so intimate. The nudity between the four of us is no longer an issue. It's natural. There's no shame, no embarrassment, only the reality of sharing a cleansing sweat bath among friends.

I am no longer struggling to breathe. Maybe my frenzied inhalations have slowed. Maybe my body has relaxed. I'm in a semi-hypnotic state. My hair is soaking wet, my skin damp, all from the steam.

Our bodies are exquisitely beautiful in the glow of the dual candles. It's as though we've been painted by Vermeer at dusk. There's no cellulite, no spider veins. The dinosaur spine motif of the scar on Paul's shoulder from a cycling accident years earlier (a marking I love, even in daylight) is graceful and full of character.

I pour a bowl of hot water over Paul's head then lather his skull with shampoo. My fingertips vibrate with life. So does his hair, like golden electrical strands tickling my palms. But as I soap Paul's back, everything suddenly goes pitch black.

"Shit!" Rachel curses. By accident, she doused both candles with a ladleful of water. "Damn it!" she yells.

Since I'm closest to the doorway, I rummage around for the *chuj's* opening. Only I can't find it. At first, we giggle in the dark like kids at a sleepover. Then I start to panic. "There *is* no opening," I tell them.

"What do you mean? There has to be," Paul says.

"I...can't find it...it's not here." My fingertips detect a slight indentation and another above it. Then I touch the thick burlap curtain that hangs in front of the opening. But there's a hard, heavy object blocking the cloth. "Juana must have pushed a stone in front of the curtain to keep in the heat," I panic.

"Can you move it?" Rachel asks.

"I'll try." With my shoulder, I struggle to push away the rock but it won't budge. "We're going to die in here," I lament.

"That's the secret ingredient in *bosh bol*," Rachel says. "Tourists!"

We laugh, in spite of ourselves. Maybe the laughter gives me more strength but I'm finally able to move aside the rock. A sliver of cool, night air kisses my face. "Juana!" I shout. "*Ayuda! Ayuda!*"

I watch Juana's feet as she runs from the kitchen to the backyard. She crawls into the *chuj's* opening, wagging her finger at us. Juana relights both candles, then leaves us to finish our soak.

We wash and steam our road-weary flesh without further incident. Then we splash ourselves with frigid water to close our pores. When we're done, we crawl out of the *chuj* to dry in the evening air. My skin feels tingly and sparkly.

~

Off in the distance, the light coming from Juana's house is wooly and fuzzy. I am nicely dizzy and drunk from the sudden hot-to-cold transition. We dress quietly. Like a drunk, I enjoy the liquidity of my limbs.

Glenn plops into a hammock as soon as we step into Juana's kitchen, lazily pumping his foot, swinging back and forth. The dinner table is set as nicely as Juana can manage. It doesn't matter that none of the cups, plates or silverware match. A pair of candles burn brightly, stuck in empty soda bottles that double as holders. The room takes on a magical cast.

Pots bubble on the stove. We alternate between taking sips of sugary coffee and *cuxa,* a potent local liquor. The clear-colored corn mash smells strong, like vodka. It's smooth going down, almost tasteless, but packs a punch. *Cuxa* is typically enjoyed with wedges of lime which you squeeze into a shot glass or suck, *"Como quieras,"* Juana says. *As you like.* She has a plate of sliced limes on the table for us too.

In the dim, mellow candlelight, Juana wonders if we are ready to eat. *"Sì,"* Glenn tells her. *"Por favor."* Magdalena serves the *bosh bol* from a big clay pot. The steamed squash leaves are a bright, cheerful green and surprisingly tender when I sink my teeth into one. At first, the salsa bath doesn't seem spicy but with every spoonful, it grows hotter. After they serve us, Glenn urges Magdalena and Juana to join us at the table. Hesitantly, they do.

A tabby cat slips in, rubbing against our legs. Oddly enough, he's called Pasquale. "He is named for a tall foreigner," Juana explains.

Glenn asks if many homes in Nebaj have cats. "I see lots of dogs but not cats," he says in Spanish. Magdalena says that cats are house pets while dogs are creatures of the street, in homes for protection. It makes a bizarre sort of sense.

As Glenn pets Pasquale with one hand and eats with the other, the cat bites him. Juana apologizes and shoos the cat. Quite earnestly, Miguel, Juana's youngest, says Pasquale has rabies. Glenn's face drops until he realizes Miguel is joking. Bilingual rabies jokes abound.

Juana tells us the condensed version of her life story, translated by Glenn. A widow with a quartet of kids, Juana's oldest daughter is grown and married. The "baby" Miguel, is 14. One of Juana's grandchildren, a tousle-haired imp, age three, named Daniel, lives with the Marcos Family as well.

Her eyes cloud as Juana recounts that her husband died four years earlier. "Of stomach troubles," she sighs. I almost choke on the *bosh bol.* "I hope it wasn't from her cooking," I say to Paul. He turns so he doesn't crack up.

At one time, Juana and her husband owned five houses but she had to sell off three to support the rest of the family. Now they only have this one and the windowless cement shack they rent out down the road.

Juana takes a bite of the *bosh bol* and chews thoughtfully. "The young these days, they don't want to keep up the old traditions," she complains, staring straight at Magdalena.

"How so?" Glenn asks.

"They're so modern. They won't wear the *cinta*. And they want to wear shoes!" Juana continues, exasperated.

Magdalena rolls her eyes in teenage disgust. Until Glenn tells her that he'd like to see her in a *cinta*. Then Magdalena dashes off to the adjoining room to wrap her head. We smile at the girl's innocent teenage crush. All except Rachel, who smirks uncomfortably then glares at Glenn. "What exactly went on the last time you were here?" she asks for the second time.

We are one big, happy dysfunctional family laughing in two languages, eating the same food at the same table in the same room in the same house but from extremely different places.

Feeling relaxed from the *chuj* and the *cuxa*, I find the courage to ask Juana if she will tie my head in the *cinta*. I'm afraid she might take offense to my request, that she might consider it an infringement on the rich customs of K'iche'. But instead, Juana is honored, proud, even. She excuses herself to find a spare *cinta* in her bedroom and returns to begin her task.

Juana stands behind me as I sit at the kitchen table. Her fingers are butterfly soft as she wraps the cloth around my ponytail then weaves the *cinta* to rest on top of my head. The *cinta* is heavy, itchy and uncomfortable. I can understand why teenagers don't like wearing it. I can't imagine how Juana dons hers all day long, cooking in it, chasing pigs in it. I guess after decades, she got used to it. But perhaps because the *cinta* isn't part of my culture, I immediately feel self-conscious wearing it.

"The *cinta* looks great on you," Paul says, while Juana beams. He poses us for a photograph. I smile while Juana is solemn as a stone. It reminds me of the African cultures who believe that a camera will steal your soul. Maybe the K'iche' people feel this way too.

I remove the *cinta* as soon as Paul takes the picture. Juana seems slightly wounded but says nothing.

Magdalena emerges from the bedroom soon after, her own *cinta* tied in a slightly different fashion than her mother's. Is this an act of defiance? A stab at self-expression amid oppressive traditions? Or just her own personal style? The girl blushes when Glenn compliments her; Rachel huffs softly and turns away.

More rabid dog jokes are passed back and forth across the table. Juana's grandson Daniel coughs and cries in his sleep in the adjoining bedroom. "Rabies," his uncle Miguel says, shaking his head sadly.

We could have spent hours longer in Juana's kitchen, eating and teasing, but it's growing late and Juana looks tired. She only asks 25 quetzals apiece for the feast, liquor and the *chuj*—roughly five dollars each—but Glenn presses more into her palm. No price tag can be put on spending a few hours in someone's home, welcomed like relatives. We promise to bring Juana a circle of cheese from the nearby factory on the outskirts of Acul after we visit it tomorrow. It's the least we can do for Juana's hospitality.

On the walk back to the Hotel Ixil, the sky is a fairy-tale shade of indigo. Paul and I sleep easily in the pitch blackness of our room, pushing the single beds together and using each other's bodies to fend off the dampness.

Day 16

Monday, December 6, 1993
Nebaj

The minute I wake up, I realize that my skin is still tingling from the *chuj*. Or maybe I've caught Rachel's scabies. I feel so spotless that I veto a cold-water shower. I'm afraid it will somehow wash away last night's magic.

The four of us breakfast on *panqueques* at a long table in an open room off the Hotel Ixil's courtyard. *Panqueques* is a popular, Guatamalacized version of American pancakes—and this is the first time it's appeared as *"panqueques"* on the menu. Except in Guate, every hotel and *comedor* makes pancakes differently. Some are thin like crepes while others are thick as steaks. But none are like IHOP's pancakes back in the States.

The Ixil's *panqueques* are served with honey dispensed from an old ketchup bottle and homemade guava jelly. There's no maple syrup—presumably because there are no maple trees in Guatemala—and we don't miss it. Although the *panqueques* at the Ixil are delicious, they're also small, about the size of powder puffs, and we are each given just three. To fill our bellies, we munch on the day-old sweet bread from Aguacatán's market.

As we pack the Samurai for the day's travels around Nebaj, Glenn tells us that last night, Magdalena asked if she could come with us. He said yes because he didn't think we'd mind. Paul and I don't; Rachel does. Magdalena's crush on Glenn is only a teenager's harmless infatuation but Rachel huffs anyhow. "What?" he asks.

"Nothing," Rachel says, turning away.

I realize that we've forgotten to ask Rachel about her scabies status and maybe this accounts for her pissy mood. "How are the scabies this morning?" I wonder brightly, although I don't really care.

"A little better, thanks," Rachel pipes, then shows me a dry lesion on her forearm. "See?" Then she picks up her pant leg to display a florid new blotch above her ankle. It's kind of gross but if it makes Rachel less sullen, I'm willing to look at her rash.

As we drive toward the Marcos compound in the compact Suzuki, Rachel starts up again about Magdalena. "Where will we put her?" she wonders.

When Paul suggests, "On Glenn's lap," Rachel scowls at him, scratching.

"She's petite," Glenn says warily. "We'll figure it out." He told Magdalena to meet us at the crossroads at ten. But when we arrive just after the hour, she still isn't there. "People are consistently late here," Glenn explains. "No wristwatches. No clocks."

We turn down the dirt road and park. Glenn goes to Juana's. He returns with not only Magdalena but with her nephew Daniel in tow. I remember the boy from yesterday, smiling timidly at us from between the slats of his *abuela's* porch and calling woefully from his bed.

As we squeeze Magdalena and Daniel into the Samurai, Glenn mentions that everyone in the house wanted to come along, including Juana, but there's barely enough room for the two we take. Daniel sits on Rachel's lap in the front seat while Magdalena wedges between Paul and me in the back. She is so tiny that the *cinta* wrapped around her head doesn't even touch the inside of the roof.

At three years old, this marks only the second time Daniel has been in a car. Unlike most toddlers, the child is unnaturally still, quiet and attentive, almost reverent. *"Coche!"* he says excitedly. *"Coche!"* Car! Car!

~

The road to Acul is especially bouncy. As Glenn attacks it more aggressively than he should, Paul's head cracks into the roof. Hard. He tries to hold his tongue because Magdalena and Daniel are in the car. "Hey, take it easy, dude," Paul snaps. When he really wants to say, "Fuck!"

Glenn's "10 minutes away" stretches into a grueling 30. With the extra weight we're carrying, he has to speed up to gain enough momentum to mount every hill. Unfortunately, the mangled roads prohibit anything beyond a jerky crawl, so we're trapped in the middle of another Guatemalan Catch-22.

After banging his skull on the inside of the Samurai's roof one time too many, Paul yells, "Stop the car!" Glenn doesn't. Then again, "Stop the car!" Paul shouts, even louder.

Glenn turns to me. "Is he serious?"

I glance at Paul. "He looks serious to me," I tell Glenn. "I'd stop if I were you." But Glenn keeps going, only more slowly now.

Just as Glenn revs the engine to tackle another hill, Paul forces him to pull over. We convince Glenn to lighten the load and let us out so we can walk the remainder of the trip to the cheese factory. It isn't far. In fact, we can see it several hundred yards in the distance.

Going by foot is a much more satisfying mode of travel. Especially for Paul's head. He and I amble through the countryside, hilly and lush as a Juan Valdez coffee ad. Cows and sheep graze lazily in the heavy *chipi-chipi* which quickly progresses into a sopping downpour. Our wet weather gear is back in the Suzuki but it doesn't matter. It's refreshing plus the rain brings out the greenness around us.

A lamb runs to its mother in a panic as we pass. Tufts of wool stick to the barbed wire which separates the fields from the road. The torrent eases into a *chipi-chipi* as the Suzuki pulls into a spot in front of the cheese factory. Paul and I catch up as everyone piles out of the car.

~

Finca San Antonio's main building is an odd bird. It's something you'd expect to find in the Alps instead of in Guatemala's Sierra de los Cuchumatanes. A handful of other white buildings surround it, none of which have the same Swiss village motif. They're boxy, utilitarian and industrial.

Although the old Italian man who owned the cheese factory recently died, Glenn tells us that his cheese lives on. The overseer who greets us is tall and light-skinned, a *Ladino* (of Spanish heritage), and is glad to give us a tour. His English is flawless.

Although they're all native Guatemalans, Magdalena and her young nephew look very different than the overseer. They are clearly Indian, with rich, bronze skin and the gorgeously-sculpted cheekbones of Mayan royalty. Little Daniel speaks no Spanish (his first language is Ixil), and Magdalena, just a bit. Indigenous people are considered inferior by those with European blood. This becomes more than evident to us on the cheese factory tour.

In the first room, we are shown a huge copper pot where the milk is heated. Glenn pretends to throw Daniel into an empty cauldron as the child squeals with glee. The boy instinctively knows that Glenn is joking and would never hurt him. But then again, could Glenn possibly be *Micolash,* the bogeyman who steals Guatemalan children to make soap out of them?

On our tour, Magdalena hangs in the background, suddenly self-conscious. It's almost as if she's afraid she doesn't belong here. Maybe the *Ladino* overseer silently makes her feel unwelcome.

Our guide painstakingly explains the cheesemaking process. Maybe a bit too painstakingly. He takes us into the adjoining room where the spongy curds are aged. The goat's milk cheese, he tells us, is made in another section, separate from the cow's milk cheese. We ask to try both.

Happy to comply, the man slices off hunks of each cheese with a large, sharp knife. He then cuts the big pieces into smaller ones for the four of us to taste. The man hands samples to me, Paul, Glenn and Rachel. But there's none for Magdalena and Daniel, who watch this transpire, embarrassed.

Glenn's face reddens with anger. "How about our friends?" he wonders. Then Glenn asks Magdalena, "Would you like some?" She nods sheepishly but won't meet his gaze. The overseer tries to cover up his ethnic blunder and gives Magdalena a piece. She shares it with Daniel, still not making eye contact. They are like small, brown mice nibbling at a snack.

Is the overseer's slight an honest mistake? Or is it because Magdalena and Daniel are indigenous people, not of pure Spanish blood like him? Did the man think they were our servants simply because they're Indians? And even if they were "the help," would this be a reason to deny them food?

Glenn clenches his jaw, still seething. "Do you believe this bullshit?" he says to us through his teeth.

When the overseer leaves briefly to check on a vat, we four have a quick conference. Our first impulse is to leave without buying anything. This will give the overseer the message that we don't appreciate the way he treated our friends. But we promised Juana a wheel of cheese and the man has given us his time.

In the end, we decide to buy two circles of cheese, one of each type. At 80 quetzals a pound (the equivalent of 16 dollars), it's expensive for Guatemala, a delicacy. One disc of cheese will be our lunch and the other, a gift for Juana to thank her for her generosity. Although they are not poor by Nebaj standards—they've traveled to Livingston and Todos Santos on trips—the cheese is a luxury item the Marcos Family cannot afford. It's our pleasure to give it to them.

~

From Finca San Antonio, we take a short walk to the village of Acul itself. In the late 1970s and early 1980s, 400 towns in the Western Highlands were completely wiped out by the Guatemalan Army. Totally obliterated. Acul was the first in a string of model villages the government rebuilt. The irony is that the very Army which originally destroyed Acul also rebuilt it.

The resurrection of villages like this was done as cheaply as possible, tin roofs and all. Acul is a sad, soulless place. Strange, but the piecemeal shacks the peasants have built themselves aren't as depressing as Acul's more modern structures. Maybe it's because the villagers' slapdash homes aren't prefab nightmares.

As we head back to Finca San Antonio from Acul, Glenn and Rachel take the opportunity to bring up Paul's old drinking habits. Luckily, it's in English so Magdalena and Daniel don't understand. "Do you remember when you crawled into my bed by mistake one night?" Glenn asks.

"How do you know it was by mistake?" Paul counters. "Besides, you loved spooning me." Glenn laughs tensely.

"How about when you brought back those two homeless guys?" Rachel chimes right in.

Glenn tag teams, "When we woke up in the morning, they were gone and so was your VCR and my leather jacket."

"How many times do I have to hear about that piece of shit leather jacket from Domsey's?" Paul sighs. "I'll buy you another one just so you'll shut up about it."

Next, Rachel brings up the frantic phone calls from Paul's longsuffering ex when Leah was working in Italy for six months. (What kind of idiot would leave Paul alone for half a year!) He was either barhopping or in an unrousable Budweiser coma when her transatlantic anguish-ridden messages flowed in. "I don't know how Leah dealt with you," Rachel says.

The subtext of Rachel's comment is: how can Carol deal with you? But Paul is a different person with me. I think. Isn't he?

Paul takes most of this good-naturedly, but when we're out of earshot, he mutters, "Heather had no problem dealing with me." Heather! This is the first time I've ever heard about any Heather. Who the hell is Heather? True, Leah is a sore spot but this Heather thing grates on me differently. She's proof of Paul's past infidelities. Which makes me wonder, *'Is he cheating on me?'*

'He's in Guatemala with you, asshole. How could he be cheating on you?' Good Carol lambasts me a second later.

My brain starts doing cartwheels. The whole element of trust, me trusting Paul, is questioned. I know you can't judge a person by their past—God knows, mine is a checkerboard. And I also know that toward the end of my marriage, I'd behaved no better than Paul did in his death-throes with Leah.

But the difference is that although I'm eager to confess my sins, Paul doesn't want to hear about my cheating history. In a sick, masochistic way, I crave every last detail about Paul's past transgressions. Why? To torture myself? No. To protect myself, maybe. To gird my loins. To be prepared for what Paul might do to me. But in another way, hearing about his lost loves wounds me. Like it would any sane, or semi-sane, person.

Cautiously, Paul submits to my "Heather questions" as we linger behind the others on the walk back to Acul. "Heather and her roommates lived next door to my parents," Paul explains. "She was young, from Ohio. And dumb enough to wear a black bra under a red negligee once."

"Whoa," I put my hands up, as if to ward off his words. "Black bra, red negligee...TMI."

Paul reels himself back in. "Okay. What else? Heather wore neckties years after *Annie Hall* made it cool. Man, how I hated that look."

"You're no fashion plate yourself," I say, gesturing to his worn-out Hawaiian shirt.

"Point well taken," Paul admits. "You sure you want to do this?" I shrug. He sighs. "Heather kept making cow eyes at me. I eventually gave in when Leah moved to Italy. Then I tried to drop Heather when Leah came back."

"And she didn't want to be dropped," I finish for him.

"Pretty much," he admits. "It was messy and ugly."

"Those things usually are."

"Speaking from experience?" Paul asks. "Wait! Don't answer that." He takes a deep breath and continues. "Leah found out, had a mini breakdown."

"Popped some more Valium?" I venture.

"I should have never told you," Paul groans. "But I can't hide anything from you, Carol."

Why does this man care for me? I haven't got a clue. Back in our San Pedro cell, Paul had told me, "You have no idea how much I love you," then promptly rolled over and fell asleep. Why do guys need to be so macho on the outside when they are as fragile and vulnerable as women are on the inside?

These past two-and-a-half weeks, Paul and I have been through so many changes. Except for bathroom time, we're constantly at each other's side. And we aren't sick of each other. Yet.

I'm starting to worry about what will happen back in the real world when we get home. Working our jobs. Weathering day-to-day struggles. But I shouldn't think about that now. I should just enjoy this. Whatever *this* is.

"Are you done with the interrogation?" Paul asks.

"I guess so," I tell him. "Enough self-torture for now."

"Carol, I…" Paul starts but doesn't finish. We head back to the Suzuki to meet Glenn, Rachel and our hitchhikers.

~

On the return ride to Nebaj, Rachel chivalrously invites Paul to sit in the passenger's seat. There's more headroom up front and little danger of banging his head on the roof. Since Rachel is at least six inches shorter than him, this should have been the seating arrangement from Day One. But anyway.

It's a quiet drive back without a cursefest from Paul. Daniel is on his lap, which is probably a wiser choice than having the kid on Scabies Sally's lap. Paul practices his Spanish on Daniel, trading words back and forth.

The boy is less wary than he was with Rachel and gets wildly excited whenever he encounters something new, like a bulldozer. But then again, almost everything is new to Daniel. He's so easy to please. I mean, he literally skipped after I gave him a Tic Tac in Acul.

"*Choo-cha!*" Daniel coos and points.

"That's Ixil slang for 'dog,'" Glenn tells us.

For a guy who says he hates children, Paul is charmed with Daniel. Which is easy considering the boy's impish smile and huge chocolate eyes.

We leave Magdalena and her nephew at the crossroads with their ring of cheese, promising to return for dinner at about seven. Our last night in Nebaj, Juana has invited us back to say a proper goodbye.

~

Glenn leaves the Suzuki at the Hotel Ixil where we weigh our lunch options. Which are limited. Weary of *comedors,* we hit the market. As we food-shop, I can't resist buying a dark scarf with Nebaj's signature geometric pattern woven into it. Then the four of us focus on produce.

The fruits and vegetables are wonderful. We choose perfect avocados, tomatoes and scallions to make guacamole. This plus sweet rolls and the cheese from Finca San Antonio rounds out our meal.

Back at the Ixil's courtyard, Paul chops our bounty with his Swiss Army knife while Glenn and Rachel stop at the hotel's kitchen to borrow plates and utensils. I slice the great wheel of cheese for *pan dulce* sandwiches.

César, the friendly neighborhood street urchin, parks himself beside me. He rubs his belly theatrically to remove all doubt that he is hungry. Glancing at Paul, I hand César the first sandwich. The child beams, his grime-smeared face lighting up, and scampers off to eat in private. "So he doesn't have to share his food with anyone," Paul offers, slicing into a second avocado.

After lunch, Glenn and Rachel go off to explore a church in a neighboring town. "I'm all churched out," Paul tells them. We opt to worship at the altar of each other's bodies. It is especially lovely— long, lingering, lazy, with teasing kisses reminiscent of dripping honey. I lay on top of Paul, rubbing, talking. The sight of this man beneath me is enough to cause me to simmer and melt. Making love has been like this with no one else. And I know that it will never be.

More than once, Paul has told me that sex hasn't been this way with any other woman. His thoughts oddly mirror mine. Should I believe him? Or is this just one of those things men always say? Like the things women always say. But still, I feel such a contentness, such a sense of peace with him it's like I've found a lost part of myself. That is, when I'm not imagining Paul committing all sorts of erotic atrocities with Heathers. And Melodys. And Barbaras. And whoevers.

What it comes down to is that I'm afraid. Afraid of losing Paul. Afraid he's lying about loving me. About there being no one else. I'm just plain scared. Of everything. Maybe this is because of all the terrible stuff I've done in my past. I was unfaithful to my ex-husband but only when there was no hope for our relationship to continue. Having a lover kept me (somewhat) sane. It made me feel like I was worth something.

With Paul, there is bliss. But there is also the fear of being lost when he's gone. Because everything ends, doesn't it?

~

With the shutters closed at the Hotel Ixil, the room is pitch black, even in the stark sun of early afternoon. I ask Paul to light a utility candle so I can study his eyes, his shimmering, caramel-colored eyes that regard me with such wonder. His gaze never leaves me while we make love this afternoon. I am suddenly bashful about being studied so intently. When I turn so he can't see me unravel, I still feel him watching me.

Afterwards, Paul and I talk about monogamy—about whether or not people are meant to be monogamous like certain animals are. Tamarins and voles, for example. Or if monogamy goes against nature. "You can't generalize about monogamy," Paul insists. "All people are different. All relationships are different."

"But we generalize about other species, like wolves and swans," I tell him. "Why not humans?"

He thinks for a second. "Maybe because human beings' free will gets in the way of our instinct," Paul suggests.

"Maybe," I say.

I couldn't leave Paul for six days, let alone six months for a work assignment like Leah did. Even to a place as awesome as Italy. Hell, I can't fathom leaving Paul for a few weeks, which is why I'm in Guatemala. But how can you leave your boyfriend for half a year and expect to come back and find everything the same? Things are always changing, whether you're in town or not. They shift, they evolve, whether or not you do.

Before Paul and after my marriage crumbled, when I got sad or lonely, I reached for the closest man (usually the worst possible man) to hold me. Not quite any port in a storm but close. In retrospect, I know it was wrong. Morally and emotionally. And I know I will never do it again. Especially not to Paul.

Why do I keep rehashing the same old fears over and over? What difference does Paul's past make to my present? It's *his* past, not even mine. Why am I obsessed with it? Maybe because I don't want it to become *my* past, *my* mistakes.

And how can I be concerned about this nonsense now? I'm on vacation, for God's sake! Here I am, happy, in love, in an "unplugged" village, nestled in the blue mountains. I'm scribbling in my journal, sitting on a bench outside our room at the Hotel Ixil in Nebaj while Paul snores blissfully in our bed. César sits on my left and the owner's son is on my right. The boys are trying to grasp what I'm writing in my notebook. Thankfully they can't read English.

César asks me questions in slow, halting Spanish. I can understand roughly half of what he says. I don't have the foreign language skills to fully answer his queries but I try. *"Qué estas escribiendo?"* César smiles up at me.

I think he's wondering what I'm writing. I dig deep into my limited vocabulary and point to my head. *"Estoy escribiendo mis… pensamientos."* I hope César gets the gist of it. *I'm writing my thoughts*.

He grins the confused grin of a clown then rubs his scruffy head against my shoulder like a kitten. César smells like soil and scallions and simple joy.

~

The afternoon's *chipi-chipi* gives way to driving rain. It storms so hard that it blows out Nebaj's electricity. When the rain stops, even though its random streetlights are dead, Glenn, Rachel, Paul and I set off to find Juana's house by candlelight. In the meantime, Juana has sent her flashlight-bearing son Jacinto to guide us to her kitchen. We meet just past the crossroads, damp but delighted to find Juana's openhearted mismatched table waiting for us.

Paul rolls scraps of paper around the candles we carry so they fit easily into Juana's soda bottle candelabras. Unlike the squalid Aguateco, Juana's home is swept and carefully tended. She may not be rich but she is clean.

With a pious expression on her face, Juana serves us a stew made with noodles, squash, potatoes, garlic and carrots simmered in a light chicken broth. The squash is different than any I've ever had. It tastes a bit like honeydew but isn't as sweet. The dish itself is golden, delicious and savory. Tentatively, Juana asks if we like her food. She swells with pride when we say we do.

Juana's kitchen is perhaps the most beautiful place I've ever been and this is perhaps the most beautiful food I've ever eaten. There's *cuxa* to ease the chill from our bodies. There's also laughter, love and hospitality to warm us.

Juana is pleased to serve us hearty second helpings of her stew. As she does, she tells us that a Swedish tourist has been in the *chuj* for over an hour. "He might be dead," she giggles.

But soon Boo materializes, skin pink and puffy from his sweat bath. He joins the rest of us, buzzed from the intoxicating heat. Juana pours Boo some *cuxa*. He tells us that he's a former professor of math and physics but is now a tour guide. Besides his native Swedish, Boo speaks Spanish and English but claims he isn't good at either. I disagree.

"I fell in love with Guatemala," Boo confesses. "And Juana." She sparks at the sound of her name but doesn't understand what Boo has said. However, she knows it's a compliment because we smile, and she does too.

Last year alone, Boo brought 40 Swedes to visit Guatemala, and a handful to Juana's house in this remote corner of Nebaj. "There's no place like it," he says. We can't help but agree.

Juana does her best to fatten up the slender Boo with her stew and adds more *cuxa* to his cup. *"Comer...beber,"* she tells him. *Eat... drink*. Boo does as Juana asks, lifting his tin fork, then his glass.

Jacinto tells us that *cuxa* is 35 proof, *"Más o menos."*

"Un cupito mas, Paolito" Juana keeps urging Paul. *One small cup more, my little Paul*. He complies. We all do.

~

As we talk and drink, Juana plucks kernels of corn from a roasted ear. She drops several in front of each of us, doling them out like bits of gold. We chew them slowly, savoring the freshness of the grain. The kernels are hard and pulpy. They taste similar to popcorn but more robust.

Juana turns to Magdalana. When she and her daughter speak Ixil, their expressions suddenly become stern. It's a guttural language punctuated with pops and clicks. They speak it quickly, as though their tongues are running a race. But when the two speak Spanish, it is slowly, hesitantly, as if they weigh every word, every syllable. Spanish is not the language they learned at the knees of their elders, at the kitchen table, perhaps at this very kitchen table. But even with their unfamiliarity, Spanish is a friendlier-sounding language in their mouths, full of amusement.

When Glenn visited the Marcos Family months earlier, Jacinto had been looking for a job. After a long search he finally found one in a health clinic, helping women learn about birth control and how to properly care for their bodies. When Jacinto speaks of the social injustice directed toward the destitute and the indigenous, his emotions spill like an avalanche.

Although Glenn translates Jacinto's words for us, he doesn't capture the young man's passion or his anger. "Jacinto says the money donated to Guatemala's poor never gets to the people it's meant to help," Glenn tells us. "Most of it's buried in the pockets of the greedy, the people who were hired to protect the downtrodden. These dishonest people become part of the problem, not part of the solution."

"How much of this money actually makes it to the Guatemalans?" Paul asks. Glenn translates for Juana's eldest son.

Jacinto shakes his head and sighs. His moving torrent continues as Glenn interprets, "Out of 50 US dollars, maybe 10 reaches the needy." We're shocked to learn this. Struck into silence by Jacinto's candor, it's words like these that cause men to be dragged out of their homes in the middle of the night, never to be heard from again. I'm glad he feels safe enough with us to be honest.

Before we leave, all four of us inscribe earnest sentiments into Juana's autograph book. (We'd forgotten to do it the night before.) Sparked by the *cuxa*, I write something nauseatingly gushy about being here with the man I love and immediately regret it. As Paul reads it, he raises an eyebrow and closes the book.

At the door, Juana approaches us and ties a hand-woven bracelet around our wrists, saying in her slow, hesitant Spanish, *"Para Navidad." For Christmas*. She repeats this four times, once for each of us, to make it more personal. Then Juana gathers us into her arms, one by one, and hugs us tenderly. It is as though she knows she will probably never see us again.

Thanks to the younger Marcoses, the rabies jokes return. Magdalena and Miguel ask permission to touch Glenn's chicken feather fuzz hair. "Why does it stand up straight like that?" they want to know. They also ask why Rachel keeps her hair cut short. She tries to answer as best she can. *"Es mas facile,"* she says in her own defense. *It's easier.*

Little Daniel cries in the next room and Magdalena runs to tend to him. A number of things transpire before we actually leave. Multiple conversations crisscross each other. Then there is the *cuxa*. There is always more *cuxa*. "This is like a Guatemalan sitcom," Paul says. "Come on down to Juana's place."

We're back at the front door and ready to leave. Again. When Glenn asks Juana the price of this supper, she responds shyly that it is 32 quetzals for all of the food and drink. This comes to six dollars to feed four people. "That's too little," Glenn says to us.

"Give her 50," Paul tells him. Juana accepts it with a grateful bow. It still doesn't seem like enough.

~

On the walk home, we notice that Nebaj's electricity is still out. Jacinto takes us part of the way with his flashlight but when he leaves us, we can barely see. We leap over puddles then stomp through others in our blindness. The VCR in the barbershop is silent. There's no sound on the muddy street except for music which grows louder the closer we get to the Hotel Ixil.

Glenn and Paul insist on investigating the source of the noise. Rachel and I beg off. "We'll never see them again," I sigh as the men fade from our sight.

"They're crazy on the *cuxa*," Rachel says. "So we might not. You know how Paul gets when he's drunk."

"Do I?" Rachel ignores my comment. She doesn't answer. The corn mash loosens my tongue and gives me the courage to say, "You seem to have it in for me, Rach...And for Paul."

"I don't think so," Rachel insists.

"Well, I do. All of that stuff about Leah." Rachel is speechless. "Paul doesn't bring up Glenn's ex-girlfriends. Why do you bring up Paul's?"

"I...I don't know," she admits.

"Well, stop. Please stop," I tell her.

Rachel nods. "Sorry," she says. "I will."

Before our silence grows too awkward, Glenn and Paul materialize out of the darkness. "It's a crazy house party," Paul reports. "The place is packed. There's a marimba band. And these humongous speakers."

"And electricity," I say.

"They must have a generator," Glenn concludes.

Rachel yawns. "It's after 12. Maybe it will stop soon."

"Looks like they're just getting revved up," Glenn tells her.

The marimba music doesn't stop. It blasts louder and louder as Paul and I brush our teeth. The songs thump as we undress by candlelight. At first, it's funny. "This is crazy," I laugh.

"This is Guatemala," Paul says, blowing out the candle.

We lay side by side. I stare at the ceiling. The music is so loud we can't sleep. It's impossible to even doze. A few times, I manage to drift off. But when I dream, it's about marimba that blares and doesn't stop. When I wake up, the music is still blasting. Even louder, it seems.

Paul's body is tense with wakefulness beside me. "This is what hell is like," I tell him.

"It's like a *Twilight Zone* episode," he groans. "Except *Twilight Zone* episodes are only a half-hour long. This is endless."

He's right.

We probably don't sleep a wink. It's too noisy to even fuck.

Day 17

Tuesday, December 7, 1993
Nebaj/Cobán

I sleep intermittently during brief pauses in the music, only to wake with a start by an explosion of sound minutes later. After a while, Paul and I burst out laughing. Either you laugh or you cry because it's both comical and sad. And the worst part is, it isn't even good marimba. The player keeps missing the same note over and over. It grates like sand against our teeth.

At about three in the morning, there's a knock on our door. It's Glenn, his hair more disheveled than usual. "I can't take it anymore," he says. "Let's get out of here."

"Now?" Paul and I pipe in unison.

"But it's pitch-black outside," Paul continues, "And the roads are shit."

"Plus, it's been raining," I add for emphasis.

"That's true," Paul agrees. "There could be mudslides."

Glenn stomps off into the dark hall. "I guess you're right," he concedes, shaking his head in disappointment.

When the music breaks momentarily, Paul flings open the shutters. *"No más! No más, por favor,"* he shouts into the night. *No more! No more, please.* But it makes no difference. The marimba cranks up again.

Days earlier, I'd asked Paul if he'd ever seen Glenn lose his temper. He's normally such a calm, reasonable person. "Once or twice," Paul admitted. "And it's not a pretty sight."

Suddenly, in the middle of our marimba serenade, I hear a familiar voice ring out into the night. In snarling, vicious Spanish. *"Cállate, tu hijos de putas,"* it spits. *Shut up, you sons of whores!*

The voice is almost recognizable, except for its wrath. "Is that Glenn?" Paul asks, astonished.

"It can't be Glenn," I reason. "Glenn would never say anything like that to anyone. Besides, he has such respect for the Guatemalan people."

But it *was* Glenn.

~

Our marimba nightmare continues. "I think I was awake the whole time," Paul croaks at about 6:30 in the morning.

"Me too," I tell him, burying my head under the sheets.

Paul and I can't stand it a second longer. We get up and start packing as the sun begins to rise. Soon, Glenn knocks on our door again. "You ready?"

"Almost," we tell him.

No sign of the Hotel Ixil's owner, who had promised us *panqueques* before we set off. "He's probably afraid to show his face," Paul says. "He should've warned us about that goddamned marimba."

"He had to know about the party," Glenn agrees. "I bet he was there."

Unable to sleep himself, Glenn poked around before dawn and managed to find out that the all-night marimba fest was part of a religious celebration—to commemorate the Virgin Mary's "immaculate conception" of Jesus on her December 8 feast day. Which is tomorrow. Apparently, this feast is a big deal in Guatemala. The lucky guy across the road had the honor of housing the Virgin's life-sized icon before she makes her appearance in church and threw a shindig to celebrate the occasion.

"This is how they observe a religious holiday?" I ask, shocked. "By getting wasted and dancing to marimba music until dawn?"

"Yep," Glenn confirms.

Sure enough, as we open our room's shutters to the gray sunlight, a handful of revelers stagger home. They scowl at us and mutter in Spanish. Somehow, they must know that we were the ones yelling out the window last night, trying to put a damper on their fun. "Screw them," Paul says.

As Rachel and I take down the laundry that refused to dry in Nebaj's persistent *chipi-chipi,* she recounts Glenn's evening performance. "He paced the floor, mumbling, 'How could that bastard miss the same freaking note every goddamned time?'"

"Right?"

Rachel continues, "I've never seen Glenn like that before and we've been a couple for five years. He wanted to go out and force them to stop but I wouldn't let him. I was afraid someone would lop off his head with a machete."

"Did he finally calm down?"

"No," she says, folding a pair of damp panties. "Eventually, he dragged his blankets out to the Suzuki and tried to sleep with the radio blasting."

"Did it work?"

Rachel nods. "Until a marimba song came on the radio."

~

We are packed and on the road before eight, giddy from lack of rest, ecstatic that the music has finally ended. "I will hate the marimba for the rest of my life," Paul says. I bet we all will.

Glenn is in rare form as he drives. Rachel grabs onto the dash as he speeds around the road's snaking curves. The usually mild-mannered Glenn is still riled up. "I mean, how could they possibly keep messing up that same note? That same freaking note? Over and over again. They'd been playing for hours!" he moans.

Glenn's tirade continues as we coil down the misty, rough roads toward Cobán. We still haven't had breakfast. Or coffee.

~

In Uspantán, Glenn insists we find a place called Comedor Kevin. "Really?" Rachel marvels. "Comedor Kevin? In Guatemala?"

"You'll see," Glenn smiles.

There's nothing remarkable about Comedor Kevin except its name. Turns out the woman who owns it has a major crush on the actor Kevin Costner. Not only did Mimi name the café after Costner but she also named her youngest son after him. A chubby toddler in overalls, Little Kevin's silly antics cheer us up following such a terrible night's sleep.

"Would you believe he's the only Kevin in the village," Mimi tells us proudly as she serves up steaming cups of Nescafé.

"He's probably the only Kevin in all of Guatemala," Paul quips.

During our meal, we are the small *comedor's* sole customers. Posters spouting inspirational Spanish sayings coupled with vivid photographs of flowers hang on the walls. There's even a framed, autographed 8x10 of Kevin Costner from *Dances with Wolves*. The kitchen is just beyond an archway. Mimi and her mother work busily, preparing our breakfast.

Mimi's two other sons materialize. The middle one is named Robinson. "Any bets he's the only 'Robinson' in town?" Glenn asks. The oldest one is Juan Carlos. They try to cajole Kevin into coming to talk with us but he feigns bashfulness. We manage to coax the trio into posing for a photo beneath the *comedor's* sign as evidence that the place actually exists. "They won't believe it back home," Paul says.

"I barely believe it here," I tell him.

Mimi serves us a sweet, runny cornmeal mush called *mosh*. It's not bad but we can't enjoy it—too similar to the "rice and water" stools on the cholera posters, we agree. So, we barely touch the *mosh*, which seems to bother our hostess but she doesn't say a word. She just whisks the almost-full cups away.

Next come our eggs, black beans and tortillas, a hearty *típico* Guatemalan breakfast. When Rachel and I ask to use the bathroom, Mimi tells us they have none. "Is it because we didn't finish our *mosh?*" I ask Rachel as we search for Uspantán's public restroom.

Through town, through the market, we manage to find the building. Crude and pungent, I force myself to pee into a stone vessel that cups the ground. Toilet paper is too much to expect in a place like this. Near the sink is a bucket and a ladle for flushing out the waterless toilet. Upon exit, we pay the man sitting at a table near the door for services rendered then head back to Comedor Kevin.

Paul and Glenn are waiting for us outside, extremely agitated. When we're closer, we see why. Marimba music blasts from huge speakers mounted to the back of a flatbed truck. An entire marimba orchestra is set up between the speakers in the vehicle's bed. In anticipation of tomorrow's Feast of the Immaculate Conception, they play enthusiastically, much to our horror. "Let's get the hell out of here as fast as we can," Glenn says.

Outside Uspantán, we pass another marimba-mobile. Glenn guns the engine and passes it at an unsafe speed, shaking his fist at them. But this time, none of us complain about his driving.

~

We're heading toward the large city of Cobán, in the center of the Western Highlands' coffee-growing region. Although it's about 40 miles from Uspantán, there's no telling how long the journey will take. The roads still aren't very good. Narrow and winding, they are increasingly treacherous, especially with trucks barreling down from Cobán, heavy with bags of coffee beans to sell.

My nose is buried deep in *The Real Guide* when I hear Paul and Rachel shout simultaneously. I glance up to see the front of a Blue Bird bus practically kissing the front of the Suzuki. Luckily, Glenn had been driving slowly enough around a sharp curve to stop before we rammed into it. There is a sheer, thousand-foot drop on our side of the road. Rachel starts sobbing quietly in the passenger seat and manages to squeeze out, "We are so damn lucky."

Glenn giggles nervously and shifts the Samurai into gear after the bus inches past us. The driver makes the sign of the cross with one hand as he finesses the steering wheel with the other. "That was close," Paul admits.

In the wake of this traumatic encounter, now Glenn beeps the horn gingerly whenever he approaches a blind curve.

Remarkably, at San Cristóbal Verapaz, the road suddenly becomes paved. Previously, if we covered 100 miles in six hours, we were lucky. Now we manage 30 miles in as many minutes. The countryside is lovely and different, still lush, but with tropical foliage thrown in as a bonus. It's reminiscent of the Rocky Mountains, except the peaks here are rounded, softer, older.

Besides coffee, the Verapaz region is famous for its succulent fruits. Trees bearing oranges, mangoes, bananas and sugar cane are planted beside the road. The verdant hills of the Verapaz are home to plentiful coffee *fincas* as well. "The green is the reason this highway is paved," Glenn tells us. "Green, as in money."

"Why?" Rachel asks.

"They want the crops to get to market before they rot," he tells her.

~

In no time, we are in Cobán. It's bathed in the Western Highlands' ever-popular *chipi-chipi*. Which is just a fancy name for drizzle. "The *chipi-chipi* is what makes the coffee so good," Glenn explains.

"This is a long way to drive for a decent cup of coffee," Paul says.

"It's excellent coffee," Glenn tells him.

After checking the hotel situation, we find one for less than 10 dollars. Of course, Glenn wants to stay in a grubby dollar-a-night *pensión* but we talk him out of it. The Hotel Rabin Ajau is on Cazalda Minerva, Cobán's main drag. All rooms have private baths, solid beds and high credenzas. But the whole inn smells musty, probably from the damp, constant *chipi-chipi*. Paul and I open the tall windows to welcome in the fresh, crisp air.

Glenn and Rachel want to "rest" (polite talk for "fuck?") while Paul lusts for a juicy steak. "I hear Cobán is also cattle country," he says.

I will be content sampling the local guacamole. I'm doing an informal compare-and-contrast and try to eat guac daily. "You never met an avocado you didn't like," Paul tells me. The product of an Italian-American household, I never tasted an avocado until I was at least 25, so I'm making up for lost time.

After our meal, Paul and I return to our room, bolt the windows and draw the shades. We French kiss and touch like teenagers, exploring each other's bodies with hesitant fingertips.

A nap and a lukewarm shower later, Paul and I are hungry again. We meet Glenn and Rachel in the Ajau's restaurant, which specializes in Italian food. Though doubtful at first—Italian food in Guatemala?!—the pizza is pretty authentic. On the wall above our table is a faded, color photograph which could easily have been taken in 1973 Brooklyn. It depicts a silver Christmas tree in a stuffy living room, plastic slipcovers on the sectional and a teased hairdo on the *nonna*. How this photo ended up in Cobán, I'll never know.

While Paul and I napped earlier that afternoon, I was vaguely aware of the sound of firecrackers but I thought I was dreaming. Rachel, who has been out exploring, informs us that Cobán is celebrating "the Burning of the Devils." She explains, "They light fireworks in front of their houses to cleanse them of evil spirits. Other people burn the devil in effigy or ignite mounds of sticks."

"Why?" I ask.

"It's a purification ritual," Glenn says. "It also marks the official start of the Christmas season."

Following dinner, we set off for a coffee shop that Glenn had been talking up our entire ride to Cobán. "Great," Paul reminds his former roommate. "We just drove eight hours for a good cup of coffee."

But it is probably the best cup of coffee I've ever had.

While we walk back to the Ajau, I spy a pay phone booth and call home. The telephone gobbles up my *centavos,* then drops the call. But it's nice to hear my father's Brooklynese accent, even for a few seconds. I hope my dad didn't think I was kidnapped and was making a ransom phone call.

Then it's back to the Rabin Ajau for reading, writing in my journal and a peaceful, marimba-less sleep.

Day 18

Wednesday, December 8, 1993
Cobán/Purulhá

Since we met up with Glenn and Rachel, we've been able to visit places we couldn't reach without a car. Off-the-beaten-track ruins. Obscure churches. Remote farms and *fincas*. Memorable villages — and forgettable ones. We never would have met Juana Marcos or experienced her *chuj* if it hadn't been for Glenn. Plus, we couldn't have gotten to Nebaj itself without a jeep. (Well, I guess we could have but it would have been enormously complicated using public busses.) And we couldn't rent a jeep without someone who knew how to drive a stick shift.

In the out-of-the-way villages, many people have never seen Westerners, especially one as tow-haired as Glenn. Their bemused expressions, their innocent questions, are priceless. Sometimes I think they get as much of a kick out of seeing us as we get out of seeing them.

In these remote cities, I'm always struck by the peculiar mix of pagan and Christian rituals. Guatemalans are devoted to celebrating the feast days of even minor saints. They set off fireworks to scare away demons. They play marimba music to please Jesus's mom. They decorate for Christmas the second December rolls around. Yet they also build shrines to pagan debauchers like Maximón and are said to practice voodoo in Caribbean villages like Livingston.

Paul and I are oddly drawn to these churches, to these rituals. On the outskirts of Cobán, we visit Iglesia del Calvario, an enormous white church set on a hill. Along the paved path leading to the Church of the Calvary itself are small recessed altars which burn inky candles. In other altars, bird feathers are stuck with wax to crosses. Sometimes coin offerings are imbedded in the wax too. "Black magic?" I ask Paul. "Voodoo?"

"Sure looks like it," he says. I step forward to snap a picture. "Whatever you do, don't touch it," he warns. "It might put a curse on you."

"I wouldn't dream of it," I swear. Our luck has been iffy enough on this vacation, so I sure don't need an evil spell cast upon me.

~

Back in Cobán, we ask a New Yorker who runs the tourist office about these unusual, devotional recesses with the crosses, black wax and feathers. Annette claims, "It works!" Way back when, she lit a candle at one of these altars and her life took a turn for the better.

Annette had been an aimless Peace Corps worker, fell in love with Guatemala, then fell in love with a Guatemalan and settled here. Their daughter speaks Spanish with an American accent and has the thick, dark, straight tresses of a native. Annette herself is dirty blonde, something of an anomaly in Guate.

We speak of what Annette misses from America: bagels and books and traffic, pizza by the slice and knishes. She tries to interest us in a tour to Semuc Champey, a national park with a gorgeous set of waterfalls. "We have a Samurai," Paul tells her. "We can get there on our own."

Annette does her best to discourage us. "Your Suzuki won't cut it," she says sternly. "You can only get to Semuc Champey in something as sturdy as a Range Rover." After our experience with the road around Lake Atitlán, we heed Annette's warning.

The tour to the falls sounds tempting but our schedule won't allow for a visit. We have to catch a flight home in three days. Our trip is quickly drawing to a close.

~

There's something I really like about Cobán but I can't figure out what. It's the biggest city we've been to since Xela, yet unlike Xela, it's charming. Because of Cobán's size, I've got to learn how to cross the street all over again. Even in off-the-grid towns like Zaculeu and Uspantán, which have a fair amount of car traffic, a stop light is a rare sight. Cobán has several.

We get lunch at the Hotel La Posada, which is filled with curious local crafts. Their Christmas tree is hung with terracotta trimmings, all hand-hewn. Waiting for our lunch to arrive, Glenn, Rachel, Paul and I grow beards, that's how long our food takes to arrive. This gives us plenty of time to study people.

For some reason, Cobán is a haven for sandy-haired Mormons intent on converting the Guatemalans. Since Mormon doctrine dictates that they must spend at least one year of their lives proselytizing, Guate is the perfect locale for evangelizing. It's briming with the poor and the impressionable.

In Cobán, the Mormons stick out more than the four of us do. Even in the tropics the men wear drab suits with starched-white shirts buttoned to the chin. Even in their twenties, the young Mormon women wear loose, frumpy, old-lady dresses, with ruffled collars and long sleeves. They're inconsistent with the lively *huipils, cintas* and burning devils. But to their credit, the Mormons do speak fluent, if not sterile, Spanish.

~

After lunch, we leave Cobán. But Glenn misses the turnoff for Otto Mittelstaedt's orchid farm and we decide not to turn back. The road is still an asphalt dream. Just before Biotopo del Quetzal, a wildlife reserve near Purulhá, we come upon a gloomy funeral procession trudging alongside the road. "That's a bad omen," Rachel says.

"You're being ridiculous," Glenn tells her.

"Be careful today," she warns him.

"I'm careful every day," he insists.

Four men carry a plain pine coffin on their shoulders, moving slowly in step. A handful of people follow them, their heads bowed. Almost involuntarily, I make the sign of the cross, lapsed Catholic that I am. It's a reflex reaction.

We're on the road only an hour today but it's a welcome change from all of the car time. As we drop off our bags at a hotel on the grounds of the quetzal reserve, we agree that Pensión Los Ranchitos looks promising. But although the *pensión* is beautiful, there's nothing to do there except wait for the coy quetzal to surface. The national bird of Guatemala supposedly only shows itself around dawn. Early the next morning, we'll hopefully have a date with the resplendent quetzal—but not before then.

"Let's try to get the word 'resplendent' back into common usage," I suggest. Being a wordsmith, I'm excited at the prospect. The others seem less enthusiastic. "You know, like 'groovy' or 'cool,'" I add.

"Let's not," Rachel replies dryly.

~

To while away the rest of the day, we head to the nearby village of Tactic. It's home to a weaving cooperative where local women sell their handiwork under one roof instead of hawking their wares on the streets. This means prices are fixed and there's no bargaining. The women take turns working at the cooperative, an open, warehouse-like shop brimming with color and possibility.

Rachel buys a cute scarf but has to borrow money from Glenn to do so. Paul considers an intricate pillowcase that doesn't match his pheasant-motif sofa but wants it anyway. The woman doing her shift at the cooperative has brought her two young daughters with her. One smiles at us as we shop. The other peeks from the back room then hides when we wave at her.

Tactic is also famous for its silver crafts but more so for the Pozo Vivo, or "the living well," a pool of water which magically comes to life whenever someone approaches. "It's like the tree in the forest," Paul suggests.

"Which one?" Glenn asks.

"The one that if it falls and there's no one to hear it, does it still make a sound?"

"What are you saying?" I push.

"If no one's there to see the Pozo Vivo, does the pond still fizz?" Paul says.

"Come on," Glenn laughs. "There's not much else to do in Tactic."

When we ask for directions to the Pozo Vivo, the woman at the weaving cooperative tells her daughters to take us. Endearing and shy, they become more animated when we ask them questions.

The girls guide us through the muck of a cow pasture, daintily lifting their skirts. We splash in the mud in our sneakers, trudging in the gummy, saturated earth. Stepping on wooden planks to avoid the deeper mud, we walk and walk until finally, we come to a dirty pool of mulch. If you look very closely, you can detect a faint gurgling near the center of the murky water.

"This is it?" Paul asks in disbelief.

The girls nod. *"Si, esto es. Esto es el Pozo Vivo."*

"I can make more bubbles farting in the bathtub," Paul comments. Luckily, our young attendants don't understand English. But Glenn still tells Paul to be quiet.

"A pipe is buried in the water, right?" Glenn suggests to the girls in Spanish.

Their expressions become reverent. *"No,"* they swear. As they shake their heads, they jangle their silver earrings. *"Es verdad."* *It's true.*

But we still don't believe them.

~

Last night in Cobán, my period started. Five days early. I'm crampy and cranky and bleeding like a stuck pig. At least, I've learned how to say, *"Donde están los Tampax?" Where are the Tampax?* But on the downside, I'm swollen, sullen and rippling with stomach pains. Our trudge back through the mud doesn't do much to help my mood.

I carefully step onto the sodden boards, wishing I'd worn my hiking boots. Despite my best efforts, I slip and fall on my ass in the mud. Everyone else is far ahead and doesn't notice. Even Paul is nowhere nearby. He walks with the weaver's daughters, oblivious. But it's probably better that way.

As I catch up to them, I hear Glenn joking, "The Exxon station on the edge of town has a switch. They flip it on whenever they see tourists coming so the pool bubbles." His cracks about the Pozo Vivo make me forget how embarrassed I am about falling. I hope no one spots the smear of mud on my behind.

~

Back in Tactic, Glenn tries to give the girls some quetzals but they refuse. "Their mother would probably be angry," he explains to us. They say goodbye and walk off arm in arm, adjusting their shawls on their shoulders as they go.

At a small silver shop, a young boy pushes an old man in a wheelchair to the front of the store. I think they want to get out so I move aside to let them pass. But the man just parks himself in the doorway, staring. "Maybe he wants a better look," Paul says.

"There aren't many Westerners here." *El anciano* just sits in his rusty wheelchair and gapes at me.

An equally-ancient woman behind the shop's cracked glass counter tries to sell us silver earrings that are cast around coffee beans. "They're too kitschy," I tell Paul. Instead, I choose a delicate pair of dangling earrings for myself. Paul buys a set of birds in flight as a gift for his sister. The wares in this shop are plentiful, one piece more elaborate than the next. But most are too ornate for our tastes. Each pair of earrings costs less than five dollars.

Annette from the tour office in Cobán told us about a restaurant run by an American woman and her Guatemalan husband. Without its name or a street to guide us, we search for it all over Tactic. When we finally locate it, the restaurant is closed. The man who rents the space next door has no idea why.

Tactic has a number of greasy *comedors* to choose from. We pick the one that seems the least offensive. There's only one choice for dinner: *pollo*. I'm so hungry that I don't give away my chicken this time; I eat it myself, like a savage. What a totally dissatisfying jump off the vegetarian bandwagon this is. The meat is dry and stringy. But I'm tired of having nothing but rice and beans and guacamole so *pollo* suits me fine.

Of course, there are tortillas to accompany them. The rice is fancy: yellow with scraps of veggies mixed in. The *comedor* is empty except for another table of rowdy, intoxicated locals. They sit nearby, making loud, unintelligible comments about *los Americanos*. We pretend not to hear them.

Glenn and Paul stand at the front door, watching a statue of the Virgin Mary travel in a procession to a church across the road. Since this is the actual Feast of the Immaculate Conception, there's a whole lot of hoo-ha throughout Guatemala. Tactic is no exception. The parade is followed by a modest spray of fireworks. Everyone celebrates the religious holiday with copious amounts of alcohol.

Soon, Rachel and I join the guys at the door. This is one of the rare times I feel like I'm intruding in this country. I'm not sure why. But the feast of the Virgin is quiet, reverent, personal—except for the fireworks. People from the village stand on one side of the street and the spectators on the other, separated by nothing but air we breathe.

~

For the past few days, I've felt like an outsider in our compact group of four. I can't say exactly when this happened. But it's profound. Maybe it comes from the awkwardness of meeting people for the first time, then spending the whole week with them. No adjustment period. Just bam! One minute they're strangers and the next, you're stripping for a sweat bath with them.

I don't know the same people Paul, Glenn and Rachel know. I don't have their common history—in fact, I have no history with the last two at all. Their private jokes don't make sense to me. I feel like I'm not nearly as bright as any of them. And I don't play cards as well as they do.

There's Paul with his natural smarts and sharp wit. There's Glenn, knee-deep in scholarships and grants. And then there's Rachel, film editor, world traveler and budding student of *Español*. Scabies and all, I still feel inadequate compared to her.

I wonder what Paul thinks of Rachel. Does he find her prettier, more intelligent and sexier than me? I'm sure he'd gotten a glimpse of her naked in Juana's *chuj*. Did he like what he saw? Did he get half a boner?

Rachel's features are more delicate than my Italian peasant visage. She has high, finely-crafted cheekbones and a perfectly-chiseled nose. She's polished, confident and not as rough around the edges as I am. Since Rachel has been to Europe "oodles of times," she and Paul can—and do!—discuss the wonders of Paris, Madrid and Amsterdam. All I can do is listen.

Plus, at 26, Rachel is eight years younger than me. And Columbia University-educated. Her wealthy parents paid her tab at a cushy private institution while I financed my way through the city college system, toughing out the semesters at Hunter by doing temp jobs.

And maybe Rachel is more confident in her five-year relationship with Glenn than I am in my dalliance with Paul. I'm still not sure where we stand after weathering a sometimes-rocky first year. Paul's assurance about how wonderful things are often come when he's drunk. But does he feel the same about me when he's sober? Paired with the mixed signals of marriage talk and "I don't want a relationship...I just got out of a relationship" talk, I am often confused.

Ghosts of ex-girlfriends are always looming on the horizon. I want to feel safe and sure and loved. Is that too much to ask? Yes, apparently it is. Sometimes I feel all three and other times, I feel none of them. Sometimes, because of my own demons, I doubt I could feel any of the above, no matter the person or the circumstances. Am I an example of the old Groucho Marx credo: "I wouldn't want to belong to a club that would have me as a member?"

~

After dinner in Tactic, we drive back to Pensión Los Ranchitos. On the edge of the quetzal reserve, it's lovely but remote, with nothing much to do. None of us want to go to sleep yet. And everyone but me wants to play Hearts. I attempt to beg out but they won't let me. "It's not as much fun with three people," Rachel whines. Meaning, 'It's more fun when someone else is the loser. Like you, Carol.'

"Sure," I finally sigh. "I'll play Hearts." The prospect of losing doesn't bother me as much as the prospect of being ridiculed. But I hope for the best.

Paul and I meet Glenn and Rachel in their room with a sixpack of *Gallo*. We sit two to a double bed as Glenn deals out the first hand. Rachel turns to me and says, "Carol, you should really try this time. The game isn't challenging if you don't."

Bitch! I *was* trying. Does Rachel think I lost on purpose? "I suck at cards no matter how hard I try," I tell her. "I know that's tough to believe but it's true."

At the Aguateco, I'd lost by a landslide, despite the 50-point handicap I'd protested about being given. What bothers me most about playing Hearts isn't losing; it's feeling like an outcast. I'm not part of their clique. I'm not one of the cool kids. It's high school all over again. It's a redux of Blackjack with my father. It's *Groundhog Day*.

These same, old emotions come crashing over me as the four of us play Hearts at the Pensión Los Ranchitos. I can't focus. It takes forever to decide which opening card I should throw out. When I finally make my move, Paul holds back a snicker. "Please don't make fun of me," I beg.

"I'm not," he insists.

"You are," I say. "You're laughing."

"Laughing isn't the same as making fun of someone."

Maybe it's the weariness of the road or the realization that our trip is drawing to a close but my eyes fill with tears. Whatever I do in this game doesn't matter. It will be the wrong thing anyhow. Paul and Rachel spout snide comments because it takes so long for me to cast out a card. "What's the difference?" Rachel giggles, echoing my fears. "It won't be the right card anyway." Glenn and Paul join in the fun at my expense.

I'm so flustered that I'm not actually *seeing* the cards in my hand. It's all a blur. I want Paul to be impressed with my card-playing ability—especially since I know how he feels about stupid women. Am I one of them?

Then it happens. I silently debate over which card to throw down as though it is the single most important decision of my life. As though the future of mankind depends upon it. Paul snorts even before I do anything. "What?" I ask.

"Nothing," Paul says, still sneering. "Just make your move." I flush with embarrassment and struggle to keep from crying. Paul is the mean boy who trips the gawky girl in the cafeteria. He is the whole class cackling at me when I don't know the answer.

I'm convinced that throwing down the Ten of Clubs would be a strategic maneuver until Paul smacks down the Queen of Spades. He laughs again, hard and cruel. I can handle losing. I can deal with not being good at something. But I can't deal with being made fun of. Especially by him.

It is all the worst moments of my childhood rolled into one. The tears rise in my throat but I don't want to cry, not in front of them—people who force me to feel inferior. They won't understand. They'll think I'm crying because I'm losing a silly card game. But it's much more than that.

Fighting to contain the quiver in my voice, I ask Paul to stop. Again. "You're going to make me cry," I say softly, wounded. But he keeps right on laughing. Laughing even harder. Laughing in my face. It's like a bad dream.

A tidal wave of memories rise. I remember all those terrible nights when I begged my ex-husband to stop—to stop tormenting me, to stop his incessant talk of suicide, to stop his constant harping that he was a failure. To stop threatening me. To stop wallowing in his unhappiness like it's a sick sort of blanket.

On one of these nights, when I could finally fall asleep, my pillow wet with tears, Alex woke me up at three a.m. by yanking a handful of my hair. "I'd kill you if I thought I could get away with it," he spat into my face.

Other times, my ex would explode into a rage in front of my friends, business associates and relatives. He would rant about his horrible life, about how he was a failure. And these people would look at me with such an utter lack of respect, as if I were somehow responsible for this man's self-inflicted misery. On the brink of tears, I would beg Alex to stop his tirades but he refused. He continued to freak out repeatedly, in bars, in restaurants when we were out to dinner with friends, at family gatherings.

It even happened in that marriage counselor's office where I was reduced to a sobbing mass in front of someone I'd met only 20 minutes earlier. "I don't give a fuck about your feelings!" Alex said. The therapist shook his head while I cried into my Kleenex.

Then there were the times when I'd be reduced to a pathetic, wailing lump on the living room floor, no one to comfort me, torn apart by Alex's dead, uncaring eyes. Another time, he pressed my face into the wall and snarled with hatred. I lost count of the nights I would cry in bed alone and pray to die in my sleep because it hurt so much to be alive. With him.

But I was afraid to leave Alex. Afraid I couldn't support myself. Afraid no one would ever love me. Afraid he would kill me if I tried to go. I was just plain terrified. Traumatized. How could I abandon this broken man who had lost everything in his life except me?

And now, struggling to play Hearts in the middle of a foreign country, being ridiculed, hovering near tears, I am confronted by the shadows of these far-flung emotional ghosts. I just can't cry in front of Glenn and Rachel. But Paul won't stop. "Please..." I tell him.

Paul takes a slug from the *Gallo* bottle. "Please, what? Please teach you how to play cards?"

Suddenly, my hurt explodes into rage. How can someone who says he loves me treat me like this? It's Alex all over again. It isn't Paul's face I see before me but Alex's.

Gritting my teeth, I lunge forward and slap as hard as I can. For a split second, it's not Paul I'm hitting; it's every person who ever tried to hurt me. Especially one.

When I smack him, Paul recoils, stunned.

Rachel gasps.

Glenn turns away.

The flesh of Paul's cheek burns under my palm. My hand
tingles, itches. I pull back, immediately shocked and regret what I have
done. I should have left the room. I should have done any number of
things. But I never should have hit Paul. "I'm sorry!" I blurt out. "I'm
so sorry!" But it doesn't matter. It's too late. The damage has been done.

"I can't believe you fucking hit me," Paul huffs.

"But I asked you to stop," I cry. "More than once."

The expression on Paul's face is indescribable. It is laced with
wrath, hurt and disbelief. And the worst part is that I already know
how he feels about being hit. "Nobody ever hits me without getting hit
back," he's often told me.

I'm terrified that it's over between Paul and me. That this
kneejerk slap has ended our relationship. We never really had an
argument before. How could it end as suddenly and stupidly as
this? Things had been perfect. Well, almost perfect, and now, if it's
finished, it would be my fault. A relationship as passionate as ours
should explode over something magnanimous and dramatic. Not over
something as ridiculous as a card game.

"You should have hit him harder," Rachel says. Glenn tries to
smooth it over with comments about how upset Rachel becomes when
he wins at chess and he gloats about it. But they don't get it. This isn't
about winning and losing. It's about so much more.

~

If we had been back home in Brooklyn, I'm convinced Paul
would have left and never come back. I'm sure he would have broken
up with me right then and there. Why? Because I shattered one of his
firmest, strongest beliefs: "People who love you don't hit you." He
says this to me back in our room at the Pensión Los Ranchitos. Maybe
it's because of all the times he was thrashed as a kid. Maybe it's
something else. But that's about all Paul says to me the whole night:
"People who love you don't hit you."

He keeps glaring at me in the most infuriated, pained way. I've
never seen his eyes seethe like this before. It's something I hope to
never see again. I can't bear it. I want to talk about what happened, to
explain it, justify it, dissect it, to settle it, understand it. But Paul can
hardly stand to be with me, let alone talk to me right now.

On top of everything else, I discover that my shampoo has
opened up in my sponge bag. By the time I clean it up in the bathroom,
Paul is already in bed. We usually sleep naked, but tonight he wears

a t-shirt and boxer shorts. It's as though he doesn't want to risk accidental contact with my skin.

I feel Paul's anger simmering as I crawl into bed beside him. I keep my distance. But in sleep, Paul keeps drawing me close, curling his body around mine. It's probably from custom, rather than from affection or forgiveness. In sleep, Paul has probably forgotten that he's mad at me.

I can't get any rest. Paul dozes fitfully. Maybe it's because of the plastic covering on the mattress underneath the bedsheet. It crackles every time I shift my weight. Is the plastic to keep out bedbugs? It's like bunking on an old Italian lady's slipcovered sofa. I cry intermittently, hoping the memory of slapping Paul across the face is a nightmare but I know it isn't.

At one point, Paul and I continue discussing the Hearts Incident in the protective shelter of darkness but our words fall flat, abandoned. There is no rationalizing what happened. There is no taking it back.

"I still don't know why I didn't hit you back," Paul admits. "Maybe that's what bothers me most of all."

Day 19

Thursday, December 9, 1993
Purulhá/Antigua

I'm foolish enough to believe that everything will be all right in the morning. In fact, the minute I wake up, I forget about the Hearts Incident for a split second. But like a hallucination, it invades my mind. My mood sinks and I can't imagine how I'll get through the day.

Without a "good morning," Paul dresses and leaves the room while I'm still brushing my teeth. Glenn stops by and is surprised Paul isn't here. Turns out, Paul has already parked himself under the Pepsi sign near the *tienda* where the elusive quetzal is said to make his post-dawn appearance.

Glenn, Rachel and I go there together to meet Paul. "Is it a mechanical quetzal?" Rachel asks. "You know, like the Pozo Vivo yesterday." Glenn shakes his head at her ridiculous suggestion. I sense their days together are numbered. Like Paul's and mine?

It's misty in the early morning light, status quo for Guatemala's Western Highlands. We wear sweatshirts zipped up to our chins and are still chilled. "I can't believe Paul is making such a big deal about last night," Rachel says. "He was asking for it." But then again, so was she.

"I'm staying out of it," Glenn adds. "But it was no big deal."

"Not to you," I tell him.

It doesn't matter what Glenn and Rachel think; it matters what Paul thinks. I'd done something to insult him worse than his insulting me. In cards, don't they call that "trumping" someone? Outdoing someone? Yes, I'd trumped Paul. All I know is that I never want to raise my hand to him again. And from the steely look he gives me as the three of us approach, I know I'll never have the opportunity. Not that I'd want to.

Paul and I speak sparingly this morning, only when absolutely necessary. And when he does talk to me, there's no eye contact.

I'm still rattled that Paul didn't listen to my pleas to quit making fun of me. Then this whole thing might have been avoided. But instead, he pushed me to the edge and I took a swan dive into blind fury for which I only have myself to blame. When it comes down to it, I'm in control of my own emotions, no one else is. I could have turned and left. But I didn't. I stayed. I fought. Literally. Maybe I should have fought my ex harder. But not Paul.

I try to apologize once more but this is a mistake. I should just let it go. Paul's response to my apology is: "What will you do the next time we argue? Stab me?" It's a valid point.

~

There are lighthearted moments with a British couple who also seek the elusive but resplendent quetzal. Bird-watchers to the core, they often travel to distant corners of the globe on the chance of spying rare birds. The six of us stand in the drizzle in the *tienda's* parking lot.

"Where does the quetzal hang around?" Glenn asks one of the hotel owner's kids again.

"It likes to land on this Pepsi sign," the boy insists, indicating the plastic placard above our heads.

We wait expectantly in the *chipi-chipi* for the bird's arrival. Every swish of the trees brings anticipation but it's usually just a wet breeze or a crow. Finally, we spot the quetzal high in the branches at least 50 feet above us. But to me, it's only a vague shadow with a long, sweeping tail. The Britishers are thrilled as they spy him through their binoculars. I, however, am disappointed.

~

Following yet another marginal *panqueques* breakfast, the four of us decide to hike through the quetzal reserve itself. Even in the gray rain, it's an impressive place, thick with vegetation and studded with dramatic waterfalls. During our three-mile trek, I'm plagued with cramps. But maybe I deserve them after last night's performance.

Paul tries his best to be civil to me, which translates into being cold and distant. I can't bear his emotional exile so I hover on the edge of tears. I want everything to be the same between us but somehow, I know it will never be.

I guess Paul can detect the discomfort in my face because he asks, "Do you feel all right?"

"Do you care?" I wonder.

"Yes," he says, and walks off.

Later, I try hugging him. While Paul doesn't push me away, he doesn't pull me toward him either. Once, he kisses me briefly of his own accord. A positive sign, I hope. Or the calm before the let-go.

When we get back from our two-and-a-half-hour ramble, I run to the bathroom. The others snack on Chikys. My whole body is rebelling. Paul returns to the room while I am still hunched over the toilet. "How are you?" he asks.

"I've felt better," I manage.

~

We pack our bags and load up the Suzuki, preparing for the last leg of our journey. Maybe Antigua's pure, broken beauty will help heal Paul's and my wounds. Maybe not.

I'm extremely uncomfortable throughout the five-hour drive, both physically and emotionally. Now I'm even more of an outsider because Paul ignores me. I understand completely but I still feel awful. When I try to hold his hand, Paul quickly moves it, as though he's been burned. Maybe he has. By me.

Hours later, I ask if I can lean on his shoulder. He considers me weightily. I try my best to look pitiful and pained. "All right," Paul finally agrees.

When we stop for lunch, my stomach is still upset. In Spanish, Paul repeats my order to the waitress to make sure I get what I want. Just a bowl of light broth. He's angry at me but at least he doesn't hate me.

Glenn's stomach is bothering him as well but for different reasons. He's horrified to find the bathroom toilet-paperless. I reach to the top of the Suzuki to retrieve the squashed roll of TP from my backpack and hand it to Glenn. I can see that Paul is impressed with my chivalry but he doesn't say a word. We finish lunch in silence.

If the emotional road is difficult at least the physical road is smooth. From now on, we travel on fully-paved asphalt, although the highway is narrow and mostly one-laned. Overtaking slow-moving fruit trucks is still perilous. Those jarring white crosses dot the sides of the roads to remind us that people lost their lives here.

~

About an hour outside of Antigua, we're pulled over by a pair of policemen. Picture a Central American take on the Keystone Cops. One is young and cross-eyed. The other is older, missing teeth and Black—a rarity outside of Livingston. He wears a dirty button-down shirt minus a button in the middle of his potbelly.

The older cop asks Glenn if any of us speak Spanish. To make things less complicated, Glenn says that only he does. His driver's license and rental papers are all in order. The man scans them and nods, but I'm not sure he can read. Smiling a chilling jack-o'-lantern grin, the cop explains that in Guatemala, every car needs to have a fire extinguisher. Do we, he wonders? They rummage under the seats of the Suzuki to see if one is stashed there. Of course, we have none.

"But we do," Glenn insists to the police officers, gesturing to Paul. *"Él es un bombero en Nueva York,"* he lies. *He's a firefighter in New York.* (In reality, Paul is an architect who works for the city, not even close.)

The cops are dumbfounded but immediately recover. They mumble something else. "They say we've got to pay a fine—right now," Glenn turns and tells us.

"For what?" Paul barks.

"For not having a fire extinguisher."

Glenn knows they want a kickback. So, to the policemen, he says, "Write us a ticket. We'll pay it in Guatemala City." But still, they're unmoved. Glenn looks at Paul. "They're obviously asking for a bribe. What should we do?"

Paul eyes the policemen then glances back at Glenn. "Fuck them," Paul says, staring down the cops. "They reek of alcohol."

The pseudo-sheriffs might not understand much English but they definitely understand "Fuck them." They eventually abandon their feeble attempt at blackmail and pardon us with a special dispensation. When Paul gives them our last pack of Marlboros, they're happy.

Back on the road, we are again stuck behind the same steer and Coke trucks Glenn had worked so diligently to pass. But being in the backdraft of a cattle car is better than being in a Guatemalan prison, I suppose.

Thanks to *The Real Guide* and Rachel's navigational skills, we get to the outskirts of Guatemala City before rush hour. There's a quick stop at a Circle K for junk-food reinforcements. Paul asks if I want anything when he climbs out of the car. He whispers, "I'm getting less angry with you," before he goes.

"I can't believe he's still pissed off because of a little smack," Rachel says, then discloses, "I had a boyfriend who used to get turned on when you smacked him across the face." Lurid details of Rachel's sex life I wish I could unhear.

As soon as Paul returns with an armload of Chikys in various flavors, we forge on to Antigua. He hands me a package of chocolate Chikys, knowing they're my favorite. Things are looking up.

~

This time, it isn't easy to find suitable accommodations in Antigua. Glenn, of course, would have settled on a flea bag youth hostel but the three of us overrule him in favor of something nicer. We compromise on La Casa de Santa Lucía. It's 10 dollars a night for a small but charming room overlooking a courtyard with a private bath and hot showers. I haven't had a hot shower in days. Although the Santa Lucía is down the street from the bus station, it's surprisingly quiet. I'm glad it comes with a *cama matrimonial* but I don't think we'll put the double bed to much use besides sleeping.

"I'm going out for a drink," Paul says. He adds on the heels of a momentous pause, "Do you want to come along?"

"Do you want me to?" I ask, slightly whiny. I'm still shaky from the events of days past.

"If I didn't want you to, I wouldn't have asked," he says, a smile creeping into the edges of his mouth. "But only if you leave that whine behind."

"I can do that," I tell him.

Rum and Cokes at the Mistral help me get rid of my whimper and my cramps. CNN blares about a madman on the Long Island Railroad who killed five and wounded 14. Suddenly, I dread going home to maniacs like Colin Ferguson. "That would never happen in Guatemala," Paul comments.

I agree. "Because someone would chop off his head with a machete in a New York minute," I say. Paul laughs, shades of the old him shining through.

The drinks are plentiful and go down easy. We need the cushion of alcohol to soften my slap. Our words come effortlessly now as we try to piece together what happened—and why it happened. Paul is still in shock that I struck him. He keeps saying, "I can't believe you hit me," over and over.

"I can't believe I hit you either," I admit. "Can you ever forgive me?"

Paul downs a shot of tequila. "Maybe in a few years," he offers.

Then he changes the subject, only to return to that fateful game of Hearts. After a beat, he suggests, "Let's forget about it and move on," then brings it up once more.

I sit on the barstool and obediently listen, reasoning that this is my penance for committing such a heinous crime.

~

Glenn and Rachel meet us hours later at the Opera Café. It's straight out of New York City's Upper West Side with *libretti* decorating the walls beside photos of legends like Maria Callas. While the pizza is good, the dessert is outstanding, simple but spectacular. Your choice of Kahlúa or amaretto is poured over a goblet of ice cream and decorated with a pirouette cookie. Paul delights in feeding me a spoonful of his. All is forgiven, it seems, at least for now.

Afterwards, Glenn and Rachel return to the Santa Lucía. They're tired, they claim. Or maybe they're just afraid I'll lose my temper again.

Paul and I continue our semi-crocked wanderings through Antigua. We're like Odysseus and Penelope, minus all of that knitting. (Knitting would be too much like Paul's ex Leah, a quilter extraordinaire, among her many faults.) As we stumble among the ruins, I try to explain to Paul about the specters of my past but he doesn't want to hear it. "I'm still trying to get my head around this," he explains. "But people who love you don't hit you..."

Maybe it's from all the rum but I start boo-hooing. A big ugly, snorty, snotty weepfest. "Don't ever say that I don't love you," I sob. "I love you more than I ever loved anyone." To shut me up, Paul kisses me and tells me not to cry. Which makes me sob more, the tears running into our mouths, bittersweet.

"When I ask you to stop doing something, please stop,"
I continue. "There are a lot of things you don't know, things you don't
want to know. You've got no idea what he did to me…" My voice
trails off.

The sky is a deep cobalt. There's no full moon this time but
the night is star-flecked and breathtaking all the same. Paul and I walk
back to the Santa Lucía holding hands. It's about two in the morning.
He jingles the keys on our ring. One is for the bolted front door and
one is for our room. However, we can't figure out which is which. And
we can't finagle either to work the gate.

We have no choice but to pound on the front door and wake up
the nightwatchman, who grumbles at us in Spanish. The one word I
understand is *borrachos*. *Drunks*. And he's right. We *are* drunk. I feel
like a tipsy teenager who's lost her keys and has no choice but to wake
her cranky father to let her in.

Back in our closet of a bedroom, more sloshed candor surfaces.
"I'm not feeling very friendly toward you right now," Paul admits.

"I respect that," I tell him. "Thank you for being honest."

In bed, we hold each other briefly. When Paul pulls away, I
back into him and curl myself into my preferred little spoon position.
"Can you move about five feet?" he wonders. "I've slept next to your
fat ass almost three weeks and I need a break." *Touché*, Paul!

In vino veritas? Maybe. But in any case, I slide to the edge of
the *cama matrimonial*, as far from Paul as I can while still being in the
same bed. If the room were big enough, I would have slept on the floor.
But then again, I guess I deserve it.

Day 20

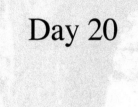

Following a restless sleep, Paul and I wake up at the same time and wordlessly make love. It's weird at first, like rediscovering an unfamiliar territory. It will take a while longer to get back to normal, if that will even be possible. But at least the anger has dissipated. Forgiveness. What a lovely thing.

Maybe this rough patch will teach me not to take this relationship for granted. The Hearts Incident has shown me how much I value "us." How much I value Paul. Since we've had no real argument for over a year, at times the union has felt too perfect, too comfortable, too easy. But not anymore.

Perhaps I just need to be reminded of how lucky I am. Of how much it—and Paul—means to me. Life isn't smooth and easy. My marriage taught me this all too well. Maybe it's so great with Paul because it had been so bad with Alex. Maybe you learn what you want in a relationship because of what you didn't have in past relationships. And what I want is Paul.

~

Rachel takes an early bus to Guatemala City (only an hour's ride) to secure a visa to El Salvador because she plans to visit there next week while Glenn is immersed in research—he has to recoup the time he lost exploring with us this week. She'll be back from El

Salvador in time to spend Christmas with Glenn in Xela. He plans to devote most of his day to research in Antigua's archives. All four of us will meet up tonight for dinner.

While our friends are off doing other things, Paul and I have breakfast alone at Doña Irena's. It has become our Number 1 spot. After moving back to the Posada Asjemenou (we'd prepaid for our final night in Antigua before we'd left for Xela the week before), Paul and I cash our remaining traveler's checks and do more sightseeing in this enchanting colonial city.

~

Near town square, a young boy tries to sell Paul a Panama-style hat. Normally, we would pass him by, but since we have the whole afternoon to kill in Antigua, we welcome the prospect of gently bargaining with the boy. Besides, he's so thin and earnest that we *have* to stop.

Paul chooses a hat with a striped band. *"Se ve bien,"* the boy tells him.

But Paul doesn't believe him so he turns to me. "He's right. It *does* look good," I insist.

The boy holds up a hand mirror so Paul can decide for himself. *"Muy guapo,"* the child says. Then, in heavily-accented English, the kid tries, "Very handsome."

"Sì," I agree. *"Muy guapo. Muy macho."*

"He's giving me the hard sell," Paul laughs. To the boy's delight, Paul ends up buying the hat.

My guy is indeed striking in the wide-brimmed Panama. It compliments his sandy beard and mustache which have filled in nicely during our time here. Paul's suntanned skin glows. The hat salesman is thrilled when Paul gives him more quetzals than he asked for. "Maybe it will buy his family a decent meal," Paul reasons.

~

Paul and I pause to take silly photos at the Tittie Fountain, making sure to get shots of our favorite maiden with the most prominent streams of water shooting out of her nipples. Then we go shopping.

Since we leave Guatemala tomorrow, we'll only have to carry our souvenirs from Antigua to the La Aurora Airport. Paul nabs three leather belts decorated with Guatemala's distinctive weaving. The trio only costs 100 quetzals, or 20 dollars.

Friday, December 10, 1993

I buy woven potholders and several pairs of kids' shorts. The first are for me and my mom and the shorts are for my young cousins and nieces back home. For myself, I also choose handcrafted hair barrettes and a woven headband plus a carved mahogany mask that's Paul's twin when he's angry.

We enjoy politely bargaining with the ladies in the market, some who nurse their babies as they wheel and deal. When one woman leaves her booth unattended to fetch a specific vase for me, Paul takes over her stall, calling out to passersby, his Panama hat pushed back on his head, *"Mira! Mira! Buenos precios!" Look! Look! Good prices!* The woman comes running back to her booth, giggling, the black lava vase I sought clutched in her hands.

During lunch, Paul and I take more pictures. Our stomachs grumble in the long wait for our meal to arrive. Paul complains to me as the café workers string angel hair floss and wooden ornaments around a Christmas tree instead of preparing our lunch. "They should be in the kitchen," he says.

To take our minds off our hunger, I snap photos of Paul holding my recent purchase, the scowling Mayan mask, in front of his face. To complete the picture, Paul puts his sunglasses over the mask's eyes. When our lunch finally comes, it's good and solid and exactly what we need.

~

Afterwards, we return to our choice Antiguan watering hole, the Mistral. We enjoy the revolving cast of characters as well as the drinks. Around dinnertime, I leave to get Glenn and Rachel at the Santa Lucía while Paul stays behind at the Mistral, bathing his wounds like a liquor-laden Lazarus. By some miracle, he's almost healed of the Hearts Incident. There might be some hope for us yet.

Dinner is especially nice our last night in Antigua. The conversation is animated yet relaxed. We talk of everything from Rachel's job editing documentary films to prostate cancer. The latter is top of mind because Frank Zappa has just died of it. The Mexican/Italian food is excellent and the restaurant is all dressed up for the holidays and reasonable. Feeling rich and fortunate, I treat. The bill is less than 100 quetzals, or 20 dollars, to feed and water our table of four.

For dessert, we return to the Opera Café. We sit at a table beneath a blindfolded *Madama Butterfly* poster. "She covers her son's eyes so he won't see her commit suicide," I softly explain to Paul. He nods, studying the dignified rendering of such a horrific act.

After arranging to meet for breakfast at a nearby bagel eatery, Glenn and Rachel head for the Santa Lucía. I'm not overjoyed with the idea of Guatemalan bagels but agree. Paul craves a nightcap while I'm content with the amaretto that doused my ice cream dessert. Slightly crampy, I go along for the ride as Paul promises to have one beer and one tequila. But I know it will be more than that.

The healing process is not yet finished. We launch tentatively into talk about what will forever be called "The Hearts Incident." If we indeed do have a "forever" together. And I think we might. We just might.

There are reassuring kisses then a walk back to our *posada*.

As usual, I lie awake while Paul drops off to dream in a sleep that is both heavy and quick. I listen to the sound of fireworks, to the lonely chime of the bell in the Santa Catalina arch and to the music of a live Christmas pageant in Spanish which goes on somewhere in the near distance. It's not nearly as offensive as the marimba assault and is over by 11.

I am gone soon after.

Day 21

Saturday, December 11, 1993
Antigua/Guatemala City/New York City

Our last day in Guatemala is a mixture of sadness and relief. I'm both sad to leave and relieved we're leaving. Thankful to have experienced this incredible, unusual place and glad to be going home. Usually, the "happy to be home" part only lasts a couple of hours after being back in Brooklyn. Seeing (and smelling!) my battleship-gray city firsthand, sifting through stacks of mail and stepping in my first pile of dog shit usually cures my homesickness immediately.

After showering and packing, Paul and I dash off to meet Glenn and Rachel in the designated place. To my relief, the bagel café is closed. But Glenn has scribbled a note and left it on the door. It tells us to meet them at Doña Irena's. We say *hola* to the armed guard posted at the front door as we spot Glenn and Rachel in Doña's courtyard, writing postcards at a four-top.

Since Doña Irena's is a favorite haven for Americans like us, barely a word of Spanish is spoken here. Except for the waitresses, most of whom wear hair nets on their ropelike black tresses. A trio of Americans sit at a table near ours. One is a Kenny Rogers clone. "Or it might actually be Kenny Rogers," Glenn proposes. "How can you be sure?"

At another table is a fluffy, nasty toy canine of some sort, a pedigreed yapping cur who never shuts up. "It's the kind of dog you want to kick when no one's looking," Paul says. One of its owners wears a cowboy hat and pretentious southwestern garb that is not worn by cowboys. For some reason, this makes the dog even more annoying.

An Australian exchange student asks us to take a photo of her and some friends. "Only if you take one of us," Paul tells the student. In it, I bet Rachel, Glenn, Paul and I will appear tense and tired. Exactly the way we feel.

Amid the jug of Log Cabin syrup and half-finished cups of coffee, Glenn and Rachel finish filling out their postcards—they want us to mail them from the States. Glenn also gives Paul a carved, painted wooden angel, a Christmas present Paul will deliver to Glenn's father and stepmother. They live blocks from him in Brooklyn. The angel is prettily wrapped in colorful tissue paper to protect her fragile wings.

After breakfast, there are kisses, goodbyes and thank-yous on the sidewalk across from Doña Irena's. The security guard watches with mild interest. "We wouldn't have been able to see all we did without you," Paul tells his ex-roommate. Glenn reddens, nods and laughs nervously. Then he and Rachel are gone, off to Quetzaltenango to return our trusty red chariot. It's a wonder he didn't flip the Suzuki with the hazardous roads and sharp turns. But there's still plenty of time for him to do that on the drive back to Xela.

~

Paul and I cram in some last-minute shopping. I find more hairclips to give as gifts—because you can never have too many hairclips. Paul buys me a *huipil* as part of my Christmas present. It's a rich burgundy and has flowers embroidered around the neckline.

And for himself, Paul can't resist getting a t-shirt with an ear of corn stenciled on the front. "Which is significant how?" I ask.

"Because corn is the essence of life here," he explains.

Back at the Posada Asjemenou, we realize that we've still got more than 500 American dollars left in our money pouches. This means that even with all of the shopping, Christmas presents, meals, accommodations, busses and such, we only spent 1,500 dollars between us in three weeks' time.

But it's impossible to put a price on what we experienced.

At the *posada*, we silently finish packing then ask the hotel to call a cab to take us back to Guatemala City. We don't want to chance missing our flight because of Antigua's iffy bus schedules.

As we carry our bags across the courtyard, there's a supreme sadness in both Paul and myself. I can see it in his eyes. The Posada Asjemenou is where we watched the full moon glow so magically two weeks earlier. But two weeks seems like an eternity now. We've seen and learned so much since then. About ourselves and about the country. About the people. About our relationship. Which is still intact. *Más o menos.*

As the taxi nears the capital, a layer of diesel fumes becomes visible in the distance. It spans across Guatemala City like a plague in a sci-fi movie. Paul and I will soon become immersed in it. But not for long.

~

After an uneventful pseudo-Guatemalan lunch at Aurora International, Paul and I check our bags. Although we have hundreds of unchanged American dollars, we only have five quetzals left. Not enough to buy anything of significance. So, Paul gives the money to a boy as we head back to the terminal area. *"Gracias!"* the child says in surprise then runs off to show his mom.

A long, slow line grows out of the check-in counter. A group of wealthy, young Guatemalans in expensive clothing try to cut in front of all of us. It's as if they think their time is more valuable than ours. In a wide array of languages, everyone else yells at them to get to the back of the line. Reluctantly, they do.

When we finally reach the gate, there's another delay before our airplane actually leaves the ground. In true Guatemalan fashion, it departs several hours late. "Now that the trip is over, I can't wait to get home," Paul admits.

"I know what you mean," I tell him. "A good trip is like a bad relationship: when it's over, it's over."

He smirks. "You have a way with words."

"That's why I have a glamorous career in publishing," I say.

As the plane sits on the tarmac, my mind blurs with thoughts of piled-up mail, telephone messages, bills, editing deadlines and life itself. All of it can wait, except for life itself.

~

Right now, I'm writing this somewhere over the Caribbean as our Lacsa flight makes haste toward New York City. I've been scribbling at a furious pace ever since the plane took off. I need to catch up on all the writing I didn't do in the past three days, since the dreaded Hearts Incident. I don't want to forget anything. Even that.

Life with Paul is good again. I think I can get used to being happy. Maybe. With a little effort, I can stop waiting for the other shoe to drop.

The captain announces that it's 27 degrees at JFK Airport. It was in the 70s when we left Antigua this morning. We're due to arrive at JFK at about 11:30 p.m., an hour or so late. I long to sleep beside my love in my pine captain's bed. There will be strong coffee, cream cheese, lox, real Brooklyn bagels and the Sunday *New York Times* in the morning.

Paul turns to me and asks what I want for Christmas. "It's only two weeks away," he points out.

My first thought is to tell him, 'I already got it.' But I consider his question and suggest, "Something foolish and beautiful." And he laughs. I'm glad I can still make him laugh. Even now.

Beside me in the uncomfortable airplane seat, Paul has just finished reading *Ever After.* He closes it with a resounding thump and looks like he wants to cry. He is misty and pensive and I love him even more for it. I'm sure the book brings to mind the losses he's experienced: of Carrie turning down his marriage proposal to grow fat and complacent in Texas, of his friend Felix who took his own life in the shadow of a harsh breakup.

I want to hug Paul. I want to tell him that it's all right to cry. Even on an airplane. But I believe he already knows this. We share a brief, pointed talk about the elusive nature of love. Then I rest my head on his shoulder, reveling in the distinct smell of his skin, in the sure, familiar weight of his body next to me.

Before I drift off, I remember the people, the faces, the ruins, the mountains, the rutted roads, the colors, the active volcanoes and the dead ones. Guatemala is a place I will never forget. And I hope it will always remember me.

Oh, and I never did finish *Huck Finn.*

Afterthoughts

When we arrive at JFK, Paul and I walk directly onto an airbus from the plane. On its tall, skinny legs, the airbus resembles a huge futuristic insect. It stands about ten feet off the ground like a big, steel spider. The strange vehicle shuttles us to the terminal itself.

It's freezing inside the airbus. Paul and I slip on our winter gear while Cancuners shiver in their shorts and suntans. Paul opens a bottle of Venado. We each take a slug of the Guatemalan rum as the airbus creeps toward the terminal. "Welcome home," he says. I groan and look out the window at the dusting of snow on the ground.

"We were walking around in our shirtsleeves this afternoon," I remind Paul. Now it's his turn to groan.

At the Customs booth, the officer asks more questions than are required. I think it's to satisfy his own personal curiosity than anything else. "Were you scared being in Guatemala?" he wonders first.

"No," I say. "It's no more dangerous than New York. Probably less so."

Next, he asks, "How were the people?"

"Really nice," I tell him. "They don't have a lot but they're happy to share whatever they've got with you."

I suppose the Customs agent is wondering why a woman from Brooklyn would want to go to Guatemala. So, for his benefit I tag on, "You should really check it out. You can't imagine how beautiful it is."

For that last remark, I receive a snort of distain. "It's not at the top of my list, but thanks," Customs Man admits. He can't possibly imagine the splendors of Tikal. Or the sunset in Flores. Or the vibrant colors of Juana's *cinta*. Or the light in Magdalena's seldom-given smile. Or the sweet weight of a street urchin's head on your shoulder.

"Was it safe?" he prods.

It's after midnight and I'm tired of the third-degree. Besides, I know this man who works at a bustling international airport will never leave the comfort of Queens. "Well," I sigh. "There was no mass murder on the railroad. In Guatemala, there is no railroad." He nods and sends me on my way.

~

The dusting of white turns to a wet, heavy snow which grinds JFK to a standstill. People are lined up at the taxi kiosk, surly, sullen and sodden. Although it's illegal for a cab driver to refuse a trip to the outer boroughs, in bad weather cabbies don't want to take passengers that far. Instead, they prefer to make a quick hop into Manhattan, then zip back to the airport for additional fares. Whereas, in Guatemala, cab drivers are grateful for any fare and in fact, like the longer trips because they mean more money.

But this isn't Guatemala, I tell myself.

JFK's longsuffering cab dispatcher, in his slick, black coat, shouts into the snow, waving his arms back and forth. "The line starts here," he cries. But no one listens to him. Travelers litter the sidewalk like scattered beads. An elderly, well-dressed man tries to cut the line, explaining "I'm a congressman."

"We pay your salary," I shout to him. "You wait in line like the rest of us." Sliding effortlessly into my bitchy New Yorker mode, I almost start a riot. But it doesn't faze the congressman, who ducks into a hijacked cab, brandishing a twenty.

"Just like those rich, young punks at Aurora Airport," Paul says.

A lady's straw hat blows off into the slush. Paul bends to retrieve it.

Welcome home, indeed.

~

The day after we get back, I fall into a melancholy funk. I miss Guatemala. Long for it, even. I liked feeling like an adventuress, an explorer. Now there's an odd sort of depression, a kind of displacement, a sense of loss. I have a difficult adjustment period. Life seemed simpler in Guatemala for everyone. Including tourists like me.

It's hard to believe how soon you take for granted things like hot showers and flush toilets. After doing pretty much nothing yet everything for three weeks, I'm amazed at how fast I become adept at meeting deadlines and editing at a breakneck speed again.

The checks from clients that should be waiting for me aren't. I'm faced with the disastrous possibility of having to get a real job, at least a steady, part-time gig. I go on an interview, am offered the position as an inhouse editor but decide to turn down the job and ride out the hard times. Freedom in exchange for security. Roller coaster as opposed to carousel. Wisely or unwisely, I choose the roller coaster and the freedom.

~

A week later, I find myself in New York City's Penn Station, en route to New Jersey for a meeting with a new client. How I long for the simplicity of an Xela bus station, crammed thick with rickety, old Blue Birds. But few will understand this. Not the Bloomingdale's lady sipping gourmet coffee from a paper cup. Not the derelict lifting his butt cheek to softly fart on a plastic chair in the PATH station's waiting room. No one will get it. No one but Paul will.

~

Just as he promised at Doña Irena's in Antigua, Paul delivers the beautiful wooden angel to Glenn's father and stepmom. And when he does, Paul says they were more taken with the paper wrappings than they were with the angel itself.

~

No one back in Brooklyn likes the Guatemalan Christmas presents Paul and I so thoughtfully chose for them. His Aunt Lorena never sets out the candy dish from Cantel Fabrica. Paul's sister sells the woven placemats at a flea market soon after they are given to her. She never wears the silver, birds-in-flight earrings. I never see my nieces and cousins wearing the colorful print clothing. No one ever wears the belts.

In contrast, I hang the burgundy *huipil* on my living room wall almost as soon as I get home. Drinking from one of Cantel Fabrica's thick-lipped, blue-rimmed glasses always brings a quiet grin to my face. Wearing my Guatemalan earrings reminds me of how the silver hoops shone on the little girls who escorted us to the Pozo Vivo. Paul in his Panama hat always makes me say, "You look like your grandfather Enrique." And he smiles because he does.

~

Maybe because of all we've been through, Paul and I don't hide our feelings from each other anymore. I'm more secure in his love for me. And I feel less and less like Groucho and his club.

In early 1994, Paul flies down to Florida to visit his parents. With him gone a week, I begin transferring my 90-page journal in the lined, fuchsia notebook onto my computer.

I don't know what will come of this. I don't know if the journal will mean anything to anyone except me—and Paul. I don't know how he'll feel about this diary or if he'll even want to read it. And if he does, I don't know if it will change his feelings about me. But everything changes. Eventually. Even us. And Guate. Especially Guatemala.

~

In early April 1994, six months after our trip, things abruptly shift down there. They start killing judges and other officials in the streets of the capital. Rumors circulate that childless American couples are stealing Guatemalan babies and smuggling them back to the States. Or that doctors are using these children's organs for transplants in sick American children.

In San Cristóbal Verapaz, in the Western Highlands, where the road suddenly becomes paved, a group of indigenous people brutally beat an Alaskan tourist into a coma, accusing her of kidnapping an eight-year-old boy. She is attacked by a crowd of 300 and has multiple stab wounds, three skull fractures, a broken arm and leg. It turns out that the child was at a religious procession and later returned home. Safe.

These incidents make Paul and I take pause. This is not the Guatemala we know. The poverty, the rage, the mistrust, is understandable, but we never experienced it on this scale. When we were there, Paul and I tried to show the Guatemalan people the respect we had for them, their culture and their customs. I hope they realized it.

Paul and I beam whenever we talk about Juana Marcos and her family, the street boy César and our boatman Roberto.

I will never look at a banana the same way, not since watching that freight ship load and unload half the night in Puerto Barrios.

I will never look at an old school bus without thinking, "Antigua! Antigua! Antigua!"

And I will always prefer a good cup of Cobán coffee over Nescafé. Who wouldn't?

And appreciate a private bathroom.

And soft, fluffy toilet paper.

And democracy.

And freedom.

Is it possible to fall in love with a country? Yes, I think it is. Because I have.

Update

As hard as Paul and I try to introduce the word "resplendent" into common usage, it never quite catches on. We're still trying, though.

~

After complaining to Lacsa Airlines about losing our luggage on the flight to Guatemala City, they give us free tickets to any destination Lacsa flies. We choose Costa Rica. But that's another story for another time.

~

I lose the hand-woven bracelet Juana Marcos gave me in Nebaj the very next day. However, Paul's hangs from the rearview mirror of his battered Calais. Some men hang garters. Some hang tree-shaped air fresheners. But not Paul. Juana's gift looks very much at home in his Oldsmobile. Like it belongs there.

It flutters defiantly in the Brooklyn breeze. Seeing it makes me smile whenever I seatbelt myself into the car. It always will.

~

The Valentine's Day after we return from Guatemala, Paul gives me a delicate gold charm. "I hope you take this in the manner in which it was intended," he says. The charm depicts a small fan of playing cards: a full house. I laugh until tears fall from my eyes. "This way, you'll always have a winning hand," Paul explains.

And also, so I'll never forget The Hearts Incident.

Whenever someone insists we play a card game, Paul says sagely, "Carol doesn't like cards."

~

And speaking of eruptions, Volcán Pacaya still manages to cause trouble. Five years after our climb, a series of explosions spewed lava and rubble. An ash column rose more than 16,000 feet into the air. The ash itself rained onto Guatemala City and Aurora International Airport.

In 2010, a number of strong eruptions again bring ash to GC and the airport. Noti7 reporter Anibal Archila, one of the first to cover the event, was killed by volcanic debris. But people still continue to hike up Pacaya. Some even toast marshmallows on its hot lava coals.

~

In the Brooklyn Museum, Paul and I discover a lintel from a Tikal pyramid in its collection. It's more magnificent than we could have ever imagined. How it got from Tikal to Switzerland to Brooklyn is a mystery.

~

Soon after Glenn returns from Xela, he and Rachel break up. No surprise there. Glenn goes on to write a well-received scholarly book about Latin America. Today, he teaches at a prestigious midwestern university. And amazingly enough, he still talks to us.

~

On a cross-country camping trip two years after our Guatemalan adventure, Paul asks me to marry him. We are in a tent on a backcountry trip, in the middle of Montana's Glacier National Park, on the shores of Otokomi Lake in Rose Basin. Out of his backpack, Paul pulls a green velvet box. And in that box is a ring that is exactly like the night sky in Antigua. A field of sapphire blue surrounded by tiny diamonds.

We are married ten days later in Las Vegas. And we're still married. Happily. Usually.

~

Decades later, we still refer to a heavy drizzle as a *chipi-chipi*.

~

These days, Paul and I don't drink anymore; it's better that way.

~

Four years after Paul and I marry, we have a son and call him Daniel. Is he named for Juana's grandchild in Nebaj? We're not telling.

~

Paul and I never did make it back to Guatemala. But maybe one day we will. We just might.

~~~

Publisher's Note

While this book is inspired by real people, places and some actual events, *Paul and Carol Go to Guatemala* is a work of fiction and in no way meant to be a historical accounting. Any resemblance to persons, either living or dead, is purely coincidental. This book is intended solely for entertainment purposes.

About the Author

Catherine Gigante-Brown is a writer of fiction, nonfiction, poetry and plays. Her articles have appeared in publications like *Time Out New York, Essence* and *Industry*. Her poetry and fiction are included in several anthologies. A handful of her films and theatrical works have been produced. Gigante-Brown's novels *The El, The Bells of Brooklyn* and *Brooklyn* Roses (aka "The El Trilogy"), *Different Drummer* and *Better than Sisters* are all published by Volossal. Born and bred in Brooklyn, Gigante-Brown, her husband and son make their home there and upstate New York in Rosendale.

Acknowledgements

This novel started as my travel journal during a trip to Guatemala in 1993 with my relatively-new boyfriend (who later became my husband). I revisited it 27 years later, inspired after reading Dan Szczesny's *The Nepal Chronicles,* which I highly recommend. There, Dan recounted his honeymoon trip to Everest Base Camp with his new bride Meenakshi. I felt my own story would be stronger as thinly-veiled fiction, staying true to the journal format. I hope you agree. *Paul and Carol...* took on a life of its own. I just followed the path to see where it led.

I'd like to thank my husband Peter for constantly putting up with me fictionalizing our lives. And for asking me to accompany him to Guatemala in the first place. A warm thanks to the people of that country for their generosity and hospitality which I still haven't forgotten three decades later.

Many thanks to my publisher Vinnie Corbo for finding value in everything I send him. (He and his wife Jackie read the manuscript aloud to each other at bedtime.) And also to my faithful readers for always asking for more. Because there's always more.

CPSIA information can be obtained
at www.ICGtesting.com
Printed in the USA
LVHW010148181021
700711LV00006B/52

9 781735 018492